Award-winni... ...s with her
wonderful histo... ...g tale where
the hunt for a lost treasure brings together two destined hearts . . .

MORE THAN HE KNEW

Rand Hamilton vows to rebuild his Charleston plantation
with the only means left to him: a long-lost treasure that
has lured and cursed two families for centuries. But to
finance his expedition, he must agree to the terms of his
wealthy London benefactor and allow his goddaughter
to accompany him. Although wary, Rand agrees to take
the woman with him, unaware that she is the one who
holds the key to a haunting riddle that will lead him
to a glorious treasure—and to a passion
he has never known. . . .

MORE THAN SHE DREAMED

London heiress Claire Bancroft is desperate to seek
hidden meaning to the terrible fate that has shattered
her life. Determined to find her missing brother and
unlock the haunting secrets of her past, she must place
her trust in Rand, only to discover that she is becoming
completely enraptured by him . . . and the promise of a
shining future together. . . .

"Jo Goodman writes with a unique and
impressive style."
—Virginia Henley

Books by Jo Goodman

THE CAPTAIN'S LADY
(previously published as PASSION'S BRIDE)
CRYSTAL PASSION
SEASWEPT ABANDON
VELVET NIGHT
VIOLET FIRE
SCARLET LIES
TEMPTING TORMENT
MIDNIGHT PRINCESS
PASSION'S SWEET REVENGE
SWEET FIRE
WILD SWEET ECSTASY
ROGUE'S MISTRESS
FOREVER IN MY HEART
ALWAYS IN MY DREAMS
ONLY IN MY ARMS
MY STEADFAST HEART
MY RECKLESS HEART
WITH ALL MY HEART
MORE THAN YOU KNOW

Published by Zebra Books

MORE THAN YOU KNOW

Jo Goodman

Zebra Books
Kensington Publishing Corp.

http://www.zebrabooks.com

ZEBRA BOOKS are published by

Kensington Publishing Corp.
850 Third Avenue
New York, NY 10022

First Printing: May, 2000
10 9 8 7 6 5 4 3 2 1

Printed in the United States of America

For Claire
Her smile dazzles us.

The Hamilton Riddle

Seven sisters, cursed every one
Seven sisters, all alone
One more lovely than the other
Each, at heart, as cold as stone

Blood will run
Flames will come
Blazing sun, blinding some
Blades lifted high across the plain
Flood waters rising, months of rain
A plague will ink clouded skies
Grieving, shadows beneath thy eyes

Seven sisters, cursed every one
Seven sisters, all alone
Await the day, when reunited
They will be placed upon their throne

The Waterstone Riddle

At the end of one God's promise
Stand seven pagan sentinels
Seven rings, but just one key
Silver, tin, and mercury
Iron bracelet, leaden chain
Treasure lost, treasure gained
Copper circlet, crown of gold
Seven sisters flee the fold
Reunited, freed of curse
Thy reward, the richest purse
Seven rings but just one key
Metals all of alchemy
With the sisters, this verse brings
Wealth beyond the dreams of kings

Chapter One

He was not surprised he hadn't noticed her from the first. She had been successful at making herself rather nondescript, though he was fairly certain it hadn't required much forethought or effort. It was her peculiarity, perhaps her good fortune, to be graced with features that did little to distinguish her. Brown hair. Brown eyes. A narrow face. Her mouth was only remarkable for its humorlessness. She was altogether forgettable, which was good. It was his most fervent wish to forget her.

He turned away again, giving her his back as he had done throughout the interview. It had been an inadvertent snub before. Now it could not be mistaken for anything but purposely rude. He leaned forward, bracing his arms stiffly on the large walnut desk. His head lowered fractionally as he took the full measure of the man sitting across from him. He had no illusions that what he had to say would be greeted with favor, and he did not try to dress it up when a single word would serve.

"No."

Evan Markham, eighth Duke of Strickland, did not blink.

Although unused to being denied, he had no startle reflex. The duke's natural reserve, bred to the bone, caused his expression to be shuttered. He raised his pale, rather fine-boned hands slowly and steepled his fingers just below the point of his chin. In spite of the positioning of his hands, the attitude was not one of prayer.

"Perhaps you did not understand," Strickland said. "I wasn't properly making a request, Captain Hamilton. I was stating the terms of the arrangement. In order to secure the funds you need, you must accept Miss Bancroft as a passenger. This is not negotiable."

Rand Hamilton did not miss the ghost of a smile shaping the Duke's narrow mouth, but he chose to ignore it. He did not care if Strickland was amused by him, and he was not going to be goaded into accepting an arrangement that was so ill-conceived. He leaned a bit more forward, his braced arms relaxing slightly. His voice and his answer remained firm. "No," he said.

The steeple of Strickland's fingers collapsed and his hands folded into a single fist. The polished surface of the desk reflected the movement as the fist was lowered. His pale blue eyes continued to assess the captain, and though his expression gave nothing away, he wondered if the conclusions he had drawn about the man's character were in error. He had expected to find intelligence and intensity. He had reasoned that Hamilton would be astute enough to understand the importance of the offer before him and desperate enough to seize it.

There were limits, it seemed, to the captain's recklessness.

Under the duke's careful study, Rand straightened. In a gesture that was less absent than it appeared, he raked back the thick, copper-colored hair at his temple and let his attention wander. There had been little opportunity to take in his surroundings. From the moment he was ushered into Strickland's London townhouse, Rand was oddly aware that he was being granted an audience, and that what he was properly expected to feel was a mixture of awe and gratefulness. That struck him as amusing. He would have allowed himself to be drawn and quartered rather than admit he felt any measure of the other emotions.

The duke's library was paneled in walnut and mounted with floor-to-ceiling shelves on the north wall. Hundreds of leather-bound volumes lent the room a fragrance that was pleasing to anyone who loved books as well as Rand. The fragrance was more than the bindings and paper and ink. It was also the hint of pipe tobacco and hand oils that had been absorbed into the leather over decades of human contact. Rand was unprepared for the stab of envy he felt. Knowing these books represented only a fraction of what the duke would have in his estate libraries did not help the sensation pass easily. He resisted the urge to view Strickland's collection more closely, afraid it would show some vulnerability on his part.

His eyes, faintly guarded in their expression now, shifted to the opposite wall, where heavily gilded frames secured the duke's English countryside and ancestry in oils. Here and there among the portraits Rand caught a glimpse of a feature now part of Strickland's own countenance. The duke's eyes were the same pale blue as those of a young woman holding a puppy on her lap two centuries earlier. The austere, even rigid line of his jaw was courtesy of another duke, this one posed stiffly on a horse. Strickland's thick dark hair was repeated in several of the paintings, most notably in a man of middle years who had also imparted the narrow shape of his mouth. Rand did not think he imagined the vaguely disapproving air of these ancestors. Certainly he did not imagine Strickland's.

Past the duke's shoulder, Rand's gaze fell on the small fire laid in the hearth. He surprised himself again by thinking of home. There, in Charleston, there would be no need for extra warmth on an April afternoon. Sunshine would have beaten back the morning chill and brightened the surface of every green leaf lifted in its direction. Bria would be sitting on the verandah, her face also lifted toward the sun. Perhaps she would be smiling. Rand hoped so. He did not like to think that she only smiled for him, as if she knew how much he wanted to believe she was happy.

It made him wonder about the woman at his back, the one

who did not smile when he had turned to look at her. She had
not seemed to care what he made of her cheerless features, nor
had she registered any surprise that he had only just become
aware of her. She hadn't blushed or in any way communicated
that she was discomfited by his scrutiny. It was almost as if
she had been unaware of it.

She did not subject him to the same study, as a bolder woman
might have done. Neither did she turn away and try to make
him out from a shy, sidelong glance. Her eyes had remained
rather vaguely focused on some point just past his shoulder,
not quite looking at him, but not quite looking at anything else.
Her solemn expression had remained unchanged.

Miss Bancroft couldn't have known, Rand realized, that she
had hit upon the very thing that might engage his interest: her
complete indifference. He wondered whether, if he turned suddenly, he would find her unchanged. Was she perhaps using these
moments to make her own assessment? Bria was fond of telling
him, a little more seriously than not, that he could afford the
luxury of not being vain. With so many women eager to surround
him, casting his reflection in their eyes, mirrors were superfluous.
He had always grinned at that observation. Bria was also quick
to point out that the secretive, self-mocking nature of that grin
did nothing to dim his appeal.

But then, he thought, Bria had not met the likes of Miss
Bancroft.

Strickland pushed away from his desk. "Please, Captain, be
seated. I think a drink would serve us well. I find that a good
Scotch whiskey clears my head. I fear I may have explained
myself badly."

Rand did not disabuse the duke of that notion. He understood
that it would not occur to Strickland that someone could simply
disagree with him or deny his wishes. He was more likely to
believe that if he fully explained the logic of his position,
agreement must follow. That his opponent might have an alternative equally sound position would not be part of his thinking.
"Scotch will be fine."

The duke nodded, pleased with what he saw as the first of

many concessions Rand Hamilton would make. "Claire," he said. "Would you be so kind?"

Rand thought that Miss Bancroft was being asked to serve them. He was aware of her movement behind him as she rose from her chair. He glimpsed her out of the corner of his eye when her path to the door cut into his field of vision. She grasped the bell pull and rang for Strickland's butler.

"Thank you, m'dear," the duke said kindly. "You may come or go as you please. I fear that hashing out the particulars will merely fatigue you."

Turning slightly, Rand noted that if Claire Bancroft was troubled by this thinly disguised dismissal, she gave no indication. Her faint smile remained reserved, her poise unchanged. When she spoke, however, her tone carried a certain amount of affection and familiarity. It took the sting out of what could have been interpreted as an admonishment.

"Have a care, your grace. Your phrasing suggests that Captain Hamilton will surrender to your dictates. Unless he changes his mind, you will never get to the point of discussing particulars."

Rand watched her slender fingers reach toward the door. He knew a moment's disappointment that she was going to leave them and wondered why that should be so. Perhaps it was because she respected his right to say no where the duke did not. She, at least, was not bent on arguing with him about the matter.

"It was a pleasure, Miss Bancroft," Rand said politely.

She fixed him with a blank stare as her fingers found the door's brass handle. "It was no pleasure, Captain Hamilton. And well you know it." Claire twisted the handle. "I will be in my sitting room, your grace." Then she let herself out.

Strickland did not watch Claire go. His attention was fully on his guest. He had not missed the captain's slight start at Claire's setdown. It was a pity, he thought, that Claire had. "I suspect you will have to make some allowances for my goddaughter's plain speaking," he said. "I have."

Rand didn't know which surprised him more: the fact that Miss Bancroft was the duke's goddaughter or that he made allowances. He commented on neither and said instead, "Has she been ill?"

"Aaah," Strickland said slowly. "My comment that she might become fatigued did not pass unnoticed."

Rand let the duke believe that was all he had observed. He could have added that except for the shadows beneath her eyes, his goddaughter's complexion was like whey. "Has she?" he repeated.

Strickland motioned for Rand to have a seat and made no response until it was done. In this way it was more of an order than a suggestion. "Not ill in the usual sense," he said as Rand stretched his legs casually in front of him. The duke doubted he would get used to this peculiar American sprawl. It came from having too much land, he thought, and almost limitless boundaries. There was a tendency, which Strickland found undisciplined, to use all the available space. Quite purposefully he sat up straighter, hoping the captain would follow by example.

"She has had rather a bad time of it lately. She has . . ." He paused, thinking of how to explain it. "I suppose it would be correct to say that she has been through something of an ordeal. She is on the mend now. All the doctors agree. As far as her being able to travel, you should have no concerns that there will be any problems. She assures all of us that she is up to the journey."

Rand's eyes were the color of polished chestnuts, but without the warmth. He regarded the duke frankly. "Do not mistake my inquiry for interest. I could not care if Miss Bancroft were fit to swim the Channel. She will not be stepping on board *Cerberus.*"

Strickland chose not to argue the point. The whiskey, after all, had not yet arrived. "Tell me, Captain, why does one name one's ship after the guardian of the gates of hell?"

"I suppose, your grace, because one is expected to name a ship something."

The duke's displeasure was in the marginal tightening of his mouth. There was an air of insolence that Rand Hamilton barely kept in check. Strickland's encounters with Americans had led him to conclude that while they took an almost fanatical pride in their commoner ways, even addressing their president as mister, they were also strangely fascinated, perhaps even a bit in awe, of the royal titles and lineage they overthrew. Thus far, Captain Hamilton was falling outside the duke's experience. "I confess I thought I understood a few things about you Yanks," he said.

"That might still be true," Rand drawled, "if you were dealing with a Yankee. We're a distinctly different breed south of the Mason-Dixon."

"Mason-Dixon?"

"Something like your Hadrian's Wall, I imagine. Barbarians to the north."

"Then it's a boundary."

"Yes, between Maryland and Pennsylvania. Though, come to think of it, a wall wouldn't be amiss."

Strickland glanced toward the door as it opened. He gave the butler no more notice than that. Emmereth's wraith-like presence was so unobtrusive, the crystal tumblers and decanter of Scotch seemed to appear as if by sleight of hand. "Really, Captain, you speak as if there are still serious differences between the northern and southern factions of your country. Your civil war is ten years in the past."

"The war's over," Rand said without inflection. "Whether anything was settled is for history to judge."

One of Strickland's dark brows rose. "Do I hear some bitterness?"

"Do you?"

The duke paused as he was raising his glass. He considered his guest thoughtfully over the rim. "It would be understandable." He took a sip of his drink and saw that if anything, the captain's eyes had grown colder. "Forgive me, but I did not invite you to come here without learning something about you. I know, for instance, that you lost everything in that civil—"

"War between the States," Rand said.

"Pardon?"

"We prefer to call it the War between the States."

Strickland nodded, understanding suddenly that the *we* Rand

Hamilton referred to was everyone south of this Mason-Dixon line. Apparently it was a point of some importance, and the duke had no wish to test the limits of his guest's patience, especially when he was maneuvering to win his own campaign. "Very well. You lost your father, your brother, your home, and your land. I believe that what you salvaged was *Cerberus*. If anyone has a right to be bitter, I imagine it would be you."

For a moment Rand did not speak. Uncrossing his boots at the ankle, he levered himself straighter in the wing chair. There was a faint tightening to his jaw, giving the planes and angles of his face even more definition. Cutting across his right cheek from temple to chin was a thin scar, the line of it whiter now than it had been a short time ago. "Your facts are somewhat confused. I didn't *lose* anyone. My father was killed at Vicksburg. My older brother David was murdered by Yankee raiders bent on raping my mother. Shelby was killed at Manassas. One of them is the brother you apparently didn't know about. My home and land were stolen by a carpetbagger for what we owed in taxes. I managed to take possession of *Cerberus*. There are plenty of people who think I was lucky. There are some days I'm inclined to agree."

"And others?"

"I think you know about the other days," Rand said. "That's why I'm here, isn't it?"

"I know what I've been told: you've dedicated the last ten years of your life to restoring your family's fortunes. Such a single-minded pursuit doesn't make me believe you consider yourself lucky very much of the time."

Rand shrugged. The white line of the scar faded so that it was almost invisible once again.

The duke's chin lifted a notch and his head tilted to one side. "You're what? Thirty? Thirty-one?"

"Thirty-one."

"I have a little more than a score of years on you, and I think I know something about what you're trying to do. Keeping what we own is a powerful driving force; getting it back after losing it can bring a man to the brink of madness." He raised his glass in the direction of the paintings. It was not a portrait that he pointed to, however, but one of the landscapes. "That's a view of the countryside from Abberly Hall. It's been fought over, pillaged, surrendered, and retaken by various members of the family for five centuries. In a royal fit of pique, Queen Elizabeth held it for most of her reign. My great-great-great-grandfather recovered it, nearly at the cost of his head. So you see, it's in my blood, too. I would do . . . no, I *will* do, whatever it takes to secure what is mine. We're not so different, you and I."

"Abberly Hall is still yours," Rand said dryly. "So nothing's been taken from you."

"Yes, you're quite right . . . about Abberly Hall."

Rand thought Strickland would go on, but the duke did not elaborate. After a moment Rand cut to the heart of the matter before them. "You must be aware that I want to accept your offer to sponsor my next voyage. I had hoped it was made sincerely and with an understanding of the terms given to my previous sponsors."

"Sponsors?" Strickland asked, his tone scoffing. "They were gamblers. I'm not. I want something in exchange for the funds I'm prepared to release to you. I need more than mere assurances that I will share in the Hamilton-Waterstone treasure. That the treasure exists at all is the stuff of legends. I'm taking a sizable risk just by taking you at your word. And you've offered no real proof that, if found, you can rightfully make a claim to it."

"I'm a Hamilton."

"There are hundreds of Hamiltons. Thousands, more likely. You can't all be descendants of Hamilton-Waterstone."

One corner of Rand's mouth curved upward. "It's worth considering, don't you think, unless you're questioning if we're all descendants of Adam?"

Strickland raised his glass appreciatively. "Very well. Darwin's notions aside, you have me there." He finished his drink and poured another, half as much as he'd had before.

"In any event," Rand continued. "Hamilton-Waterstone is not one man, but two, and I believe you know that. Did you think I wouldn't?"

"I had to be sure. You're an American, after all. The treasure is *our* legend."

"And it's *my* legacy. James Hamilton was my grandfather times seven greats. It was his grandson who settled in South Carolina in 1626. His son, grandsons, and all the greats, were born there, most of them at Henley."

"Henley is your plantation."

"Was," Rand corrected. "It's been renamed Conquered by the current owner."

"Conquered?" Strickland asked, frowning.

"Did I say that?" Rand's dry smile appeared briefly and there was a touch of feigned innocence in his eyes. "I meant Concord. Believe me, the similarity of the name is no accident. Orrin Foster gave the renaming of Henley a lot of thought before he arrived at one that suited him." And he had wasted no time in making certain Rand found out about it.

"All the more reason for you to find the treasure," the duke said. He stood and walked to the fireplace. Placing his glass on the mantel, Strickland poked at the fire, then added another log. When he turned, his brow was knit thoughtfully. "Tell me, if Henley were still in your possession, would you have this interest in locating the treasure?"

Rand did not have to consider the question before he answered. "No. Finding the treasure was Shelby's idea of adventure. David and I humored him. As children the three of us would play at treasure hunting, and it was Shelby who was always allowed to find the booty." Rand leaned forward and rested his forearms on his knees. He rolled his drink in his palms in an absent gesture. "The truth is, your grace, for a long time I didn't believe there *was* a treasure. I'm not certain that my father did either. I never knew my grandfather, but there's some indication that he and Shelby were of a like mind. I don't know how far you'd have to go back after that to find someone who gave the treasure much credence. Uncles. Great-uncles. No one that I knew did any actual treasure hunting."

"Until you."

Rand nodded, his smile a little grim now. "Until me."

"And now? You believe it exists?"

"I have to, don't I?" he said carelessly. "Else it would make these last ten years of looking for it a lie."

The duke's expression was considering. "You don't strike me as a man who chases a legend down at a whim. Such a man as that would have given up the quest years ago. Surely there would be more practical ways of taking Henley back."

Rand shrugged. He wondered if Strickland considered murder a practical method. "You may be right."

"I'm certain I am," he said gravely. "And just as certain that you're privy to more information than you're willing to impart. That much of the legend, then, is true. Hamiltons don't trust anyone."

"We prefer to think of ourselves as cautious. You only have to look at the Waterstones to understand why the Hamiltons chose a different course."

"You're referring to the fact that the Waterstone family made no secret about their connection to the treasure."

"I'm referring to the fact that the Waterstone family no longer exists. The last of them died twenty years ago, right here in London, set upon by thieves who hoped to gain the riddle."

The duke watched Rand closely. "Some people say the thieves went by the name Hamilton, or were at least in the employ of Hamiltons."

Rand shrugged. "I've heard that. It's natural, given the animosity that grew between James Hamilton and Henry Waterstone, that stories like that would attach themselves to the legend. To hear my family tell it, the reason Henley Hamilton left England was to protect his wife and children from coming under a Waterstone knife. I think it was more likely that Henley wanted to be certain that none of his children attached themselves to any Waterstone through marriage."

The duke approached his desk again, this time ignoring his usual seat in favor of taking the companion chair closer to Rand. "And that brings me to this," he said. "Is it really possible for you to find this treasure without a Waterstone to assist you?"

"You're talking about the Waterstone riddle."

"Yes," Strickland said. "Is it in your possession?"

Rand chuckled softly. "Now *that* would be giving something away. I don't think I'll answer."

"But you have the Hamilton riddle? It does exist?"

It was not clear to Rand if Strickland was asking for a confirmation or simply fishing. It was time to cut line. Rand placed his drink on the side table and settled back in his chair. "What is the precise nature of your interest in the treasure, your grace?"

"It belongs here," he said.

"The Spaniards would disagree, I think. The story goes it was their treasure first."

"Yes," the duke said gruffly. "But then they should have bloody well taken care not to lose it."

Rand laughed out loud. "And my ancestor and Henry Waterstone? What did they do but lose it?"

"Safeguarded it, Captain. If they had not had a falling-out, most of the treasure would have found its way into the queen's coffers."

"Perhaps that's what they wanted to avoid." He saw the duke start. "That never occurred to you? Surely they would not be the first privateers to try to hold back something from the queen. Perhaps you're thinking I shouldn't say it so easily, or at least that I should be embarrassed by the admission, but it was a long time ago, your grace, and being more thoroughly American than English, there's some bit of pride among the Hamiltons that our common sire got away with it."

Because Strickland looked as if he might choke, Rand got up and retrieved the duke's glass from the mantel. He filled it with another finger of Scotch and handed it over. "I can't say that it doesn't trouble me that you'd want to turn over your share of the treasure to the British Museum, or even that you'd give some part of it back to the queen. But then, if you support my next voyage and it's successful, you may do anything you like with your portion."

"And what of the claim the Spanish government will make?"

"What of it? No court but a Spanish one will take the claim

seriously. As you said, they should have bloody well not lost it."

The duke's mouth lost some of its stiffness as he smiled thinly. He raised his glass in salute. "Damn if I didn't. And bloody good for me." He finished off the drink in a single swallow. "So this leaves us precisely where?"

Rand wondered if the effects of the Scotch on the duke would work in his favor. "I imagine at the point of discussing your stake."

"My offer of three thousand pounds remains unchanged."

Rand said nothing. It was a generous contribution and Strickland knew it. It was also in the nature of a bribe.

"Very well," Strickland said after a protracted silence. "I can give you as much as four thousand. But no more."

"The terms? Are they also unchanged?"

"I'd expect a full third of the treasure, not a quarter. And I still expect you to take my goddaughter."

Rand came out of his chair in a fluid motion. "No." He glanced over his shoulder, almost expecting to find her there in the background again, silent and watchful, effortlessly making herself unobtrusive. Impatient now, believing there could be no resolution or compromise, Rand's fingers raked his copper hair as his eyes settled on the door.

"Are you not even going to ask why?" Strickland said.

Rand looked frankly at the duke. "You've missed my point if you think the why of it matters to me. My answer is no. It will remain no. I'm not playing nursemaid to Miss Bancroft, and I won't ask it of my men. She needs to stay right here in England and recover from her broken engagement, stubbed toe, hangnail, or—"

"You're referring to her ordeal, I believe."

There was a certain cutting edge to the duke's tone that Rand did not miss. Clearly Strickland was unhappy with his characterization of Miss Bancroft's experience as being of little account. "I apologize," he said stiffly, the words and manner not coming easily to him, not in these circumstances. "It was unfair to trivialize Miss Bancroft's affliction. It is none of my concern and I would not have you make it so. She can be no part of this voyage.''

"If she were my godson, Captain Hamilton? What then?''

"My answer would be the same.'' Strickland's skepticism was evident. "You don't believe me?'' asked Rand. "Then make the same request for yourself.'' Rand saw that this rejoinder captured the duke's full attention. "You know it's true. No man who has put up money has been allowed to make the voyage; no man who has staked me couldn't afford to lose it. You sought me out. I would have looked for financing closer to home. John MacKenzie Worth has expressed interest. Carnegie. Vanderbilt. Rushton Holiday.''

"Apparently you have no qualms about accepting Yankee money.''

"None whatsoever. But they have to accept my terms. That means no one looking over my shoulder, tracking my route, or trying to cut me off from the treasure.''

"My God,'' Strickland said softly. "You Hamiltons are a suspicious lot. That's not why I want my goddaughter to go with you.''

"No?'' As soon as he heard himself say the word, inadvertently inviting an explanation, Rand held up his hand, palm out. "Don't tell me,'' he said. "I don't want to know.''

"Then you're willing to pass on this opportunity to secure new backing?''

"Your letter said I could expect to be reimbursed for the costs associated with my trip here.''

"Yes. Yes, of course. I'll write you a draft immediately if that's your wish.''

"It is.''

Strickland rose slowly. "I can't say that I'm not disappointed, Captain. I had hoped you would not be so intractable.''

Rand's slight smile did not touch the polished chestnut color of his eyes. "I also had hopes.''

The duke's gaze shifted away uncomfortably. He cleared his throat. "Yes, well . . .'' Strickland rounded his desk and opened the middle drawer. He pulled out the ledger he kept there and in short order presented Rand with a draft.

Rand glanced at the amount. "This is too generous. It's more than my costs."

"I hope you will take it. And you need not worry that I expect something in return." He watched Rand fold the cheque and place it inside his jacket. "When will you be leaving London?"

"I've allowed myself and crew two full weeks. They may agree there is nothing to be gained by waiting it out, but I'm in no hurry. The Royal Geographical Society has invited me to speak about my voyages to the South Pacific."

"I had heard that," Strickland said. "Congratulations. The Society is particular about their lecturers. Not many explorers outside Britain are given that opportunity."

Rand was fairly certain the duke had played a part in extending the invitation. Someone in his family had been a fellow of the Society since its inception. Apparently Strickland wanted no credit or thanks. "The honor for me is in having my small contributions to the natural sciences recognized."

"I would hardly characterize them as small."

"I'm not a particularly modest man," Rand said. "My observational writings will not have the impact of Darwin's, and my explorations are not so exciting as Burton's, but in my own way I have advanced the understanding of man's influence on the environment."

Strickland's expression turned thoughtful. "Listening to you talk now, l could almost believe the Hamilton-Waterstone treasure is a diversion, not a purpose unto itself." His pale blue eyes considered Rand again, this time taking the measure of the man with a different yardstick. "But then, you began your training as a naturalist, didn't you? Here in England, if I'm not mistaken."

Rand imagined the duke knew very well that he wasn't mistaken. Strickland did not strike Rand as having made too many mistakes in his research. He would not have offered four thousand pounds and his goddaughter to just anyone. "At Oxford," Rand said. "My studies were interrupted by the war at home."

"You never returned?"

"No. I've studied on my own."

"Then you didn't complete your formal education in America?"

"I completed it on board *Cerberus.*" And in the fields at Gettysburg, he could have added. He'd made a study of the nature of man on that occasion, but it was not something he wanted to write about. It was not something he even wanted to remember.

"Do you regret not finishing at Oxford?"

"What I regret is that I did not have the opportunity to study under Abernathy or Bancroft or Sonnenfeld. They taught third-year students and—" Rand stopped. His eyes narrowed on Strickland, and for a moment his mouth flattened. "Bancroft?"

The duke gave nothing away. "Yes?"

"Sir Griffin Bancroft taught botanical sciences at Oxford. He is credited with the discovery of seven varieties of medicinal orchids."

"I should say it's well over two dozen by now," Strickland said amiably. "He's been away from his chair at university for almost seven years, and I expect he made good use of it. He always was a prodigious talent."

"He studied in the South Pacific."

"That's correct. That's where he returned when he left Oxford."

Rand reached inside his jacket and removed Strickland's draft. He held it out. When the duke made no move to accept it back, Rand laid it on the desk. "You couldn't let me leave here without knowing," he said. "So much for expecting nothing in return." He crossed the room and opened the door. He was on the point of leaving when he heard Strickland's quiet, mocking response.

"So much for expecting it not to matter."

Rand Hamilton did not immediately return to his rented house on Beecher Street. He met with his crew on the *Cerberus* and informed them they could expect little in the way of remuneration this time out. He would not have blamed them if they had deserted on the spot. He didn't expect them to, but he wouldn't have held it against them. Instead they pooled their meager resources and took him to a waterfront tavern. They let him get stinking drunk and bought him a whore.

Or at least Rand hoped they had paid for her. Levering himself up on one elbow, Rand slowly tugged at the sheet that covered the whore's face. Her brow puckered as the material brushed her skin, but she didn't wake. She had a wide face, vaguely heart-shaped, and dark hair. Her lips were parted and she made an abrupt little sound reminiscent of a snore when Rand covered her again. At least she was not a child. Rand had to be thankful his men used some discretion in choosing a diversion for him. That only left him to wonder if she was diseased.

He sat up and immediately put his head in his hands. "God," he said softly, closing his eyes. "What swill did they pour down my throat?"

"They didn't have to pour it down, guv'nor. You managed to toss the rum back on your own."

Rand slowly turned sideways, keeping his head as steady as possible. He lowered his eyes just enough to take in the whore. "I thought you were sleeping."

"Wasn't I just," she said. "Then you commenced your inspection of the goods." She smiled and revealed a remarkably healthy, though slightly crooked set of teeth. "I don't disappoint, do I?" She pushed herself upright, completely unconcerned that the sheet slipped to her waist. "Here's a pair, ain't they, guv'nor? Go on, you can touch 'em, seein' that they're out and all."

"That's kind of you, Miss . . ."

She giggled and tossed her head back. Her hair fell behind her shoulder so there could be no mistaking she meant for Rand to have an eyeful. "Jeri-Ellen. Two names, don't you know. After me dad and mum."

One name for each breast, he thought muzzily.

"Go on, sir. Take 'em in hand. I don't mind a little squeeze now and again."

"Well, Jeri-Ellen, just at this moment my hands are needed

to secure my head to my neck. But it's as good an offer as I've ever had.''

She thrust out her lower lip, not at all placated by his rather off-handed compliment. "Then you don't want a poke?"

He started to shake his head, groaned, and used words instead of gestures. "Not this morning."

Jeri-Ellen fell backward in a dramatic swoon and covered her eyes with one forearm. "I suppose this means you'll be wanting your money back. And where does that leave me, I'm thinking. Charles knows I've spent the night here. He's going to expect something for my services. I can't show up with nothing, now can I?"

"Then you've been paid?"

She raised her forearm and looked at him. "Right off. You mean you don't remember?"

"Not a thing," he admitted.

Jeri-Ellen smiled widely. She nodded once, satisfied, and leaped out of bed. She began gathering her clothes, oblivious to the fact that her quick exit had shaken the bed and almost brought Rand Hamilton to his knees. "That's all right, then. Who's to know? You were a wonderful lover, guv'nor. Poked me three times and it's still like you was inside, though I don't mind a large one like yours from time to time. Keeps me company the rest of the day, if you know what I mean." She continued to move spritely about the room, slipping into her chemise and shift, giving lie to anything but the fact that she'd had a good night's rest. "I think I gave as good as I got," she said, expanding on her theme. She added, winking at him, "Leastways, you had no complaints."

Rand discovered it hurt to smile and also that he couldn't help himself. The thought of taking this saucy whore three times over would have brought outright laughter if he could have survived it. "Three pokes," he said softly. "Imagine that."

"I'll have to." She sighed, giving up the pretense. The coins she'd been given jingled pleasantly in the pocket of her dress as she pulled it on. "No need to help with the hooks. I'll find one of my friends to do me up. Like as not I'm not the only one sleeping in this morning. Won't Charles just be apoplectic?'' She lifted her skirts high and raised one slender leg to pull on her stockings.

"Charles?" Rand asked. "You mentioned him before."

"He takes care of me."

"Your pimp."

"There's some that call him that. He prefers protector." She forced her feet into shoes that were a bit too tight for her. "Oooh. That's the first thing I'm going to do with my coins. A new pair of leathers for me feet."

"Drawers wouldn't come amiss," Rand noted dryly. He'd gotten another eyeful when she threw up her skirts.

"Now what would I be needing new drawers for? Mine are right here." She slipped the toe of her right foot under one corner of the bed and it came out dragging her drawers at the end of it. In a rather bawdy display of acrobatic grace, Jeri-Ellen kicked high and the drawers sailed upward. She caught them in her hands, held them open, and stepped in, wriggling like a harem dancer until they were in place under her shift. "Admit it, guv'nor, there's not many that would give you a show for the price of a poke."

"I fear I'm not the appreciative audience your talents deserve."

"That's all right, sir." She patted him on the shoulder and dropped a kiss on his forehead, nearly spilling out of her bodice in the process. "You show a bit more temperance with your drinking next time and come and see me. I shouldn't be at all surprised if we go for four pokes."

"I would."

Jeri-Ellen was philosophical. "Men just don't have the stamina of women, do they? More's the pity." She shrugged. "Mornin' to you, guv'nor." She was out the door and deaf to his entreaty not to slam it.

Rand lowered himself back on the bed very slowly. It was a small comfort that he didn't have to worry that he'd contracted the pox.

* * *

It was two hours after Jeri-Ellen's departure before Rand felt fit enough to leave. He wasn't at all surprised that he was no longer at the tavern where the drinking had started, but the effect was disorienting. He ignored the knowing looks he received from passersby as he took a moment to get his bearings. When he caught sight of Lloyd's, he began walking in the opposite direction.

The house on Beecher Street was a luxury he could no longer properly afford. Just now it was difficult to remember exactly why he'd considered it necessary to leave Strickland's cheque behind. It hadn't seemed a precipitous action at the time, but he couldn't help thinking he'd acted hastily.

Rand let himself into the foyer, shutting the door softly behind him. He stamped his feet, shaking droplets of muddy water free of his boots, and flung his coat over a chair in the corner. The noise was enough to rouse Cutch from the kitchen below stairs.

"You're back," Cutch said, looking Rand over. "And none too worse for a night's drinking and whoring, I reckon."

"That's because you're not inside this head."

Cutch stood almost seven feet tall. He was one of the few men capable of making an assessment of Rand from a superior height. He made the most of it now, stepping in closer and forcing Rand to bend his neck back while he examined his eyes and the pallor of his complexion. "Wouldn't surprise me at all if you swallowed some bad liquor. Anyone else feeling as poorly as you?"

"I don't know. I didn't see anyone from the crew this morning. They deserted me. I didn't get the money, Cutch." He saw Cutch's black brows lift and belatedly realized how what he'd said could be interpreted. "I don't mean they deserted me because I didn't get the money. They took me drinking and whoring because I didn't get the money. They deserted me because they had duties back at *Cerberus* and I wasn't fit for traveling."

The high furrowed plane of Cutch's forehead became smooth

again. "You're not fit for receiving visitors either, but you've got one." He smiled widely, his large white teeth a startling contrast to his dark skin. His deep chuckle vibrated pleasantly in his chest. "Money's got to come from somewhere. I wouldn't turn this one away."

Rand swore softly. The last thing he wanted was to face Strickland in his current condition. "I have to change."

"In anticipation of your arrival, I drew a bath for you. Of course that was over an hour ago, but the water might still be warm. Go on. Your guest's not leaving without talking to you. Very particular about that. I'll bring you something for that head." Cutch stepped back and gestured toward the stairs. "You want me to carry you?"

Rand gave the older man a sour look. "I think I can manage from here, thank you."

Cutch watched him mount the stairs anyway, silent laughter in his coffee-colored eyes. He had just the remedy for what ailed his captain.

The water was a few degrees cooler than tepid, but Rand didn't care. For once he drank down Cutch's foul-tasting concoction without asking what was in it. On the few occasions he had required it before, Cutch had never been forthcoming with the recipe. Rand had no reason to believe that would change. He preferred not to think beyond the obvious ingredients of tomato and raw egg. It was probably better not to know what gave the drink its peculiar tang and made him sweat rum as though he were a tapped keg.

While he soaked, he heard Cutch moving about in the bedchamber, laying out fresh clothes. Rand had no recollection of a time when Cutch hadn't been looking out for him or some other member of his family. He was of an indeterminate age, though his long history with the Hamiltons suggested he was now in his late fifties. It was Rand's father who had given Cutch his manumission papers, making the slave a free man twenty years before the Emancipation Proclamation required it. It was not a thing Andrew Hamilton had done lightly, but Cutch had saved young David from drowning and there was no better way to thank him. Cutch didn't go anywhere, though.

He celebrated his freedom by shaving his head and kept it that way just because he could.

Rand felt almost human by the time he finished dressing. He looked over his reflection in the cheval glass while Cutch pronounced himself satisfied with the transformation. Rand raked back his hair and felt the lingering dampness in the dark copper strands. He tugged on his collar and let the overlong curling ends drop against his skin. Cutch brushed off the shoulders and back of his jacket and adjusted the fit.

"Don't be too proud to take the money," Cutch said.

Rand's eyes lifted to meet Cutch's in the mirror. "There might not be another offer."

Cutch shrugged his broad shoulders. "Can't imagine someone going to all the trouble of coming here unless there's an offer in the waiting."

Rand remained unconvinced, but he was in a better frame of mind to meet the duke. "We'll see. Will you bring us some tea?"

"I already have."

There was no hesitation in Rand's step this time as he retraced his trail down the stairs. On the threshold to the sitting room he gave Cutch an encouraging sign, noticing only at the last moment that the other man was smiling perhaps a little too broadly. Rand was completely inside the room before he understood why that might be so.

"Good morning," he said. "It's Miss Bancroft, isn't it?"

Claire Bancroft nodded. She had started to rise when she heard the door open; now she lowered herself back into the corner of the sofa. "Your man said you wouldn't mind if I waited for you."

Rand dismissed the apologetic undertone. If she knew that it was a bother for him, she should have left her card and taken herself off. Apology now was a waste of breath. "Cutch doesn't always know my mind." He saw her head jerk up and a faint wash of color touch her cheeks. It was an immediate improvement on the pallor of her complexion.

Rand went to the side table where Cutch had placed the tea service. He poured himself a cup and added a small amount of milk. Claire Bancroft, he noted, seemed interested in his movement, although she did not appear to watch him directly. He also saw that she avoided looking him straight in the eye. "Will you have some more tea?" he asked.

"No, thank you." Her hands settled quietly in her lap. She turned her eyes in their direction.

Rand sat opposite her on an overstuffed armchair. He took his first sip of tea and wished to heaven that he had asked Cutch for coffee. Miss Bancroft's English taste buds be damned, he thought. Darjeeling was no fit substitute for the heady pitch that Cutch brewed. "What can I do for you, Miss Bancroft?"

"Stickle says you've refused him."

Rand blinked. "Stickle?" He couldn't have heard her correctly. "You are permitted to call Evan Markham, the Eighth Duke of Strickland, *Stickle?*"

Claire felt heat in her cheeks again, but she managed to keep herself from touching them. "He *is* my godfather," she explained. "It was the best I could manage as a child. And he's not so high in the instep as he'd like to have you think."

"Then we already have a difference of opinion," said Rand, "but I'll accept that you believe it. Did he send you here?"

"Oh, no," she said quickly. "I doubt if he knows I'm gone. He wouldn't approve. He thought that I should invite you back to his house, but I didn't think you'd come." She paused and risked a glance his way. "Would you?"

"I don't know."

Claire nodded. "Then it's good that I didn't leave it to chance. Luck is overrated, don't you think?"

"I'm inclined to believe we make our own," he agreed.

Her smile was tentative and did not reach her eyes. "Yes, well, that's what I've come to realize." At her side was a small beaded bag. She reached for it and opened it, extracting Strickland's cheque. "We both want you to have this," she said. "You shouldn't feel that it obligates you in any way." She held it up. "Please, won't you take it?"

Claire held it out for what seemed an eternity to her. At last she felt it being tugged gently from between her fingers. She let out her breath slowly and settled back against the sofa.

"Thank you. I confess that I was afraid you wouldn't deign to accept it. It's all very well for us to say there is no indebtedness, but that cannot account for your own feelings. I explained to my godfather that by drawing the draft too generously, he had placed you in an awkward position. He was not trying to purchase your services, Captain Hamilton, only recompense you your full due."

Claire fell silent and the silence stretched uncomfortably. Had she said something to offend him? What had happened? "Captain?"

Rand turned over his hand and let the small, torn pieces of the cheque flutter to the carpet. Not once did her eyes follow their movement. There was a slight tremor to his hand as he picked up his cup and saucer.

"When were you going to tell me that you're blind, Miss Bancroft?"

Chapter Two

Claire Bancroft's smile held a touch of irony. "You're the one with a pair of good eyes, Captain. It wasn't something I was trying to hide. I thought you could see for yourself."

He could, now that he knew what to look for. On brief acquaintance she was clever at disguising what set her apart from others. When she had never quite met his gaze fully, he had considered it a measure of her shyness. At the moment she seemed to be intuitively aware of his scrutiny, but she didn't flinch from it. Instead her chin came up a notch, almost defiantly, inviting him to take his fill.

Rand did not think she had been blind from birth. Her almond-shaped eyes were as deeply brown as bittersweet chocolate, the irises and pupils clear of any obvious imperfection. He imagined her blindness had come upon her gradually, over the course of years. He guessed she was not yet twenty-five. When was the last time she had seen anything clearly? he wondered, and what was the last thing she saw? "How long?" he asked.

"Eighteen months," she said. "I suspect that surprises you. It does most people who aren't afraid to pose the question."

Was this the ordeal Strickland had spoken of? Rand wondered. ''Was there something you wanted this morning? Besides to return Strickland's cheque.'' There was no point in mentioning what he had done with it. The duke would suspect a problem when it was never presented to his bank for cashing. Claire Bancroft did not have to know.

She hesitated. She had carefully considered what she would say on the carriage ride to his townhouse. She'd had further time to refine her plea while she waited for him. Now, given this opportunity, she found that her mouth was dry and the words were a tangle in her head. Sightlessness had not made her especially courageous when facing someone down. She found that her imagination still worked too well, and what she encountered in her mind's eye was far more intimidating than anything her healthy eyes would have confronted. Or at least she hoped that was the case. There was cause to wonder when she'd made the acquaintance of the one called Cutch. The giant had called a great obsidian obelisk to her mind, and she could not remove the image.

It was not so very different with Captain Hamilton. She had witnessed how his quietly confident manner could border on arrogance, and he had already proved he could be uncompromising. She had immediately envisioned the stone sentinels she had seen on Easter Island and throughout Polynesia. Claire embellished this tiki to be larger than its companions, with a face more aggressively carved but every bit as implacable.

''I came to ask you to reconsider,'' she said. ''You're a man of science as well as adventure. I hope you will be a man of reason.''

''Thus far your attempt at flattery is falling short of the mark. I am *always* a man of reason.''

Beneath his words the tone was as dry as bleached bones. Claire could almost imagine there was a hint of a smile at one corner of his mouth. Perhaps the captain was not as obdurate as stone after all. If she was wrong, he could always crush her to prove himself. ''Stickle told me you recognized my father's name.''

''I didn't remain long enough to identify the relationship between you and Sir Griffin, but yes, I recognized the name and the fact there was a connection. The duke says your father's in the South Pacific.''

''Yes, that's right.'' Claire paused. ''The last I knew that was true.''

Rand frowned and realized the expression was lost on her. ''Miss Bancroft, if what you're looking for is to mount an expedition to locate your father, then why not just do that? Why do you need me?''

''Because I can think of no one with so great a chance of being successful.''

''Your flattery improves.''

''I have no wish to flatter you, Captain. I state what I have because I believe it to be the truth. I also cannot allow you to consider my request under any pretenses. It's unlikely that my father is still alive, and while I find I cannot give up my last hope, I have made some peace with it. My desire to return to Solonesia is not so those fears can be confirmed or relieved.''

''Then why?''

''My brother's there. Or at least I hope he is. While I don't think my father is alive, I believe that Tipu is.''

''Was there some accident? Illness?''

Claire shook her head. She touched her temple and said faintly, ''I'm not certain.'' This was met with silence. ''Are you glowering, Captain Hamilton? Or is your expression merely confused?''

Rand was fairly certain he was glowering. ''Confused, I'm afraid.''

''Then you have some idea what I feel. I have no clear memory of the events of my last days in Solonesia. It may be that I am missing only a few hours or as much as a week. What I can recall clearly begins as I was being lifted from an outrigger by islanders at Raiatea.''

''Raiatea? But that's almost six hundred nautical miles from the Sun Islands.''

''Closer to seven. Stickle plotted it out for me on a map.''

''You did this alone?''

Claire didn't fault Rand for his disbelief. She found it difficult to credit herself and she had been the one to do it. ''Apparently so,'' she said. ''I say that because I can't be certain. I'm told there was an empty skin in the boat which probably held water. There were crumbs on the floor that I hadn't found. One paddle was missing. There was no one with me at Raiatea. My exposed skin was burned and I was dehydrated. I weighed quite a bit less than I do now.''

That would have made her very nearly insubstantial, Rand thought. For a moment he pictured her at the taffrail of *Cerberus*. A gentle Pacific breeze would lift her hair—and the rest of her—right into the water. He quickly revised the image. She would never survive the cold Atlantic crossing to meet up with those breezes again. Certainly she would never encounter them on the *Cerberus*. ''How long ago was that?''

''A year and a half.''

Rand made the connection to the onset of her blindness. ''Was it the sun?'' he asked.

''Most of the doctors say that. Stickle has taken me to more than a dozen. Almost to a man they say the same thing: the sun's glare off the water, the steady exposure to the bright light, burned the retinas. These same physicians hold out no hope. The condition cannot be reversed.''

He almost said he was sorry. Those words, coming from a person of no account in her life, such as himself, would give little comfort and might even be construed as pity. Besides, he had heard something else, something that made him believe Claire Bancroft might hold out some hope. ''You said almost all,'' he told her. ''What do the others say about your condition?''

''Not others,'' she said. ''Only one. A physician in Paris, Dr. Anton Messier, believes there may be another explanation. He says the one offered by others is too facile. The condition of my eyes is not consistent with what I report to have suffered. He thinks my blindness is here, in my head.'' She tapped her temple lightly. ''In my thinking,'' she went on. ''Not in my eyes.''

Now Rand realized he could feel pity for her. She was quite literally groping in the dark, accepting one irresponsible physician's opinion against the prevailing wisdom of all the others.

Claire knew how to interpret this silence. "Your skepticism is understandable. His grace thinks no differently, but he *is* my godfather and he believes it's his duty to indulge me."

"Forgive me, Miss Bancroft, but I can't help but point out—"

She held up her hand. "When you begin a sentence with *forgive me,* it's a sure sign that the rest should be left unsaid. Do I seem spoiled to you, Captain? Have I given you the impression that I must have my own way? I have yet to throw a tantrum because you've turned me down. If you were the sightless one in this room, can you honestly say you would not reach for the carrot Dr. Messier has offered?"

As Claire warmed to her subject and as her agitation increased, she moved closer to the edge of the sofa. "I know what I am risking by holding out this hope, but I am accepting a life of darkness if I risk nothing."

Rand watched her come to her feet. A year or more ago, he thought, she would have paced the floor, perhaps gone to the window and turned her back on him while she spoke. Her short, impassioned speech had given rise to a certain restlessness that she could not properly express in an unfamiliar room. She stood in front of the sofa, her hands at her side, the fingers alone betraying something of what she was feeling by curling and uncurling against the dark fabric of her gown.

"I am at six o'clock," he said quietly. "There is a window bench twelve paces behind you at twelve o'clock. You must only skirt the sofa and side table."

Surprise stilled her fingers. Her head lowered and her eyes narrowed in Rand's direction, as if she could peer through the black curtain of her vision and see him clearly. She smiled faintly as she realized what she was trying to do. "Thank you," Claire said. "I never oriented myself to this room. I was afraid I would break something."

He considered how difficult it must have been for her to sit in one corner of the sofa while she waited for him, when what she wanted to do was explore. "There's nothing in it that can't be replaced," he said. "Of course, since I'm renting the house, none of it's mine." He watched her feel her way carefully around the side table. The cup and saucer she had placed there rattled momentarily as her fingers brushed them.

"Twelve paces?" she asked, rounding the table.

"I think so. Unless you have a mannish stride, Miss Bancroft. Then I make it to be ten."

Several strands of Claire's dark hair had fallen forward across her cheek. She brushed them back impatiently, tucking them behind her ear until she could repair the knot that held the rest in place. "I shall endeavor to comport myself as a lady," she said wryly.

Rand found himself grinning. It was odd, he thought, watching her. He had not yet revised his first impression of Claire Bancroft, but he was open to the possibility that he might have to. As on the occasion of their first meeting yesterday, she had taken no pains to draw his attention to her appearance. He considered that it might be related to her blindness, but he dismissed that idea almost at once. He doubted she ever gave her appearance more than an afterthought. Someone might have chosen the plain navy-blue day dress for her to wear today, but he suspected her wardrobe was filled with gowns of an equally nondescript nature. She would have had a hand in selecting her new gowns when she returned to England, and apparently practicality ruled the day.

Perhaps it was the gown's very simplicity that drew Rand's eye to the figure in it, but for whatever reason, he found himself looking at the slender line of her back and shoulders, the curve of a high waist that his hands could span, and the suggestion of legs that went on just about forever. There was nothing remotely mannish about her stride. Claire Bancroft carried herself with casual gracefulness, the slight hesitation in her step her only concession to blindness.

She found the window bench with the toe of her shoe, then found the window with her hand. She laid a palm flat against one of the panes and felt the coolness of the glass. "Is there still fog outside?"

Rand rose from his chair and walked over to the narrow rectangular window. "Yes. It looks to be a gray morning and afternoon. How did you know about the fog?"

"My driver mentioned it when he was helping me into the carriage. He said he didn't think he'd be able to see a thing." She shrugged lightly. "I offered to drive . . ."

Rand laughed. "You have a rather droll sense of humor," he said.

"Do I?" She considered the observation seriously for a moment, her wide mouth flattening. A small vertical crease appeared between her dark brows. "I suppose I may be acquiring one," she said at last.

Rand was not entirely certain that she wasn't pulling his leg again. Her tone was so arid, it was difficult to tell. "Would you like to sit or continue pacing?"

Color touched her cheeks. "I believe I will sit," she said. "I do not intend that you should always rile me so easily."

"I didn't try to do it earlier." Rand felt her stiffen as he touched her elbow to guide her onto the bench, but he didn't release her. "I can't promise that I won't do it again."

Claire removed her arm from his light grasp. She hoped it had not been too obvious that the contact had distressed her. People were never quite certain how to be helpful.

"I should have asked if my assistance was desired or even needed," Rand said.

Claire felt along one edge of the window bench and scooted herself backward a few inches. The direction of his voice told her that Rand Hamilton was no longer standing above her, but was sharing the bench with her. She looked away, toward the window she couldn't see, finding the space suddenly confining. "Yes, thank you. That would be appreciated. I find it disconcerting to be . . ." She paused, searching for the right word. "To be *handled*."

Rand's eyes skimmed her three-quarter profile thoughtfully. Her eyes were so dark a brown that they could almost be black, and the almond shape gave them a faintly exotic look. As if she could feel his appraisal, the color in her cheeks deepened. "Then I'll tell you the next time I'm going to touch you," he said.

It was the way he said it, Claire thought, that raised sensations at the back of her neck and sent the parade marching down her spine. For a moment she was afraid she was actually going to shiver. She clamped down on her teeth, tightening her jaw, to contain the reaction. She recalled to her mind the aggressive countenance of the great stone tiki and found she could substitute one kind of fear for another.

Rand removed himself from the window seat and took up a casual perch against the back of the sofa. He folded his arms across his chest and crossed his legs at the ankle. "I think I'd better hear the whole of it from you," he said. "The duke's explanation, I'm finding, was not entirely factual."

Claire turned her head toward him. Her hands settled quietly in her lap again and she realized that taking a breath was easier now that the captain had placed some distance between them. "I believe his facts were in order but that he left some things unsaid," she told him. "That would have been at my insistence, so I hope you won't think less of his grace."

"After today I hope to never think of him again," Rand said. "And I don't suppose for a moment that he cares a whit for my good opinion."

Claire's folded hands tightened almost imperceptibly. The bones of her knuckles stood out whitely against the background of her dress. In every other way she ignored Rand's terse comments. "Strickland has had an interest in the Hamilton-Waterstone legend for as long as I can remember. I learned of it at his knee. He has a collection of artifacts at Abberly Hall from all over the world. Necklaces and armbands from Egypt. Mandarin ceremonial swords. Indian sculptures. Manuscripts. Tapestries. There are few pieces that are not encrusted with gems. Lapis lazuli. Rubies. Diamonds. Stickle is particularly fond of sapphires, no matter their color. He has arguably a finer representation of the variety of sapphires than the queen has in the Crown Jewels."

"Your godfather mentioned museums," Rand drawled. "I didn't realize he was talking about his own."

"This is not public knowledge, and it's not meant to be. I'm telling you now so that you know the duke's interest in your exploration is genuine. He's been following your progress for years."

"Why am I only learning of it now?"

Claire simply stared in his direction, allowing him to work out what he could for himself.

"You?" he asked. "The duke's revealing his interest because of you?"

Claire was surprised and not a little disappointed that he had attached his thinking to the simplest explanation. He was proving Stickle right. Rand Hamilton deserved to know no more than he was capable of considering. "Yes. Because of me. Dr. Messier has hypothesized that if I return to Solonesia I may be able to recreate the events that led to my blindness. In confronting my fear—if indeed that's what it is—then I may be able to regain my sight."

"There is some precedence for this, I take it."

"Dr. Messier cited three cases of unexplained, spontaneous reversal of blindness."

"Did any of them mention Jesus Christ?"

Claire almost came to her feet again. At the last moment she recalled the promise she had made to herself not to take the bait he dangled. "I believe the doctor looked for examples outside of the New Testament," she said coolly.

"This documentation," he continued to probe, "has it all been in the last fifty years?"

"In the last five hundred years."

Now Rand invoked the Lord's name again, this time by cursing softly under his breath. "Three examples in five hundred years," he said incredulously. "*This* is your best hope?"

"It's my *only* hope."

Rand fell silent for a time. "Tell me more about your father and brother."

"My father left Oxford in '68 to return to the South Pacific. He received a grant from the duke to research the flora around Tahiti and farther north to the Sun Islands. His earlier work in Polynesia, around the Cook Islands, had led him to some promising medicines for hemophilia. The queen, naturally, has been interested."

Rand understood Queen Victoria's interest. Her children all suffered with the disease that kept the blood from clotting and made even a bruise potentially life-threatening. "That's why he received his knighthood," Rand said slowly, thinking back. "He wasn't Sir Griffin when I first encountered him at Oxford."

"The honor was conferred on him in '63. Her majesty was very grateful."

"Grateful to the duke as well, I'd imagine." When Claire frowned, he added, "For his financial support of the research."

"Oh, yes. He's a favorite with her." At the nape of her neck, just below the place where her hair was swept up into its smooth coil, Claire felt a band of heat touch her. She bent her head forward a fraction, exposing more of her skin to this hint of the sun's warmth. She could not know it, but the man watching her found the gesture sensual and vaguely erotic. "The sun's come out," she said. The lift of the corners of her mouth was so slight that it could not properly be called a smile, yet Rand thought she was fairly thrumming with pleasure.

"Yes, it has," he said.

Claire lifted her face and the band of sunlight slipped to her collar. She continued as if there had been no sybaritic pleasures to distract her. "I accompanied my father on both his voyages to Polynesia. I was very young yet when he was exploring Tahiti and the Cook Islands, but I have many vivid memories of that time. I had no hesitation about going back with him." Her voice dropped to a near whisper. "I have no hesitation now."

"No," Rand said without inflection. "Apparently the hesitation is all on my part."

"Make no mistake, Captain Hamilton, if it isn't you, it will be someone. I've already explained why it should be you. My father is not of the revered stature of Dr. Livingston, and Solonesia is not the Dark Continent, but if you should be the one to find him alive, you can be certain fame and a considerable fortune would follow."

"Like Stanley? Rather a difficult task, I should think, since you've already made it clear that Sir Griffin is probably dead. I don't suppose I can expect fame or fortune for locating your bastard brother."

Claire sucked in her breath. "You have no—"

"No right? Perhaps not, but that doesn't make me wrong. You said his name was Tipu. That suggests to me that he has an islander mother. If he was on Solonesia when you left, then he was probably born there, and I make his age to be no more than a few months past six. I don't suppose he has Stickle for his godfather."

This time Claire did stand. Anger made it difficult to think clearly and that disoriented her. She had learned it was possible to be blind and still be blinded by rage.

"I've remained at a six o'clock position," Rand said easily. "The door is at nine. Your reticule is on the sofa. Do you want it?"

"Yes."

"Then you'll have to come here to get it, won't you?"

Claire's lips changed their shape around the word *bastard.* She took a step forward and was brought up short by Rand's light laughter.

"Careful, Miss Bancroft. That word is apparently the one that got me into trouble with you. What would be served by both of us being in a snit?"

Claire walked forward again, less confidently this time, afraid that Rand would place himself squarely in her path. She felt the edge of the sofa, sensed his nearness, and moved around. She forgot about the side table and bumped it hard with her leg. She bit her lip rather than cry out, and when she tasted blood on the inside of her mouth she had the satisfaction of knowing that at least she'd kept it from him.

Her bag was on the cushion exactly where she'd left it. Claire held it in both hands and walked toward the door at the nine o'clock position.

"I'm going to touch you."

His voice was very near her ear. She'd had no sense of how he came to be so close. She hadn't heard him move from his place at the back of the couch. Claire stopped so suddenly that inside her chest it was as if her heart was still moving forward. There was a hard, sustained beat, then a slow return to normal rhythm.

Rand slipped his hand around her upper arm. "Are you

really going because I've offended you?'' he asked. ''Or is it something else?''

Claire raised her face. ''I don't know what you mean.''

He couldn't tell if that was the case or not. Yesterday he had been hard pressed to notice her; this morning he couldn't seem to help himself. There was an *awareness* here that he did not think he was mistaking. Certainly he felt it. Rand was only willing to lay so much of the blame on last night's rum and the lingering effects of Jeri-Ellen's stale perfume.

Rand changed the subject. ''Where would you go on board *Cerberus?* If you walk away at every slight, then you'll be in the water before we make Charleston.''

''I imagine I'd go to my cabin, Captain,'' she said levelly. ''Not walk the plank.''

Rand eased his grip slightly. ''Will you have a seat, Miss Bancroft?'' He felt her agreement in the relaxation of her body. If not a complete surrender, it was at least some measure of progress. Rand helped her find the sofa again. She sat but did not let go of her reticule this time.

''I wasn't wrong about your brother, was I?'' he asked.

Claire shook her head. ''No, not wrong. But you made Tipu sound as if he were of no account. He's my brother and I care very much what's happened to him.''

''Perhaps more than your father?''

She didn't answer immediately and when she did, she didn't deny it. ''Differently than my father.''

Rand waited, prepared for her to say more, certain she was on the verge of it. He watched her hold it in, almost as if she was absorbing the silence to withdraw into herself. She was paler than she had been a moment before, drained by the effort to contain what she felt.

''Solonesia is a chain of more than twenty islands and atolls,'' Rand said. ''How will you know if we come upon the right one?''

''Eight are inhabited. When I left, my father was working on one that was not. The one the natives call Pulotu, the spirit land.''

Rand shook his head, wondering at Sir Griffin's folly in

choosing to set foot on what was no doubt sacred ground. "Then it's guarded by tikis."

"Seven tiki women. I call them the sisters."

Rand felt his heart lurch. "Seven sisters," he said quietly, as if he did not fairly resonate with the deep chord she struck. "That's *your* name for them?"

"Yes," she said. "Like in the Mother Goose rhyme. It seemed an obvious name for seven goddesses. I'm certain I didn't hear it anywhere else. The natives of Solonesia don't willingly talk about the guardians or set foot on Pulotu. There is a very powerful tapu there."

"Sacred spell."

"Yes."

"But your father risked going there anyway."

"He didn't believe in the tapu. He said the tikis were there to warn navigators away from the shoals."

Rand was coming to the conclusion that Sir Griffin was a talented botanist but a poor historian and sailor. The sandbars that created the shallows around some of the islands would have posed no problem for the outrigger canoes used by the Polynesians. They would not have placed the sacred stone images to warn fellow explorers about the shallows.

He did not mention this to Claire. Instead he asked, with a trace of humor, "Shoals? I have to also worry about grounding my ship? Is there anything else that should concern me and my crew? An abnormally large population of sharks, for example. Or wild boars once we're ashore?"

Claire's voice contained hope she had not thought she could realize. "Do your questions mean that you'll take me? Am I to return to Solonesia with you?"

"I believe we can come to terms."

For the second time in two days Rand was a guest at the Duke of Strickland's London house. This occasion was dinner. The invitation to join Strickland and Claire had arrived that afternoon, not long after Claire would have returned home and informed her godfather of Rand's capitulation. To Rand's way of thinking, she hadn't let a moment pass between telling Strickland and arranging Rand's own presence at the house. Clearly she wanted to come to terms quickly.

He wondered if they believed he would change his mind.

Rand was seated to the right of his host at the dining table. Claire, he immediately noticed, had made a point of dressing for dinner and sat across from him. As each course was served, Claire unobtrusively ran her index finger along the rim of the plate, feeling for the placement of the meat, or fish, or vegetable. The only real concession that Rand could observe Claire making was in her contribution to the conversation. With her concentration fully engaged in managing the cold soup, the steamed trout, and the lemon sorbet, she was able to offer little.

Or perhaps it was simply that Strickland gave so few opportunities for her to slip in a word. The duke, Rand realized, might be willing to indulge his goddaughter by supporting the voyage, but he had a list of conditions of his own. All of them apparently leading up to the one he proposed over the port.

"I want someone to attend Claire," Strickland said, leaning back in his chair. He swirled his glass, considering the port's deep color and bouquet. He glanced at his goddaughter. "I really wish you would leave us now, dear. You cannot enjoy this."

Claire smiled with genuine amusement. "And miss you haggling over what concerns me the most?" she asked. "I think I'll stay just where I am, thank you. Please don't let my presence keep you from enjoying one of your cigars." To prove that she meant it, Claire rose from the table and went to the sideboard. It only took her a moment to find the duke's intricately carved cigar box. She carried it back, nudged open the lid, and held it out for Strickland's choosing. The duke took one and Claire came around the table to make the same offer to Rand.

"Captain? His grace informs me these are the finest cigars in London."

"That may be, but I don't smoke." He turned back to the duke as Claire withdrew the box. "Miss Bancroft seems eminently capable of attending to her needs as well as everyone else's," he said. "I'm not prepared to take another passenger."

The duke chuckled. "You're referring to Claire's little display of independence. I beg you not to be misled. Before you commit yourself to any position, you should know that she practiced just that action for a large part of the afternoon."

Rand saw Claire fumble with the box as her godfather gave her away. She placed it on the sideboard with enough force to make Rand wince; then she turned on both of them.

"I practice everything," Claire said without apology. "I've had to learn how to walk again and how to feed myself. You would have me remain helpless, your grace, dependent on your staff for my most basic needs. I told you at the outset that I would not have it so. I am not so independent as I would like, but I have no need for someone to be my crumb catcher."

Claire pushed away from the sideboard and took up her chair at the table. "I won't have my place on board *Cerberus* jeopardized by your conditions, your grace. I told you Captain Hamilton would have terms of his own. I've yet to hear them."

Rand did not believe there was anyone in all of the British Empire who could speak to the Duke of Strickland as Claire just had. He made allowances for her that he would grant no one else and Rand suspected this was not a recent turn of events. Rand hoped she did not expect the same license from him. On board *Cerberus* his word was the last word and there was rarely a time when he entertained discussion.

Rand set his glass on the table. Candlelight flickered across his hand. "I think I should tell you, Miss Bancroft, that my first term is that you never speak to me the way you just did to your godfather. To do so privately will get you confined to your quarters. In front of others will get you keelhauled."

Claire's cheeks pinkened as Rand began speaking. When he was finished, they were ablaze with high color. Still she spoke evenly, one dark brow lifted in cool inquiry, "Do they still do that? Keelhaul, I mean."

"*I* do."

Claire was quiet a moment. "Is his grace smiling?" she asked finally.

Rand glanced at the duke, then back at Claire. "Yes, he appears to be amused."

Her mouth flattened disapprovingly. "Traitor," she whispered.

Still smiling indulgently, the duke shrugged and held up his cigar. One of the dining room's attendants peeled himself away from the wainscoting and came forward to strike a match. Strickland drew deeply on the cigar and released a puff of smoke that immediately sought out the room's four corners with its heady aroma. "Well, Captain?" he asked. "Do you still disagree that she needs a companion?"

What Rand thought Claire Bancroft needed was a keeper. He imagined that saying so would only raise her hackles. "I didn't say that I disagreed with your suggestion, merely that I was unprepared to grant it. Did you already have someone in mind to accompany her? What accommodations would be required? *Cerberus* has limited space."

"Soon after Claire arrived in London I hired Mrs. Webster from the Academy for the Blind to privately tutor her. She is a widow and was able to accompany us when we met with physicians on the Continent. Claire's complete recovery has always been foremost in my mind. I admit, however, to having some reservations about her ability to see again and it was with this in mind that I retained Mrs. Webster's services." Strickland looked over at Claire, taking in her stoic expression. "Are you certain you won't leave us, my dear? This can't help but be painful for you."

"This is nothing you and I haven't discussed before," she said. "I know what you think of the chances to reverse my condition. I told Captain Hamilton this morning that you didn't hold out much hope. I can bear to hear you say it again."

Rand realized she had spoken to relieve the duke of just that onerous task. Claire may have been at odds with her godfather's wishes, but she was sensitive to the awkwardness of his position: wanting only that she should see, while acknowledging that his prayers, his power, and his great wealth might be insufficient to make it so.

"Then it's Mrs. Webster that you'll want to join us?" Rand asked.

Strickland shook his head. "I do not believe she would be

willing to make such a journey even for what I would be prepared to pay her.''

"Mrs. Webster has grandchildren she would not want to leave," Claire explained. "The trips to Paris and Rome were exciting for her, but she always grew homesick after a few weeks."

"That's understandable. Who is your candidate, then?"

It was Strickland who answered. "I will be interviewing companions up until the time you're prepared to sail. Mrs. Webster will be certain to supply a list of qualified teachers from the Academy. I will be looking elsewhere as well. I think Mrs. Webster can be persuaded to assist me with the interviews. She will have certain expectations about Claire's new tutor. I will have others.''

"And what about Miss Bancroft's participation?" asked Rand.

Claire sighed. "Limited, I'm afraid, to accepting whomever Stickle approves.''

"I think you can appreciate, Captain," Strickland said, "that Claire's presence at the interviews would not be helpful.''

Rand was forced to agree. "The person would strictly be Miss Bancroft's companion. Is that correct?"

"She would be my teacher," Claire interjected. "I can admit there is still a great deal for me to learn. What I cannot accept is that this person should feel bound to provide conversation and diversions. The former will only tire me and the latter will place me at wit's end.''

Rand could not help himself. He offered dryly, "Perhaps she will permit you to twiddle your thumbs and talk to yourself.''

"I assure you, I would prefer it. At least I would not be stupifyingly bored.''

The duke cleared his throat and drew Rand's attention. "Mrs. Webster was a fine instructress, but her conversation was limited to her own health and her grandchildren. I believe her health remained forever fair to middling and her grandchildren were singularly unremarkable in their accomplishments.''

"His grace is saying that he suffered her presence because

I required her services. He put himself away from us at every opportunity.''

"Now, dear," Strickland began to protest, waving his cigar. "I don't really think—"

"I, on the other hand, had no choice but to have her living in my pockets."

The image she placed in Rand's head brought his smile to the surface. "That must have been powerfully motivating."

Claire actually welcomed the humor she could find in the situation now. Her lips quivered slightly. "Precisely. I learned more quickly than anyone—even Mrs. Webster—could credit. My lessons are now limited to a few hours each day."

She had every reason to be proud of her accomplishments, Rand thought. He imagined that upon longer acquaintance she would prove herself to be extraordinarily capable. It caused him to wonder whether there could actually be a long acquaintance. Claire Bancroft's physical appearance could not be described by anyone as robust. The only color he had observed in her cheeks was when she was embarrassed or angry, and those emotional states were hardly conducive to her recovery. He wondered how often she had been permitted out of doors for her lessons. The Widow Webster might have believed her pupil was not ready for walks in the park and public display. Miss Bancroft herself may have been against it.

Her hair, as dark as burnt sugar, was not without some depth and highlight as he had first thought. Coiled at the back of her head, it reflected the candlelight's orange tones and absorbed the golden ones. The same strands that had come free of their anchoring combs that morning had freed themselves again. Claire brushed at them absently, her mouth puckering as she softly blew away the last stubborn one.

The question could not be avoided. "What about Miss Bancroft's physical health?" he asked Strickland. "Have her doctors really confirmed she can make this voyage?"

"You may put that question to them yourself. The two who have seen her most frequently since her return to London are immediately available in the city."

Claire added, "I also had the benefit of a physician on board

HMS Mansfield. My recuperation began there. I returned to London by way of Australia, India, and Africa. There was a great deal of time to become accustomed to my condition, if not accept it.''

Strickland shook his head. ''She makes it sound as if she was all of a piece when she arrived. That voyage was not without its own hardships, though efforts were made to accommodate her. Her physicians will tell you she has had relapses. They suspect some recurring island malady.''

''Like malaria.''

''Yes, like that. But not malaria. That's been ruled out. Her first bout with the disease was the worst, but her survival then has given her something with which to fight subsequent bouts. At least that's what I'm told. I don't understand it. I'm not a scientist or a physician.''

''Actually, I'm not sure they understand it.''

''My thought exactly,'' Strickland said, gesturing with his cigar again. ''Claire may be able to fight these odd attacks, but not at some cost.''

Claire tapped her tea cup with the bowl of her spoon, drawing the duke's attention. ''Leave off, your grace, before Captain Hamilton reconsiders. You are not supporting the position that I am fit to travel.'' She turned to Rand. ''You must talk to my physicians yourself. They will tell you that this voyage poses no more danger to me than remaining here in London. Dr. Phillips will tell you further that the sea air will be an improvement on these close city quarters.''

''We could always return to Abberly Hall,'' Strickland pointed out.

Claire rendered him silent with a sour look. ''Well, Captain? Has his grace succeeded in raising more doubts?''

''Let's say he hasn't laid any to rest.'' But Rand also knew he wouldn't deny her passage, and that he would do everything in his power to make certain she lived long enough to lead him to Pulotu and the seven sisters.

Rand addressed Strickland. ''I've personally chosen every man who sails with me on *Cerberus*. Miss Bancroft and her companion can be no different. I've already agreed to your goddaughter. I want final approval of her teacher."

The duke's pale blue eyes widened a fraction over his wineglass. He sputtered momentarily, making vague noises of protest until he actually choked on his last swallow of port.

Watching him, Rand merely raised one eyebrow. Claire left her chair and found the duke's shoulder. She patted him lightly on the back until he recovered his breath and his wits.

"I take it you have some objection," Rand said.

Strickland patted the hand Claire rested on his shoulder, indicating that he was sufficiently recovered. She did not return to her seat, but remained at his side. "I don't believe his grace considers you qualified to make a judgment on the matter."

Rand shrugged, unconcerned. "That may be, but I'm going to exercise my right to do it anyway. If I'm unsatisfied with her performance on the first leg of the voyage, I'll find someone new in Charleston and send her back to London at my own expense."

Beneath her hand Claire felt Strickland's shoulder stiffen. He was not accustomed to this sort of high-handedness from anyone save her. She felt a moment's sorrow for him, but it did not make her smile any less genuine.

Strickland did not look up at Claire. He asked Rand, "Is she smiling?"

Rand glanced at her. "I believe she's amused, yes."

The duke sighed. "You have me then. I may as well demonstrate to my goddaughter that there is no shame in giving in gracefully. Of course, you may have the final approval. I don't believe you will have any concerns with my selection."

Rand nodded. "Very well. That brings us to the funding for this expedition. I have considered all of the requirements, and I can accept no less than six thousand pounds."

Strickland gave Rand Hamilton full marks for naming his price with a straight face. "I mentioned that four thousand was my limit."

"I'm agreeing to accept Miss Bancroft and her nursemaid, undertake the search for her father and brother, all the while trying to extend my research into Solonesia."

"And the Hamilton~Waterstone treasure," the duke said after a moment.

"I hadn't forgotten. I wondered if you had. I'm firm at six thousand."

"Bah," Strickland snorted, grinding out his cigar in a cut-glass ashtray. "The money is not the issue. Being dictated to, is. You're arrogant and ill-mannered, and I question how well you will serve me on this expedition. But Claire wants you, and I am of no mind to refuse her."

"Claire wants me," Rand said softly, testing the sound of it on his own lips.

"An unfortunate turn of phrase," Claire said. Her voice snapped as her eyes could not. "His grace meant—"

"I know what he meant," Rand interrupted. "I know I am more your choice than his." At least in some things, he told himself. "If we're agreed on the figure, then it only remains—"

Strickland held up his hand. "It only remains for you to show me some proof that you are in possession of the Hamilton riddle. That *is* what you were going to say, is it not? I need to be certain you are as you represent yourself. Claire cannot convince me to put her in your care otherwise."

"I don't carry the riddle with me," Rand said. "After three centuries the paper is in no condition to be placed in my pocket. But I've committed it to memory."

"I've committed fourteen of the bard's sonnets to memory," said Strickland. "It doesn't make any of them the Hamilton riddle."

"Then we are at an impasse because I certainly won't allow you to view the riddle in its entirety."

"Why not? What good can it possibly do me?" The duke paused, thoughtful. "It's because you don't have the Waterstone half, isn't it? You're afraid I may."

Rand said nothing and gave nothing away.

Strickland pressed. "How can you be certain you're searching anywhere close to the treasure without having both riddles?"

"I can't."

"My God," the duke said. "Do you even know what you're looking for?"

In answer, Rand quoted from the poem:

> *Blood will run*
> *Flames will come*
> *Blazing sun, blinding some*
> *Blades lifted high across the plain*
> *Flood waters rising, months of rain*
> *A plague will ink clouded skies*
> *Grieving, shadows beneath thy eyes*

Strickland looked at him blankly. "A curse?" he asked at last. "Your riddle is a curse?"

"It may be. Others before me certainly thought so. The few attempts made at finding the treasure ended in tragedy. But there may be an alternative explanation. Curses are often put in place to serve as warnings."

"Tapu," Claire said softly. "Sacred spells."

"Yes, like tapu and tiki. I believe the curses may reveal another meaning. They represent precious stones. That's what I'm looking for." Rand let the duke consider that, watching him try to recall the exact words of the riddle.

"These are the gems King Philip II of Spain intended for Pope Gregory. They were offered as tribute for the Pope's continued support in uniting Catholics across Europe against England and keeping the New World under Spain's domain. The gems nearly bankrupted the Spanish war chest, but there is no evidence that they made it to Rome or the Pope's private collection. In fact, they may not have existed at all. They could simply be another legend concocted to explain those empty state coffers. Philip would not admit that any ship carrying this treasure was captured by the English. The loss was too demoralizing, and it made him seem a fool for entrusting that fortune to a water route."

"If there was such a fortune," the duke said.

Rand lifted his glass and sipped his port. "I could be wrong. The story of the Hamilton-Waterstone treasure makes no mention of the exact nature of the Spanish prize. Perhaps it is something as mundane as gold. I could be content with discovering a chest of gold.'' His hooded glance took Strickland's full measure. The duke's own expression was guarded. ''Could you?'' Rand asked.

Strickland's austere features relaxed. ''A third share of a chest of gold? Yes, that would satisfy me.''

''A quarter share,'' Rand said. ''Plus the complete return of your investment, of course.''

''Of course,'' the duke said, his smile fading. ''I find this bargaining is tiresome and better done by cits and Yankees. I will accept a quarter share, but only because of my goddaughter. You would not find me so amenable to your changing terms were it not for her.''

Rand bowed his head slightly, acknowledging the truth of the duke's statement. He came to his feet as Strickland stood.

''You will both excuse me,'' the duke said. ''I find I am weary of terms and conditions.'' He bent his head and kissed Claire's cheek. ''G'night, m'dear. You'll see the captain out, I trust.''

Claire nodded, letting her hand drift delicately from the duke's shoulder. ''I'll look in on you before I retire.''

He smiled and patted her forearm. ''Yes, you do that.''

Claire waited until he was well beyond the room before she dismissed the servants and rounded on Rand. ''A quarter share?'' she demanded hotly. ''He told me yesterday that he had proposed a third.''

''He did. But I didn't accept,'' Rand said. ''Yesterday I hadn't agreed to any of this. Stickle could have proposed to take half and I wouldn't have protested.'' Rand gently pushed out the chair that separated him from Claire with the toe of his boot. He took a step toward her, silent now, barely breathing. His gaze fell away from her eyes only to watch her mouth.

''Don't call him Stickle. That's *my* name for him and I don't give you leave to use it.'' She drew in a sharp breath, aware of how priggish she sounded and quite unable to help herself. ''You must know that he's agreed to these terms because of me. I'm sure you were more generous to others who have financed you. You know very well I'm not going to be a hardship for you or your crew. You won't have to entertain me or—''

Rand's mouth settled over hers, swallowing her words, then her thoughts.

Chapter Three

Claire recoiled from the pressure against her mouth. Her step backward and her arching spine set her off balance. She reached for the chair to steady herself and found Rand's arms instead. She felt his hands on her waist, and each finger was like the separate bar of an iron cage. Claire brought her own arms up between them, then pushed against his chest with all the strength panic lent her.

It was enough for Rand to release her but not enough to move him away. She was the one forced back by her efforts. She stumbled again, this time catching her hip on the arm of the duke's displaced chair. Uncertain what had touched her, Claire struck at it with enough ferocity to tip it on its side. Rand couldn't stop it from thudding heavily to the floor.

Claire's small cry was something between surprise and pain. Instinctively she moved away from the fallen chair and bumped hard into the table. The hand that she put out to find purchase found Strickland's weighty glass ashtray. She picked it up and flung it hard in Rand's direction.

It was because Rand was in the process of bending over to pick up the chair that the ashtray sailed harmlessly over his head. It did, however, spell the end for a Sevres vase and a bouquet of fresh flowers. Water, pale pink blossoms, and shards of heavily decorated French porcelain spilled and scattered over the sideboard.

"What in the—" Rand looked over his shoulder as he straightened the chair and himself. It was the wrong direction in which to be interested. A dessert plate came spinning at him like a loosed circular saw blade. The impact on his chest was sufficient to make him suck in his breath. He made a grab for the plate, missed, and watched helplessly as it shattered on the floor.

Rand was only slightly better prepared for the second missile Claire threw at his head. His sideways dodge allowed him to avoid the wineglass if not the wine. Port stained the shoulder of his jacket and dripped onto the sleeve.

"Enough, Claire! Have off! I'm not going to—" Rand broke off when he saw Claire's head cock in his direction and unerringly make his location from the sound of his voice. She groped along the edge of the table for abandoned plates, bowls, and silver, and came up with a very fine fork. She let it fly. Her aim was off, but so were Rand's reflexes. He stepped right into the tines of the miniature pitchfork. "Bloody hell, Claire!"

She had an arsenal of silver at her disposal now. She held up a handful of utensils to show what she could do. "Stay precisely where you are, Captain."

He was four feet away and his hands were slowly coming up. "I'm surrendering," he told her. Rand saw her hesitate. He was encouraged that she didn't toss her fistful of ammunition at him. "Really, Claire. My hands are up."

Claire was taken by the notion, but she was also wary. "I don't believe you," she said. Then, as an afterthought, she added, "And I haven't given you leave to call me Claire."

Both of them turned toward the entrance as the sliding panel doors were pushed open. It was Strickland's butler who stood on the threshold, taking in the scene with virtually no expression. "Shall I be informing his grace of this row on the premises?"

Claire lowered her fistful of weapons slowly. "No, Emmereth. That won't be necessary."

"Very good, Miss Bancroft. I thought it might not be."

She nodded, a glimmer of a smile touching her mouth. "Thank you." She heard the doors start their slide shut and stopped the butler suddenly. "Emmereth?"

"Yes, miss?"

"Does Captain Hamilton have his hands in the air?"

"And a napkin," Emmereth said dryly as Rand waved his white linen flag. "You have him, Miss Bancroft. Like Wellington at Waterloo, I should think."

"Thank you," she said cheerfully.

Emmereth nodded and backed out of the room, closing the doors as he went.

Claire found the edge of the table and replaced the utensils. "Emmereth may not inform his grace, but we're certain to be all the servants talk about this evening."

"And the next evening," Rand said. "Unless I mistook the gleam in Emmereth's eye."

"Gleam? Was there truly? I remember him as being so dour. He frightened me when I was a child."

"I think it was a gleam. Or a tear." Rand glanced at the broken vase. "For the Sevres, perhaps."

"Oh, God. Is that what I broke?"

"Afraid so. The ashtray appears to be in one piece."

Claire sighed. "I think Stickle cares more for the Sevres."

Rand suspected that was so. "May I lower my hands now?"

"You still have them up?"

"I certainly do."

"And your flag of truce?"

"I'm waving it."

"Well, you may stop that nonsense, but leave your hands just where they are."

Rand let the napkin flutter to the floor. "As you wish," he said, then he lowered his arms.

Claire turned and leaned back against the table, her fingers holding the edge on either side of her. "I should like to hear why you kissed me," she said evenly.

"Tried to," he corrected. "Tried to kiss you. What happened cannot properly be called a kiss."

"No, it can't."

So she *did* know something about it. Rand had wondered. What was disconcerting, however, was that Claire seemed to read his thoughts.

"Did you think I'd never been kissed, Captain? I assure you, I am not without the usual experiences for a woman my age. I'm twenty-four, you know. I've quite literally been around the world, and in some cultures I'm considered tolerably pretty. I admit, yours is the first kiss I've had since I've been without sight. I don't think Stickle's peck on the cheek counts, do you?"

"No," Rand said quietly. "It wouldn't count."

"So." There was a certain finality in her tone, as if she'd drawn a conclusion and only needed him to confirm it. "I have no illusions that you find me particularly desirable, Captain Hamilton. I have every reason to believe that yesterday you failed to notice me. Did you mean to warn me off by taking me unawares? Can I expect more of the same sort of groping on board *Cerberus?*"

Rand's complexion had taken on a ruddy hue. The last time he had been set down so firmly, he was still a great green youth, stealing kisses in the stable loft and behind the slave quarters. He was thirteen when Mammy Komati caught him trying to expand his experience. She sent Jennie Ann flying out of the fruit cellar and walloped his backside good with a wooden spoon. The spoon hurt a lot less than the lecture she delivered. *Some folks is born to privilege,* she'd told him. *That makes dem more responsible to look out fo' others, not less. There ain't no achievement in taking what can't be refused, and there ain't no pleasure in winning what can't protect itself. You know what's right, boy. You been raised better than that. I surely know it.*

Her voice came to him so clearly that Rand wouldn't have been surprised to feel the wooden spoon again.

"Well, Captain?" Claire asked when he didn't reply.

Rand realized the only way he could honor Mammy Komati's memory was by telling the truth. It was no easier now than it had been at thirteen. "It was a test," he said.

"A test?"

"It occurred to me that perhaps you were only pretending to be blind."

Claire's lips parted as her jaw sagged slightly. This answer wasn't anything that had occurred to her. "I suppose I should be grateful you didn't simply stick a foot out. Tripping me would have served the same purpose."

"It was not my intention to hurt you."

Claire snorted indelicately. "Were you the sort of boy who pulled the wings off butterflies?"

"No," Rand said. "That was my brother David. Before you ask, it was Shelby who bedeviled the cat."

"And your target?" She waited. "You'll have to speak up, Captain. It's a myth that blindness improves one's hearing. It only makes me sensitive to sounds; it doesn't make them louder."

Rand cleared his throat. "Girls," he said with some effort at contriteness. "I liked to chase girls." This confession was followed by a rather prolonged silence, then the unexpectedly fresh resonance of Claire's hearty laughter. Rand felt another wave of heat rush his cheeks even as he found himself grinning. "I liked to pull their pigtails."

"When you were six," Claire said, catching her breath. "I suspect your interests changed."

"They did. But so did theirs."

"Yes," she said slowly. "That seems to be the way of things." Claire wondered if Rand Hamilton was a handsome man, and if she asked him, if he would tell her the truth. She had learned that handsome people generally knew themselves to be so. Her mother had been beautiful and required no mirrors to support that opinion. It was as if she had absorbed the appreciation of others from the time of her birth and needed no further confirmation. A mirror was no substitute for her reflection in the eyes of an admirer.

"Did you have to force your attentions often?" asked Claire.

Rand thought of Jennie Ann. He had not forced himself on her, but Mammy Komati had also seen the truth of it. Jennie Ann had not considered that she could properly refuse him. "No," he said. "There was never any force."

"Droit du seigneur? Right of the lord? Do they have a name for it in South Carolina?"

Perhaps they didn't always, Rand thought. Not when it was perpetrated on female slaves. It could be it was one of the things the war had actually changed that the South would be better for. "They call it rape," he said.

"That's what they call it here," Claire said. "I had a need to be clear on that."

"You have nothing to fear on *Cerberus*. At my hands or those of my crew. You won't come to any harm."

Claire believed him but she was compelled to point out that he had already lied to her. "You promised me this morning that you would warn me before you touched me. I expect that consideration from now on."

"You have it."

"As for any questions you have about my blindness, I hope they're answered now."

"Completely."

"Good." She nodded once. "You may put your hands down, Captain, and you're free to go. I'm not taking prisoners."

Rand glanced down at his arms. They had been folded against his chest for some time. "Yes . . . thank you. I was getting tired holding them up."

"I forgot about them."

"I thought as much."

"Would you be so kind as to mention to Emmereth that some attention is needed to this room? On your way out, I mean." She sighed. "I suppose I shall have to apply myself to fabricating a story about the vase."

Rand watched Claire's face lift and brighten as though the explanation had just come upon her. He winced in anticipation of what he would hear.

"I know," she said. "I'll tell Stickle I'm blind. That should serve me well enough. I can't be expected to know the position of every one of his valuables."

"Miss Bancroft," Rand drawled softly, *"you* are a piece of work."

Claire was stunned into silence as the captain bade her good evening and left the dining room. She stood just where she was, leaning against the table more for support than protection. She stared sightlessly in the direction of the closed doors, a faint frown pulling at her features.

Claire Bancroft did not think she had mistaken admiration in his tone.

Strickland closed the lid on his writing desk when he heard the light rap on his door. "Enter!" he called.

Claire pushed open the door. She was carrying a tray of hot milk and brandy. Behind her one of the servants hovered, anticipating a collision, a spill, or some other disaster. "When you say that so importantly you make me feel as if I'm being granted an audience."

"You are," the duke said. His narrow, finely carved features softened somewhat. He waved away the servant. "Miss Bancroft has proven herself to be quite capable. And where's the harm if she spills some on the carpet? It can be cleaned or replaced."

Claire thought that if the carpet was of the Egyptian design she remembered, then it could not be replaced easily. It was said to have been one used by Napoleon in his encampment at Alexandria. The duke found some perverse pleasure in trampling it on his way to bed. "Do you feel the same way about the Sevres vase in the dining room?" she asked. Claire relied on his voice to guide her to a place to set the tray.

"The Sevres? On the sideboard, do you mean?"

"Yes, that's the one. It's come to a rather bad end, I'm afraid."

"Chipped?" he asked somewhat hopefully.

"Shattered."

"Here, let me take the tray now, m'dear. You've done admirably, Sevres vases aside."

Claire let Strickland remove the tray from her hands. She put her arm out and found the wing of a nearby chair. She seated herself almost gingerly. She had not been able to arrive at a feeling of security when she lowered herself onto a chair or sofa. Mrs. Webster chided her for it, finding this bit of trepidation most odd. *It's not as if someone is going to pull it out from under you,* she had said. But that was exactly the feeling Claire had about it. She did not confide in the widow that it was not an unfamiliar experience. It was only since she had become blind that she had extended the feeling to tangible objects. Before that it was confined to matters of the heart, like love and trust.

Claire held out one hand and felt the warm mug of milk being pressed into it. "Thank you."

"You're welcome." Strickland leaned back in his chair. He rubbed his jaw with the back of his hand, massaging away the hard line of tension there. "Tell me about the vase."

"An impassioned speech," she said. "I was standing at the sideboard and flung my arms wide."

"Impassioned?" The duke's steady gaze was thoughtful. "Does the captain inspire that sort of emotion in you?"

Claire's mouth twisted wryly. "Perhaps angry describes it better. The captain certainly inspires that."

"I'm not sure I like that any better. You should be careful, Claire. I don't entirely trust him."

"I wish you had been able to strike a better bargain, Stickle."

"I hope to God you've never called me that in front of him. It's precisely that sort of comfortable and cozy familiarity that gives Hamilton an advantage. What good is cultivating a countenance that can etch glass if one is known as Stickle?"

Claire brought her mug to her lips quickly. "I don't believe I've used it," she said over the rim.

Strickland sighed. "What a horrid liar you are."

Claire shrugged.

"I'm not sure I believe you about the vase either."

This time Claire managed not to choke, but only just. She could feel her godfather's eyes boring into her. They would be like ice chips as he attempted to freeze a confession out of her. "What were you doing when I came in?" she asked, changing the subject. "You mentioned retiring, but you're here working at your desk."

"I was composing an advertisement for the paper. For your next teacher."

"What a horrid liar you are."

Strickland's eyes widened a fraction; then he chuckled appreciatively. "Very well, I was trying to write down the riddle, if you must know."

Claire nodded. "I thought as much. That's why you excused yourself so quickly after hearing it. How much have you remembered?"

The duke opened the lid of the writing desk just enough to remove one piece of paper. *"Blood will run. Flames will come.* Something about the sun."

"Blazing sun, blinding some."

It was understandable, Strickland supposed, that that particular phrasing had caught Claire's attention. "Then he mentioned a flood and a plague. That's it. That's all I can bring to mind."

"I don't understand the connection he makes to the gems. Do you?"

"No, but then we only heard a portion of the riddle. It may be there is a clue elsewhere in the text."

Claire noticed that the duke was not questioning the riddle's origin. He didn't appear to believe Rand Hamilton had created the message for his own ends. "His story about the treasure nearly matches your own theory."

"I didn't think you would fail to notice that. Captain Hamilton has either thoroughly researched the legend and history or he has some intimate knowledge to guide him. It may be all of that. I don't believe he used his time at Oxford only to study the natural sciences. The library there is the same place I found some intriguing similarities between the legend and the capture of the Spanish galleon *Frontera.*"

Claire smiled. "It's unraveling the mystery that's exciting to you, isn't it? Finding the treasure is so much gilt on the lily."

Strickland's brows rose a notch. "I would not go so far as to say that, m'dear. I won't mind at all adding these stones to my collection."

"A quarter of them," Claire corrected. "That's the bargain you struck."

"Yes," he said after a moment. "Just a quarter. Go on, you should take yourself off to bed. There's a lot to be done in these next weeks. You will need the voyage to rest from the frenzy of the preparations for it."

Claire laughed and held out her mug. "G'night, Stickle. Pleasant dreams." She squeezed his hand as he took the mug.

"Do you require assistance?"

"Ten paces to the door and another fourteen after the third room on the right. I can manage, thank you."

He watched her progress across the room just to satisfy himself of her safety. When she was gone, his eyes dropped to the blank piece of paper in his hand. He had had no need to make a record of the captain's poem. The lines were unimportant. The fact that they numbered seven was enough to convince him that Rand Hamilton was on the right course, closer perhaps than he had been.

Seven lines. Seven curses. One curse for each sister. The captain might well know what he was looking for after all.

Evan Markham, eighth Duke of Strickland, crumpled the paper in his fist and tossed it into the fireplace. He opened the desk and took out the correspondence he had begun. At this juncture there was no sense leaving anything to chance.

The next twelve days were every bit the frenzy for Claire that her godfather had predicted.

At the duke's insistence, there were fittings for a new wardrobe. Claire was left with no choice but compliance and almost no choice in the fabrics or fashion. Strickland was pleased to discover that Mrs. Webster had a rather keen eye for what suited his goddaughter. After the first day of witnessing her veto the fussy ruffles and ruching that served no purpose but to draw attention to the dressmaker's skill, the duke was happy to place Claire in her teacher's hands. His visit to the drawing room on the occasion of the initial fitting was enough to assure him that all would be completed by the time *Cerberus* left London.

Claire was also the recipient of more lessons with her cane. She despised the thing as a crutch that only called attention to her. It did no good that the duke tried to ease her discomfort by having it made of ebony and calling it a fashionable affectation. *She* was the one affected by it. Mrs. Webster had been unsuccessful in making Claire see the use of it until now. Claire, she pointed out, would be subjected to more hazards on board *Cerberus* than she had encountered on *HMS Mansfield*. On her voyage back to London, she had been largely confined to quarters by illness or choice. She had learned enough skills since that time to be made a bit overconfident. It was the surest way, Mrs. Webster warned, for her to be lost overboard.

Claire accepted the truth of this and practiced daily, first in the familiar surroundings of the townhouse and later, as a test of her skill, in the less inviting twists and turns of Abberly Hall. It was there that she again toured the duke's vast collection of artifacts. He had been very clear that Mrs. Webster could not join her in the room, and Claire did not invite trouble by disobeying him. She wondered that her godfather trusted her at all after the destruction of his Sevres vase.

Strickland's private museum was a gallery some sixty feet long and a third as wide. It was located on the second floor in Abberly's west wing. The heavy doors to the gallery remained locked at all times. Strickland and his housekeeper of thirty years were the only ones with keys. To Claire's knowledge no other household staff had ever entered the room.

Mrs. Novak opened the doors for Claire and set herself to dusting while Claire cautiously made her way along the perimeter of the room. She lifted the lids on glass cases that held ancient weapons of knights and the more ornamental, jewel-encrusted daggers of their fierce ladies. Even older were the Roman broadswords and Druid blades etched with runes to make them strike true. Claire found a favorite Egyptian arm bracelet lying atop one of the cases. She ran her fingers over the delicate silver band, coiled to circle an arm like a snake. Her fingertips touched each of the eyes and recalled that these tiny stones were rubies. Claire slipped the bracelet on as far as her elbow and pretended to admire it. When she had visited Abberly Hall as a child, Strickland had allowed her to wear the bracelet as he guided her and her mother through the gallery. Even then, she thought, he had indulged her.

Claire paused as she came upon the tapestries hanging on the walls. She could only touch them now, not stand back and view the stories they told. She was disappointed that her fingers could not distinguish between the woven pictures, nor raise their colorful threads to her mind's eye. She recalled that one displayed the Battle of Hastings; another depicted Sir Gawain's search for the Holy Grail. Now, without asking Mrs. Novak for assistance, they might as well have been the duke's bedcovers.

Claire felt some of the joy of her exploration fade. She recognized the jade figures from China and the exquisitely fashioned bowls and vases from a dynasty she couldn't name, but they merely seemed cool to her now. The delicately hand-painted patterns had no power to capture her attention. She passed the duke's collection of sapphires altogether. Each stone would only feel like another when she could not hold them to the light and remark on their clarity or color.

But it was at the books that Claire truly felt the depth of what she had lost halfway around the world. She ran her hands lightly over the edges of the illuminated tomes. The covers were soft with age, and except where they were embossed, the texture was smooth. She opened one carefully, wondering if she was looking at a monk's painstaking copy of Plutarch's *Lives* or one of Homer's epic poems. Her godfather, she knew, had all of that and more. Claire turned the pages gingerly, respectful of both the age and the content. To pass too quickly seemed somehow disrespectful.

She stopped when her hand fell on a piece of paper whose texture was different from the one preceding it. The page moved as she withdrew her fingers. Claire's first thought was that she had clumsily torn it free. She almost slammed the heavy book closed to hide her blunder. That reaction was more suited to a child, she decided. It also occurred to her that the housekeeper might have already witnessed the destruction.

"Mrs. Novak?"

"Yes? I'll be done here in a moment. What do you need?"

Claire could tell by the location and pitch that the house-keeper was turned away from her. She was willing to accept that for now she could behave as a child. She closed the book. "Are you dusting armor?" she asked.

"Why, yes, I am. You're a marvel, that's what you are."

Then she was easily on the far side of the room, Claire thought. "I wondered if I might trouble you to tell Mrs. Webster I'll be ready to go shortly. I think she's in the conservatory. If she's found a comfortable place to nap, I should like to give her some notice. She might wish to refresh herself before we leave."

"Of course. Will you be all right, then?" Mrs. Novak made a last pass across the knight's helmet, then joined Claire at the books. "These were always a mystery to me," she said. "I don't read a word of Latin and that's what his grace tells me these are. I don't suppose you can read something to—" Her hand flew to her mouth as she realized what she was saying, and to whom. "Oh, I'm truly sorry, Miss Bancroft. It's just that you haven't changed with your . . . that is, with the . . ." She hugged her duster. "What a foolish woman I've become. My tongue's as knotted as my laces."

"It's all right, Mrs. Novak." Claire found that apologies were much worse than the unintended thoughtless remarks that preceded them. "Please, just see to Mrs. Webster."

The housekeeper was happy to leave quickly.

Claire opened the book as soon as Mrs. Novak was on the other side of the door. It took her a few moments to find the page again. This time she removed it completely. Her heartbeat resumed a normal rhythm when she traced the edges of the paper and found it smooth on all sides. Even though the quality of the page suggested it was not part of the manuscript, it was good to confirm it another way. She wondered if the duke had placed the paper in the book as a mark. She tried to imagine him reading the heavy book for his enjoyment and couldn't. This possession wasn't meant to be read, but admired for the craft that had produced it. Strickland had readable volumes of these books in several of his libraries.

Claire ran her hand over the paper much as she had the tapestries and the embossed covers, with no expectation that she would recognize anything beneath her fingertips. It startled her when she felt the small holes that had been pushed into the paper.

Each hole was larger than a pinprick but not a great deal. Had the paper not been lying pressed between the pages of the manuscript, the holes would have caused tiny bumps on the obverse side. The holes were not cut out but had been made by poking an instrument through the paper.

Claire felt the page in its entirety again. She wondered how noticeable these small punches would be if she could see the paper. Would they have even come to her attention? It seemed unlikely. Using the manuscript to house the paper had nearly obliterated evidence the holes were there.

Letting her index finger run gently over them, Claire counted seven. They were located near the bottom right corner of the page as she held the paper. She had no idea if she was holding it upside down or on the reverse, but she was careful to hold it in the exact manner she had taken it from the book.

She wondered if Strickland knew of its presence, and she felt the small thrill that accompanies every discovery. Perhaps it was something placed in the manuscript by the monk who had worked on it. His prayers. His dedication. His Latin laundry list.

Claire smiled, tracing the path of the holes a third time. No, probably not a list at all, she thought. Something celestial instead. The placement of the seven holes was more familiar to her as the most easily recognized grouping of stars in the night sky: the Big Dipper.

She replaced her discovery in the manuscript, she hoped just as she had found it. Mrs. Novak's clipped footsteps were approaching from the hallway. Claire met her at the door. "I'm prepared to leave," she said. "Thank you for letting me in."

"As to that, Miss Bancroft, it's a pleasure. His grace doesn't visit often enough, and while I don't begrudge him these wonderful things, it's always seemed a shame to me that he doesn't invite more of his acquaintances to view them. Why, I can count on my fingers and toes the number of times he's brought visitors here." Mrs. Novak locked the door, then continued her theme as she fell into step beside Claire. "Not that I can't imagine there'd be trouble sooner or later from the traffic. We'd have our share of thieves trying to scale Abberly's walls. Can't say that I'd want to invite that, so his grace's caution is understandable. Do you know that there's never been a piece come up missing in all the time I've been in the duke's employ?"

"There is no question that he trusts you," Claire said kindly.

"Until now," Mrs. Novak went on.

Claire frowned. "Do you mean he no longer trusts you?"

"No, I was referring to the missing pieces. One's going to come up missing now."

Claire's frown merely deepened. Had Mrs. Novak seen her with the paper after all? Did the housekeeper believe she had removed it? Claire began to deny that she had taken anything when Mrs. Novak interrupted her.

"Don't trouble yourself," she said. There was nothing accusing about her warm tones. "I realize you simply forgot it." She stopped at the lip of the stairs. "May I?"

Claire was bewildered. "You'll have to be clearer, I'm afraid." She laid her left hand over the banister, prepared to make her descent down the wide staircase. "What is it you wish to do?"

"Take the bracelet back," Mrs. Novak said. "That awful snake is still on your arm."

Laughing, Claire held out her arm. "Oh, please. Yes, take it back. I should have been very put out to find it on the journey back to London. His grace would not have been at all happy with me."

As it happened, the journey back occupied Claire's mind in other ways. It was unlikely she would have given a thought to the bracelet.

"A penny for them," Mrs. Webster said. "You're so quiet, dear."

Claire was surprised her teacher noticed. There had been a long, one-sided account of Mrs. Webster's recent bout with some stomach distress. Her comment was an indication that she had finally exhausted the topic. "Is Captain Hamilton a handsome man?" she asked without preamble.

The carriage continued to roll forward smoothly. A rut in the road could not be found to explain Mrs. Webster's sudden jerk. Claire would not have appreciated her teacher's surprise or the knowing smile that came on its heels. "So that's the way the wind blows," she said.

"It's merely a question," Claire said tartly. "Not an indication of any particular feeling."

Mrs. Webster's smile faded. "There's no need to be prickly, Miss Bancroft. As it happens, I do have an opinion about the captain's countenance."

Claire was weary of apologies and she did not offer one now. She did, however, make an effort to soften her tone. "Please, I should like to hear it."

"Well, it's not that I've been formally introduced to him, you understand. I've only observed him on those occasions he was coming and going from his grace's house. I have to say that I thought him rather formidable."

"Yes, I gathered that." It fit well with Claire's image of him as a large stone tiki, fierce and forbidding. "But it's not very descriptive. What else can you tell me?"

"His hair is the color of a copper. Not a new coin, mind you, but something that's been in your pocket for a while."

"Tarnished?"

"Oh, but not green, dear." Mrs. Webster chuckled at the thought. "It's brown and copper and burnt orange. A dark sunset, I suppose. Does that bring it to mind?"

Claire found that it did. "Yes, what else?"

"He has dark eyes," she said. "Not so dark as your own, but some shade of brown. He has strong features: a hawkish sort of face with a hard chin and a Roman nose. Not so different from his grace, if you'll forgive the comparison, when he was a younger man.''

Claire could remember that. The Duke of Strickland had always been able to turn heads with his compelling looks. Their close association had not made her immune to them. As a young girl she had offered him a proposal of marriage. Claire could smile at the memory now. It had caused her some embarrassment at the time, and her mother no small amount of distress. Stickle was the one who had recovered first, declaring himself heartily flattered by her declaration.

''Then he *is* handsome,'' said Claire.

''That's a fair assessment,'' Mrs. Webster allowed. ''But it just misses the mark. It doesn't account for the scar.''

''The scar?''

''The captain has a thin scar running from under his hairline at his temple to his jaw. I couldn't say what put it there, and I'm certain I don't know how long he's had it. He appears perfectly comfortable with it, so I don't believe it's a recent acquisition. By rights the scar should be disfiguring, cutting across his cheek the way it does, but with Captain Hamilton it merely keeps me from pronouncing him beautiful.''

Claire blinked and her lips parted in wonder. ''Why, Mrs. Webster, I wouldn't have—''

''Because I'm a widow?'' Mrs. Webster interrupted. ''And old? Neither of those characteristics keeps me from appreciating fine things when I see them.''

''Now who's being prickly?'' teased Claire. ''Are you certain you won't accompany me on this voyage, Mrs. Webster? It could be that you and the captain would—''

Mrs. Webster leaned across the carriage aisle and tapped Claire on the knee, stopping her in mid-sentence. ''It could be that casting my eye in the captain's direction is the cause of my stomach distress. My constitution would not tolerate the close quarters of the voyage.''

Claire smiled as she was meant to and said nothing. Mrs. Webster could have been speaking for her as well.

*   *   *

"You're in a mood this evening," Cutch said. He looked pointedly at the book that lay open on Rand's lap. It had been placed there ten minutes ago when Rand grew tired of holding it. Up until that time he had at least made a pretense of reading it. Cutch folded his newspaper into quarters and put it on the side table. He picked up his brandy. "Second thoughts?"

Rand knew exactly to which thoughts Cutch was referring. "I'm long past second ones," he admitted. "I've talked myself in and out of taking her a dozen times over."

Cutch nodded. He couldn't remember when Rand had ever given this much consideration to a decision already made. "Women have never been more than trouble on a ship."

One of Rand's brows lifted skeptically. "You don't believe that any more than I do."

"I thought if you were looking for an excuse . . ." Cutch shrugged, letting his voice trail off.

"We sail the day after tomorrow. It's a little late. There's been quite a bit of preparation already. If the comings and goings of dressmakers, milliners, and seamstresses are any indication, Miss Bancroft's new clothes are going to require a cabin of their own. Today I made my choice on the teacher who will accompany her."

"What is she like?"

"He. Miss Bancroft's teacher is male."

"Oh." Cutch did not try to hide his disappointment. It would have been a pure pleasure to have two women on board *Cerberus*. Not that either of them would have paid him any mind, but they couldn't stop him from appreciating their company. "Wasn't expecting that."

"Neither was I." Rand closed the book and laid it aside. "Until yesterday, all the candidates for the position were women. Then Strickland introduced some new ones whom he had interviewed while Mrs. Webster was at Abberly. She met them this morning and found them acceptable. We all agreed that one was exceptional."

"Then that's good."

It would have been better if he had been female, Rand thought. He didn't voice his misgivings because there was no substance to them. He was not willing to credit that his personal preference might be rooted in jealousy. "We'll have to rearrange the accommodations. I was anticipating that Miss Bancroft and her teacher would share quarters."

Perhaps they would, Cutch thought. And perhaps that was what disturbed Rand. "Hmmm," was all he said.

Rand cocked an eyebrow but didn't challenge Cutch to say what was on his mind. "His name is Macauley Stuart. *Dr.* Macauley Stuart."

"A physician?"

"Yes. Scots. He had, by all accounts, a fair practice in Aberdeen. He treats everything but he's had a particular interest in treatments for the eye. He is not optimistic about Miss Bancroft's chance of recovery. In fact, he went so far as to say that his French colleague, Dr. Messier, should not be allowed to make such claims. Mrs. Webster agrees that he is not as knowledgeable as other candidates in being able to further Miss Bancroft's skills, but his medical background is something no one else can offer. She also believes he will not bore Miss Bancroft."

"Why does he want to make this voyage? Money?"

"I don't think so. He appeared to be comfortably settled. I think it's the adventure. He has a romantic's idea of sea travel."

"That might be tolerable. I expect I'd feel differently if you told me he was a do-gooder. I can't stand do-gooders."

Rand was aware of Cutch's sentiments and shared them with only a bit less fervor. "He doesn't have a missionary's zeal, and it won't take him long to realize the poets and writers have vastly overrated the sea's romance."

Especially if Rand took *Cerberus* on a choppy North Atlantic course. Cutch imagined the good doctor couldn't provide much in the way of conversation if he was spilling his guts over the taffrail. "What does Miss Bancroft think of him?"

"When I left the duke's, she was out. She's meeting Dr. Stuart this evening."

"And her reaction?"

"She'll either hate him because he was my choice or love him just to spite me."

"Hmmm."

Rand nodded, staring at his hands. "Yes, that's what I thought."

Cerberus was a clipper that Rand had saved from being refitted as a steamer after the war. He borrowed money and raised funds to buy and refurbish her. She was a fine Remington ship out of Boston, with sleek lines built for speed and so many sails when she was fully rigged that it seemed a following wind couldn't catch her. She had been part of a Yankee blockade around Charleston and was captured early in the war because of a well-placed Confederate cannonade. Her crew was forced to abandon her, and eventually she was towed in and repaired. She ran the blockades after that and helped bring relief to a city that was being cut off from every supply imaginable.

Rand appreciated that *Cerberus* had begun her life as a Boston clipper. He liked the notion of having taken something from the Yankees and put it to his own use. Too often the period known as Reconstruction was merely the North reconstructing the South in its own image. It pained him still that as much as he was able to raise to repair and outfit the clipper, it was only a fraction of what he had needed to pay the taxes assessed on Henley.

Rand stood at the rail and watched the traffic on the wharf. Behind him his men moved with the ease of long practice, taking on the last of the perishable supplies and making the ship ready to sail. Rand's attention could have been elsewhere, but Cutch was competent to see to the details while Rand looked for the duke's carriage.

He would sail without her. There was no question of that. Rand didn't know if Strickland or his goddaughter would have even considered such a thing possible. The seven sisters, be damned. He could find them on his own now that he knew to look on Pulotu. Claire's presence was not strictly necessary, and that would free him from having to bother with Dr. Stuart.

It was not that he had to hurry the departure. An hour, even more than one, would not seriously impede him. He was not on a schedule to deliver goods or passengers. *Cerberus* was fast, too. Given the right conditions, she could ply the Atlantic waters from London to Charleston in just under two weeks. Anxious as Rand was to see Charleston, Henley, and Bria, he was not of a mind to put his ship through her paces or create problems for the crew.

He was, though, willing to leave these shores on time as a matter of principle, and begin the first lesson that Miss Bancroft needed to learn. In all things that happened on *Cerberus,* he bore the responsibility and the command.

Rand watched a wagon being unloaded of the last crate of fresh fruit. He followed its progress up the gangboard, then motioned to Cutch.

"Pull the gangboard!" Cutch ordered. The rich bass notes of his voice rumbled like distant thunder over the heads of the men. "Make ready!"

"Make way! Make way, I tell you! Out!"

Rand's attention was caught by the hack driver who was not only whipping at his horse, but at anyone who got close to his cab. The pedestrians who could not jump out of his way fought back with raised fists and blue language. The number of angry people seemed to increase exponentially as the hack drew closer to *Cerberus.* Rand thought a brawl was a distinct possibility and was almost sorry he would miss it.

Then again . . . He paused in turning his back as the door to the hack was flung open and the Duke of Strickland stepped out. Rand's eyes narrowed and their chestnut coloring gleamed a little brighter as he surveyed the hired hack and the duke's flustered features. He was quite certain this equipage was not what Strickland had proposed to arrive in.

"Stay!" Rand called to the men hauling in the gangboard. "Let it rest." He moved to the opening as Strickland helped Claire down from the hack. The duke was also giving orders for the driver to hurry with the trunks. Rand counted them with something akin to wonder. He thought they'd taken on all Claire and the doctor could possibly need last night. He sighed. "Find room for them, Cutch."

Cutch scratched his bald black head for a moment. "If that ain't a sorry sight." He grabbed one of the crew as the hapless man walked in front of him. "Diggs, you heard the captain. Find room for those trunks." Over the man's head, Cutch grinned widely at Rand. "Always someone smaller to pass the problem on to."

Rand nodded, taking in Cutch's full height. "In your case, that's true." He looked over the rail. Claire was on her godfather's arm, but she was holding an ebony cane. He had never seen her with it before, and his first thought was that she had injured herself. He called himself a fool when he realized what service she would be putting it to.

Macauley Stuart was the last to alight from the carriage. Rand acknowledged the doctor's raised hand with a curt nod. He had no wish to become the man's friend.

Strickland escorted Claire up the gangway. "Steady, m'dear. You're doing fine. You should try to use your cane."

Claire clutched the duke's elbow a little more tightly. "Not just now," she whispered. "Not yet."

He nodded. "Of course. When you're settled. Dr. Stuart will help you."

"That I will, Miss Bancroft. You're in good hands."

"She'll be in my hands," Rand said as Claire and Strickland reached the top. "I'm going to take your arm, Miss Bancroft." She offered it without hesitation, which Rand took as a good sign. "Welcome aboard."

Claire found herself feeling shy all of a sudden. "Thank you. I apologize for our lateness."

"It's not her fault," Strickland said gruffly. "She doesn't have anything to apologize for. The damn carriage threw a wheel not a block from the house. Had to hail a cab and transfer the trunks. Bah! What a scene. Most of the residents were peeping out their windows and pretending not to. What a story for their dinner table: the Duke of Strickland standing at the curb flapping his arms for a hack while his driver tried to fix the wheel. I looked like some ungainly bird, I'll wager."

"I'm sure you didn't," Claire said gently.

"An ostrich," he went on. "Or . . . what's the other one I told you about at the zoo?"

"An emu."

"Yes, a damn emu. Not pretty birds. Not pretty by a long shot. Hmmmpf."

Claire reached out and found the duke's forearm. She tugged on the sleeve of his jacket until he moved closer.

"What are you about, girl?"

She smiled. He only called her girl when he was working hard at being irritable. "I shall miss you so very much," she said. "Dr. Stuart promises he will help me keep a journal and write letters. I will record every aspect of the voyage in such detail, you will think you've been part of it. I'm coming back to you with my eyes wide open, my brother in hand, and offering up your share of the treasure. You'll see, dear Stickle, it won't be long." She stood on tiptoe. Her ebony cane brushed against his leg as she kissed him on the cheek.

He blustered a bit at this public display of affection, but Strickland's ice-blue eyes had taken on a watery edge.

Claire removed herself from the duke's embrace. She found Rand's elbow again.

"God's speed, Claire," Strickland said. He turned and hurried down the gangboard. It was pulled up as soon as his feet touched the wharf.

"Is he going to his carriage?" Claire asked.

"Yes," Rand told her.

She nodded. "I didn't think he could bear to just stand there and wave me off. Still, I'd like to stay here until we're away."

"Of course, as long as you like." Rand watched Claire raise her face. Her smile held the kind of serenity he did not associate with her. He wondered whether Claire could sustain that rare calm if she knew what he was thinking.

Chapter Four

Cerberus was ten days out of London before Macauley Stuart acquired his sea legs. "Perhaps you would like to take a turn on deck," Claire suggested as he escorted her into the companionway. It was really very encouraging that the doctor had not bolted from the captain's table during the meal as he had on the occasion of every other dinner.

"A turn on deck," he repeated, assessing the steadiness of his legs and his stomach. "Just the thing. Shall we get your cane from your cabin?"

Claire shook her head. "As long as you stay at my side, I'll be fine."

"Very well. Lead on."

"I believe it's you who should lead on," she reminded him. She squeezed his elbow lightly to show that she was in position a half step behind him.

"Quite right, Miss Bancroft. You make it so easy to forget."

Claire accepted that as a compliment. She was also of the opinion that she had managed a confident transition from land to sea. It was something of a feather in her cap that she had accomplished most of it without the aid of Dr. Stuart. When he was not leaning over the rail in the choppy Atlantic waters, he had confined himself to his quarters, and Claire was largely left to her own devices.

When they rose from the companionway onto the deck Claire lifted her face eagerly into the rush of wind. "It's like flying, Doctor."

"You'll forgive me if I don't share your enthusiasm."

Claire laughed. In short order she had her bearings and pointed Stuart to the starboard side. "I believe we'll start in the weather," she said, "and finish in the calm."

Stuart wondered what she meant by calm. "It's been my experience that there is no calm on these seas, only less weather."

Claire smiled. "You may be right."

From his position on the quarterdeck Cutch watched the doctor and Claire begin their turn. Moments later Rand appeared from the main companionway.

"Appears he survived his dinner this evening," Cutch noted when Rand joined him. Out of the corner of his eye he watched his captain carefully. "Of course, the evening isn't over."

Rand's eyes followed the couple's progress. "Hmmm."

"That's what I thought. Why don't you send the good doctor off?"

"I can hardly make him walk the plank," said Rand.

Cutch chuckled deeply. It occurred to him that Rand might not have realized he'd spoken aloud. Cutch seized the opportunity anyway. "I'll think of something." He started off toward Claire and the doctor before Rand could call him back.

Watching him go, Rand shook his head. He had no choice but to follow. If Cutch succeeded in removing Stuart from Claire's side, then Claire would require some assistance. Not that she wouldn't have her pick of the crew as a companion. There wasn't a man on board *Cerberus* who wasn't willing to spend time with her. Had she been able to see, she would have witnessed men all but tripping over themselves to reach her when she arrived on deck alone. They practically formed a protective circle around her as she circumnavigated the ship.

He had had to warn the men privately that if they continued in such a fashion, he would be forced to curtail Miss Bancroft's deck privileges.

He did not require Cutch to point out to him that he was no longer enjoying the same degree of popularity among the crew as he had in the past.

"Miss Bancroft," Rand greeted her as Cutch led Stuart away. The doctor was making some protesting noises but Cutch, at seven feet, was insistent.

Claire's fingers eased their grip on the rail. "Captain."

Rand heard relief in her voice, but he suspected it had little to do with him and everything to do with the fact that she had not been abandoned. "You're not carrying your cane," he said.

Claire made a face. She cocked her head in the direction of the departing doctor and first mate. "I thought I had an escort."

"And so you do. May I?" He took her hand when she nodded and placed it at his elbow. "What did Cutch say to Stuart that took him off in such a hurry?"

"You don't know?"

"I wouldn't have asked."

"Odd. I was under the impression that you and Cutch were standing together on the quarterdeck just before he approached us."

Rand knew her *impression* had been courtesy of Stuart. He wondered if the doctor had only been describing the activity on deck or whether she had specifically asked after him.

"I was inquiring into Mr. Cutch's whereabouts this evening," Claire said.

Rand winced a little at this revelation but he took it on the chin. Cutch had clearly made himself a favorite with Claire. While the doctor was indisposed, Rand had lightened Cutch's duties so he could spend more time with her. "He tells me he's been reading to you," said Rand.

"Yes." A heavy lock of hair whipped across Claire's cheek as they made the turn at the quarter gallery. She pushed it back but didn't attempt to secure it. "I don't suppose he'll be able to do that this evening. He took Dr. Stuart off to examine him for stomach cramps."

So *that* was Cutch's diversion. Rand could only shake his head. "Perhaps the doctor will read to you. Now that he's recovered, it would seem to be his responsibility."

Claire was not successful in hiding her lack of enthusiasm. "Of course. You will want Mr. Cutch to return to his full duties. I understand. I don't think I've expressed my gratitude to you for allowing him to assist me."

Until now Rand hadn't thought she realized any of it was his doing.

"Mr. Cutch told me you made it possible," she said. "It was kind of you. Before we left London you made your feelings clear about providing me with a nursemaid. I know it went against your grain."

"I felt some responsibility, Miss Bancroft. I had the final say in choosing Dr. Stuart. I thought that between the duke, Mrs. Webster, and me we had covered every important question in determining his suitability. None of us inquired into his fitness for sea travel."

Claire considered reminding him that she had not been allowed to interview the doctor, then let the opportunity to take him to task pass. She wouldn't have thought to ask the question either. Anyone signing on for months of sea travel should have taken some stock of their constitution to do so. "The waters have seemed unusually rough," she said in mild defense of the doctor.

Rand's shrug was communicated to Claire. "It hasn't been so bad. They haven't bothered you."

Claire tugged on Rand's elbow, holding him back. She turned toward the open water and let her hand fall away. She laid her palms flat against the rail. "Is it dark yet?" she asked.

"No. Not yet. We're chasing sunset."

It took Claire's breath away. Rand had captured so perfectly the speed of the clipper and the sun's great orange arc balanced on the horizon. "How long can we stay like this?"

"A half hour," he said. "Not much beyond that. *Cerberus* never quite catches her." Rand saw Claire shiver slightly beneath her mantel. "You're cold. Perhaps I should escort you below."

"Oh no, not just now. Really, I'm fine." *It was not that kind of shiver.* Claire pulled her mantel more closely about her shoulders. "There, it only takes a bit of adjustment."

Rand looked over her fine profile as she turned away again. The wind had beaten some roses into her cheeks, but he knew it didn't account for all of her favorable coloring. He had witnessed the pallor fading from Claire's complexion even before they left London, and on board *Cerberus* her health continued to improve. Rand came to realize the woman he had first seen in the duke's study was the shadow of this one. He had long ago dismissed the possibility that she would not be noticed in a sea of people. His eyes would invariably find her.

The wind pushed strands of Claire's dark hair forward again. This time she didn't bother to repair them. They tickled her cheeks and the sides of her throat. Rand could hear the soft hum of her pleasure above the chuckle of the water. "You left your hat behind," he said.

"Hmmm," she murmured. "I did. Shall I tell you why?"

"If you wish."

"They're impractical. The ones with no ribbons to secure them will simply be blown away. I would require pins the size of anchors to keep them on my head up here. The ones with ribbons will choke me." She raised one hand to her throat to show him how the ribbons would catch her under the chin. "It's better that they remain in my cabin."

"Apparently so."

"Are you wearing a hat?"

"No."

Claire imagined the wind beating back his copper hair. "You don't have some sort of captain's hat?"

"I'm not that sort of captain. *Cerberus* is a research vessel, not a military ship."

"I understand that." Cutch at her side, Claire had explored almost all of the ship these last ten days, including Rand Hamilton's workroom. *Cerberus* was equipped with microscopes and slides, chemicals for specimen preservation, and all the tools for probing and dissection. Cutch had allowed her to run her hands across the dozens of journals where Rand kept account of his studies, and he explained in some detail what the glass jars secured on the shelves contained. The older man was clearly proud of what the master of *Cerberus* had accomplished. Claire did not think she allowed her own discomfort at being in the room to show. "But you were a captain during your war, weren't you?"

"Actually, I was a lieutenant. In the army, not the navy. And I didn't keep the hat."

Claire heard the lightness Rand forced into his tone. His war experiences were not a subject for discussion. "How is it that you came to command *Cerberus*? Why not hire someone to do it for you?"

"I'm not especially good at taking orders."

Claire raised one hand to her lips to hide her smile. She could believe that. "But you've sailed before?"

"Only as a passenger before I bought this ship. I studied under some real salts while *Cerberus* was being repaired. They pronounced me fit to take a skiff out to Fort Sumter and back." One corner of his mouth lifted in a half smile. "I've done a little better than that."

"You haven't run her aground."

"I didn't say that." He laughed outright at Claire's open-mouthed surprise. "Once. In the shoals at Avarua. It took quite a feat of engineering and two hundred strong backs to pull her free. The natives extracted a high price for their help. Since then I've learned to read the charts better and exercise more caution around the islands."

"I should hope so."

"You have nothing to worry about, Miss Bancroft. At least on that account. Come, take my arm again and let's continue. It won't be long before you won't be able to stand the chill."

Claire found his elbow and fell into step. "You know how to guide me," she observed. "Dr. Stuart is not quite as good at it."

The doctor hadn't had the benefit of Mrs. Webster's instruction, Rand reflected. "I suspect it comes naturally," he said.

Claire laughed. "That is really too bad of you. Mrs. Webster told me you made some inquiries."

Rand tried to remember if he had asked the widow to keep it a secret. "She wasn't supposed to," he said at last.

"Why?" she chided him. "Are you afraid I'll suspect some interest on your part? I think that's hardly likely. Save for a few dinners, this is the most time you've spent in my company since I came aboard. I'm not complaining, Captain. I told you before that I do not require entertaining."

Rand drew Claire around a large coil of rope and sail that was being repaired. "Are you satisfied with Stuart?" he asked.

"I hardly know him. I've learned a good deal about Mr. Cutch, though."

"Cutch."

"Pardon?"

"Just Cutch. No one calls him Mister."

"I do. He doesn't seem to mind. Besides, it confers respect."

"Cutch knows I respect him."

"I didn't mean that you don't. He's your friend, isn't he?"

Rand didn't answer immediately. To call Cutch his friend didn't do justice to the relationship that existed between them. Mentor, helper, pundit, sage, supporter . . . father. "Yes," he said. "He's my friend."

"He's a fascinating man."

"He likes to think so," Rand said dryly.

Claire smiled. "He's reading *Around the World in 80 Days* to me."

"Our trip won't be that fast."

"That's all right. I brought lots of books."

"So I learned. I thought those last trunks that arrived with you were filled with more clothes."

"More clothes?" She shook her head, not quite able to credit that thinking. "I can't wear what I have now." Claire paused a beat. "At least not all at once."

Rand recalled that under her dark mantel she was wearing a promenade dress of blue and white striped silk. It was a vast improvement on the dull gown she had worn at their first meeting. "Your godfather ordered you an entirely new wardrobe."

"He hated the things I had chosen before," Claire admitted.

"He said I was self-pitying and mourning the loss of my sight. I couldn't even argue that I was grieving for my father and brother. That would have meant I had abandoned all hope of finding them."

"Was he right about you being self-pitying?"

"Yes. And it's no pleasure to admit it."

"That he was right or that you were self-pitying?"

"Both."

Rand laughed. He stopped and pointed out that they had made another turn. "Would you like to take the wheel?"

Claire's eyes widened. "And be responsible for running us aground?" she asked. "I think not."

"This is very open sea, Miss Bancroft."

"An iceberg then."

"We're well south of them now."

"I could set us off course."

"Not so that it couldn't be set to rights."

"What if she heels? I could sink her."

Rand's dark brows lifted as he searched her features. Her eyes gave nothing away, but the small parenthetical lines around her mouth did. "Are you afraid, Claire?"

"Certainly not."

"Liar," he said softly, goading her.

"You'd better put my hands on the wheel, Captain, else they're apt to find your throat."

"I suppose I should be lucky you have nothing to throw." Rand motioned Paul Dodd to remove himself from the deck chair as he guided Claire toward the wheelbox. He placed her hands on the wheel and let her feel the power that ran through it. He stood behind her, palms lightly on her slender shoulders. "You don't have to do anything," he told her. "She knows where to go. Easy and steady does it."

Sheltered by Rand's lean frame at her back, Claire's skirts beat against her legs less frantically. Overhead she could hear the pyramids of white canvas strain the rigging. The steady rush of wind filled the sails. They would be like blossoms on the seas, she thought, forever being opened and carried off by updrafts and cross breezes. If it were not for Rand's hands on

her shoulders, Claire thought she might be carried away as
well. The harnessing of so much energy, the power of it, the
speed, all of it touched a chord in her. Her body fairly vibrated
with it. She had never known the like of it before.

Rand's nostrils were filled with the fragrance of her hair. He
was close enough that strands of it touched his chin, There was
lilac in her bath salts, he thought. He liked it.

"Tell me what other books you brought," he said. He did
not want to think about lilac right now, but he couldn't deny
her this pleasure.

"*Through the Looking Glass. Middlemarch. Uncle Tom's
Cabin.* Hugo's *Ninety-Three. The Count of Monte-Cristo.*" She
paused, thinking. "Those are the ones that stand out. Oh, and
The Moonstone by Wilkie Collins."

"You are going to keep Dr. Stuart very busy."

"I suppose," she said, sighing. "Unless you'd permit Mr.
Cutch to keep reading to me."

"Did Cutch suggest that?" Rand asked suspiciously.

"Oh, no. But I confess, I like his voice. He does the characters, even the female ones. And he has an ear for accents."

"A man of many talents, our Cutch." Rand's smile was
wry. "What am I to do with Dr. Stuart? Now that he's better,
some effort should be made to see that he earns his keep."

"I'll think of something."

Rand didn't doubt it. "We'll see," he said, promising nothing. "Dodd, take over." He let his palms slide from Claire's
shoulders to her upper arms. He noticed it was with some
reluctance that Claire loosed herself from the wheel. "You've
made a good run of it, Miss Bancroft. It's time to return to
your cabin."

Claire took the elbow he offered and allowed herself to be
led toward the main companionway. She was silent until they
reached the door to her quarters. It seemed that Rand filled the
small space even beyond the length and breadth of him. Some
odd sense of self-preservation had Claire pressing herself
against the door. She groped behind her for the handle and
found Rand's fingers already there. "Thank you, Captain. I
can see myself in."

"Of course." He straightened but did not remove his hand. He noticed that neither did she. She was looking at a point just past his cheek. She might not have been blind at all, simply shy. Rand touched her chin with his free hand and saw her flinch. "I'm sorry," he said. "I forgot to warn you." He left his fingers where they were, though, and gently nudged her face toward his. "Have you really been kissed so very often, Claire?"

Her mouth was dry. It occurred to her that she could be insulted by the question. How he expected her to answer was not immediately clear. She had no idea how the truth would serve her.

Claire was saved from saying anything. A door farther down the companionway opened and Dr. Stuart stepped out. "Aaah, Miss Bancroft," he said genially. "And Captain Hamilton. How kind you are to have seen after her when I was called away. I gave Mr. Cutch some peptic salts that should ease his stomach cramps. I think he'll have no complaints on the morrow."

Rand's hands remained in his coat pockets, just where he had placed them when he heard the first stirrings in the companionway. He searched the doctor's face for some sign that he had been caught out. There was nothing about Stuart's cheerful features that said everything was not as it should be. The doctor was not boyish in his looks, but he appeared younger than his twenty-nine years. His widely spaced eyes held a certain good humor and he smiled easily, with warmth more than amusement. Even when he had been doubled over the rail—and once, unfortunately, on the weather side of the ship—Macauley Stuart had been determinedly philosophical about the experience.

He was not an especially tall man, barely passing Claire in height, but he had a slender and wiry frame and carried himself well. He admitted to have taken up boxing when he was at Edinburgh, which Rand thought explained Stuart's particularly light tread. His hair was orange, not the penny copper of Rand's, but aggressively orange, like the fireball of the sun at daybreak. Every time Rand looked at it he thought of the old salty chant: *Red sky at morning, sailor take warning*. It wasn't fair, Rand knew. He could just have easily recalled the rest: *Red sky at night, sailor's delight.* But he didn't, and he made no apology for it.

"I'm about to go topside," Rand told Stuart. "You may join me if you like."

"No, I'll stay here with Miss Bancroft," he said. He looked at Claire. "If that suits you."

"He's talking to you, Miss Bancroft," Rand said when Claire made no reply. "Not me."

"Oh." She flushed, embarrassed at not having known.

A muscle worked faintly in Rand's jaw. He knew Stuart had not had Mrs. Webster's years of training with the blind, nor had he spent a great deal of time in Claire's company, but Rand thought his training as a physician should have made him less of an idiot. "You have to use her name, Doctor, if you wish her to know she's being addressed."

Stuart's fair, freckled complexion flamed with almost as much brilliance as his hair. "Of course," he said. "Forgive me."

Claire frowned. Rand had not needed to make so much of it. She would have explained it to the doctor, given the chance. "Don't give it another thought," she said. "Please, and call me Claire. Miss Bancroft is such a mouthful when we'll be spending so much time in each other's company." Opening the door to her cabin, Claire invited Dr. Stuart inside. She wondered if she imagined that the captain's receding footsteps were just a bit heavier than usual.

Cerberus made Charleston harbor four days later. A skeleton crew was left with her while the rest of the men scattered to make the most of two weeks on solid ground.

Cutch rode ahead to Henley to announce the arrival while Rand rented a horse and buggy to carry him, his passengers, and a small fraction of their belongings out to the plantation. Rand took the driver's seat and kept the mare steady as Dr. Stuart assisted Claire. Claire was comfortably situated, but the doctor was barely seated when Rand snapped the reins.

"Are you all right?" Claire asked him. She heard his start of surprise and felt the awkwardness of his position beside her.

"Yes, yes. No harm," he said warmly, pushing himself upright. "The captain's impatience is understandable. You and I will feel the same way on our return to London."

That might be true, she thought, but Dr. Stuart was unlikely to leave anyone so literally in the lurch. Claire kept this to herself. She had no wish to draw Rand's attention to her. There had been talk among the crew that Rand Hamilton was better left to himself. Anyone in his sights ran afoul of him sooner or later. His men, even the formidable Cutch, made a point of going about their duties silently.

"Tell me what you see, Macauley," said Claire.

Ahead of them Rand did not listen. He had no wish to hear the city he loved being described by someone who had no connection to it. It would not be the same place through this stranger's eyes. The doctor would not tell Claire about the twisting lanes beneath them or that beautiful gardens lay beyond the aged walls they passed. He couldn't invoke the history of the stucco homes or find the right colors in nature to portray their pastel tones. He didn't know young women sometimes stepped out on the wrought-iron balconies to be wooed by their suitors. It was not only merchants who prospered and built mansions in the Battery, but almost every planter along the Cooper and Ashley rivers boasted an architectural wonder in the city proper. It was here in the relaxed social splendor that was Charleston in the summer months, that the owners of the rich rice and indigo fields could escape the oppressive heat for sea breezes and choose good health over the risk of malaria.

The landscape quieted as they left the city. The steady clopping of horses' hooves faded and the mellow voices of passersby vanished. From time to time the wide, spreading crowns of towering white oaks shaded their passage. Sweetbay blossoms and spruce pine added their fragrance to the route while Carolina wrens added their chatter. *Tea-kettle, tea-kettle, tea-kettle, tea.*

They passed plantation homes that had been restored to some semblance of their former splendor following the war. What the Yankees hadn't destroyed, carpetbaggers tried to swindle.

Proud families, their ranks reduced by battle, used every means at their disposal to keep their land.

Rand Hamilton's own family was no exception. He needed no reminders of that as he turned the mare into the long drive leading to Henley. There, at the gates flanking the entrance, a new marker had been set into the bricks: *Concord*. Rand felt his heart being squeezed.

Claire sat forward in her seat when Macauley told her they were approaching the house. She tried to imagine how Rand saw his home after so long an absence. It could not merely be the symmetrical collection of red brick, white columns, and window shutters that the doctor described. What about sunshine reflecting on the glass? Did it wink at them? Warm the brick? Was smoke curling from either of the chimneys? Had anyone come out to the second-floor balcony to wave Rand in?

Rand slowed the buggy as Henley filled his vision. "The bricks came from England," he said quietly. "Carried here as ships' ballast. The story goes that it required seven separate vessels and five years before Henley had matched enough brick to suit him. He and his bride lived in a log cabin by the river while they cleared and worked the land and made plans for their home. The cabin's gone now. My grandfather cleared it out to expand the gardens at the front of the house. There wasn't much left to it by then. It was burned by Tory sympathizers during the Revolution."

Claire would have liked to hear other stories about the house, but Rand seemed suddenly more aware of his audience, almost as if he had been speaking solely to himself before, and stopped abruptly. She heard the whalebone whip whistle in the air as he snapped the mare's haunches. The buggy rolled ahead quickly now, and there was no further reflection.

It had been enough, Claire thought. She knew what the captain saw when he looked at Henley: history and heritage.

Jebediah Brown ran up to hold the mare steady as Rand jumped down from his seat. "Welcome home, seh," he said, beaming. "It's a fierce pleasure havin' you back."

"And it's good to be here, Jeb." He glanced toward the

steps, expecting to see someone come out of the house. "Where's Mother? Bria?"

Jeb's smile faded as he followed the direction of Rand's puzzled glance. "Miz Foster ain't feelin' all that well today, I reckon. Miss Bria ... well, she took herself off to the river when Cutch said there'd be visitors beside yourself. You know she shy and don't like no fuss."

"And Orrin? Where can I expect to find him?"

Jeb merely pointed to the last window on the first floor, a window that opened on the master's study, then made a pantomime of knocking back drinks.

Rand merely nodded. "See to the horse, will you?" He turned and saw that Claire and the doctor had alighted from the buggy and were now standing awkwardly beside it. He wondered if Stuart had explained Jeb's gesturing to Claire. Did she realize the man who had laid claim to Henley was no better than a drunk?

"Welcome to Concord," he said without inflection. This was not his home, he thought. This was not Henley. "Come, I'll show you to your rooms."

Addie Thomas met them at the door and ushered them inside. Her welcoming smile was less broad than Jebediah's but no less deeply felt. "Your mama wants to see you straightaway," she told Rand. "No dallying. She's fretting because she's not here to greet you herself."

"Go on," Claire encouraged him.

Rand hesitated. He was saved having to make an unpleasant choice by Cutch's appearance at the top of the stairs. He left Claire and Stuart in those capable hands and hurried to his mother's room.

Elizabeth Hamilton, now Foster, was comfortably propped at the center of her wide bed. Ruffled pillows bolstered her arms on either side and another supported the small of her back. She was a petite woman with dark coppery hair that was graying at the temples. Her complexion, fiercely protected from the sun for years by shaded verandahs and a hundred different parasols, was pale and creamy—except for the yellowing bruise laid flat across her cheek like wet parchment.

Her hand went to the bruise as soon as she saw Rand's eyes fall on it. She felt the coldness in his gaze all the way to her heart. "It's not what you think, dearest," she said softly. "I fell on the stairs and caught my cheek on the banister. Here, give me a kiss and forget about it."

Rand sat on the edge of the bed and leaned toward his mother. He kissed the unmarked cheek she offered him and didn't resist the arms she put around his shoulders. He touched her back lightly, held her to him. She had always seemed so fragile. How was it, he wondered, that she had never broken? He didn't argue with her story about the banister but neither did he accept it. Helplessness made his nerves raw.

Elizabeth Foster held her son at arm's length and regarded him critically. "Your face is too thin and brown," she said firmly. "And I don't think I like how Cutch is cutting your hair." She squeezed the work-hardened muscles of his upper arms. "And ropey besides. You're like a strip of deer jerky, nothing but meat and little of that."

Rand laughed. "Sssh, Mother. You'll turn my head with those compliments." His assessment of his mother, bruise aside, was that she was as lovely as ever. "Why are you still in bed?" he asked. "Surely it's not because of your . . . accident. Have you become vain, Mother?"

"I've always been vain," she said without apology. "I simply have so much less to protect these days. No, of course it isn't the bruise. I sprained my ankle in the fall. It's giving me more pain today then it did last week."

"Have you had Dr. Edwards examine it?"

She hesitated and glanced briefly away. "I didn't think there was reason to send Jeb for him."

Rand suspected the truth was a little different. Either his mother was honoring her husband's express wishes, or she had reason to fear reprisals if she summoned Edwards. "Then it's fortunate indeed that Dr. Stuart is one of our guests. I'll have him attend to you as soon as he's settled in."

"A guest attending me? I should say not."

Rand took his mother's delicate hands in his and squeezed

them gently. "You have no say in it at all, Mother. Now, let me tell you about our other guest."

It was after sunset that Cutch introduced Claire to the banks of the Cooper River. He escorted her on one arm and carried a blanket under the other. Their walk took them out the front of the mansion, across the verandah, and through the expansive gardens that joined the house to the river. The air was redolent with new blossoms, their fragrance cut by the crisp scent of the water.

Cutch snapped the blanket open and laid it smoothly on a shallow incline. "Don't think you can just wander off," he warned her. "No one wants to fish you out of the Cooper."

Claire raised the book she had in her hand. "You're not going to read to me?"

"Not this evening. I . . . I, umm, got some things to do my first night back."

"Why, Mr. Cutch. I believe you have an assignation. And you've been so quiet about it."

"Like the sphinx." He looked over his shoulder. "But here's Miss Bria. She's volunteered to take my place."

Claire stiffened a little. Bria Hamilton was an unlikely volunteer. Her welcome had been restrained to the point of being cold and she had made no effort at supper or dinner to thaw. Claire would have much rather been left alone. She gave herself better than even odds of returning to the house safely if she was left alone. With Bria at her side, Claire speculated she was likely to arrive dripping river water.

"Good evening, Miss Bancroft," Bria said quietly.

"Claire. Please." She had made the same offer before, but Rand's sister insisted on addressing her formally. Claire patted the space beside her. "Won't you join me? Mr. Cutch has brought a spread big enough to entertain the crew from *Cerberus*." Her smile faltered in the wake of Bria's silence. She wondered at what looks passed between Cutch and Rand's sister. "Mr. Cutch?" she said uneasily.

"I'm leaving now, Claire. You're in Miss Bree's fine hands."

Claire heard the grass fold softly under Cutch's feet, then the rustle of Bria's skirts as she settled herself nearby. The doctor had informed Claire, with a richness of expression he had not applied to anything else, that Bria Hamilton was a singular beauty. Her hair was the color of dark honey, smoothly coiled in an intricate knot behind her head. Her eyes, he told Claire, warming to his subject, were as blue as sapphires and shaded by long lashes that kept her glance remote and somehow mysterious. Claire imagined she also commanded what was now the fashionable line of beauty: a short waist and long legs; all of it confined rigidly in a whalebone corset that fit her like a cuirass. Only Bria's hands were flawed as far as Macauley Stuart was concerned. The backs of them were brown and the palms were coarsened. The nails were squared off and short. If she applied creams, they failed to eliminate the chapped skin.

"I'll take your book," Bria said. "If you want me to read, I need to begin now. There's not much daylight left."

Claire started to hold out the book, then withdrew it again. "I'd rather not. Would you mind very much just keeping me company?"

Bria drew her legs up and stared at the river over her knees. "This is one of my favorite spots," she said.

Which, Claire supposed, was Bria's way of saying she was trespassing. Rand's sister was as determinedly difficult to get along with as Rand. "It's lovely," Claire agreed. "Is it—"

"How could you know? You can't see."

"I don't need you to remind me," Claire said evenly, carefully holding her temper. "But no one I know has a favorite spot that doesn't have something to recommend it. I can smell the greening of the garden here. There's a sigh in the branches above us, and the sound of lapping water is always pleasant. Forgive me, but I don't think I've really intruded on your private place. The vision I have of it, the one I'll carry away, is no doubt different from yours."

Bria said nothing but neither did she move away. At least Claire Bancroft was not without a backbone. "What has Rand said about me?" she asked at last.

The question startled Claire. "Precious little," she admitted.

"But your brother seldom spoke to me during the voyage, and hardly at all about his family. Mr. Cutch told me scarcely any more."

"Then you asked."

"I admit I was interested when I learned we would be stopping here. When I first heard your name mentioned I thought you were the captain's fiancée."

One corner of Bria's mouth turned up in a smile that was startlingly similar to Rand's. "My brother must have found that amusing."

"Oh, I didn't tell him. He would have made too much of it, I think. Or deliberately misled me to try to prompt a reaction."

"And would he? Prompt a reaction, I mean?" Bria turned her head sideways to study Claire's profile. "Would you have been jealous?"

Claire hoped there was enough dusk to cover her immediate discomfort. "I think it would have only made me more curious about you. Your brother is . . . well, he's . . . he's unusually—"

"He's a bastard sometimes," Bria concluded matter-of-factly.

"Yes," Claire agreed. "There's that."

Bria laughed. "Have you said as much? To his face?"

"Only once. To his face. Several times behind his back."

Bria's smile widened. "Good for you, Miss Bancroft . . . Claire." Bria sat up and inched closer to Claire, narrowing the gulf of blanket between them. "I love him to distraction, you understand, but we're all opinionated Hamiltons here and we don't always share the same opinions. He thinks I should get married and leave the running of this place to Orrin. As if that's an answer to anything. Letting Orrin run the plantation is the surest way to run it into the ground."

"Your brother must have his reasons."

"Oh, he does. My best interests, he calls them. Getting married would get me away. He doesn't understand that I couldn't leave Mother." Bria's voice dropped to a whisper. "He doesn't understand I'm saving Henley for him."

Claire wondered if Bria imagined she was an ally—all

because she had been able to call Rand Hamilton a bastard. "I'm not certain why you're telling me this," she said. "I don't have any influence and I don't even know if I disagree with him. Perhaps he doesn't want to feel responsible for the sacrifice you're making."

"Sacrifice? This is . . . was my home, too. I have a right to determine the lengths I'm willing to go for it. There's no reason for Rand to feel responsible or guilty."

"Have you told your brother this?" Claire asked gently.

The passion in Bria's voice faded and she only sounded tired now. "Twenty minutes before I came down here," she admitted softly. "I wasn't quite recovered when I joined you."

"I see," Claire said slowly, unaware of her companion's thoughtful regard or the hint of admiration in her eyes.

"Yes," Bria said. "I think you really do."

Claire saw a lot more over the course of her first week at the plantation. Orrin Foster was a drunk. Not a sloppy, slurring, stumbling drunk, Claire realized, but a steady, serious one. He began applying himself to this single-minded pursuit when he rose for breakfast, usually around ten, and he paced himself throughout the day, taking time to ride into the fields or oversee the small stud. That he managed to do this without breaking his neck was a measure of his horsemanship or proof that God watched over fools.

The master of Concord—and he liked to refer to himself that way at times —was largely genial during the day. He had an open, affable countenance: a round face, wide smile, and the steady pink of drink in his cheeks and broad nose. He was by nature loud and expansive in his expressions, spreading his arms wide in conversations, slamming his hand down when he was crossed. It was toward evening that he tired, and that tiredness made him just plain mean.

What Claire could not see for herself, she saw through the eyes of others. The tension as evening approached was palpable. Elizabeth Foster made efforts both to placate her husband and excuse his behavior. Bria often simply excused herself. Dr.

Stuart usually followed her, offering his escort into the gardens and along the riverbank. Claire and Rand stayed, the hours passing interminably, until Elizabeth retired to her room or Orrin took himself off to the study. Rand's presence, as far as Claire could tell, had virtually no effect on Orrin's drinking or his manner. Orrin seemed unconcerned by his stepson and made no attempt to affect consideration for consideration's sake. He did not make a pretense of extending kindness to Elizabeth or Bria for Rand's benefit, but Claire doubted that he treated them any worse. Orrin Foster was not given to posturing. He was what he was and he appeared to relish the idea that Rand had no countermeasure for that.

It was nearing the end of a particularly grueling Sunday, a full week after their arrival, that Claire decided she could leave Rand and Orrin alone in the parlor and nothing would come of it. There might be some words exchanged, but they would probably not trade blows. Exhausted from the tension that Orrin raised like a dust cloud around him, Claire excused herself soon after Elizabeth. She was surprised, though, to hear Elizabeth still making her halting way up the stairs.

Claire swept her cane in an arc in front of her and moved confidently across the large foyer to the bottom of the stairs. She climbed only a third of the steps before she was at Elizabeth's side. "Is it your foot?" Claire asked. "I think it must be bothering you more than you've admitted."

Elizabeth's hand tightened on the banister and she let her slight weight be supported on her uninjured leg. "It's really nothing," she said. "I have no tolerance for pain, I'm afraid."

"I doubt that's true," Claire said softly. A woman who subjected herself to Orrin Foster's savage tongue and boorish manners, Claire thought, had a great deal of tolerance for pain. It occurred to her that in some ways, Elizabeth Hamilton Foster was very nearly numb. "Here, take this." She handed Elizabeth her cane. "Use the banister on one side and this on the other."

Elizabeth did not grasp the cane until Claire quite firmly put her fingers around it.

"Here," Claire repeated. "Use it, or I promise I'll call for Rand." It was then that Claire felt it being seized like a lifeline.

She matched Elizabeth's careful steps until they reached the top of the stairs. "Let me take your elbow now and you use the cane. We shall manage nicely, I assure you."

Elizabeth offered her arm, but it was Claire who provided the support. They made their way down the hall slowly. At the entrance to her room, Elizabeth tried to return the cane.

"Keep it for now. I suspect you will need it tomorrow more than I."

"Oh no, I couldn't let them see me—" Elizabeth broke off. "I don't want Rand and Bria to suspect how much it still pains me."

Claire heard in Elizabeth's voice what measure of pride it cost her to admit that. "I don't know that either of them believes your assurances to the contrary. What does Dr. Stuart say?"

"He's only examined it once," she said. "The day of your arrival. I haven't asked him to look at it again. He says it's a sprain, a bad one to be sure, but still, merely a sprain." Elizabeth opened the door to her room and hobbled inside. She invited Claire to join her.

"Will you permit me to look at it?" Claire asked.

Elizabeth's brows lifted. "You? What do you mean, dear? How can you *look* at it?"

Claire held up her hands. "With these." It was not difficult to imagine Elizabeth's surprise and skepticism. "I spent a great deal of my time on the islands with native healers. I was able to identify illnesses of the stomach and heart. A broken bone presented no problem to me."

"But you had your sight then," Elizabeth said warily. "And they were *natives.*"

"I'm not suggesting that we use charms or amulets or tiki to relieve your pain, but perhaps there is some herbal remedy that will be more helpful than the patent medicine Dr. Stuart gave you."

Elizabeth sat down slowly on the edge of her bed. "How did you know he had given me anything?"

"The hint of anise and alcohol on your breath."

Elizabeth's hand flew to her mouth. "Oh, my."

"I shouldn't be at all surprised if there's not opium in it," Claire told her. "And it hasn't been effective, has it?"

"No, not nearly as much as I'd hoped."

"Are you sitting on the bed, Elizabeth?"

"Yes."

"Then lie down."

Elizabeth placed the cane at the foot of the bed and eased herself back. She winced as Claire's weight depressed the mattress. Such a small movement should not have hurt so badly, she realized. She bit her lower lip when Claire's delicate hands moved lightly over the tautly stretched skin of her lower calf, ankle, and foot.

"Is your skin still a purple hue here?" asked Claire. "Or is it fading to yellow?"

"Indigo," Elizabeth told her. "Just there . . . and there."

Claire nodded. She lowered Elizabeth's foot gently. "I'm not sure this is a sprain, Elizabeth. You may have some sort of fracture. You need to stay in bed and keep your weight off the foot. The color in your skin is because of swelling and poor circulation. You do not require any medicine with alcohol. It will only serve to further the problem." She leaned forward. "And in the event you think I learned that from an island witch doctor, I know that from my father. He's made a study of the blood and medicines that might affect its flow and humor. Some children have picture books read to them. Sir Griffin let me sit on his lap and look through his microscope. He read his journal entries to me as though they were chapters in a Dickens novel. For a long time I thought a corpuscle *was* a character." She smiled when she heard Elizabeth's small chuckle. "When my father and I returned to Solonesia, I was his assistant. I was helping him with his work on hemophilia."

"I think you would be wise to listen to Miss Bancroft, Mother."

Elizabeth and Claire turned simultaneously toward the door. For all that Claire prided herself on being able to attend to extraneous sounds, she had not heard Rand's entry into the room. Now she was aware of his footfalls as he approached the bed.

"If it's privacy you want," Rand told them, "then you have to close the door. It was not my intention to—" His eyes fell at that moment on his mother's discolored ankle. He swore softly.

"Rand!" Elizabeth reprimanded him. "There is no need to be coarse."

Claire smiled. She believed that Rand had made some effort to hold himself back. She had overheard the full range of his salty expressions on board *Cerberus,* and this bit of cursing was only mildly seasoned. "You mustn't scold him on my account," Claire said innocently. "I've heard much worse."

Rand wished that Claire was not oblivious to the acid glance he cast in her direction. He snorted derisively to convey what he thought of her comment.

Elizabeth's eyes, so much like her son's in their chestnut color but infinitely more warm, darted between Rand and Claire. She wondered if they knew they wore their antipathy like armor. "Why don't you take Claire outside?" she asked Rand. "It's not too late for a walk in the gardens. I believe Bree and the doctor are out and about. And there's nothing to be gained by all three of us examining my foot." She arranged her petticoats and taffeta skirt over the offending appendage. "Send Addie to me. She can help me prepare for bed."

"I'd like to make you a poultice," Claire said. "Leeches would not be out of the question."

Elizabeth made a face. "Absolutely no leeches. A poultice will be fine. But not just now. Please, enjoy what remains of the evening and don't give another thought to me." She smiled sweetly at her son.

Rand wondered when his mother had become as oblivious to his acid glance as Claire.

Chapter Five

"I'm afraid Mother can be rather obvious," Rand said as he and Claire stepped onto the verandah. "She would quite willingly sell her soul to see me married."

"As long as she doesn't sell *your* soul," said Claire.

Rand's step faltered and Claire was brought up short beside him. "What do you mean by that?"

Wishing she could retract her words, Claire simply shook her head. A light breeze from the river made strands of dark hair flutter at her temples. She pressed them back self-consciously. "No."

At first Claire thought Rand was forbidding her to touch her hair. Her hand dropped to her side before she considered why she was obeying him. When it occurred to Claire that he could command her so simply, she raised her hand again, this time with a small wave of defiance, and pushed back another forward-falling strand of hair.

Rand frowned at Claire's fiddling. He saw it as a way for her to avoid his question. "Tell me what you meant," he said more harshly this time.

Claire could not have been more startled if he had taken her by the shoulders and shook her. Her hand fell back to her side.

"I only meant that it seems you've given up quite a lot of yourself already," she whispered.

"What do you know about it?" he asked. "Who have you been talking to? Bree?"

"No, not the way you mean. Not just about you." She released his elbow and took a step away from him. Without her cane Claire was unable to move more than this small distance. She had relied heavily on it to cross the verandah with its scattering of furniture and hanging and potted plants. "Of course I've talked to Bria, but about David and Shelby . . . and your mother and father."

Rand stiffened. "What about them? What has Bree been saying?"

Claire raised her arms in front of her. Suddenly chilled, she hugged herself. "Nothing."

"Hardly nothing."

"Just stories," Claire amended. "That's all. Just stories from your childhood and growing up together."

Rand regarded her for a long moment. Claire always seemed to hear more than was said. Now she had put her own construction on what she'd learned. "I'm going to take your arm," he said at last. The meager light cast from the house was sufficient for Rand to see her flinch. He may as well have touched her as warned her.

Claire felt Rand's fingers circle her wrist. He placed her hand under his arm. She adjusted her grip so that she held only the sleeve of his jacket. When he began to lead her away from the house, she followed. She could feel the tension in his stride.

"Why are you so angry?" she asked.

"I don't like being the subject of your speculation."

Claire said nothing.

"I wish you would not become Bria's friend."

If he had said it arrogantly, prohibitively, Claire would have turned on him angrily and challenged his right to make such a statement. Instead she was touched by the quiet resignation in his tone and felt something akin to sadness. "And I wish such a thing were possible," she said. "But your sister is not amenable to friendship."

"You've spent a great deal of time in her company."

"It signifies nothing. Bria is very insular."

"I've seen her with you," Rand said. "She's warmed to you. She smiles in your company and she's eager to take you off alone."

"Perhaps she thinks it pleases you. It's true that she's warmer than on the occasion of our first meeting, but Bria is hardly sharing confidences." Except once, Claire thought. After Bria's first failed attempt to gain an ally, there had been no more overtures. "So you see, Captain, I have not become your sister's friend. You have nothing to take me to task for."

Rand had taken a path straight through the gardens. Now he and Claire stood at the lip of the gentle slope that leaned toward the river. Fifty paces away was a gazebo. He turned in that direction. "Do you think I want Bree to have no friends?" he asked Claire.

"No," Claire said with credible calm. "Quite the contrary. I assume it's something you find lacking in my character that makes me unsuitable for your sister."

Rand sighed. "It's nothing like that. Don't goad me with that absurd line of reasoning."

Claire did not find it absurd at all. Rand had scarcely been complimentary. "Then explain yourself," she said.

"I thought it was evident. In seven days you'll be leaving. You can hope for no more contact with my sister than through an occasional letter, and since Dr. Stuart is the means through which you compose your letters, I imagine it will only encourage him."

"Encourage Macauley? In what way?"

"To continue his hopeless pursuit of Bree."

"Pursuit? He has only made himself available to take a few walks with her."

"Bree leaves the house to get away from him."

"She leaves the house to remove herself from Orrin's presence."

Rand stopped at the edge of the gazebo. "Stairs," he said. "Three steps." He took them carefully, watching Claire, then he led her to the bench that ran along the gazebo rail on six of its eight sides. "We can sit here. The river's behind you. Henley is visible through the trees in front of us. There is lamplight outlining four of the windows on the second floor. I think my mother must be reading in her room."

"If she is," Claire said, "it's to take her mind off the pain."

Rand was quiet. He leaned back against the rail and became aware that Claire's fingers were still curled in the sleeve of his jacket. He glanced sideways at her shadowed profile. She was staring toward the house, just as if she could see through the trees to the lamplighted windows. "Do you think my mother's ankle is broken?"

"It's difficult to know at this juncture," she said carefully.

"Stuart examined her the first day."

"I know. He told me it was a severe sprain. It's a moot point. Her problem is blood flow now. Elizabeth should have an herbal poultice applied to relieve the swelling, leeches if she would cooperate, and be made to keep her leg elevated and immobile. She should not have been out of bed this past week." She also should not have been given the bottled alcohol and opium mixture, Claire thought. It was unfortunate that physicians did not know as much about the workings of the blood as her own father did. "You will have to persuade her. Orrin will want her up, and she will not want to be confined during your visit."

Rand nodded. His voice, when he finally spoke, was strained. "He pushed her, you know. Struck her across the face hard enough to make her fall. That's how she hurt herself."

"I thought it was something like that. Macauley mentioned a bruise on her cheek."

"Sometimes I hate her for marrying him." The bitter words came out in a rush, as if Rand had lost a battle to hold them back. "She defiled my father's memory, taking him to her bed."

"She saved your father's legacy," Claire offered quietly. "Elizabeth saved Henley. She bought you time."

Rand rubbed the back of his neck, massaging the corded muscles. "There's no difference between my mother and Jeri-Ellen."

"Jeri-Ellen?"

"A London whore."

Claire's hand fell away from Rand. "How dare you," she said with soft menace. "It's acceptable to lie with one but unacceptable to *be* one. Is that what you're saying? Your mother used the only means she had to keep Henley in the family, and in your heart you revile her for it? Tell me, do you feel the same way about Bria?"

Rand jerked upright. "What do you mean? What have you heard?"

Claire recoiled from the heat of Rand's barely leashed anger. She did not have to understand the thinly veiled accusation to feel cut by it. "I haven't heard anything. Bria manages the plantation. That was all I meant. She stays here, removes herself from everyone in Charleston to oversee Henley. It matters not at all that Orrin Foster owns it now and calls it Concord. Is she sullying your father's memory because she runs Henley for another man, a surly clod who can't appreciate what she's doing?"

Rand simply stared at her. "Are you talking about Orrin or me?" he asked finally.

"I don't know anymore, but if the shoe . . ." She shrugged. "Shall I tell you what I really think, Captain?"

Since she had yet to mince words, he wondered what she could possibly have left to say. "Only if you call me Rand."

"Pardon?"

"If you're going to tear another strip off me, I'd prefer you called me Rand."

"What I think, Captain," she said quite deliberately, "is that you believe that you have somehow failed to protect both your mother and sister and the memories of two brothers and a beloved father. You blame yourself for not being able to take Henley into your own hands after the war. You blame yourself for the decision your mother made and for the course your sister's life is taking. You want Bria married and away from here as a balm for your own conscience, regardless of her wishes. It pains you to look at her calloused hands the same way it pains you to see your mother's injuries. You see those things and you feel your failure more keenly. The problem is, it belittles what Elizabeth and Bria have accomplished.'' Claire drew in a calming breath. ''And that's what I think,'' she finished softly. ''Captain.''

Rand rested his forearms on his knees. His fingers were folded and the balls of his thumbs tapped lightly together. His head was bent. He stared at the gazebo floor a long time before he felt the ache at the back of his throat. Swallowing was hard. Pressure built behind his eyes and he blinked. Along the rim of his lashes he felt the welling of tears. When had he last cried? he wondered. Had he shed any tears for David or Shelby? Had he cried when he read his father's name on the dead rolls? Not even for Bria, not even when he had learned what had been done to her, had he cried.

''Rand?''

It was the concern in her voice. Just that. There was no pity or sympathy. No pretense of understanding. It was simply concern and it undid him.

Rand felt the first tear slip over the edge of his lashes and drip to the floor. It was quickly followed by another. He sucked in a shaky breath and held it in until he felt Claire's hand rest lightly on his forearm. She barely touched him, laying her fingers across his sleeve more than his arm, but he recognized her presence in spite of that. She kept her hand still. She didn't stroke or pat him like a child or make any soothing sounds, yet her touch acted on Rand like a lightning rod, grounding him while the emotional storm struck and vibrated through him.

He turned on her slowly, careful not to dislodge the hand that was his lifeline. ''Let me,'' he said on a reedy thread of sound. ''Say yes.''

She had no clear idea what he was asking, but Claire also knew she wouldn't refuse. ''Yes,'' she said. When she felt the heat of him, heard his breathing change as he bent toward her, and understood what he wanted of her, Claire's answer remained unchanged.

''Yes,'' she said again. And this time his mouth closed over her softly parted lips.

She could have been anyone, Claire thought. It was closeness he needed, not *her* closeness. She should remember that, she cautioned herself, but it was difficult from the very first. These were *her* lips opening under the pressure of his mouth. *Her* breath that was caught at the back of her throat.

His hands came to rest at the small of her back. He gave her only a moment to accept him there, then she felt Rand's strength in the tension in his forearms and fingers as she was inexorably pulled toward him.

He held her tightly. One hand slid up the length of her spine until Claire's breasts were flattened against his chest. Her fingers found purchase at the level of Rand's shoulders, and she held on. The pressure on her mouth increased. His tongue swept the underside of her lip. The breath she would have taken was taken from her.

It was not enough for him. He traced the ridge of her teeth, then withdrew and kissed the corner of her mouth. He held her still, one hand buried in her coil of dark hair while the other slipped between their bodies and found her breast. His thumb passed back and forth across the taut material of her bodice. She whimpered against his lips.

The pins were removed from her hair. She heard them drop one by one to the floor of the gazebo, and with the part of her mind that could think of nothing else than what was about to happen to her, she counted them. At six her hair cascaded over Rand's wrist and across her back. His fingers twisted in the thick strands and he tugged gently. Her face was lifted, raised and tilted so that his mouth grazed her cheek and chin and the underside of her jaw. The line of her throat was exposed to him. In the evening's velvet shadows it had acquired a milky radiance. His lips touched her skin, first just behind her ear, then lower until they found the pulse at the base of her throat. He drew on her skin there, sucking gently until he had a shivering response from her. His mouth grew more heated then, and the touch of it was like a brand on her flesh. He could not seem to get her close enough or kiss her quite hard enough. She simply held on.

He was breathing roughly when he dragged himself away

from her. There was only the briefest pause before he stood and pulled Claire to her feet in front of him. She came without protest or fear and her forehead rested against his shoulder while he unfastened the back of her gown. He pushed the opened neckline over her shoulders and tugged on the wide straps of her chemise. Claire took a steadying breath as the strings of her corset were loosened and Rand's fingers slipped under the stiff stays to touch her skin.

She could not look down at herself and see where he was going to touch her next. Eyes opened or closed, Claire had only the anticipation of his touch to guide her. His hands on her breasts, at her throat, at the small of her back, this was expected. She accepted his mouth on her forehead, at her ear, and again slanting across hers. It was only when she was being lowered to the floor that she felt a moment's panic.

He whispered against her mouth, *"Shhhh."*

It should not be so easy for him, Claire thought. But she did not think it for long. Tension dissolved as he laid her back. She felt his face just above hers, and she was the one who lifted her mouth this time.

The kiss was hard and deep and hungry. He did not cradle her head as much as restrain her. His fingers were threaded in her thick hair, and the pads of his thumbs pressed against her temples. His mouth moved over hers, and on the next foray his tongue pushed past her teeth and thrust deeply alongside hers. Even though she did not resist him, it became less of a kiss and more of a battle, and when Rand lifted his head, Claire's fingers came up to press against the open wound of her mouth.

She felt the length of Rand's body shifting. His leg nudged hers. His arms moved lower and his fingers disentangled themselves from her hair. He kissed her throat and she felt him draw in a deep breath, absorbing the fragrance of her skin and hair. Claire's fingers still lay across her lips, and they muffled her small, surprised cry when Rand's mouth closed over her breast. He took the turgid nipple between his teeth, worried it gently, then flicked it with the tip of his tongue. The arching of Claire's body invited him to do it again. This time he captured her with the hot suck of his mouth.

She twisted, but not far, and with no intent to escape. He captured her wrists anyway and held them flat against the floor on either side of her head. He kissed her again, softly at first, as if he could oppose the forces that kept him tautly strung at her side, then harder, desperately, as though surrendering to them was against his will.

Claire took a long draught of air when he released her mouth and expelled it sharply as he claimed her other breast. The edge of his tongue was hot and damp. He drew it across her skin slowly, raising awareness of where he had been but not of where he was going.

His knee raised the hem of her gown. Petticoats were lifted above her ankles and then above her calves. Her skirt bunched around her thighs, and the space between her legs widened. He seemed to move across her without exerting any pressure or weight. He was able to make her raise her knees without offering direction or encouragement, and when he released her wrists her arms did not come up to ward him off or cover herself.

He removed her corset and lowered her bodice and chemise to her waist. Her breasts and midriff were almost translucent. He kissed the flat plane of her abdomen and felt her skin retract slightly under the pressure of his mouth.

Claire felt a tightening in her chest as Rand's mouth and hands moved across her flesh. She was hot and cold at once, and between her thighs she was damp. His hands moved with rough impatience, yet his mouth was tender. She had no fear of what was being done to her, only that she was not returning the full measure that he expected. It would be easier if he expected nothing.

Claire's hips lifted as her drawers were dragged over her thighs and her skirt was pushed higher. She closed her eyes for the first time since Rand had lowered her to the floor. She had no time to think why it would be that she saw herself more clearly now; she only knew that it was so. It was as if a mirror had been raised above their tangled bodies.

The abandonment of her posture both alarmed and aroused

her. She saw one arm flung wide and the other curving near her head. Her hair fanned away from her face like a dark penumbra. One finger twisted in the disarray but with no attempt to smooth it. It was a beckoning gesture, she thought. That was her hand, her hair, and she was stroking herself, inviting Rand to touch her in just that same way.

Her complexion was pale, tinted by the blue-silver of moonlight. A band of shadow covered her eyes, but her mouth was clearly visible and it was damp and parted. The slender stem of her neck was arched. Rand's head lay between her breasts, and what she felt as his lips moved lower, she also saw in her mind's eye.

She heard herself cry out softly and saw her body lift. Rand's fingers were dragged lightly across her thighs before they dipped between her parted legs. Her head fell to one side as he stroked her, first with his finger, then with his tongue. His copper hair was darkened by moon shadow to the color of rust. Claire watched her knees being raised and bent until the backs of them rested on Rand's shoulders. Her slim calves lay across his back.

She could be anyone, she reminded herself. But it was difficult to think so when it was happening to her.

Claire's fingers curled and her open palms became fists. Liquid heat traveled the same course as her blood, and she felt it pool around her heart and between her thighs. It had weight, and it sat heavily on her as the pressure built in both places. A sound passed her throat, something incoherent, and she wondered what she wanted to say. She wondered if it mattered to him.

Her legs fell to the side as he lifted his head then raised himself over her. There was a pause and she moved restlessly, not recognizing the sound of Rand fumbling with his clothes for what it was. He took her wrist and drew her hand toward him. He pressed his thumb against her pulse to open her fingers. When they closed again, they closed around the hot, hard length of his penis. It filled her hand.

She heard his soft groan near her ear, then felt his lips on hers. She thought she tried to speak, but she couldn't be certain.

The voice she heard didn't sound like hers. The things it said she wasn't sure she wanted to say.

"No!" The cry was thin and reedy. It should have been a robust refusal but it vibrated with so much fear that it was robbed of strength. "Don't touch me. Please. I'm going to be sick."

In one swift motion Rand pushed himself away from Claire and lurched to his feet. He repaired what was necessary but took no time to close his jacket or tuck in his shirt. Blood still pounded in his temples, and it was like having the roar of the ocean in his ears. He shook his head to clear it and spoke tersely to Claire. "Stay here."

Claire felt him step around her and heard him cross to the gazebo stairs in two heavy strides. He leaped over the steps and landed with a soft thud on the grass. He was running in the direction of the other voice, the one that wasn't hers. He was running to Bria.

As Claire sat up she heard Bria's cry again. This time there was a rawness to it that spoke of pain. Claire felt a slight tremor in her hands as she pushed her petticoats and skirt over her knees. She yanked at her chemise and bodice and covered her breasts. On her hands and knees she swept the floor for the discarded corset and drawers. Tears stung her eyes but didn't fall. Her own humiliation warred with her fear for Bria.

Crouching low, Claire slipped into her drawers. The corset she took to the river side of the gazebo and flung it as hard as she could. It made a satisfying splash in the water.

It was difficult to traverse the gently rolling landscape from the gazebo to the path without her cane or a companion. Claire relied on sounds from the river to her right and the raised voices directly ahead.

Rand found his sister backed against the thick trunk of a cottonwood. At either side her fingernails dipped into the furrowed bark. She held on to it with the tenacity of a treed cat.

Dr. Stuart was standing a good ten feet from her, his hands raised in the air, palms extended out. It was not so much a gesture of surrender as one meant to calm or quiet.

"Bree?" Rand said her name in question. He could have

been asking anything. Was she all right? Had anything happened? What was going on? It didn't really matter because Rand didn't wait for an answer. He launched himself at Macauley Stuart before there was an explanation from that quarter. Just now he didn't care what anyone had to say.

Macauley was easily toppled and thrown to the ground. Rand grabbed him by the collar, hauled him up, and threw a hard right that put the doctor down again.

"Rand!" It was Bria who shouted. "No! Don't hurt—" She didn't finish because it was useless. Macauley Stuart's howl of pain left no doubt that he had been hurt.

"Bloody, bloody hell!" the doctor swore. "You broke my nose!"

"Are you sure I didn't *sprain* it?" Rand's demand came through a tightly clenched jaw. He ducked Macauley's punch and landed another of his own, this time on the doctor's midsection.

Stuart's breath was forced out of his lungs. He doubled over, but instead of falling to his knees he ran full tilt at Rand. His head butted Rand in the stomach.

"So much for Queensbury rules," Rand said hoarsely. He recovered his balance and set Macauley back on his heels with an upper cut. The doctor's head snapped up as his bottom teeth met his top ones.

"Rand!" Bria cried again. "Rand! Please!" Out of the corner of her eye, she saw Claire approaching. "Can you make him stop, Claire? He's going to kill Dr. Stuart!"

At the sound of Claire's name, Rand's head swiveled to find her. Stuart didn't waste this advantage and drew back his fist for a superior roundhouse punch. The swing was so powerful, it bruised the doctor's knuckles. It also dropped Rand to his knees. He fell against Stuart more than tackled him, but the effect was the same. The physician went down and dragged Rand with him. They rolled on the ground, each looking to land the definitive blow that would end the fight, if not settle anything.

Claire took a step backward when they brushed her gown. She held out one hand. "Bria?" she called. "Where are you?"

Bria detached herself from the cottonwood. "Here," she said, stepping closer to Claire. "I'm here." She took Claire's extended hand and drew her back again when the two men widened their ring.

"It's Macauley, isn't it?" Claire asked. "Rand's fighting with the doctor."

"Yes."

Claire realized her own hand was steadier than Bria's. "Are you hurt? We heard you cry out."

"No. I'm all right." She raised her voice so that it could be heard over the pained grunts of her brother and the doctor. "I'm all right! Nothing happened, Rand! I was foolish and frightened and—" She squeezed Claire's hand tightly as Rand found a fistful of Stuart's shirt and used it to lever him against a tree.

Rand was breathing heavily and his tongue seemed to be tangled in his head, but he managed to make himself understood. "You . . . leave . . . my sister . . . alone . . . you don't . . . touch her . . . or walk behind her . . . you don't sniff after . . . her skirts. She's no whore. Next time . . . I'll kill you."

To punctuate his warning, Rand knocked Stuart's head against the deeply ridged trunk once; then he rose from his crouch and shook himself off. He glanced into the shadows where Bria and Claire stood huddled together. "Bree, go to the house. I'll escort Claire back in a few minutes."

Bria looked at Macauley. His head was lolling at an uncomfortable angle against his shoulder. "What about Dr. Stuart?"

"A dip in the river will bring him around."

"You don't intend to drown him, do you?"

Rand paused long enough to let her know it had occurred to him. "Not this time," he said under his breath. "Go on, Bree. I'll speak to you later."

Bria tried to release Claire's hand and realized she was the one being held now. "Claire?"

"I'll return with you," she said quietly.

Rand's fingers raked his hair. Frustration made his voice more brusque than coaxing. "Stay with me, Claire. This will only take a few minutes with the doctor."

"I'm going with Bria. I've heard everything I want to." She tugged on Bria's hand. "Please." The appeal that could not be seen in her eyes was in her voice and in the tightening of her fingers.

Still, Bria looked at Rand for direction. He nodded once, stiffly, making no effort to mask his unhappiness with Claire's decision. "Take my elbow," Bria told Claire.

The grandfather clock in the entrance hall chimed once on the half hour. Claire turned over in bed and drew the covers up to her shoulders. She tried to remember if she had heard the two o'clock chimes. Perhaps she had fallen asleep at the very moment she thought it would never happen. No matter, she was awake again.

Propping herself on one elbow, she reached for the cool compress on the bedside table. She lay back and placed it over her eyes. Beneath the damp cloth her lids were still swollen, the edges of them red. Claire had never cried prettily, and she had no expectation that being blind changed that. Her complexion would have pinkened but not with perfect roses in her cheeks. The color would be there in asymmetrical blotches, across her forehead and along her neck.

She sniffed rather inelegantly and found the handkerchief tucked in the cuff of her nightgown. She blew her nose and winced when she rubbed the tender tip. If she didn't gain some control of herself, it would be a beacon by morning. That was enough to make Claire toss the handkerchief toward the table. Chances were, she thought, she wouldn't be able to find it again if she *did* need it.

Claire added her forearm to the weight of the compress across her eyes. She felt the cloth dampen her sleeve but she didn't remove it. The extra pressure seemed to keep the tears at bay. For now it was all she cared about. It was one thing to allow herself the freedom to weep, something else entirely to let others know she had.

Lost in a muddle of thoughts and images she had no defense for, Claire did not hear the door handle turn. She was deaf to the whisper of her door passing across the fringed rug. It wasn't until she heard the first creak of floorboards that she realized she wasn't alone.

She lay very still, hardly breathing. Perhaps her visitor didn't know she wasn't sleeping and this small advantage she kept to herself. By the time the intruder crossed the room to her bedside, she knew who it was. She decided that pretending to be asleep was the only solution.

"Claire?"

She thought Rand's ragged whisper might be her undoing. There was part of her that longed to bolt upright and slap his face. If he said her name again in just that way, his voice somehow sensual and urgent, she might do it.

"I know you're not sleeping," he said. He sat on the bed and raised the candle he held above her. Golden light flickered over her but she didn't move. "Claire, please." He thought she might continue to play at being asleep then he saw her lips part softly.

"Go away." It was not a petulant command but an order that was not meant to brook refusal.

"I've just left Bree," he said. "Or I would have come sooner."

"I wish you wouldn't have come at all. I didn't think I had to lock my door." She turned on her side away from him and rested her head on her damp forearm. The compress dropped on the pillow.

Rand shifted the candle so he could better see what had fallen. The presence of the compress immediately raised his concern. "Is it your eyes, Claire? Is there pain?"

Under her breath, Claire called herself a fool. She should have known he had a candle or a lamp when he didn't miss a beat on his way to her bed. "Put out the candle," she said.

For a moment Rand thought that it was the light that bothered her eyes, then he realized she only meant for him not to see her. He wet his index finger and thumb and suffocated the flame. The wick sizzled and a thin spiral of acrid smoke leapt into the air. "It's out," he said when he didn't feel her turn on the bed.

''I know.'' She remained exactly as she was.

''What about your eyes, Claire? Should I wake Stuart?''

''Then you let him live,'' she said dully. ''How clever of you to realize I might need him.''

''Claire.''

She could not miss the admonishment in Rand's tone. Claire sighed somewhat impatiently. ''I'm fine. There's no reason to disturb Macauley.''

Rand reached for her. Intent upon turning Claire onto her back, his hand hovered just above her shoulder. Through the small space of air that separated them, he felt her stiffen.

''Don't touch me,'' she said. ''Don't you dare touch me. I couldn't bear it.''

He withdrew his hand slowly. ''I'm sorry.''

Claire had no sense of what he was apologizing for. Did he mean that he was sorry for almost touching her now or that he regretted everything that had come before it? She supposed it didn't matter. If apology was why he had come, then it was finished. ''Fine,'' she said. ''Good night.''

Rand was silent for a long time. ''Perhaps it was a mistake to come here,'' he said quietly. ''I needed some assurance that you were all right.''

''Well, you have it. You can rest easy.''

He swore softly. ''Nothing's settled, Claire. Apparently you believe you have some right to be angry at me. I don't know that I deserve that. I didn't do anything wrong this evening.''

That statement had the power to take her breath away. It was a moment before she could answer. ''No. That's right. *I* did. You made that very clear.''

Rand frowned. ''What are you talking about? I never said—''

''You told Macauley he had no right to touch your sister.''

''Claire, I only—''

''She wasn't a whore, you said.''

''I didn't mean that *you* were.''

''Didn't you? Wasn't that just the conversation we were having before you . . . before . . .'' She didn't finish. She couldn't. The ache in her throat effectively blocked her voice.

Rand turned slightly on the bed, drawing his knee up so that it rested near the small of her back. He wanted so very much to touch her. To keep that from happening, his fingers curled into the loose bed sheets. "That's not how I remember it," he told her, his own voice not much above a whisper. "It's not how I think of you."

Claire did not believe it. "No? You're here now, aren't you? Or would you have me understand you often visit Henley's female guests in the middle of the night?"

"Now you're twisting things. You know that's—"

"I know *nothing*." Claire yanked hard on the coverlet, pulling it closer about her shoulders like protective armor. "Perhaps this is something you and your brothers all played at. Were the other women allowed a choice, or did they have to accept your attentions once you barged into their bedchambers?"

Rand's head snapped up as if he'd been slapped.

Unaware that she had struck her target, Claire went on. "What would you do to Macauley Stuart if you found him like this in your sister's room? The only difference between Bria and me is that she has someone to protect her."

Rand removed himself from Claire's bed. He stood beside it a moment, staring at her shadowed profile. "You're wrong," he said finally. "There's another difference. Bria said no. That word never once crossed your lips."

Claire's hand made a fist in her pillow. "Get out," she said hoarsely.

"As you wish."

Because it was his custom to rise late, Orrin Foster was used to eating his breakfast alone. What he found disconcerting this morning was the unusual quiet of his home. When he inquired about the whereabouts of the others, he was told his wife was having another lie-in, Bria and Claire and Dr. Stuart had all requested breakfast in their rooms, and Rand had gone fishing with Cutch at dawn.

Orrin accepted this information without comment. He masterfully hid his annoyance by closing himself in his study and starting his first drink two hours ahead of his usual schedule.

Unaware that his stepfather was applying himself early to a superior state of drunkenness, Rand lay back on the grassy riverbank and closed his eyes. It was not so much that he was relaxed, just that he was tired. Beside him Cutch sat with his legs folded tailor-fashion, plucking thick blades of grass, then holding them up to his mouth to whistle through them. Almost forgotten, the fishing poles were propped on forked branches so their lines could meander in the river with the current.

Cutch eyed one of the poles as it bowed a bit. "Could be you got a bite," he told Rand.

"Mmmm."

Cutch shrugged. "Probably you'd just toss it back in like the others."

"Pro'bly."

Lowering the blade of grass from his lips, Cutch looked down at Rand. "Don't seem right, somehow, you yankin' me awake this morning to come out here. Trampin' all this way from the house just to fish, then not carin' if you catch a thing."

"I wanted the company."

"I can see that." Cutch nodded slowly, his wide mouth pursed to one side in a wry smile. "You've been downright loquacious."

"I didn't say I wanted to talk. I just didn't want to be alone."

"Then you probably want me to sit here all quiet like."

"Pro'bly."

"No whistlin' through the grass."

"No whistlin'," Rand said.

Cutch turned his attention back to the river. He dropped the blade of grass in his hands and plucked a new one. Instead of trying to make a reed of it, he simply fanned it back and forth across the bottom of his chin. In deference to Rand, he kept his thoughts to himself.

A shaft of sunlight broke through the umbrella of willow leaves above Rand and touched his face. He laid his forearm across his eyes to shade them. He remembered that Claire had been lying in bed in much the same posture when he had entered her room. Rand frowned slightly, wishing he hadn't remembered that. He'd made Cutch tramp two miles along the riverbank to get away from memories of Claire. Apparently distance had nothing to do with it.

"What time do you make it?" Rand asked.

Cutch glanced through the willows to the angle of the sun in the sky. "Ten-thirty or thereabouts. Why? You have some pressin' appointment you only recollected now?"

"No. No appointment."

"Didn't think so." It seemed to Cutch that what Rand needed to do was sleep. Judging by what he'd heard last night, there was precious little of that going on. He hadn't asked about it. That wasn't his way. He could wait for Rand to tell him. "I suppose everyone's up at Henley. Could be they're wondering where we are."

"I told Jeb." Rand felt the slant of sunlight change. He moved his arm. "You were in Charleston yesterday. How soon do you think we could be ready to sail?"

Cutch realized he wasn't surprised by the question. He'd sensed a certain restlessness in Rand throughout the morning. They might still be walking if Cutch hadn't thrown down his pole under the willow and announced it was the perfect fishing spot. "Supplies have been ordered but nothing's been loaded. The men think they have a week yet to make ready."

"I know that. Can it be done in two days?"

Cutch whistled softly. "Two days. The men won't like it."

"I didn't ask if they would like it. I asked if it could be done."

Cutch's high brow furrowed. "If I leave this afternoon and put the order to those on *Cerberus,* yes, it can be done. The remainder of the crew will have to be routed from their homes. They think they have more time with their families."

Rand nodded. He stopped short of giving the order. There was some peace to be found simply knowing what could be accomplished in two days' time. He would not push toward that end now. Rand sat up. There was no possibility that he would sleep this morning. He rubbed the bridge of his nose with his thumb and forefinger, sighed softly, then selected a blade of grass and held it up to his lips. The sound was short and sharp.

Cutch countered with a deep warbling whistle and the competition was begun. The impromptu woodwind selections included recognizable versions of "Dixie" and Stephen Foster's "Camptown Races." Rand admitted defeat when Cutch offered up several measures of "Ode to Joy."

Laughing, Rand tossed his blade of grass aside and leaned back so he was braced by his arms. He crossed his ankles. "You're quite something, Cutch. 'Ode to Joy.' Where did you learn that?"

"Same place you did, I expect. Your father used to play it. Bria, too, now that I think of it. Been a long time since there was music coming from Henley."

Rand nodded slowly. The Yankees might as well have destroyed the piano when they tramped through his home. Instead they'd left it untouched. The same could not be said of the piano player. "Were you in my room some time yesterday?" he asked.

Cutch took Rand's deliberate change of subject without blinking. "Just before I left for Charleston," he said. "But you were there then. Why?"

Rand shrugged. "I thought maybe you had gone through some of the papers on my desk."

"Not while you were there. And certainly not while you weren't. Something missing?"

"No. They're just not the same way I left them. Or at least how I thought I left them."

"Orrin," Cutch said. It was not a question. "Still looking to get his hands on the riddle."

"That occurred to me. I suppose he thinks I wouldn't keep it on the ship when I'm here."

"That would be a logical assumption."

"I don't know. I used to believe he didn't think it really existed, but Bria told me that even when I'm not here he searches the house for it from time to time. It seems he can't make up his mind where I might be hiding it."

"He's afraid of it."

Rand wasn't sorry about that. "Good. He should be."

Cutch didn't reply. Even if he had thought one was necessary, his attention now fully rested on another matter. His pole was bobbing in earnest and in danger of being pulled free of its support. "Look at this!" he grabbed for the pole just before it slipped through the forked branch. "Seems like I've caught me some bragging rights!" He stood up and snapped the pole toward him. His line stretched and the pole arced, but nothing came to the surface.

Unperturbed, Rand stayed where he was. "You hooked a rock," he said. "You can brag all you want to about that. I'll be happy to make certain everyone knows."

Cutch snorted. "Don't be so quick to judge." He ducked out from beneath the willow and walked a few feet to his right, then his left. Something was definitely tugging on the end of his line. He could feel the current pulling him. It was *not* a rock. Cutch tugged on the pole again and sensed the give. He drew in the line as he walked down the bank to the river's edge. Water lapped at his bare toes and the rocks were cool under his feet.

"It's coming, Rand!" The line stretched taut again as Cutch heaved. He danced sideways over the rocks, looking for the angle that would land his fish on the bank. Veins stood out on his forearms like cords when he heaved again. This time his catch gave in. Cutch almost fell backwards as it leaped out of the water and sailed over his head, flapping and dripping water all over him. Behind him he heard it flop heavily on the grass.

Cutch scrambled up the bank to examine his prize. Rand was already kneeling beside it, trying to release the hook. Cutch's eyes went from his catch to the man trying to free it. The faint ruddiness of Rand's complexion couldn't be properly explained by his sudden exertion.

"Seems like I caught a rare *Femina corsetus.*"

Rand didn't look up. "Appears that way."

"Probably originated somewhere upstream."

"Pro'bly."

"Near Henley, I expect."

Rand's grunt was noncommittal. He knew a surge of satisfaction out of proportion to his accomplishment when he finally pulled Cutch's hook free of the material. He took off his jacket, folded Claire's corset, and stuffed it into one of his sleeves. He draped the jacket over his arm and picked up his pole. Without a word to Cutch, he began walking in the direction of Henley.

Cutch grabbed his own pole and caught up quickly, falling into step beside Rand and matching his long stride. "Don't suppose there's anything to brag about after all."

"No," Rand said quietly, his eyes on the uneven ground. "I don't suppose there ever was."

Orrin was holding court in the entrance hall when Rand and Cutch arrived. Elizabeth stood on the stairs, supported by the banister on one side and Claire on the other. Her face was pale and pinched with pain. Claire's features only held concern. In contrast to both of them, Bria was stoic. She showed no distaste or pleasure for the proceedings, no anxiety or apprehension. Her beautiful face was simply expressionless, as if she had ceased to hear or see anything, or as if anything she saw or heard had no impact.

Dr. Stuart stood at the foot of the stairs. The bandage across his nose was only a few shades paler than his freckled complexion. His left arm was stretched out at his side, his hand resting on the newel post. His posture suggested he was shielding the women from any drunken physical advance Orrin might make. At the end of the hall Rand saw Jebediah, Addie, and two other servants hovering around the doorway, afraid to interfere, afraid to move away.

Rand gave his jacket and pole to Cutch. "What's going on, Orrin? Why is my mother out of bed?"

"She's not much good *in* it, is she?" he snapped. The edges of his words were only slightly slurred.

Rand started forward, his hands clenched at his sides.

"Rand, no!"

It was his mother's voice that brought him up short. "It's the drink," she said. "It will pass."

Orrin chuckled. "Always the peacemaker, your mother. Well, I've got my own peacemaker." Until now his left arm had been partially concealed from Rand. He raised it enough for Rand to see that he was holding a Colt. He waved it in the direction of the stairs. Elizabeth and Dr. Stuart cringed. Claire's reaction came a moment later in response to Elizabeth's shudder. Only Bria remained unmoved.

Rand knew he could get the weapon away from Orrin, but not perhaps without it discharging. He held his ground. "Put it down, Orrin. You can't enjoy Henley if you're swinging from a rope."

"Concord," Orrin said, jabbing the gun in Rand's direction now. "Concord, damn you. That's what it's called now, you bastard. That's what I named it and that's what it's called. No more goddamned Henley. No more goddamned Hamiltons. This is *my* house and I'll be goddamned if any one of you will go into *my* study, through *my* things. Did you think I wouldn't know? I know everything that goes on around here, do you hear? Everything!"

"Orrin," Rand tried to inject his voice with calm, but even to his own ears it sounded more like a warning.

"Shut up," Orrin snarled. His grip on the Colt tightened and he leveled it a bit more solidly at Rand. "Unless you want everyone to know what I saw last night. Would you want that, Rand? Would you?"

Rand was careful not to look at Claire. If she was not giving herself away, then he was not going to do it with a guilty glance. Hoping that his stepfather could be redirected, Rand asked, "What's this about someone being in your study? Is that why you've summoned everyone?"

"Ain't it just," Orrin drawled. "Someone's been lookin' through my books. I know the order. I know when they've been misplaced on the shelves. My desk, too. Always keep the letter opener one particular way on top of my papers. It wasn't the way I left it. Seems no one here knows anything about it. You're late to the party. Could be it's you."

"It was me," Cutch said.

Orrin's brows rose. He wavered a bit on his feet, startled by Cutch's rumbling baritone, almost as if he'd forgotten the towering presence of the black man. "Well, damn," he said softly. Then he fired.

Chapter Six

Cutch staggered backward, but the bullet did not put the big man on the floor. His soft grunt of pain was covered by Elizabeth's scream and the sound of the Colt being discharged. Before Orrin could squeeze off another shot, Rand tackled him, taking him out at the knees. The Colt fell heavily and spun away from the combatants. Macauley Stuart bent to pick it up, but it was Bria who reached it first. She rose slowly, holding the weapon in a steady, two-handed grip, and pointed it at where Rand had Orrin pinned to the floor. Her eyes, like her hands, were unwavering.

Bria's voice was eerily calm. "Get away from him, Rand."

Rand glanced at his sister, struck by her tone as much as her order. Her expression was cold, her beautiful sapphire eyes remote. She could kill, he thought. Had she been anyone else, he could have let her. "No, Bree. Give the gun to Stuart."

On the stairs behind Bria, Rand saw that his mother had sunk to a sitting position. She was crying softly, almost soundlessly. Claire was still beside her, one arm around Elizabeth's narrow shoulders. Rand knew it was Claire's presence, her offer of comfort, that was keeping his mother from a well-deserved fit of hysterics. His eyes darted to Stuart. The doctor hovered near

Bria, looking as if he might try to take the Colt from her. He'd made no move toward Cutch to examine the injury.

Rand glanced backward. Cutch was leaning against the door, stemming the flow of blood from his shoulder with one hand. He had finally dropped Rand's jacket but still held both fishing poles. Rand shook his head slowly, the smallest smile playing on his lips.

"Cutch is going to be fine," he told Bria. "Orrin only winged him." When Bria's stance did not falter and her eyes remained unmoving, Rand wondered if she had even heard him. "Bree, look at him," Rand said more loudly, this time with a touch of urgency. "Look at Cutch." It seemed to Rand that even Orrin was holding his breath, waiting to see what Bria would do. Rand's weight bore down a little harder on his stepfather, just as a reminder that he was paying attention.

"I'll be right as rain, Miss Bria," Cutch said. His deeply melodious voice had a soothing cadence. "Right as rain. I've been hurt worse than this tumblin' out of bed."

Bria's eyes narrowed. She hesitated, then risked a glance at Cutch.

He winked at her.

The gesture was so unexpected that Bria blinked owlishly. Her eyes refocused, first on Cutch's injury, then on the weapon she held. The cool remoteness of her expression vanished, replaced by one that was almost like surprise.

Rand saw his chance. "Stuart, take the gun. Bree will give it to you."

Macauley held up his hand. It hovered just above Bria's wrist for a moment. She lowered the gun slightly and relaxed her grip. He took it from her loose fingers easily.

Orrin released the breath he was holding. Rand reared back from the sour reek of it. He got up slowly and brushed himself off. Stepping over Orrin as though he were so much offal, Rand went to Cutch. He took the poles from his friend's hand and propped them in the corner. "Jeb," he called to the servant still hovering at the far end of the hallway. "Help Cutch to one of the rooms upstairs."

Orrin had recovered sufficiently to sit up now. He also found his voice. "No nigra is going to use one of my bedrooms," he barked. "Take him to the servant quarters."

Rand turned on his stepfather. "Shut up, Orrin." He gave the order without rancor.

Cutch made a quiet protest. "You don't have to put me up in the big house. I can—"

"Shut up, Cutch." Rand waved the hesitant Jebediah forward. "Now, Jeb. Give Cutch some support. Stuart, help him." He took the Colt as the doctor lent his assistance to Jeb, then stepped out of the way. Motioning to another servant in the hallway, Rand gave orders for her to supply Stuart with whatever he needed. "Go on, Kate. Follow them up and make yourself useful. Mother, help Claire down a step so they can pass without trampling her."

Elizabeth swiped at her tear-stained face with the back of her hand. She regarded her son with a mixture of wonderment and admiration. "Yes, Captain," she said quietly. She guided Claire to the step in front of her. "Just for a moment, dear. Then you can help me back to my room. We'll be the caboose to this train."

Orrin lurched to his feet. "Like hell, Elizabeth. I want to see you in my study."

Rand stepped forward and leveled the barrel of the Colt at Orrin's head. "I won't let Mother talk me out of it again," he said. He sensed that the parade on the stairs had halted momentarily to see if the drama would be played out this time. Rand indicated the study's paneled doors with a quick gesture of his gun hand. "Through there, Orrin. Get drunker. Pass out. No one wants to hear from you any longer."

Orrin's hesitation cost him. Lightning quick, Rand shifted the position of the weapon and struck Orrin in the back of the head with the Colt's butt. Orrin grunted hard and collapsed in stages, falling to his knees first, then forward on his hands, and finally flat-faced on the floor at Bria's feet. She stared down at him just long enough to make certain he was out cold.

Bria stepped around Orrin to open the study doors; then she bent at the waist and grabbed him by his boots.

Elizabeth leaned forward and placed one hand lightly on Claire's shoulder. "Bria's dragging Orrin inside his study."

Claire nodded. She had followed most of what happened, right up to the moment Orrin's body thudded to the floor. Beside her she noted that Jeb, Macauley, and Cutch were on the move again. She waited until they passed before she returned to Elizabeth's side and offered her help.

Rand watched Claire's shoulders brace to take his mother's weight. He didn't like what he saw. Elizabeth was almost wholly dependent on Claire just to be able to stand. It looked as if Claire was lifting his mother, not merely supporting her. Rand thrust the Colt back in Bria's hands as she came out of the study and took the steps two at a time.

"Let me," he said. He felt Claire stiffen as he inserted himself between her and his mother. "You can't carry her, Claire."

Elizabeth looped her arms around her son's shoulders and was lifted easily in his arms. "Take his elbow," she told Claire. "Come with me to my room."

Claire could not explain that she had no wish to take Rand's arm. She imagined he felt the same way. He did not pause overlong waiting for her to come to a decision. Claire reached for him, expecting to be able to curl her fingers in his jacket. Instead, her hand rested solidly against the sleeve of his shirt. The thin cotton was no barrier to the warmth of his skin. She felt his corded muscles tense beneath her palm. Claire almost pulled away, but some sense of self-preservation kept her attached. Releasing him now, she thought, would be a kind of admission that she was disturbed by his closeness. Claire was not prepared to acknowledge that openly to herself or to Rand.

At the foot of the stairs, Bria watched her mother, Rand, and Claire turn on the landing. The Colt was still heavy in her hand. She emptied the chamber of the remaining bullets and pocketed them; then she laid the gun on the entry hall table. She did not think it looked terribly out of place next to the vase of flowers she had arranged only yesterday. It looked . . . handy.

Bria was on the point of joining everyone above stairs when she noticed Rand's discarded jacket on the floor. It lay there

in a creased heap, but was untouched by the drops and spat-
terings of Cutch's blood. She backtracked, stooped, and picked
it up, smoothing the collar and pressing out the sleeves with
the heel of her hand.

Her curiosity was caught by the dampness of one of the
sleeves. At first she thought she had been mistaken about
Cutch's blood and that it had not only stained Rand's jacket,
but soaked the sleeve through. When she risked looking at her
hand she saw it was not red at all, but merely damp. Frowning
now, Bria raised the sleeve and found the weight of it more
than could be explained by its wet state. She opened the jacket
and slipped her hand inside the sleeve. Her fingers touched the
ridged edge of the object that had been thrust inside.

Looking at the corset and surmising it could only have
belonged to Claire, Bria was left with the notion that what she
had stumbled upon in Rand's jacket was another Hamilton
riddle.

The breeze-cooled verandah was the location Rand had chosen to have his confrontation with his sister. He knew the timing
of it was poor. It was easily after nine o'clock, and the course
of the day's events had made everyone at Henley long for sleep.
As far as he knew, only Orrin and Cutch had found that blissful
state. Orrin had been removed to his room after another bout
with his bottle in the afternoon. Cutch was resting after his
surgery.

Bria watched her brother for a few moments from the doorway before she stepped onto the wide porch. He was sitting
stretched out in a wicker chair, his posture more indicative of
sheer weariness than relaxation. His hands rested lightly on the
arms of the chair but his fingers were quiet for a change, not
tapping out an accompaniment for the crickets in the hedgerow
or the owl in the pine boughs. He was staring off toward the
gardens, and beyond that to the river. She wondered if his
vision had gone as far as *Cerberus* and the ocean. She hoped
so. He needed to leave.

She joined him, taking the companion chair beside him. He

raised one hand a few inches, acknowledging her presence, and she reached for it. Bria squeezed his hand gently. "Addie said you wanted to see me."

Rand nodded. "I thought we might talk."

"Argue?" she asked.

"Talk," he repeated.

Bria waited. When Rand didn't offer a subject for discussion, she said, "What were you thinking just before I came out here?"

"That Macauley Stuart is an ass."

"Oh," Bria said softly, tempering her smile. She withdrew her hand from around his. "I thought it might have been something else."

Rand pushed himself a bit more upright. "He should have been able to remove the slug from Cutch's shoulder himself," he said. "What sort of physician has no experience with bullet wounds?"

Bria's soft drawl was absent as she said in crisp accents, "Apparently a veddy proper English one."

"He's Scots," Rand said dryly.

"Och, then a ver-r-r-a proper Edinburgh mun."

Rand was forced to laugh. "You do miserable impressions."

"I know." But she had made him laugh and it was enough. "I don't suppose Dr. Stuart has had much opportunity to deal with bullets in his practice. He told me that it certainly wasn't something he had to perform at medical school. You said yourself that his specialty is in the matter of vision."

"Yes, but he had a general practice. Don't the Scots shoot each other from time to time?"

"I think they still hack about with broadswords and those spiked clubs. What are they called?"

"Maces."

"Yes, maces."

Rand smiled. "I think their weapons have improved, even if their physicians haven't kept up with the times."

"It was good that Dr. Edwards could come out. I wasn't certain he would operate on Cutch. He doesn't feel so differently than Orrin about the blacks."

"I didn't give him much choice."

Bria had thought it might be something like that. She didn't ask what manner Rand had used to persuade the doctor. She had noticed, though, that the Colt had gone missing. "Dr. Stuart attended to Orrin's head wound," she pointed out. "And his hangover."

"Sobered him right up," Rand said, refusing to give Macauley his due. "Got him ready for the second round. I think the Scots have experience with hard drinking and hard blows."

"Is that why you had Dr. Edwards check Mother? You didn't trust Macauley to recognize the difference between a sprain and a fracture?"

Rand did not miss the ease with which his sister called the Scottish physician by his Christian name. She also seemed willing to defend him. "Mother appeared in too much pain for it to be a sprain. I thought it might require a splint."

"Only to keep her fast to her bed," Bria said. "Dr. Edwards confirmed precisely what Macauley said in the beginning. Mother needed to rest and keep her leg elevated. She has not followed his orders. You can hardly hold him accountable for that."

"He didn't mention phlebitis, did he? Edwards diagnosed that. Even Claire knew something else was wrong." His mother had railed against the treatment Edwards prescribed—the same treatment he had overheard Claire suggesting just yesterday. Elizabeth wanted no part of having leeches placed on her swollen ankle and lower calf, but it was only when Dr. Stuart lent his opinion to the matter that she had complied.

"Macauley helped bring Mother around, Rand. You know he did."

Rand's grunt was noncommittal. "What are your feelings for the doctor?"

Bria deliberately misunderstood. "I wish Edwards had a less self-important bedside manner, but I find him competent."

"Bree."

She sighed. "Very well. The truth is, I have no feelings."

Rand waited to hear more, but when Bria was silent he

realized that she believed she had explained it all. A chill went through him as he understood what she was really saying. His initial reaction was to deny it. "That can't be so, Bree."

"I don't know if you can appreciate how sincerely I meant it. I'm not like you, Rand. I'm not like anyone else I know. I playact at emotion. I have for a very long time. Sometimes I capture the nuances perfectly—the expression, the tone, the exact gesture—but it comes from the outside, not from within."

"But last night . . . when you were with Stuart . . . you were clearly terrified."

"Was I? I know you told me that when we talked afterward. I accepted it because you said so, not because I felt it. I didn't want him to touch me, that's true enough, but whether I felt anything about it, I couldn't say."

Rand turned sideways in his chair and studied his sister's shadowed profile. He remembered how she had looked in the entrance hall while Orrin held them all hostage. It was as if she was distanced from what was going on, as if she had somehow come to stand outside her physical self and could watch the drama without fear of being touched by it. Even when she had taken the gun, it was as though someone else were commanding her. Bria had been capable of pulling the trigger. He hadn't doubted it then. He'd heard nothing that made him revise that opinion now.

"Come with me, Bree," Rand said. "Leave Henley. Join Cutch and me on *Cerberus*. Claire will appreciate the company and you and I can find the treasure together. You've never once sailed with—"

Bria reached across the space that separated her from her brother and touched Rand's hand again. "I'm not leaving Mother."

"I don't intend that you should. Neither of you is safe here with Orrin. You can both come. We'll make room aboard. I'll give up my cabin. I spend most of my time on deck anyway."

Bria shook her head. "Stop, Rand. I'm not coming with you. Neither is Mother. We're not going to leave Henley, so there's no sense in you making plans to the contrary. I came to realize this morning that I can protect Mother. I'm not afraid of Orrin

Foster, Rand. I saw it in his eyes. He's afraid of me. I don't think he presents the same threat to Mother as he did before."

"What about you?"

She shrugged. "He's only ever been a nuisance to me. A fly in the ointment. I think of Orrin differently than you. I don't manage Henley to spite him; I manage it *in* spite of him. It still requires his Yankee money to keep things going. This will be only the third year we can anticipate a profit since the war."

Rand's cheeks puffed slightly as he released a long breath. Bria didn't need to remind him that she had been supervising every aspect of Henley just five years. Before that, Orrin Foster's money had not been enough to save the plantation from his own mismanagement. At nineteen, Bria had taken over the reins, subtly at first, merely countermanding Orrin's directives with more suitable ones of her own. By the time she was twenty, she was in control in every way that mattered. Orrin never acknowledged that he knew perfectly well what was going on, and no one had ever faulted him for being stupid. The truth was that after four years of trying to restore Henley to its former grandeur, he had lost interest. As long as there was liquor, details could be left to others. He claimed full ownership and not a whit of responsibility.

"Perhaps I should leave Cutch with you and Mother," Rand said.

"So Orrin can take another shot at him? I think that's a poor plan. Cutch would think so, too."

Rand's elusive smile flickered briefly. "All right. It was a bad idea. But I don't know how I can leave this time."

Bria shot to her feet. "No, Rand. Don't even consider staying, or staying longer than you planned. Nothing good can come of it. Besides, you entered into a business arrangement with Claire and her godfather. You can't renege on that."

"God, Bree. What would you have me do? How am I supposed to—"

Bria dropped to her knees in front of Rand. She took his hands in hers and held them. "You don't belong here," she said earnestly. "It's not a sacrifice for me to be here, Rand. It never has been. I can't explain it, but Henley is the only place

I feel truly safe. I don't expect you to understand. I don't myself. After what happened to me here, it would be natural to think I'd be happier anywhere else. But it isn't like that. Not for me. I'm not giving anything up by staying at Henley. *You* would be.''

Rand shook his head, denying that she spoke any part of the truth. "You're wrong, Bree. Name one thing that I'd be giving up that I couldn't live without."

Bria did not hesitate. "Claire," she said. "You'd be giving up Claire."

Tearing his hands away from Bria, Rand stood. He stepped around her kneeling figure and stopped on the lip of the verandah. "For someone who insists she has no feelings, you take some peculiar romantic notions to heart."

"I don't have to feel it," she said, rising to her feet. "I only have to know what it looks like."

He glanced over his shoulder. "What are you talking about?"

"Love. You're in love with Claire."

"Jesus, Bree." He shook off her attempt to place one hand on his forearm. "You need to make another study of the matter before you try acting on it yourself. I was in a room with her godfather for upwards of thirty minutes before I even noticed her."

Bria's smile was gentle. "I didn't say it was love at first sight," she said. "But you notice her now. You notice everything about her. If she knew how your eyes follow her, she wouldn't be able to cross a room without her knees buckling."

"You're confusing me with the good doctor."

"Not for a moment. He watches her, yes, but not as you do."

"You're mistaken, Bria."

"About which part?"

"All of it."

She laughed lightly, mocking him. This time when she patted his arm, he did not pull away. "You go ahead and think so," she told him. "Perhaps a magician's greatest trick is to hide his own heart."

Rand's brows drew together. He raked back his hair impatiently. "What is that supposed to mean? I'm a magician now?"

"What else am I to think?" she continued gently. "I picked up your jacket this morning, Rand, after Cutch dropped it. It seems that you always have something up your sleeve." With that parting shot, Bria turned on her heel and neatly dodged her brother's attempt to capture her. She ran into the house and slammed the door on him, locking it for good measure. The tumbler fell in place with a satisfying click.

"Bree!" Rand called after her. "Bree!" Through the window he watched her sashay down the lighted hallway, pausing just once to toss him a mischievous smile over her shoulder. "Damn you! I'll get—"

The sound of a throat clearing brought him up short. He spun around and saw Claire's slim figure limned by moonlight. She was standing on the lower step of the verandah, holding her cane in front of her. Her hands rested one on top of the other and covered the gold-plated knob.

"How long have you been there?" he asked roughly. If she took exception to his tone, Rand noticed, she hid it well.

"I came up through the gardens," Claire said. "I was sitting on the riverbank."

Which was not an answer to his question. "I didn't see you."

"No? I suppose because you were occupied with tormenting your sister. Did she lock the door?"

"Yes."

Claire nodded. "I thought perhaps she had. I'll go around to the other side." She turned and extended her cane to guide her off the step. She was brought up short by Rand, who not only halted her progress but lifted her over the next step and set her on the verandah.

"Stay here. I'll go. Unless I miss my guess, Bree's locked the other door by now. There's no point in you going."

Claire was seated in the chair previously occupied by Bria when Rand returned. He leaned against one of the porch's fluted columns and crossed his arms in front him. "Apparently she's rallied everyone to her cause," he reported with ill humor. "I couldn't get anyone's attention to let me in."

"There are windows, aren't there? Perhaps one of them is open."

"I thought of that. They're open on the second floor but not on the ground. The last time I was boosted through a window that high, I had my brothers' shoulders under me."

Claire smiled, imagining the acrobatics involved in that maneuver. "Did you make it into your room safely?"

"I didn't say it was my room I was trying to get into."

"Oh," Claire said thoughtfully. "Then what was *her* name?"

Rand found his black mood shifting. "Miss Emily Tipping. The Tippings own the neighboring plantation to the west. She was really David's love. I was sent as an advance guard just to prove it could be done. She practically tossed me back through the window."

"Were you hurt?"

"Only my pride. I had a bit of a schoolboy crush on her. I thought she might throw David over for me."

"Instead she threw you out."

"Hmmm." Rand wondered when it had started to hurt less to talk about David. Had it been happening so gradually that he hadn't noticed or was it just a recent turn of events, further proof that he found Claire's company good for his soul? He pushed away from the column and sat down. "I hadn't thought of that for a long time." More importantly, he hadn't minded thinking about it now.

Claire smoothed the skirt of her gown where she felt Rand brush it as he passed. The gesture had more to do with the state of her nerves than the condition of her dress. She couldn't help wonder how amenable Rand would be to what she wanted to say. "If David and your father had survived the war, they'd be managing the plantation now."

Rand shot her a glance. "Yes, that's right. David would have married Emily, and she would have come to live at Henley. He knew just about every aspect of running the place."

"The heir apparent."

Rand nodded. Belatedly he realized Claire couldn't see his acknowledgment. "Yes," he said. "The heir apparent."

"And Shelby?" asked Claire. "What would he be doing now?"

"That's easy. Shel only ever wanted adventure. He'd be in Africa, paddling up the Congo."

"Really? What about the Hamilton treasure?"

The slow smile that curved Rand's mouth was rueful. "He would have found it years ago, Claire. Shelby knew more about it than any of us back then. He was going to follow me to Oxford and research the legend there. Instead he proved himself too impatient. He couldn't wait until he was of an age to come to England. He begged me to start the research and complete detailed correspondence of what I found."

Claire remembered that Strickland had thought Rand had done research on the treasure in the Oxford library. He had only been mistaken that it had been Rand's real purpose for being there. "And did you?" she asked.

"As time allowed," said Rand. "Never as much or as thoroughly as Shel would have done himself, but I admit I found it fascinating."

Claire could easily believe that. "I imagine Shelby saw the riddle as a means to an end, while for you it was an end in itself."

Rand wondered what he had said that helped Claire arrive at that conclusion. He shrugged. "I suppose that was true then. It's been some time since I regarded the riddle so differently from Shelby."

"I know," Claire said quietly.

There was an odd metallic taste in Rand's mouth. It was the hook, he decided, that Claire was using to reel him in. "What is it you think you know?" he asked.

She didn't answer immediately. Claire pushed a stubborn strand of hair behind her ear. "David was on a course to secure Henley for a new generation of Hamiltons. Shelby's course would have put the treasure in the family's hands. It seems to me that they're still on course, Rand. Death hasn't altered their plans at all. They're managing quite nicely through you."

Her words had the power of a blow. It was as if the air had been driven from his lungs. What he wanted to do was strike back in a real physical sense. What he did was not move at all.

"Rand?" Claire said his name uneasily. She cocked her head and listened for the faint sounds of his breathing. "Are you still here?"

"I'm here, Claire," he said after a moment. Rand wondered if he could have reacted so strongly, so immediately, to her words if they hadn't resonated with truth.

"Are you angry?"

"It's passing."

"Should I leave?"

He sighed. "No. The doors are still locked anyway."

"Oh. I'd forgotten."

Rand's short laugh was without humor. "No easy escape. This time you have to finish what you started."

Claire did not call attention to her flaming face by raising her hands to her cheeks. Rand would know his barb struck home without confirmation from her. She waited to speak until she was certain her voice would not quaver. "If your brothers had survived the war," she said, "what would you be doing now?"

Rand decided there was no sense in pretending he didn't know the answer. Claire probably knew it as well as he. "Studying," he said. "Collecting. Cataloging. I haven't abandoned it entirely, Claire, in spite of what else occupies me these days. You've been in my workroom on *Cerberus*. You know that's true."

"I know it's an afterthought most of the time. And once you have the treasure in your hands, it will be less than that. You'll come back here and pick up the threads of David's dream . . . marry Emily Tipping or someone just like her. You can't even see beyond what David would have done to recognize that Bria is not only capable of managing Henley, but that she actually *wants* to."

"Did Bria put you up to this?"

Claire shook her head.

"Then why the hell should it matter what I do or why I do it?"

"It matters," Claire said quietly. "More than you know." Wishing she could retract her last words, she stood. There was no warning as Rand's fingers closed around her wrist. "Don't." The single word was more plea than protest. She offered no resistance as Rand drew her between his splayed legs and removed the cane from her hand. Claire heard it drop to the floor beside him. He kept steady pressure on her wrist until she was sharing the chair with him, more of her on his lap than not. He raised her hands to his shoulders and Claire held on, feeling the warmth of his face close to her own.

The click of the lock was like a gunshot. Claire pushed herself off Rand's lap in spite of his intention to hold her. She found her cane just as the doors to the verandah swung open and Bria stepped into the breach.

"It was my intention to let you fend for yourself, Rand," Bria said. "Then I realized I had locked Claire out as well."

One of Rand's brows was arched skeptically. Light from the hallway flickered across Bria's face. Her smile was too sweet to be sincere, just as her timing had been too good—or too bad—to have been anything but deliberate. "You'd better go, Claire," he said.

Claire did not require Rand's encouragement. She was halfway the distance to Bria when a voice intruded in her thoughts: *You notice her. You notice everything about her.* Claire's steps faltered, but her knees held. She tamped down a smile. Apparently she possessed a bit more stamina under Rand's scrutiny than Bria had given her credit for.

There was little opportunity for Claire to be mindful of her knees over the next several days. Rand left for Charleston to oversee the preparations for the next leg of the voyage. Cutch complained mightily that he did not need to lie abed, but no one, least of all Rand, paid him any heed. Claire helped him feel moderately useful by bringing in *Through the Looking Glass* and insisting he read to her. She wasn't at all bothered that he fell asleep from time to time.

Cutch's own rumbling snore woke him up. He slapped at

the book lying open on his chest as if it were a pesky fly. Grumbling, he brought himself to wakefulness and looked over at Claire. She was staring straight ahead, her brow furrowed as she concentrated on her knitting. "I hope you're not making that for anyone I know. Don't think I could stand looking at someone wearing it."

Claire's fingers flew over the stitches on the needles, counting them for the third time. "What are you saying, Mr. Cutch? Is it badly shaped?"

"Shape's fine, I guess." With some effort, he pushed himself upright and stuffed a pillow at the small of his back. "It's a scarf, isn't it?"

"I suppose it could be." She held it up. "Is that what it looks like?"

Cutch examined Claire's work critically. She had managed about sixty rows but it was now much wider at the bottom than at the top. "It looks like a triangle."

"A triangle? Really? That means I've been dropping stitches." She lowered the knitting so Cutch could see she was having him on. "I know perfectly well it's a mess," she told him. "Every color of the rainbow, too, I should imagine."

"There's a fact. Only not as soothing. Hurts my eyes."

"It's a good thing I'm blind, then."

Cutch was silent a moment. Then sharp laughter erupted from his chest. "You're a piece of work, Miss Bancroft. Just like Rand says."

"I think that's Shakespeare," she said dryly.

"Shakespeare was referring to all mankind. Rand says it about you."

Claire ducked her head quickly and ran her fingers over the stitches again. It was useless. Sighing, she found the basket at her feet and tossed the knitting into it. "*That* is a piece of work."

Chuckling, Cutch picked up *Through the Looking Glass*. "Do you want me to read more?"

"No, that's all right. I wondered if we might talk?"

Cutch closed the book carefully and set it away from him. "What did you have in mind?"

"You didn't really go through Mr. Foster's books and papers, did you?"

Now Cutch knew he should have resisted waking and slept on. "No," he said. "I didn't."

"Who did?"

He shrugged. "I don't know."

"Then you weren't protecting Rand?"

"Oh, I was protecting him, but not because I thought he'd gone through Orrin's study. His stepfather would have shot him if I hadn't said anything. Orrin was working himself up to it."

"I wasn't certain. I could follow most of what happened, but not everything. When the gun went off, I wasn't sure who was . . ." She let her voice trail off, and it was another moment before she spoke. "You must suspect someone."

"Most likely it was Orrin."

"Orrin?"

"It would not be the first time he's done something and forgot about it later."

"I hadn't thought of that."

"Then perhaps you have a suspect of your own."

Claire shook her head. "No. I don't." She could almost feel Cutch's skepticism. "I really don't. I don't know what's so important about Orrin's books."

"The riddle."

"The Hamilton riddle? But Rand has that, doesn't he?"

"Does he? I've never seen it."

"But he quoted a portion of it to my godfather. I was there."

"I didn't say Rand doesn't know the riddle. I think he grew up knowing it."

"You mean it doesn't exist on paper at all? It's been passed down orally for three hundred years?"

"Could be."

Or not, Claire thought. Cutch wasn't really saying, was he? "You wouldn't tell me under any circumstances," she said.

"No," Cutch said. "I wouldn't. I figure that's Hamilton business. Anything I've learned by living with them all these years, well, I figure it's still their business. Besides, you might have been the one tearing up Orrin's study."

That raised Claire's eyebrows. "Did that really cross your mind?" she asked. "Even for a moment?"

Cutch wondered at Claire's earnestness. "It occurred to me," he admitted. "A little longer than a mere moment."

Claire leaped from her chair and felt along the edge of the bed until she came to the head. Crawling halfway on board, her striped poplin gown fluttering upward, she threw her arms around Cutch's massive shoulders. "You dear man," she whispered, blinking back tears. "You dear, dear man."

He smiled broadly. "I'm happy for the compliment, but uncertain what I've done to deserve it."

She drew back. Her fingers swept across Cutch's collarbone, then went higher. She laid her palm against his broad cheek. "You thought I could do it," she said. "You don't know what that means. It didn't matter to you that I was blind."

Cutch moved her hand so she could feel the wide smile that split his face. "Actually, it did," he said. "It's the reason I decided it wasn't you. You would have made a better job of it. Nothing would have been left out of place. Orrin wouldn't have known anyone was there."

Claire laughed. "I'm not so careful about where I put things as you might think, Mr. Cutch. I spent a frustrating ten minutes trying to find my hairbrush yesterday, and the book I meant to bring was *Frankenstein*. My trunk is partially packed and it seems nothing is where I put it."

Cutch made a clicking sound with his tongue, shaking his head disapprovingly. "Mrs. Webster will be disappointed you've forgotten so much."

"I couldn't agree more."

Claire sat up straight as Rand's voice came to her from the doorway. "You should learn to knock," she said crisply. She smoothed Cutch's nightshirt across his shoulders and retucked his blankets.

"That's better," Cutch said, grinning at her primly set mouth and busy fingers. Perfectly at his ease, he smiled happily in

Rand's direction. "She's taken very good care of me in your absence."

Rand did not return his friend's wide smile. "Apparently," he said. He crossed the room to Cutch's side just as Claire was patting down the covers in search of her book. Before she placed her hand squarely on Cutch's groin, Rand picked up the novel and gave it to her.

"Thank you, Mr. Cutch."

"I'm sure you're welcome," Cutch said, taking the credit and blithely ignoring Rand's sour look.

Claire tucked the book under one arm and bent to get her basket of knitting. "If you'll excuse me, gentlemen, I'm sure you have business to discuss."

"Tomorrow, then," said Cutch. "We'll finish—"

Rand interrupted. "On board *Cerberus*. That's my business. You may stay, Miss Bancroft. It concerns you as well."

Claire felt anxious and eager at the same time. She dropped her book in the basket and sat down slowly. "We're leaving tomorrow?"

Rand brushed a fine film of road dust from his sleeve. He hadn't taken time to make himself presentable upon returning home. He'd found Bria in the stables looking not much better than himself. Her riding habit was stained with dirt and sweat from a hard morning tour of the plantation. She looked as if she had checked the progress of every rice seedling personally, then ridden hard across the fields to celebrate her accomplishment. Her face was shiny with perspiration—glowing, he would have said if she had given him the time. Instead she had anticipated his news, half laughing, half crying, and threw herself into his arms.

His mother had not greeted his announcement with Bria's enthusiasm, but neither did she try to dissuade him.

"We leave Charleston tomorrow morning," Rand said. "We leave Henley tonight."

Claire knew that Rand's trip to Charleston was in aid of making *Cerberus* ready, but she hadn't expected it to move their departure forward by three days. "So soon," she said.

"I wasn't aware you had other plans."

Although it confused her, Claire chose not to react to the soft sarcasm in his tone. "I thought I would have more time to pack."

"I overheard you say you already started."

"Then you also heard it's a rather bad start."

"I'll find someone to help you."

"Have you told Bria? Your mother?"

"Just before I came here," Rand said.

Then he had already started his good-byes, Claire thought. She had been delaying hers. "I should go," she said.

"We'll have dinner here. We go immediately after."

Claire nodded and bent for her basket and her cane. Holding them both in front of her somewhat protectively, Claire bade them good day.

"What do you make of that?" Cutch asked when Claire was gone. "Seems like she isn't so happy to leave."

"She's torn, Cutch," Rand said. "Leaving Henley means she won't be able to find much respite from my company."

Remembering the corset, Cutch scratched his hairless head. There was obviously something he didn't understand. He made a mental shrug. Like the riddle, it was Hamilton business.

It was barely morning when *Cerberus* made her way out of Charleston harbor. Her white sails spread wide, she carried the wind and the rosy-hued light of dawn in her canvas. Rand stood at the helm, his copper hair windblown and glinting like fire. Inside of thirty minutes, he thought, they would be making ten knots, perhaps twelve. In a few days they would pass through the Caribbean and on to the warmer waters around the equator. He could anticipate this leg of the journey would be smooth, just as he could predict foul weather as they headed into winter on the underside of the world.

He would not dare imagine how the same journey might go with Claire. Rand only thought it safe to suppose they would not experience the doldrums.

Below, in her cabin, Claire lay awake. The change in the ship's pitch, the steady beating of water against the hull, raised her from an already restless sleep. Turning on her side, Claire hugged the pillow to her breast with one arm and rested her head on the other. She extended her fingers to the wall and traced a furrow in the wood paneling.

What had Bria meant, she wondered, by her parting words? *Have a care,* she had whispered in Claire's ear, *I won't be on board to draw the doctor's attention.* Had Bria set out to do that at Henley? Quite purposefully? Claire had never considered that. It appeared to her that Macauley Stuart had been attracted to Bria from the outset. His poetic description of her features certainly seemed to indicate that was so. Bria had not always been encouraging to him, or at least not past a certain point.

With a heavy sigh, Claire fell on her back. Why had Bria wanted to draw Macauley's attention to herself in the first place? Had she imagined she was doing her brother a favor? Or was it something else?

Claire closed her eyes. How like a Hamilton, she thought, to present her with a riddle.

Over the next week Claire played with the puzzle in her head. She spent much of her time with Cutch, caring for him almost exclusively until Macauley pronounced him fit for light duties. If anyone was especially attentive to her during that time, it was Cutch himself. He found ways to keep her at his bedside, and once or twice she suspected he was better than he would allow. Claire didn't mind his fakery, if that was what it really was. He read to her with more animation than Macauley and his conversation was less taciturn than Rand's. The morning that he reported himself for duties on deck, Claire knew that a measure of the peace she had enjoyed was at an end.

As the weather grew warmer and the wind softened, Claire spent more time topside. The crew was watchful of her—she always sensed that—and at times they were even friendly. Paul Dodd taught her how to do rope work. She learned the difference between bends, which joined knots, and hitches, which anchored a rope to an object. He showed her how lines could be joined by lashing them together side by side, or by splicing them, unraveling the ends, then weaving them. Making a half hitch was no more complicated than tying a shoe. The square and thumb knots took her more time. Claire worked for half a day on a double carrick bend. She found infinitely more patience for the task than the knitting Macauley Stuart wanted her to practice.

She had no skill for mending sail, though several different members of the crew tried to help her. The tools were too unfamiliar. If there was a large repair to be made, it was not so simple as whipping a needle and thread through the canvas. It could require mallets, hooks, and a tapered wooden pin called a fid for opening up the strands of rope. The men also wore a leather strap which fit over the thumb and around their palm and held a metal needle pad. None of them fit Claire's small hand properly. She was not particularly sorry.

Claire lost her concentration for the sheet bend she was working on when someone rapped lightly on her door. The two ropes separated, one in each hand, and she was holding them that way when Rand stepped inside her cabin.

"I don't think I said you could enter," she told him.

He looked at the ropes she clenched, then the frustration that pulled her mouth tight. "I suppose what I mistook for your welcome was actually several pointed curses."

"Hmmm." Claire dropped the ropes and rested her elbows on the small writing table where she sat. She propped her chin on her fists and waited for him to state his business. It didn't seem likely that he had sought her out for companionship, or meant to provide her with any. He had not done anything so overtly pleasant since leaving Charleston.

Rand shut the door and leaned against it. He crossed his arms and ankles at the same time, his eyes never leaving Claire's face. A strand of dark hair had fallen forward across her brow. Disdaining to repair it in any real way, Claire simply blew upward to make it flutter to the side. Fascinated by the artless gesture, Rand watched the shape of her mouth soften.

"Yes?" Claire asked.

Her cool tone brought Rand around. Her mouth might have softened, but butter wouldn't melt in it. "Did you know it was me at the door?" he asked.

She couldn't imagine why it was important. "You have a

sharp rap," she said. "Two rapid bursts. Like gunfire. Very much to the point. Mr. Cutch, for all that he's half again your size, taps with his fingertips. Dr. Stuart knocks with the back of his hand. It makes a different sound somehow, and it's usually done in sets of three." Claire's brows rose a notch. "Shall I tell you more or is that satisfactory? Mr. Cutch and Dr. Stuart are my most frequent visitors, but I can sometimes recognize others."

"I've heard enough, thank you. May I sit down?"

"Of course." Claire's position in her chair changed slightly as she followed Rand's progress across the cabin. He could have perched on the trunk at the head of her bed, but when she heard the mattress ropes give, she knew he had chosen the bed itself. She tried not to think of that.

"Dr. Stuart said you were not feeling well this evening. You declined to join us for dinner."

"It was a headache." She found the ropes and held them up. "These, I think."

"You've been tenacious."

She dropped them again and returned to resting her chin on her hands. "I have."

"At avoiding me, I was thinking."

Surprise made Claire's mouth open a fraction. No sound came out.

"You probably thought I was referring to something else."

"You know I was."

"But I'm not mistaken, am I? You have made a point of staying away from me."

"You *are* mistaken. I've left you to the running of this ship and found ways to occupy myself. You didn't want me on board in the first place, Captain. I've never forgotten that and I've tried to be accommodating. I should think you'd be grateful for not having me underfoot."

"It's Rand, Claire, and underfoot is not exactly where I want you."

Chapter Seven

Claire straightened slowly. Her hands folded on the edge of the desk and her chin lifted a mere fraction. Rand's announcement brought no rush of color to her cheeks. The effect was quite the opposite. Claire felt unnaturally cold. "You would not want me under your thumb," she said. "It would be like pressing on the wrong end of a tack."

Rand didn't doubt it. But again, it wasn't what he had in mind. "Are you being clever?" he asked. "Or purposely naive?"

"I was giving you an opportunity to change the course of this conversation, perhaps even the direction of your thinking. It occurs to me, rather belatedly I admit, that you believe I should be flattered by your remark. The truth is, I hardly welcome the idea of being under you." She smiled without humor. "There. I said what you would only allude to. You can dismiss it from your mind that I'm naive. I suppose that leaves clever."

Rand stared at her, silent. From temple to chin, the thin line of his scar stood out whitely. A muscle worked rhythmically in his jaw.

"Captain?" His silence unnerved Claire. Her head cocked to one side, she strained to simply hear the sound of his breathing. "Rand? What are you doing?"

He still did not answer immediately. He waited until the first full rush of hurt had passed. "Licking my wounds."

"Oh." She slumped a bit in her chair.

The mattress ropes creaked as Rand stood.

"Where are you going?" asked Claire.

"Out."

Claire followed his progress to the door. It was when she heard Rand twist the handle that she came to her feet. She put out one hand. "Wait." She could almost feel his hesitation. "Please," she said quietly. "Please wait."

Rand released the door and turned to Claire. His eyes fell on the hand she had extended as it was slowly brought back to her side. "I'm still here, Claire."

She nodded. Her heart was in her throat and her voice never rose above a ragged whisper. "Can you comprehend how humiliating it is for me to have held your penis in my hands and never once been invited to touch your face?" Tears washed her eyes. They lay thickly on her lower lashes until she knuckled them away impatiently. Claire sucked in a steadying breath but it didn't help. It shuddered through her like a half-sob and she realized that she was in danger of crying in earnest. She quickly turned away from Rand. Her arms were crossed and raised in front of her, part for protection, part for comfort.

"Claire."

His voice came from just behind her and Claire realized she had been deaf to the sound of him crossing the cabin. She took a step forward, away from him, and was brought up short by the edge of the desk.

"Claire, please."

She could feel the heat of his hands as they hovered near her shoulders. Claire's head bowed, exposing the nape of her neck. She was not trying to avoid him now; it was a gesture of surrender.

Rand's palms fell on the curve of her shoulders. He bent his head so his mouth was near her ear. "God, Claire," he whispered. "I'm so sorry. I didn't . . . I never meant . . ." He didn't finish his thought. Instead he turned her so that she was facing him. His hands slid from her shoulders to her elbows and finally to her wrists. She offered only the slightest resistance as he unfolded her arms. He raised her hands to his face. "Look at me, Claire."

She hesitated a moment, telegraphing all her uncertainties.

"I have no expectations," Rand said quietly. "This will not end in your bed or mine." He felt Claire's knuckles brush his cheeks as her fingers unfolded. Rand released her wrists and let his arms fall to his sides. "Go on," he encouraged her. "I want you to see me."

His skin was warm under her fingertips and stretched taut across his cheekbones. Claire pressed her palm to his forehead and made out the gentle ridge of his brow. She felt the slight indentation of his temples. His lashes fluttered against her fingers as she passed over his eyes. She had never forgotten that Mrs. Webster told her they were brown, but she wondered about the exact shade. Were they more like teak or hickory bark? Dark as coffee or light as sand?

Claire traced the line of his nose once, then again to judge the faint arch that gave it its aggressive character. She felt the flare of his nostrils as he anticipated her touch. Her fingertip fit perfectly in the groove between his nose and upper lip; then it tripped past his lips and rested briefly on his chin.

Rand captured her wrist again and brought her hand back to his mouth. "Here, too," he said.

Claire felt the soft rush of his breath on her fingers. When he released her, her hand stayed in place and she explored the shape and texture of his lips. His mouth parted slightly and there was heat and dampness on the tip of her finger. Her own breath caught and she withdrew, this time cupping the underside of his jaw. Lowering her hands, she could feel the pulse beating strongly in his throat. She paused, then raised her fingers to just behind his ears. Her thumbs grazed his cheeks.

Rand held his breath as her thumb passed over his scar. He made himself stand without moving while her nail traced the length of it from just beneath his hairline to his jaw.

"Your beautiful face," she said softly. There was compassion in her voice but not pity. "How did it happen?"

"A Yankee saber."

"You might have been killed."

A glimmer of a smile lifted Rand's mouth. "I believe that was the Yankee's plan."

"How did you escape with only this?"

"A lead ball cut him down before he finished pressing his swing. I passed out under him. Instead of being left for dead, I ended up in a Yankee field hospital. After that, prison."

"Oh, Rand." Claire's hands fell to his shoulders, then slid lower and rested against his chest. "I didn't know. Were you there long?"

"Until the end of the war. About eighteen months."

Claire could only nod, trying to take it in. Rand's experience was outside her imagination. "I knew about the scar," she said. "Mrs. Webster told me."

"I thought perhaps you were expecting it," Rand said. "When you weren't repulsed . . ." He shrugged. "I guess you had prepared for it."

Claire frowned. "I didn't have to prepare myself, not the way you think. Frankly, I was curious." Her voice dropped to a whisper and she went on in the manner of a confession. "Intrigued, actually."

Rand stared at her, fascinated himself by the faint wash of pink that colored her cheeks. Her head was turned slightly to one side, and if she could have seen, she would have been staring at some point past his shoulder, her posture vaguely shy and uncertain. "What exactly did Mrs. Webster tell you about me?" he asked.

"She said the scar merely kept her from pronouncing you beautiful."

Rand ran a hand through his coppery hair. His weight shifted from side to side.

"I've embarrassed you," said Claire. She was smiling softly now, taken by the notion that Mrs. Webster's observation had made him uncomfortable. "Would it help if I told you that I've always imagined you as a great stone tiki?"

Rand thought about all the carvings he had seen in the South Pacific. None of the images flattered the human face and form. The features were usually cut broadly, somewhat aggressively, and the spirits that lived in them were not always friendly. "I think I prefer Mrs. Webster's description," he said dryly.

"I thought you might." Claire removed her hands from his chest. She expected Rand to take a step back and place some distance between them. He didn't move.

Rand studied Claire's fine features. The hint of a smile still hovered about her mouth. "Tell me something," he said. "Was Mrs. Webster's description offered spontaneously, or was it perhaps prompted by someone's interest?"

Claire's smile vanished. "I don't think I remember," she answered coolly.

"What a terrible liar you are."

"Stickle says the same thing."

"And I thought there was so little the duke and I could agree on." He chuckled as her mouth pursed. "You asked her what I looked like, didn't you?"

"It signifies nothing. I ask the same about many things."

"What color is my hair?"

"I'm sure I don't recall."

"You never forget anything."

"Oh, very well. She said it was like a dark sunset. Brown and copper and burnt orange."

Both of Rand's brows lifted. He grinned. "I always think of it as a tarnished penny."

"So did she until it occurred to her I might think it was green."

"Then I'm grateful she elaborated. And my eyes?"

"Brown."

"That's all? Just brown?"

"Not so dark as mine, I think she said."

"Bittersweet chocolate," he told her. "Yours are that dark and fine. Mine are the color of chestnuts. At least that's what my mother has always likened them to."

"Chestnuts. That would make them a close match to your hair."

"Some people say an exact match."

"Women," Claire said. "Only women would say that."

Rand pretended to think about it. "You could be right."

Claire fell silent, her features drawn and remotely troubled. She did not shy away when she felt his fingers under her chin. Neither did his gentle encouragement alter her distant and thoughtful expression. "I haven't forgotten what I look like," she said. "My mother was beautiful. I know I'm not. I never particularly minded before, and I find myself wishing I didn't now. But I do mind, Rand. I'm realizing that I'm minding it terribly. I don't have the experience to accept your attentions casually. I'm afraid I'll make too much of it, expect more than you're offering. I won't know how to go away gracefully. I've never had any practice."

Rand's fingers brushed her cheek. He tucked a stray lock of Claire's dark hair behind her ear. "What about the woman who told me she'd been kissed before? The one who's quite literally been around the world?"

"It wasn't strictly a lie," she said.

"A bit of an overstatement, then."

"Yes."

"So what do I do, Claire?" Rand asked. "Stand by and watch while you cut your teeth on Macauley Stuart and Cutch and half of the crew? Do I have to see you learn to walk away from everyone else before you'll walk *to* me?" He shook his head. "I hope that's not your proposal. I couldn't do it. Seeing you with them now is very nearly painful."

"But nothing's happened," she said. "Nothing."

"I know. I said *very nearly* painful."

Claire did not hear any humor in his tone. She reached up and touched his mouth. There was no smile edging the corners upward. He was perfectly serious. Claire's hand fell away. She held on to the desk on either side of her to keep her fingers steady and her arms from slipping around his neck. "I think you should leave."

He stared at her face. For all that her voice was a husky whisper, the set of her mouth was resolute. "Very well."

It was only when the door was closed quietly behind him that Claire released the breath she hadn't known she was holding.

* * *

"They're called right whales," Cutch said. He stood just behind Claire at the side rail, protecting her from pitching about on the slippery deck. *Cerberus* rolled under them, and it was Cutch's sure footing that kept them both upright. They were well south of the equator now, away from the warm trade winds. Here the beginning of July meant the dead of winter. The sun shone brightly, but it was a cold light. Still ahead of them were the treacherous waters around Cape Horn at the tip of South America, where gales would strain every inch of sodden canvas, and masts could topple before the winds.

Water dampened the hem of Claire's hunter-green gown. Even weighted down, it whipped against her legs and the side of the ship. Layers of petticoats were turned upward by the wind. She turned her head to make herself heard above the crashing waves and creaking masts. "Why right whales, Mr. Cutch? Why do they call them that?"

"A whaler once told me it's because they're right for hunting. They're the only ones that float after they're killed."

"How many in the pod?"

"I make six. The largest is fifty-five feet from spout to tail."

Claire had seen whales before and the sight of them clustered together had never failed to thrill her. She leaned forward, bracing herself at the rail, straining to see through the veil of her blindness. "Are there calves, Mr. Cutch?"

"Two. Snortin' and blowin' just like their mamas. One of them's diving!" Cutch described the scene to Claire: the whale's beautiful arc in the water as the powerful tail drove the animal out, then down; the spray that surrounded her and captured a fleeting rainbow in the sunlight; and the mournful cry of her sibling, who immediately followed in her wake. "They're chasing each other. Mama's going to take them both in hand."

From his place near the wheel, Rand watched Claire lift her face into the salt spray. The waves were cresting sharply, and the clipper was pushing twelve knots. The sea would sting like nettles, yet he noticed that Claire did not turn away and seek shelter in the crook of Cutch's shoulder. The hood of her cape had fallen backward and her hair was no longer confined by its anchoring pins. Every lock distinguished the current of air that caressed it.

She was wrong, he thought. She was beautiful. Not in any standard way; not in any way that he found easy to define but nonetheless knew to be true. He couldn't imagine that a man looking at her now would not be moved to want her.

Rand turned to Diggs at the wheel. "See *Cerberus* rides the waves, Mr. Diggs. Don't wrestle her under like she was a plow and you had the lower forty to clear."

"Aye, Cap'n," Diggs said. But he didn't think he was heard. His captain was already walking away.

Out of the corner of his eye, Cutch saw Rand approaching. Claire did not have the same advantage. When Rand spoke, Cutch had to steady her.

"She needs to be below," Rand said. His glance speared Cutch's large hands at Claire's waist. "Before she goes over."

Claire leaned away from the rail. "Mr. Cutch was telling me about whales."

"That's fine," he said shortly. "And now it's ended."

Cutch nodded. He watched Claire struggle for composure in the face of Rand's coldness. "Very well, Captain. Claire. This way."

It was not until she and Cutch reached her cabin that Claire spoke. "He's come to hate me," she said quietly.

"No."

"He doesn't speak to me except to ensure that I'm removed from his sight."

"What would you have him do?" asked Cutch, watching her closely. Her hurt was almost palpable. "Follow you around like a lovestruck stripling? He has pride, Claire. And sense. He's keeping you at arm's length for a reason. You should thank him, not tempt him."

Claire's head jerked up. "Tempt him? But I—" *Seeing you with them is very nearly painful.* Rand's words came back to her. Had she been asking him to prove he'd meant what he said? Not consciously, she hadn't. Not deliberately. She was not so cruel, Claire thought. She was *not*.

Cutch said nothing as Claire let herself into her cabin and shut the door. She seemed unaware that she had left him standing alone in the companionway, or even that she had left the remainder of her last thought unsaid. Whistling softly to himself, Cutch returned topside.

Claire sat on the edge of her bed and unfastened the frog closure of her cape. She let it fall back on the quilt. Bending, she began to untie the laces of one shoe. The lace was nearly as cold and stiff as her fingers. She swore softly when it confounded her efforts.

The faint sound of breathing that was not her own caused Claire's head to lift suddenly. She cocked her ear, listening hard. Outside her cabin waves beat steadily against the ship. She forced herself to block out that roar and wait for a different pitch. "Is someone here?" she asked. "Cutch?"

But it wouldn't be Cutch. He would never have followed her inside without making his presence known. The sound was not repeated. Had she imagined it or had she surprised an intruder into holding his breath?

Claire stood slowly. She always left her cane on the right side of the door so she could pick it up on her way out. Six paces from the bed to the door. Claire was only a step away when she heard the sound again. Groping for her cane, she found it and swung around. She poked the air, jabbing right and left, high and low. The cane banged the trunk and rattled the desk chair. Books thudded to the floor; papers scattered. Her frantic, sweeping search brought her up against the bed and she hit the armoire with enough force that the cane vibrated in her hands. Claire thrust her cane deep inside the wardrobe while she yanked her carefully arranged dresses out. Nothing she swung at swung back. Nothing groaned.

Claire stumbled on the discarded pile of clothes as she turned away. Her cane slipped out from under her and Claire went to her knees. She patted the floor with her palms, searching for the cane. She found it partially hidden under the bed and realized that was one place her search hadn't taken her. Instead of retrieving her cane, she shoved it deeper and made a strong arc that covered the length of the bed. Nothing obstructed the movement.

Claire stopped. Her heart pounded and her own breathing was loud in the quiet room. She laughed a little uneasily as she sat up, wondering at the damage she had inflicted on the room. There were clothes and bed linens under her, and she remembered toppling books from the desk. She would not be able to put it right again without assistance. Claire stood, vaguely surprised her legs held her so surely when she was still shaking inside. If she had been sighted, she asked herself, would she have been so frightened? Would her mind have even played this trick on her? Angrily, Claire shoved the scattered clothes out of her way and left the cabin in search of Macauley Stuart.

She rapped her cane loudly on the doctor's door. When there was no response, she called for him. Hoping to rouse him if he was napping, Claire pushed his door open and said his name again. There was still no answer. Claire considered the possibility that he could be attending to one of the crew somewhere else on the ship. The doctor also liked to frequent the galley. Occasionally he had been invited to use Rand's workroom for his own study, though Claire had not known him to take advantage of it often. The most likely place Macauley Stuart had gone was topside. Ever since *Cerberus* had been riding the choppy, colder waters of the South Atlantic, the doctor's difficulties with his sea legs had returned.

Claire did not stop in her own cabin to retrieve her cape. She had no plan to be on deck above the minute or so it took to find Macauley. As it happened, she was topside even less than that.

The only warning that she was about to be taken in hand was Rand's sharp order, "Seize her, Mr. Cutch! Now!" Claire was not given the option to retreat into the companionway on her own. Cutch's large hand circled Claire's arm and pressed hard enough to leave bruises. Her fingers opened on the knob of her cane and she dropped it as she was thrust down the stairs she had just come up. Her skirts tangled in her legs and she stumbled backward, saved from a hard fall only by Cutch's grip on her.

Claire's cry went unheard above the resounding crash on deck. The entire ship seemed to shudder in the aftermath. Pressed against the companionway wall as she was, Claire felt the vibration run through her. She was finally glad for Cutch's hand on her arm. It felt less restraining now than it did steadying.

There were shouts topside and more scrambling as Rand's orders were carried out. *Cerberus* rolled suddenly, and Claire felt a sickening sensation as the floor seemed to fall away from beneath her. "Mr. Cutch?" His hand was still tight around her, but Claire had a need to know his presence in some other way.

"I'm here," he said deeply. He could see out the companionway that the opening was partially blocked by the splintered mast and sodden canvas. Water dripped on the stairs as steadily as if it were raining. He eased his grip on Claire's arm but did not release her. "It was the main topgallant mast," he explained. "The wet sail and wind proved too strong for her. She's lying across the companionway hatch now."

Claire nodded slowly, finally understanding the urgency of Rand's order and Cutch's response. "You saved my life," she whispered.

"No. Captain did. I only grabbed you. He's the one who saw you needed grabbing."

Before Claire could respond, there was more shouting overhead and a call for the doctor. Cutch yelled back that he would fetch Stuart.

"He's not in his cabin," Claire said. "I was going to look for him on deck. He was the only reason I went there."

"I don't remember seeing him topside."

"Rand's workroom, then," Claire suggested.

Cutch let go of Claire's arm so she could place her hand on his elbow. "Where's your cane?" he asked.

"I don't know. I had it."

Cutch looked around and didn't see it. "I'll find it later. Come on. I'll return you to your cabin and get the doctor."

Claire lost her footing again as the ship lurched forward.

She squeezed Cutch's elbow. "Are we going to sink, Mr. Cutch?"

"No. We're not even going to slow down much. These repairs can be made at sea." When they reached Claire's cabin, it was Cutch who opened the door. He hesitated on the threshold, his eyes narrowing as he took in the ransacked condition of her cabin.

Claire responded to the sudden stillness of her companion. "It's all right, Mr. Cutch. I know how it looks. I'll explain later, after the important things are taken care of. You should find Dr. Stuart now."

Cutch was not as certain as Claire that the disorder of her cabin was unimportant. He helped her negotiate her way to the bed. "I won't be long," he assured her. "You'll be safest if you just lie here."

Claire didn't argue. It seemed to her that she had lost her bearings back in the companionway and had yet to regain them. She lay back and closed her eyes. It wasn't until Cutch was out of the room that the first of Claire's tears pressed her lids.

She was sleeping when he entered her cabin. It was late and the room was dark, but her breathing gave her away. Cutch had warned him about the disarray. He stepped over the scattered clothes and books. The toe of his boot caught one corner of a blanket that had partially slipped off the bed. He started to drag it with him, shaking it off just before it uncovered Claire's legs.

He removed a lantern attached to the wall near the desk and lighted it. He held it up, surveying the damage with a keener eye before he replaced it on the wall. Tipping the desk chair on one back leg, he spun it around and straddled it. He sat down, folding his arms across the top rail, and waited.

Claire lay very still, caught in the groggy, undefined state that exists between sleep and full waking. She knew something was different—not necessarily wrong, only different. She told herself that she would not be so quick to panic this time, that she would not allow her mind to play her the same trick as before.

Strain as she did, she could not hear any breathing save her own. What she felt was a presence. She remembered that she no longer had her cane. As little help as it had been the last time, she recognized her vulnerability without it.

"I'm here, Claire," Rand said.

There was no conscious brake that Claire could apply to her startled response. At the first sound of his voice, she stiffened. The rush of adrenaline set her heart to flight-or-fight speed, and she leaped out of bed. At her sides her hands were clenched in bloodless fists.

Rand's stomach lurched sickeningly as he realized how badly he had frightened her. He should have left as soon as he became aware that she was sleeping, not waited her out, remaining for his own selfish pleasure. "Claire, it's Rand." Afraid to approach her, he did not rise from his chair. "I'm at your desk."

She backed away, raising one hand to ward him off.

"I'm sitting," he told her. "I'm not coming after you."

Claire hesitated, testing the truth of his words. Wary, she cocked her head to one side and listened.

"I'm not moving, Claire," he said to give her the direction and distance she needed. "I won't go anywhere until you tell me I can."

Claire shifted her extended hand and pointed toward the door. "Then leave now."

Rand shook his head. "I came here to talk. It wasn't my intention to frighten you and I apologize for it, but I'm not leaving just yet."

Without warning, Claire dropped to her knees. She groped around her for a misplaced book. Finding one, she pitched it hard in Rand's direction and knew a measure of satisfaction when he grunted as it thudded against his chest. She swept her hands across the floor looking for another missile. What she came up against was Rand's foot. He had moved after all.

Rand hunkered down and captured Claire's wrists. "You didn't think I would sit there and take that, did you?"

Claire tried to jerk away but he held her fast. Anger gave her strength she had never used and didn't know how to control. This time when she yanked, she fell backwards. Her momentum was not enough to free her, but it did pitch Rand forward and bring him down on top of her. Claire squirmed, pushing at him in earnest, arching her slender frame with enough ferocity to lift him momentarily. He swore softly when her knee jammed his thigh but he was still careful not to hurt her. With little additional effort he was able to force her back and press her wrists to the floor.

Claire sucked in her breath and tried to slither out from under him. One of his legs trapped both of hers. She pushed upward again. This time Rand wouldn't be budged. "Let me up," she said, her voice strained.

"In a moment."

She turned her face away from his. "Now . . . please."

Rand was not proof against the tears that Claire tried not to let him see. He watched her blink them back. Her teeth had caught her lower lip, and now she was biting down on it, accepting pain in place of what she thought was weakness. Rand eased his hold, then rolled off her. He lay on his back, some of the earlier wreckage under him. His fingers curled in a soft cotton petticoat. His head rested on a dark wool day dress. He watched Claire sit up and draw her knees toward her chest. Her arms circled them. She bent her head. She looked very alone, hugging herself in that manner, offering herself this small measure of comfort. Rand had no illusions that she would accept his.

"What happened?" he asked, looking at the clothes, books, and papers strewn across the cabin. From his new vantage point on the floor the scene appeared even more cluttered.

"You frightened me."

"No, before that. What happened before I got here?"

"You mean the mess." She raised her head. "I did that."

"I guessed as much. I thought you only threw things at me."

A glimmer of a smile touched Claire's mouth. "As far as I know that's still true." Her earlier fear seemed so misplaced that she was reluctant to explain what she had done. If she had thought for one moment that Rand would let it rest, she would have avoided the explanation. Instead she told him what he wanted to know.

Rand listened without interruption. The small vertical crease that appeared between his brow was the only evidence of his mounting concern. He was silent for a long time after Claire finished. Without once accusing him, she had made him understand why she had been so extraordinarily frightened to discover him in her cabin.

"Do you think someone was really here?" he asked finally. "Or did you imagine the sounds?"

"I didn't imagine the sounds," Claire said. "I may have put the wrong cause to them, but I don't believe I imagined them."

"Could someone have slipped out while you were in the middle of your search?"

"I thought of that later." And she didn't like thinking it might have happened that way. "I made a lot of noise crashing about. I could have missed the door opening and closing."

"Why didn't you leave?"

"I suppose because I didn't want to appear foolish, running away from nothing."

Foolish was not a word he had ever associated with Claire. "I'll speak to Cutch about it," he said. There would be a duty roster that would explain the whereabouts of most of the crew. It would not be difficult to maintain a more thorough watch. "Someone will rig a lock for your door."

"Will it keep you out?" she asked wryly.

"Probably not."

"Then don't go to the bother."

Rand let the comment pass. He pushed himself upright. Scooting backward, he leaned against the bed frame. Claire, he noticed, stayed exactly as she was.

"Who was injured when the mast fell?"

"Matt Barcus."

"Badly?"

"A dislocated shoulder and a broken leg. Stuart couldn't mistake them for what they were this time."

Claire didn't point out that the doctor had not been completely wrong about Elizabeth's leg. Rand didn't want to hear it. "Then Mr. Cutch found Macauley," she said, relieved. "I had been looking for him myself. Was he on deck after all?"

"In his cabin, I think."

"No, that's not possible." She waved her hand, dismissing the contradiction from her mind. "It's not important." Claire rocked back slightly, hugging herself a little tighter. "Thank you for what you did today," she said.

"What I did?" Rand was genuinely puzzled.

"Saving me from the falling mast."

"Cutch's reflexes did that."

"I thanked Mr. Cutch. Now I'm thanking you."

"Then you're welcome," he said quietly.

A rare comfortable silence settled between them. Claire turned her head again, resting her other cheek on her knees. "Is it late?" she asked after a while.

The watch had changed while he was waiting for Claire to wake. "After eight."

She had slept far longer than she would have thought possible. "I missed dinner."

"Most of us did. Are you hungry?"

"Not really." Her stomach protested the outrageous lie.

Rand chuckled. He leaned forward. "Will you accompany me to my cabin? I have fruit and cheese there."

It was on the tip of her tongue to refuse. The answer that came out, though, was yes.

Rand's quarters were only marginally larger than Claire's. He did have a padded bench along the stern wall and a table big enough to seat eight. Claire had never been invited to explore the cabin and the little familiarity she had with it was because of the dinners she often had there.

Claire waited by the door while Rand lighted two lamps. She smiled to herself, thinking she could have found her way to the table or the bench without his assistance and without any light.

"Where's your cane?" he asked.

"I lost it when the mast fell. Mr. Cutch said he would find it and bring it to me. I don't suppose he's had much time to look for it.'' Claire sat on the bench and smoothed her gown over her lap. While Rand cut thin slices of gouda and apples, Claire fiddled with the collar and cuffs of her dress, straightening them both. At her feet the hem was finally dry, but she knew it was stained with saltwater from her earlier foray on deck. Her shoes would be similarly watermarked. Self-conscious of her wrinkled gown and tangled hair, Claire ran a hand over both.

Rand's fingers closed over Claire's wrist, stopping her. He lifted her hand and placed the stem of a wineglass in it. ''Burgundy,'' he said.

''Thank you.''

He hesitated. ''You look fine, Claire.''

Embarrassed, she ducked her head. ''I slept in these clothes. My hair is—''

''Tousled.'' Just the way he imagined it would be if she woke up beside him. ''Don't touch it again.''

''I don't think even a captain can properly order that,'' she said.

''Humor me.'' He nudged the bottom of her wineglass upward with his fingertips. ''Drink.''

She did. The burgundy was cool and dry. It eased down her throat and erased the metallic taste that had been on her tongue since her first confrontation with fear that afternoon. She murmured her pleasure against the rim of the glass. The vibration tickled her lips. Claire smiled and lowered her glass. Her mouth was damp.

''Here,'' Rand said, his voice husky. ''Open.''

Claire's lips parted. A bit of cheese was pressed between them. She chewed on it, washed it down with a sip of wine.

''Again,'' Rand said. This time he gave her a small wedge of apple. His fingers touched her lips. Claire did not flinch. ''More?'' he asked.

''Yes, please.''

Rand smiled. She had spoken so softly that it could not properly be called a whisper. He had read her lips more than heard her. ''Cheese,'' he said, alternating the bites.

Claire took it, then another bite of apple. She drank deeply from her wineglass. She pressed her lips together and ran her tongue along the inside, tasting the burgundy again.

Watching her, Rand's eyes darkened. "Open," he repeated.

This time it was his lips he placed across her mouth. The taste of the wine was on her tongue. He drank from her mouth. She never once pulled away.

Rand pushed the plate of cheese and fruit out of the way. Without raising his mouth from hers, he removed the empty wineglass from her hand and put it aside. He lifted her hands to his face and pressed her palms against his cheeks. He raised his head a fraction and spoke against her mouth. "Look at me, Claire. You don't have to be afraid."

She had never been afraid of what he might do to her, only what she might do to herself. This tightening in her chest, the unfamiliar sensation of never being quite able to catch her breath around him, of always being off balance—Claire wondered if it was already too late for her. A more experienced woman would have known if she were in love. "I'm not afraid," was all she said.

"Liar." On his lips, then against hers, it was an endearment. Claire's fingertips traced the line of his cheekbones; her thumbs brushed the corners of his mouth. His skin was taut. There was no smile. A muscle worked faintly in his scarred cheek. She laid her palm there and leaned into him. This time she initiated the kiss.

Her tongue swept the underside of his upper lip and darted along the ridge of his teeth. She opened her mouth wide to accept the sound that rose at the back of his throat. When he pressed for more, she pressed back.

It was a slow, deep kiss, lingering and exploring. There was pleasure intrinsic to the waiting, to keeping urgency at bay. Rand's fingers sifted through her dark hair, touched the sensitive nape of her neck. He lifted her hair away, drank in the fragrance that was unique to her as it spilled over his hand. Claire hummed her pleasure against his mouth. When he broke the kiss, it was to place his lips at her throat.

Her hands drifted to Rand's shoulders and lay there lightly while he made small forays across her skin. She tugged on the

collar of his jacket, hanging on as much as wanting him closer.
More by accident than design, her fingers brushed the first
button of his shirt. She twisted it. The material parted under
her hands.

Claire paused, uncertain. For a moment Rand did not move.
Then he said her name, his voice a mere whisper, and the
words, ''Go on.''

She touched his skin so carefully that except for the warmth,
it might have been crystal under her fingertips. Her thumb
found the next button, and she opened it in turn. Hands splaying
wider, Claire helped Rand shrug out of his jacket. Her palms
ran along the length of his arms. She heard the jacket slide off
the bed and land on the floor. Her attention returned to his
shirt, and this time there was a hint of a siren's smile on her
lips.

His eyes on that smile, Rand turned so he was under her.
Claire pushed at his shoulders and sat up. She found his wrists
and drew his hands to his sides. She didn't tell him not to
move, but his stillness, except for the movements he couldn't
help, was exactly what she wanted. Claire pulled the tails of
his shirt free of his trousers. She finished unbuttoning it and
spread the material open. Her palms crossed his chest from the
flat of his abdomen to the base of his throat. Her fingers traced
his collarbones and learned again the breadth of his shoulders.
She felt the defining tautness of the muscles of his arms and
the ridged plane of his chest. Beneath her hand, Claire felt the
steady beat of his heart.

After a moment, her hand moved lower.

Claire felt along the waistband of his trousers. She felt him
suck in his breath when her fingers dipped under the material.
Leaning forward, her hair a dark curtain on either side of her
face, Claire kissed Rand at the base of his throat. His pulse
was unsteadier now, his breathing a little ragged. Through the
material stretched tautly across his groin, Claire's knuckles
brushed the rigid length of him.

At his sides Rand's fingers curled into fists. He watched
through heavy-lidded eyes as Claire levered herself upward
again, and this time moved farther down the bed.

She tugged on his boots, first the left, then the right. He started to help her, but she felt him rising and waved him to lie back again. There was a certain unexpected pleasure, she thought, in this role of handmaiden, undressing him while she remained fully clothed, moving over him while he did not move at all. One boot thumped to the floor. Then the other.

Claire removed Rand's thick socks before she stretched over him. For a moment, as her body unfolded sinuously across his, the cleft of Claire's breasts held the rigid outline of his penis. Only his soft groan gave her pause. She raised her head as if to search his face, but it was her fingers that did this work. Claire touched his forehead, the plane of his scarred cheek. She brushed his eyelashes and knew that he was watching her and that his eyes would be intense. Her thumb passed across his lips. There was no smile there, but a tension instead. Beneath her fingers she felt the cost of his self-denial in the shape of his mouth and the tightness of his skin.

She replaced her fingers with her own lips. He let her press the kiss, control its desire and its depth. Between them her hands fumbled with the buttons of his trousers. The only assistance he offered was to lift his hips. Claire broke the kiss long enough to remove his trousers and drawers. When she returned her attention to his mouth, she was his covering.

She liked that he let her do as she wanted, that the exploration was at her instigation and leisure, but in time it wasn't enough. Her breasts were tender, and between her thighs, where she was warm and damp, there was also a hollow ache. It was as if in learning the planes and angles of Rand's body, she became more intimately aware of her own.

Claire's mouth lifted. Her breathing was uneven and in her chest her heart hammered. "Please," she said.

The single word was enough. He knew.

Rand grasped Claire at the waist as though to steady both of them. His hands slid to her bottom and he cupped her in his palms, urging her to bear down on him. Her petticoats and gown did not seem so substantial a barrier now. He began to unfasten the tiny buttons at the back of her gown. It required

Jo Goodman

only six to be released before Rand was able to spread the neckline over her shoulders.

The thin lawn straps of Claire's chemise were eased lower. He searched for the strings to her corset and discovered she wasn't wearing one. Rand found he still had the capacity to smile, although this one was brief and vaguely wicked. He caught her by the back of the neck, his fingers threading deeply into her thick hair, and kissed her hard.

His tongue swept her mouth and this time sweet battle was engaged. He turned, bringing Claire under him now, and pressed his advantage. He kissed the corner of her mouth, her jaw, and closed her eyes with the touch of his lips. His hands slid under her bodice and lifted her breasts. First it was the rough edge of his fingers that flicked over her nipples, then it was the rough edge of his tongue.

Claire's neck arched. Her response surrendered the slim stem of her throat to him. Rand kissed her there, sipping on her skin, taking in her heady fragrance as if he could absorb her through his mouth and fingertips. She made a small sound that was part submission, part encouragement, as his mouth closed over her breast again. Her hands cradled his head, her fingers tightening when she felt the first hot suck of his mouth.

Rand raised Claire's gown and petticoats to her knees. She squirmed under him as he pulled on her drawers. They joined all of his clothes on the floor beside the bed.

Rand sat up long enough to remove Claire's shoes. His fingers traced a path from the arch of her foot, over her calf, to just above her knee, where her smooth stocking gave way to even silkier flesh. He bent his head and kissed her inner thigh. The scent of her was musky and her skin was warm. He left her skirt and petticoats bunched around her thighs, and lay across her again, this time levering his weight with his elbows. Her hips moved under him as if she resented the restraint of her clothes.

Slipping his hands under her back, Rand tugged at another button, then another, and Claire was finally able to pull her arms free of her gown. They closed around the small of his back. Her index fingers pressed the dimples at the base of his

spine. She heard him groan when, as if against his will, he
ground his hips against the cleft of her thighs. She palmed his
buttocks.

"It's all right," she whispered. "I'm not afraid."

Rand couldn't say the same. She seemed so small under him,
every line of her body as supple and slim as a willow whip,
but somehow more fragile. "I'm going to hurt you," he said
thickly.

"I know." But she did not think they were talking about
quite the same thing. She raised her knees on either side of his
hips. One of her hands drifted away from his buttocks and
slipped between their bodies. She was prepared for the length
and thickness of him this time. She was prepared for the catch
in his breath as her fingers curled around him. What Claire was
not prepared for was the pressure she felt at his entry.

She tensed, breathing shallowly. Her hands returned to his
shoulders, and this time her fingers dug deeply into his flesh.
She sensed that he was holding himself back, waiting for her.
She nodded slowly and he pushed again, this time deeply and
swiftly, covering her mouth with his own so that he absorbed
her cry of pain.

Claire's fingers eased their grip. Rand's kiss was sweet now,
languorous, as if they shared nothing but time. She felt herself
stretching inside and out to accommodate him. He did not urge
her to this end but let her arrive at it on her own. Except for
the movement of his mouth over hers, he was still.

Claire's hands slid to his neck. Her thumbs brushed the
underside of Rand's jaw. She pushed gently, raising his head
and ending the kiss. "No matter what you think," she said
thickly, "I won't break." It was Claire's body that surged
upward. Beneath her fingertips she felt the cords of Rand's
neck tighten first, then the entire length of his body.

He moved in her, over her. His first withdrawal took her
breath away, and his thrust gave it back. She was not so different
than the sails overhead, she thought, unfurling in a following
wind. Rand filled her, pressed her, and the response of her body,
arching and sighing, defined his presence, his very existence.

It was as if she were standing on deck again with Rand

behind her, holding her while she held the clipper's wheel. There had been exhilaration then, an unfettered joy that was not so different from what she felt now. What had changed was how it came over her, not in a rush, but slowly, in increments, so that she seized each bit of pleasure and guarded it selfishly, giving it up only when it was replaced by a fuller, richer version of itself.

In this way she opened to Rand, surrendering herself, if not to him, then to what he could make her feel. In the end the distinction blurred.

Claire's fingers curled in the coverlet under her. Her breasts were faintly swollen, the aureoles flushed darker than rose, the nipples engorged and erect. They scraped against Rand's chest as he moved. His breath was hot against the curve of her neck. Their bodies rocked, the intimate rhythm underscored by the pitch and roll of *Cerberus*.

Claire felt the tempo of Rand's thrusts change. He seemed to struggle against it, fighting the quick and shallow movements. The words he whispered against her ear were mostly incoherent, but the tenor of them was angry. Instinctively she soothed him, running her hands along his back. She was whispering his name when his entire body stiffened and he cried out. Claire felt the tremor of his muscles as he spilled his seed into her. She held him, hardly daring to breathe as his own ragged breathing quieted.

She felt strangely tense, uncertain. "Rand?"

He levered himself away from her and turned on his side. "Shhh," he whispered. Cupping the side of her face, Rand kissed her. Then, without breaking the kiss, his fingers laid a trail from her cheek to her thighs.

Chapter Eight

Claire's legs closed at the first touch of his hand. Rand waited, his palm rubbing the length of her thigh. He raised his head a fraction and said against her mouth, "Open for me, Claire."

The words tickled her lips and tripped down her spine. Her small shudder was a prelude. When Rand's fingers slipped between her parted thighs, he touched off a fire-storm. Stroking her intimately, he forced her to give up all the tension and pleasure she had been hoarding in equal measure. Her skin was like liquid velvet under his fingers, damp and warm. When her body arched, it was as if he controlled the single nerve that could pull her taut and create a slipstream of pleasure in her rushing blood.

Now it was Claire who cried out as Rand brought her to the very brink and pushed her over. She groped for him, needing to find his solid frame as her dark world melted. At first she could not hear him clearly, deaf to everything but the roar of her own blood, but then she felt his mouth close to her ear and felt his breath against her skin. She was not afraid. She was not alone.

He said her name. "Claire. Look at me." Rand found her wrist and lifted her fingers to his face.

She explored his features with her fingertips. The tension was absent from the line of his jaw. The muscle no longer worked in his cheek. She brushed his lips and relearned the shape of his mouth when it was relaxed. A smile hovered at the corners. Her own was tentatively offered.

"You can show more pleasure than that," he said. "You did a moment ago."

Claire's capacity to blush had not changed. She felt the heat creep into her cheeks. Her hand dropped away from his face and she pushed at the gown self-consciously, covering her legs. Smiling to himself, Rand lifted the neckline of her bodice and chemise over her breasts. His hand lingered on the high curves even after they were modestly hidden from his view.

"Better?" he asked.

"Hmmm." She turned slightly, curling into him. Claire rested her hand on his hip. "You don't mind being naked?"

"As long as you don't take advantage of me."

It seemed like an invitation. Claire's fingers dipped over his thigh.

"You have no shame," he told her. Rand caught her hand as it brushed his groin. He placed it back on his hip. "No peeking."

Claire turned her face into the pillow to muffle her laughter. It took her several moments to compose herself. "You have a wicked sense of humor," she said with credible sobriety.

"Do I?"

She nodded. She thought he seemed genuinely surprised by her observation. "Not many people would dare find humor in my sightlessness. In fact, you and Mr. Cutch are the first. My condition makes so many people uncomfortable . . ." Claire shrugged. "It never seemed to bother you that way. You treat me as if I were any woman."

"Not *any* woman."

Claire's small smile edged the corners of her mouth. "You told me once you liked to chase girls."

"I remember," he said. "As you pointed out, I was six then."

"Some things don't really change."

Rand touched her cheek with the back of his hand. His knuckles brushed the line of Claire's jaw. "That did," he said quietly. "I've spent most of the last ten years on *Cerberus* or raising money for her next voyage. Those activities never lent themselves to other pursuits."

"Until now."

He frowned. "Claire, I'm not—"

"I'm a convenient sort of woman."

Rand's brows rose. "That's the *last* thing you are."

Claire lifted her hand from his hip and touched his mouth. It was narrow and flat. There was a ridge across his brow. "You're glowering," she said. She let her hand fall away. "I wasn't being serious . . . well, not entirely. I'm not so experienced with what one says . . . afterward. It's not easy to be as certain now as it was when you were kissing me."

His cupped her cheek. "There's a remedy for that, you know." His mouth was close to hers. Claire's murmur of agreement vibrated against his lips. He kissed her slowly, deeply, reacquainting himself with the taste of her. Her mouth moved under his with the same languor. It was hard to remember who had initiated this kiss and more difficult still to think why it mattered. When Rand started to withdraw, Claire's lips held him for just a moment longer. "Feeling a little more confident?" he whispered, his voice husky.

"Hmmm." Eyes closed, Claire lay on her back. She doubted it was seemly to be so satisfied, or at least to show it, yet there was nothing she could do about her smile. "Do I surprise you?" she asked at last.

"Yes," he said. "Often."

Claire nodded, thinking this over. "I surprise myself," she admitted. She opened her eyes, her smile fading at last. "When I realized that I might be blind for the rest of my life, one of my first thoughts was that I would never know this experience. It struck me as odd at the time because it had never been much on my mind before. When I considered it at all, I supposed that I would meet someone very late in my life who wouldn't care that I had spent my youth in the South Pacific staring into a microscope and gathering and cataloging plants for my father. I never thought beyond meeting that gentleman. I never thought of marriage or the marriage bed. I didn't think of lying under him. Even though I understood the biology of conception and the mechanics of passion, I never applied either to me. Yet, when I was struck by blindness, I could only think that what was taken from me was so much more than my sight.''

Rand studied her face. Bitterness was absent from her features, and her voice held only a faint ironic note. ''Was there never anyone, Claire?''

A small crease appeared between her brows as she considered Rand's question. ''No, not really.''

''What about all those kisses you told me about?''

''There were not so very many of them,'' she admitted. ''And none so very recently. The last time I returned to Solonesia with my father, he had a paid assistant, a student, who accompanied us. He was rather handsome, I suppose, in an intense sort of way. Trenton spent a lot of time with me, but it was more in an effort to learn what I knew. He wanted to make himself indispensable to Sir Griffin. Any other interest he showed in me was because he thought it would please my father.''

''Did your father encourage him?''

''I couldn't say if my father even noticed. Except for what I knew about his work, I was not so very interesting to Sir Griffin either.''

Now Rand heard something creep into her voice that wasn't there before, a kind of resignation that let him know she had accepted this as fact, even if she had no peace with it. ''What happened to Trenton?''

''He followed my father's example and took a native mistress. Several of them actually.'' Her slight smile held no humor. ''I'm not certain Sir Griffin would have approved of his profligacy, and I'm quite certain Trenton didn't know I was aware of it, but I don't think he could have helped himself in any event. The Solonesian women are as lush and beautiful as their islands, and to Englishmen who take no notice of any culture save their own, the women seem more than welcoming and gracious. They appear available. Trenton took what he thought he was being offered.''

Rand nodded. He had seen it happen time and again, on occasion with members of his own crew. There had yet to be a voyage where *Cerberus* did not leave a man or two behind. Even before the first sloe-eyed, honey-skinned young women came out to meet the ship, the South Pacific islands seduced men with cerulean waters and emerald landscapes. ''So Trenton has six wives and a herd of children now,'' he said.

''No, he never married any of his mistresses and I'm not aware of any children. He contracted a disease of the blood.''

''Syphilis?'' asked Rand, struck again by Claire's ironic tone. Rand knew the Europeans had brought syphilis to the islands along with smallpox and typhus. There was some justice, he supposed, if Trenton had gotten the disease from one of his mistresses.

''Yes,'' she said. ''Trenton was diagnosed about six months before I left the islands. My father was treating him but did not hold out much hope that it would not eventually kill him. I can't say what's happened to Trenton now. Perhaps he left Pulotu in a canoe as I did, or perhaps he stayed behind with my father. I have no expectation of seeing him again, or caring if I do.''

If she had said the last with passion in her voice, Rand would have wondered if she spoke the truth. Claire's voice, however, had no inflection. ''You still have no memory of what happened to make you leave?''

Claire shook her head. Her eyes narrowed and she drew in her lower lip, worrying it.

Watching her, Rand could see that she was agitated by this turn in the conversation. He bent his head and kissed her lightly on the forehead.

''Why did you do that?''

''I didn't know I required a reason,'' he said. He saw that she would not be put off. His fingers threaded in her hair. ''You looked as if you were in need of reassuring.''

The urge to deny it was strong. She wondered at her reaction and paused long enough to think better of it. It was true, she thought—she *had* needed something from him. Reassurance was as good a word for it as any other. "How did you know?" she asked quietly.

Rand turned his palm so Claire's dark hair spilled over it. He shrugged in answer to her question. Her hair slipped through his fingers. "You have an expressive face," he said finally.

"Do I? Even without my eyes?"

"Even with your eyes closed." He added dryly, "Claire, you've never shown much reluctance to say what was on your mind."

"I suppose you wish I were more circumspect."

"What I wish is that you were more tired."

"Oh." With a mixture of naivete and bold curiosity, she asked, "Do you want to sleep now?"

"One often does . . . afterward."

"I didn't realize."

"It's not something one learns studying—what did you call it?—oh, yes, the biology of conception and the mechanics of passion."

"Do you commit everything I say to memory?" she asked.

"Yes," he said, smiling. "I think I do."

Claire's response came to nothing as Rand's mouth covered hers. She fell asleep wondering how he always knew the right thing to do.

When Claire woke, she was alone and with no clear idea where she was. She didn't know if she had slept to daybreak or well past it. Sitting up slowly, she began orienting herself to her surroundings. Her fingers ran across the distinctive pattern of the quilt beneath her. She recognized it as her own, not the woolen blanket she had lain on in Rand's cabin. A vague memory returned to her, that of being carried in Rand's arms.

"Put your arms around my neck," he had said.

Smiling sleepily, she had complied without protest. Her head had fallen against his shoulder and she had closed her eyes, quite secure in the cradle he made for her.

Claire touched her throat. Her fingers came in contact with the warm brushed cotton of her nightdress, not the satin neckline of her gown. She remembered something else: Rand had undressed her.

"Stop wriggling," he had said. "I'll never undo all these buttons."

And he hadn't. Some of them had been scattered to the floor when she pushed impatiently at her gown. She had pulled at the ribbons securing her petticoats and let them form a puddle of fabric at her feet. He had tried to help her with the chemise, but she brushed his hands aside and managed the thing on her own.

Claire had fallen on the bed, her bed, and he had joined her, first to remove her stockings, then to lie between her open thighs.

He had said her name in question, his mouth very close to her ear. "I don't think you're even awake," he had said a moment later.

He had been right, of course; she hadn't been. Not fully. But she hadn't acted against her conscious self. There was no denying, then or now, that she had wanted him.

Claire lowered her head and rubbed her temple. There was the beginning of an ache behind her eyes. She wondered what Dr. Stuart might carry in his black bag that could ease it.

Straightening slowly, Claire came to her feet. Rand had fired up the small stove in her cabin and the floor was not unbearably cold. She found her robe in the armoire, slipped it on, and belted it. Claire padded soundlessly to the writing desk and sat down behind it. Folding her hands, she raised them, and propped her chin on the fist she made. She tried to make her mind a blank, or at least think of something else, but it was impossible.

How could she, she wondered, when her skin carried the lingering scent of his? Even a small movement of her head lifted her hair and made her think of how his fingers had sifted through it. She could still feel his hand on the flat plane of her belly and his mouth on her breast. She did not have to touch her lips to secure the sensation of his kiss.

He had asked her once, teasingly, if she had any shame.

Now Claire wondered if there wasn't some substance to the question. He did not seem to mind that she had drawn him onto her bed, that she had invited him to take her, but then, she had not been able to see his face. What her travels had taught her was that different standards were often applied. Trenton Sinclair, while welcoming the lack of inhibition of the Solonesian women, would have been repulsed by Claire's advances. He would have berated her for acting in any way like the island women he found so fascinating. If he had followed her onto the bed, he would have treated her with the contempt he reserved for whores.

Rand hadn't done that. Not at all. He had . . . *adored* her. Claire blushed, closing her eyes, wondering if she was putting too fine a point on it. But no, she thought, remembering the way his fingertips dragged lightly across the underside of her elbow, there were times when his touch had seemed almost . . . well, reverent.

Had he loved her?

Claire shook her head, forcing herself from her reverie. She would not think of the unfamiliar ache between her thighs, or the sensation of feeling him there, moving in and out, carefully at first, then more forcefully, hard enough at last so that she had dug her heels into the mattress and gripped the bed frame above her.

The picture would not be banished. "Oh, God," she moaned softly. The words echoed for a moment, until Claire finally heard herself and understood that she had spoken aloud. She had said those same words earlier, she recalled, but with a very different cadence. That she had used them just now brought a slight smile to her lips. She laughed, under her breath at first, then harder, with genuine amusement. "Oh, God."

The rap at her door sobered her. Claire had been too caught in reflection to identify her caller. "Yes?" she asked.

"Dodd, here. Cap'n sent me with fresh water for your bath."

Claire went to the door and opened it. "Fresh water?"

"Been saving it a little at a time from the rains. This morning the captain said there'd be enough and you might like it."

"Oh, yes. Please."

Paul Dodd's cherubic face reddened under the fierce pleasure he saw in Claire's. He motioned to the men behind him carrying the copper tub and cask of heated water. "This way," he told them. "Step lively."

Claire laughed as they marched past. She thanked them individually while they set up the bath and again as they were leaving.

"Sure wish the cap'n could see you," Dodd said. "He's been like a man with a sore tooth since he stepped topside. Seems like your smile would be pure clove oil to him."

Claire heard the other men laughing as they headed up the companionway, probably winking and poking one another in the ribs, but she thought it was a very pretty compliment. She touched the seaman's arm. "They're wishing they could have thought to tell me something as nice. Thank you, Mr. Dodd."

Dodd shifted his weight from one foot to the other. "I'm supposed to see about a lock for your door later," he said. "Cap'n Hamilton was specific that it should be done today."

"Give me an hour," she told him. "And perhaps you would bring my breakfast."

"Yes, Miss Bancroft." He turned on his heel and headed off, ticking off his duties under his breath. "An hour. Breakfast. Lock."

Claire poured one full quarter of the jar of lavender bath salts into her water. Kneeling beside the tub, she stirred the salts with her arm to dissolve them. The knock at her door was not a welcome reprieve this time.

"What is it, Macauley?" she asked when Dr. Stuart put his head in the door. Claire made an effort to hide her displeasure as the door was pushed open. "Yes?"

"It's time for our—" The doctor stopped, surveying the scene. "Have you just awakened?"

"A short while ago." Claire did not ask the time. If he had arrived for their lesson, then she knew it was half past ten. "I think I'll pass on our work this morning."

"Are you feeling quite all right?"

It was a reasonable question given the lateness of her rising, but Claire found she resented it. She did not want to tell him about the ache behind her eyes just now, or anything else about her physical condition. The last thing she wanted was an examination. "I'm fine. I'd like to take my bath now. Mr. Dodd brought me hot fresh water."

Macauley Stuart did not move. He rubbed his chin thoughtfully. "Dodd. He's the one who looks after you with those puppy eyes."

"Does he? I wouldn't know."

"You should exercise caution, Claire, when dealing with members of the crew. Mr. Cutch included. They can be rough men, given to loose tongues and temperament. Captain Hamilton informed me what happened last night."

Claire's hand stilled and her head jerked up. "He did?"

"Of course. My duties here include more than caring for your health. The duke expects me to offer my protection as well. I'm afraid I failed in that last evening."

Claire's throat was dry. She slowly withdrew her hand from the water and gripped the edge of the tub. It was barely enough to steady her. "I don't know what—"

Stuart interrupted. "I should have thought of a lock for your door myself. I understand you were under the impression that someone may have been inside your cabin."

Claire's world righted again. "Yes. As you said, it was an impression. It frightened me, but nothing more. I looked for you afterward."

"Hamilton mentioned that. I was surprised to hear it. I was in my cabin."

Claire's dark brows drew together slightly. "But I knocked. Pounded, actually. How could you not have heard me?"

"I don't know. I was sleeping for a while. Perhaps it was then."

She had no choice but to accept it. "Very well."

"You don't believe me," the doctor said. It wasn't a question. Something of Claire's reluctance had shown on her face. He watched her closely, a faint flush shading his freckled complexion.

"It's just that I called your name," she told him. "I was quite loud. I even put my head inside your door and inquired again. I was so certain you were not in your cabin that I went on deck to look for you.''

"But you can't look, can you, Claire?'' he pointed out. "At least not properly.''

His statement, for all that it was true, rubbed Claire the wrong way. Often she appreciated the doctor's directness, but not just now. "You're right,'' she said. "I couldn't see that you were lying abed.''

"To my lasting regret,'' he said softly, taking some of the sting from his earlier words. "I shall endeavor to make myself more available to you from now on.''

"I think I will find the captain's precaution sufficient,'' she said. "There's no need for you to trouble yourself.''

"No trouble. It's hardly a burden to be in your company.''

Claire's grip on the tub eased. She dipped her fingers below the water and tested its temperature. "Would you mind leaving me now, Dr. Stuart? I wish to take my bath in warm water, not cool.''

Stuart was not unaware of Claire's sudden formality toward him. "I apologize if I offended you with my plain speaking,'' he said. "A man can tolerate many things, but being called a liar is not one of them.''

"Oh, but I never—''

He did not let her finish. "I'll leave you to your bath.''

Listening to his steps receding in the companionway, Claire felt strangely deflated. She hadn't meant to suggest he was lying. She couldn't imagine why he would. Perhaps he was embarrassed that the rough winter seas had put him under again. After all, her godfather had certain expectations that Macauley Stuart would act as her companion and protector. The doctor was probably afraid she would tell the duke he had failed her in some way.

Claire stood and shrugged out of her robe. Raising her nightshift, she stepped into the tub. It was still hot enough to afford pleasant relief. She pulled the shift over her head, let it fall on the floor, then eased herself into the water. She wondered if her sigh was audible topside.

It was not. On deck Rand's eyes scanned the horizon without

the aid of the telescope in his hand. For all intents and purposes he was occupied with the storm front. He doubted there was anyone among his crew, even Cutch, who thought otherwise. They believed it was the portent of a gale brewing that kept him occupied this morning. No one suspected his mood had anything to do with Claire.

Rand had only to look at Paul Dodd's face as he returned topside to know Claire had been pleased with the gift of rainwater. Her appreciation, if Dodd's beatific expression could be used as a measure, had been warmly given.

Now she was enjoying this small pleasure while he was left with disturbing images that all but robbed him of his concentration: Claire with her head tipped back against the lip of the tub, her damp throat exposed, her complexion flushed with heat and beaded with steam; Claire with her dark hair in a loose topknot that was already slipping to one side; Claire with a sponge in one hand and a slender leg raised, resting at the foot of the tub. She would drizzle fragrant water over the length of that leg, across her other arm, and again between her breasts. She might push the sponge under the water and touch it to her waist or the curve of her hip. She would draw it along the edge of her inner thigh.

Impatient with himself, Rand's fingers raked his hair. The image faded slowly; his head cleared. There was nothing about the night with Claire that he regretted. Only that morning ended it.

"That's a deep scowl," Cutch noted, coming up beside him. "You're making the men nervous. Are we in for it even before we round the Horn?"

Rand handed his second the telescope. "Judge for yourself."

Cutch lifted the scope and eyed the same view as his captain. He whistled softly. "She'll come up on us fast."

"That's what I'm thinking."

"Someone should warn Dr. Stuart and Miss Bancroft."

Rand nodded. "You can tell the doctor now, but let Miss Bancroft enjoy her bath. There's time yet."

"As you wish."

Watching Cutch go, Rand thought to himself that it was not

as he wished at all. Given a choice, he would have elected to go to Claire himself and tell her what the next few hours would bring them. The storm might trap them for the better part of the day. And there was always the chance *Cerberus* wouldn't survive it.

Rand realized he knew nothing of Claire's experiences at sea. Had she been through a storm like the one they were about to face? The high wind and crashing waves could be terrifying for sighted men. What would it be like for her to face in the dark, without the comfort of family nearby?

Then there was no more time to think on it. The wind shifted, this time coming from the east, and *Cerberus* rode the waves into a thick bank of fog. When Cutch returned to the wheel, rain was already pelting the deck. He handed Rand an oilskin like the one he was wearing now. In a few hours the covering would serve no purpose. With the deck awash with seawater and the skies opening up above them, there was little protection from being soaked to the skin or feeling the cold all the way to the bone.

Rand ordered most of the men below. The sails were fixed, and any man left on deck was in danger of being swept into the sea. Cutch lashed Rand to the chair at the wheel. It was time for *Cerberus* to ride out the gale, hoping she could stay high in the water and not take this journey on a leeway cant.

Cutch had to raise his voice to be heard. The bitterly cold Antarctic wind flattened the oilskin against his body and kept him upright even as he tried to lean forward. "She'll be fine," he told his captain. "She's come through it before!"

Rand didn't know if Cutch was speaking of *Cerberus* or Claire. Perhaps he was referring to both. He didn't ask, because he felt he couldn't. "Below, Cutch! You and everyone but the watch!"

Nodding, Cutch waved off the last of the men who weren't tethered to the masts like yard dogs. They struggled to the companionway opening across the treacherous deck, then, one by one, dropped out of sight. The doors were closed behind them to keep out more seawater.

Icy droplets of water clung to Rand's hair at his forehead

and nape. The deck ran with foamy water that turned to a thin sheet of ice in places. In an hour the rigging was a great iced spider's web. Rand's fingers ached to the joints with cold. He worked them spasmodically to keep them from stiffening unbearably. He thought they had taken on a bluish cast but he couldn't be sure. The steady spray of water churned up by the sea and the wind all but blinded him.

Men on the first watch shouted their status and reported at regular intervals on the condition of the ship. Occasionally there was work to be done in the icy rigging. As hard as the work was there, it was preferred by many men to remaining on the foamy deck. They would line up on the weather side of the yards and work the nearly frozen canvas free. In this way the wind pressed them hard against the rigging, and not away from it. In contrast, on deck, they could be washed overboard with a moment's inattention.

In her cabin Claire sat on the bed, her back against the wall and her knees drawn toward her chest. The fire in her stove had gone out, and the cold that swept over the ship had finally penetrated her underbelly. Claire had her mantle drawn over her like a blanket, but she still felt the fingers of cold air seep under the material.

Cutch had brought assistance with him to remove the copper tub. He also checked her cabin to make certain that everything that could be secured in fact was. Dr. Stuart, she'd been informed, was already feeling the effects of the high seas and pitching ship, and could offer no companionship. Claire was willing to go to Macauley's cabin to help him through the storm, but Cutch was not encouraging. "You're safer here," he'd told her. "Where everything is familiar. Someone will come by from time to time to check on you."

In spite of Cutch's promise, no one had come since then. It was not so much that Claire required attention, but that she wanted to know that *they* were safe. Rand would be on deck, she knew. Cutch told her the captain would not be removed from his place at the wheel. He would ride out the storm with *Cerberus,* keeping her bowsprit in his sights.

The ship pitched sideways. Claire's stomach lurched as she was tumbled out of her cocoon. She heard her heavy trunk slide across the floor and slam into the dresser. The chair under the desk tipped sideways and crashed. Claire groped for her headboard and held on, even when *Cerberus* rolled back. She wondered what Cutch would think if he checked on her later and found her curled under the bunk. She would tell him she had gone there in search of her stomach.

The storm—really a succession of gales—lasted for days. *Cerberus* rounded the Horn with her sodden canvas and icy yardarms intact. The seas gave up more water, pressing it into the ship's hull until the pumps jammed. The skies gave up snow. It swept in little eddies across the deck and settled on the eyelashes of every man on the watch. Stiff sails were caught in frozen gaskets and had to be loosened by hand. Men hauled themselves painfully into the rigging to do the work. All their attention had to be for their task, none at all for whether they would survive it.

Claire knew bits and pieces of what was happening above her. Now and again someone would arrive at her door with a plate of cold food—the galley fires no longer burned—and information from topside. She was aware that one of the crew had been swept away during the changing of the watch. If not for a momentary lull, the ship would have sailed on. Even so, Claire understood that making the decision to rescue the man would have been agonizing for Rand. It meant pitting six men in a lifeboat against the high seas to save one. He had to have known the outcome was not guaranteed. A decision that he would have to live with the rest of his life had to be made almost instantaneously. Claire wondered how she would act if given such terrible choices, and she prayed she would never have the opportunity to learn.

Measuring from calm sea to calm sea, it took eight days for *Cerberus* to weather the storms, round the Horn, and move from Atlantic to Pacific. Claire knew as early as day five that she was becoming ill. By then she could discern the different forces that were working on her body. She knew when discomfort was caused by the pitching ship and cold food and when the nausea had nothing to do with either of those things. The icy squall was responsible for only part of Claire's bone-chilling ache. On day six she knew the kind of cold that no amount of blankets could ward off. It was only a matter of time before fever and delirium would follow.

Rand stood at Claire's bedside, looking down on her unnaturally flushed face. He watched Macauley Stuart wring out a compress and lay it over Claire's forehead. "Is that the best you can do?" he asked in a harsh whisper. "Cutch says it's been hours since she could be roused."

"And like to be hours yet," the doctor informed him calmly. "I'm following the treatment exactly as Miss Bancroft's London physicians prescribed."

"Then you've never treated this yourself."

Macauley looked up from his patient. "No. One doesn't have occasion to see many tropical diseases on the moors," he said dryly. "I availed myself of the knowledge gleaned by her other doctors. As I understand it, Captain Hamilton, Miss Bancroft's malady has many peculiar characteristics. There *are* no experts. The physician who cared for her on the voyage back to London made copious notes to chart her progress. He turned those over to her godfather, who made a search for doctors to treat her. I believe everyone involved learned as they went. Protocols for this illness do not exist except as they apply to Miss Bancroft."

Rand did not like anything he heard. During the course of the storm he had held fast to the hope that there was always something he could do. In the face of rising seas and powerful winds, there was always some order he could bark out that might alter nature's impact on the ship and the lives of his men and passengers. This was different. He had no knowledge or skills that might alter the course of Claire's illness; he had to rely on someone else, who seemed only marginally more competent.

Rand's response to helplessness was anger. With Macauley Stuart he felt little compunction to temper it. "I hope to hell you know how to follow their instructions," he said.

Stuart didn't flinch, although his complexion reddened. "I think I can be relied on to do that much."

Rand turned to Cutch, who was standing in the doorway. "I want a man posted outside her cabin to fetch anything the doctor needs and keep the fire going in her stove. If I find it was allowed to go out again, I'll throw the man responsible overboard myself."

Cutch stepped aside to let Rand stalk past him. "I'll post Adams here," he told Stuart when Rand was gone. "How are you holding up?"

The doctor shrugged. "As long as the sea stays calm I should manage. I regret I couldn't attend Miss Bancroft myself until now."

Cutch didn't reply. Stuart would do more than regret it if his own incapacity resulted in further complications for Claire. Cutch had reported Claire's illness to the doctor as soon as he became aware of it. He had his own regret to reconcile, namely that he had allowed Claire to convince him nothing was wrong with her when his suspicions were first roused. With three quarters of the men seasick at one time or another, all of them veterans of white squalls, it was easy for Cutch to believe that Claire would be similarly affected. He knew now that it wasn't so much that she lied, but that she hadn't told all of the truth.

He had to discover that fact when he learned from one of the crew that Claire was found lying unconscious on the floor of her cabin. *Cerberus* had not yet reached calm waters. Stuart was weak himself from days of sickness and incapacity. Cutch half dragged, half carried the doctor to Claire's cabin to examine her, but it was pitifully clear that Stuart could do little in his state. He had neither the stamina nor the stomach to stay with her. Following his instructions, it was Cutch who nursed her in the beginning and poor Paul Dodd who had to walk across the wave-washed deck to inform the captain.

Alone in his cabin, Rand sat at his desk and filled out the ship's log. In the past eight days he had had little time away from the wheel. He slept intermittently, sometimes while wind and water pounded him in place, other times in his cabin. He had made a point of looking in on Claire twice, but only briefly.

She seemed surprised by his visits, as if his need to reassure her was unnecessary. He couldn't be certain if it was because she placed so much trust in his command to see them through the storm, or because she thought they were all better served if he was on deck.

He never explained that he was drawn to her cabin as soon as he dropped into the companionway, that it was his need he served by making certain she was all right. He doubted she would have been flattered if he had explained it to her. It was more likely that he wouldn't have been believed.

On neither of his visits did he touch her. Their lovemaking, more than thirty-six hours in the past when he first saw her again, had already been shaded by a sense of unreality. On the second visit it was even more so.

Rand wished now that he had reached for her. He might have known that she was becoming ill. He knew the texture of her skin, after all. He knew that her lips should have been warm under his mouth. But the opportunity had passed. Twice. He didn't touch her because he needed her to be less real to him, not more. The only way he could ride out the storm was not to think of how much was riding on it.

Rand closed the log book, stood, and stripped out of his clothes. Still damp from his last command on deck, they slapped the floor hard. Rand fell naked on top of his bed and, lulled by the gentle rocking of *Cerberus* on the Pacific calm, was asleep in minutes.

Claire's own sleep was disturbed. Over the next few days, as her illness ran its course, she drifted in and out of consciousness, though no one who sat by her side was certain which state gave rise to the most peculiar statements. To varying degrees they understood some of it. It was not surprising that she spoke of Sir Griffin and her brother. Stickle was mentioned from time to time. Once, when she was particularly agitated, she called out Trenton's name. Most often, however, what Claire whispered were phrases and words peculiar to Solonesia. She spoke of tapu and over and over, like a mantra, of Tiare.

"What does it mean?" Stuart wanted to know when Rand

came to relieve him. "Have I mistaken the words? Was she speaking of her brother again?"

"Tipu is her half-brother," Rand said. "Tapu is a spell . . . a curse."

The doctor came to his feet. He stretched and massaged the back of his neck. "And Tiare?"

"I don't know. There's a flower with that name. She could be talking about it."

"It makes no sense."

Rand shrugged. He was anxious for Stuart to be gone but not willing to show it. "Were you able to get her to eat anything?"

"A little broth."

"And her medicine?"

"She spat that back at me."

Rand found he had no patience for that answer. "Go on, Stuart, I'll see that she gets it."

"I wish you more luck than I had," he said. "It's in my bag."

Once the doctor was gone, Rand pushed the chair he'd occupied aside and sat on the edge of the bed. Three blankets covered Claire up to her shoulders. Someone—Cutch, he suspected—had taken the time to brush her hair and neatly plait it. Tendrils of it lay very darkly against her pale forehead and temples. Her skin was as pale as he remembered from their first brief encounter in her godfather's study. There were violet shadows beneath her eyes and a bluish tinge to her lips. She looked as if she had just been found sleeping on a glacier, yet Rand found her cabin uncomfortably warm.

He rooted in Stuart's bag until he found the bottle of medicine. He did not bother with a spoon. There was no sense in trying to ladle it into Claire's mouth. Instead, Rand uncorked the bottle and held it up to her lips. With his free hand he pressed on either side of her jaw, forcing her mouth open, and tipped some of the medicine into her mouth. Claire tried to grimace and push it back out, but Rand held her firm. She swallowed most of this first dose and all of the second.

Rand put the bottle away. He poked his head into the companionway long enough to hand over Claire's bowl of cold broth.

It wasn't long before a warm serving was returned to him. Using the same technique he'd used with the medicine, Rand was able to get most of the liquid down Claire's throat. Satisfied, he gave the bowl back and dismissed the crewman from his post. Rand quietly locked Claire's door and returned to her bed. He pulled off his boots and lifted the blankets. Nudging Claire closer to the wall, Rand stretched out beside her. He placed one arm across her waist; the other rested under his head. She didn't stir as his body heat was added to the warmth of the blankets.

He knew he slept for a time. It wasn't until he heard Claire's faint whisper that he knew what woke him.

"No tapu, Tiare. No tapu. I don't . . . I don't believe this. There is no tapu."

Rand watched her lips move around the words and wondered at their meaning. He raised his hand from her waist and touched her cheek. Her skin was warmer now—not fevered, just warm. He gave a small start, blinking once when Claire's eyes opened suddenly. There was such intensity, such focus in her gaze, that for a moment Rand believed she could actually see him.

"Tiare!"

Rand heard both horror and pleading in her tone. Claire's breathing took on a labored quality, as if she had paused in the midst of a hard run; then she was quiet. A shutter was drawn over her eyes, then her expression. Almost instantly she was asleep again, this time peacefully.

He had occasion to wonder what it all meant as *Cerberus* moved without incident toward the South Pacific islands. Three more days passed before he could ask Claire.

She was sitting up, propped against the wall and the headboard, surrounded by pillows and a tangle of blankets, when he strode into her room.

"I suppose I shall have to use the new lock after all," she said. "No one knocks any more."

Rand's smile was faint. He stood at the foot of her bed, his eyes moving over her face, her hair, the open neckline of her nightshift. A hint of color had returned to her cheeks. Her collarbones looked fragile beneath skin that was stretched tautly over them. He swallowed hard. There was a slight catch in his voice. "It's Rand," he said.

"I know. I heard you coming down the companionway."

"Mr. Dodd reported that you've finally deigned to join us."

Claire made light of it. "If you mean the living, yes, I'm finally among you. It seems *Cerberus* weathered the Horn better than I did."

Rand found he did not want to look away from her. Somehow his feet had become rooted to the floor. "Claire."

Pushing at the blankets impatiently, Claire rose to her knees. She thrust a hand forward, palm up, fingers outstretched. It seemed an eternity before her hand was filled with his.

Rand stepped around the corner of the bed and hauled Claire flush against him. She seemed impossibly delicate in his rough embrace, but she didn't shy from it or murmur anything that could be mistaken as protest. He kissed her hair, her brow, her closed lids. He laid his mouth across hers. And when he drew back, it seemed that no words were necessary to say what he felt, or what he had felt for interminable days and nights. Claire was holding him now, her fingers stroking the coppery hair at his nape, and whispering against his neck, "I know. I know."

His fingers loosened on her waist. She drew him onto the bed. He kissed her again, lightly this time.

"Careful," she said. "The door's not locked."

"Hmmm." He held her face between his hands, his thumbs touching the corner of her lips. "I remember."

"I suppose everyone became accustomed to barging in here while I was ill."

"Not everyone. Stuart, Cutch, and Dodd. They did the lion's share."

"And you. I know you were here."

He wondered that she had sensed his presence. He couldn't recall a moment when she had seemed to be aware of him. "Did you?" he asked.

Claire nodded.

"You never once said my name."

She turned her head a fraction and kissed the pad of his thumb. "Rand," she said quietly.

A shiver went through him. He lifted Claire and placed her back among the pillows and blankets. He drew them around her, tucking her in. Her vaguely disappointed look drew a deep chuckle from him, just as he suspected she knew it would. "You're only just recovered," Rand told her, though he doubted Claire had forgotten. "Stay there. Would you like some tea?"

"Yes, please."

A tray had been set out earlier on the desk. Rand felt the pot and found it still warm. He poured Claire a cup, added a little sugar, and gave it to her. She sipped it gratefully.

"You called me Tiare," he said. The tightening of Claire's fingers on her cup would have been imperceptible if Rand hadn't been looking for it.

"You must be mistaken," Claire said with credible calm.

"No, I don't think so. Stuart heard you use the name. Perhaps you called him that as well. I didn't ask." He continued to watch her closely. "Who is he?" he asked. "Who's Tiare?"

"It's a flower," she said. *"Tiare apetahi."*

"I know the flower," Rand said. "It's native to Tahiti . . . a sacred white flower that can be grown nowhere else. There's a legend to it. Something about a young girl dying of a broken heart."

Claire's smile was wry. She chided him gently. "For someone whose life has been caught up in a legend, you speak rather dismissingly of this one. The petals are her five fingers. The flower unfolds at dawn and dies at nightfall. And the beautiful girl of the legend fell in love with the son of a royal chief. It was because she couldn't hope to marry him that her heart was broken."

"I like the Hamilton-Waterstone tale better. Privateers . . . cutlasses . . . treasure."

"And treachery. Don't forget the treachery."

"The best part."

Claire smirked. "You *would* think so."

Rand wondered if she thought she had put him off his original question. He repeated it now. "What about Tiare?"

Lifting the cup to her lips, Claire did not respond directly. "Did I talk a lot during my illness?"

"A lot? I don't know if I would say that. Mostly it was about your father and brother. Occasionally about Stickle."

"Oh, dear. Then I suppose Mr. Stuart knows about my pet name for him."

"He does but I doubt he'll ever have occasion to use it. You mentioned Trenton."

"I did?"

Rand saw that Claire seemed genuinely surprised by that. "Only once that I'm aware of."

"I must have been having a nightmare," she said. "It's the only context in which I can imagine bringing Trenton to mind."

"What about Tiare?"

Claire frowned. "Why is it so important to you? I'm sure I don't remember saying anything like that."

"You mentioned him in the same breath as tapu."

Her mouth flattened, and this time Claire was almost mutinously silent. The tips of her fingers were white on her teacup.

Rand eyed the cup, wondering if she could break it. Thinking she might just throw it in his face, he didn't try to take it from her. "You must know your prevarication and silence has me intrigued, Claire. You would have been better served to tell me at the first."

She was realizing that now. If anything, it made disclosure more difficult.

"Is he someone to you?" asked Rand. "A suitor, perhaps? The son of a royal chief?"

Claire's flush deepened. "No. That's ridiculous."

"Is it? Are you saying that no man among the islanders ever tried to court you?"

"Yes . . . no . . . I mean it's ridiculous that you think his name would be Tiare. It's a woman's name."

Rand's brows raised a fraction. "A woman?"

Claire nodded. "Tiare is Tipu's mother. My father's mistress."

He considered that a moment, wondering what lay behind

Claire's reluctance to tell him at the outset. "What was her tapu?" he asked at last.

"Her tapu?"

"Her spell," he explained. "Was she the one who cursed your eyes?"

Chapter Nine

Claire thrust her teacup in Rand's direction. *Was she the one who cursed your eyes?* "Take this," she said, urgency in her tone. "Please."

Rand realized that Claire's hands were shaking too badly to hold the cup any longer. He grabbed it in time to keep it from falling out of her hands. "Claire? What is it? Are you all right?"

She shook her head. "I think I'm going to be sick." She drew her knees toward her chest and hugged them. Her stomach churned. The nausea was only marginally relieved by the change in her position, and bile began to rise in her throat. She choked it back. Her heart seemed to be tripping over itself in a race to escape her chest, and a deep flush colored her skin from her breasts to her scalp. Claire was trapped into stillness by an overwhelming sense of fear. It was made worse by her inability to name the thing that frightened her.

Rand pulled Claire closer to the edge of the bed. He reached for the basin on her commode and placed her hand along the rim so she could sense its position. Her shoulders heaved once and she retched dryly. Rand held her steady.

"Go away," she said miserably. There was no comfort in

having him hold her now, only a keen sense of embarrassment. His presence did not lessen Claire's fear; it merely reinforced the irrationality of it. She should feel safe, she thought, yet there was no sense of well-being. "Please," she whispered. "Go away."

Rand did not doubt the sincerity of her request, but its reasonableness made him hesitate. "I'll get Dr. Stuart," he said. It was a compromise he could live with.

Claire shook her head. The motion made her heave again. "I don't want—"

Her wishes were of little concern to Rand now. He wished he had not been so quick to dismiss the man posted at her door. Pressing the basin more fully into Claire's grip, he told her he would only be a moment. He strode to the door, threw it open, then went in search of Macauley Stuart.

When he returned to Claire's cabin it was to discover that she had locked the door. "Claire! Open up!" The door rattled under his hard knock but it didn't give. "I have Stuart here. I think you should see him."

Inside, Claire was standing at the commode, pressing a cool cloth to her face. She shook her head in response to Rand's orders but she said nothing.

Rand gave her a few moments to come to the door. When she didn't, he repeated his demand for her to open it. This time he and Stuart heard her faint reply that they should leave her alone. Rand looked sideways at the doctor, one of his brows arched in question.

"Let's give her some more time," Macauley suggested. "She doesn't sound as though she needs me this very minute."

"You didn't see her. The illness could be starting again."

The doctor rubbed his chin. "Well, if it's a relapse, there's little I'll be able to do in the way of helping her. The sickness has to run its course. The medicine's to ease her way. It's not a cure." He saw that Rand didn't like his answer, but he didn't apologize for it. "I left the tonic with her. She can take a dose herself as well as I can give it to her."

Rand gave him a sour look. "Some days I wonder why the

Take 4 FREE Books!

We created our convenient Home Subscription Service so you'll be sure to have the hottest new romances delivered each month right to your doorstep — usually before they are available in book stores. Just to show you how convenient Zebra Home Subscription Service is, we would like to send you 4 Kensington Choice Historical Romances as a FREE gift. You receive a gift worth up to $24.96 — absolutely FREE. There's no extra charge for shipping and handling. There's no obligation to buy anything - ever!

Save Up To 32% On Home Delivery!

Accept your FREE gift and each month we'll deliver 4 brand new titles as soon as they are published. They'll be yours to examine FREE for 10 days. Then if you decide to keep the books, you'll pay the preferred subscriber's price of just $4.20 per title. That's $16.80 for all 4 books for a savings of up to 32% off the publisher's price! Just add $1.50 to offset the cost of shipping and handling. Remember, you are under no obligation to buy any of these books at any time! If you are not delighted with them, simply return them and owe nothing. But if you enjoy Kensington Choice Historical Romances as much as we think you will, pay the special preferred subscriber rate of only $16.80 each month and save over $8.00 off the bookstore price!

We have 4 FREE BOOKS for you as your introduction to **KENSINGTON CHOICE!**

To get your FREE BOOKS,
worth up to $24.96, mail the card below.
or call TOLL-FREE 1-888-345-BOOK
Visit our website at www.kensingtonbooks.com.

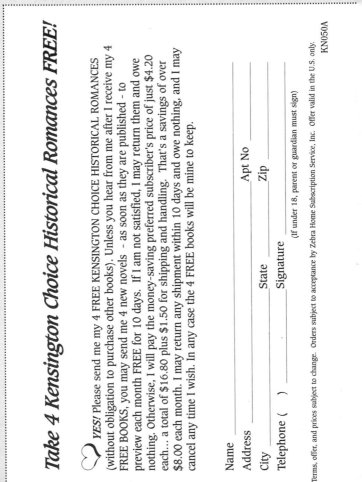

Take 4 Kensington Choice Historical Romances FREE!

YES! Please send me my 4 FREE KENSINGTON CHOICE HISTORICAL ROMANCES (without obligation to purchase other books). Unless you hear from me after I receive my 4 FREE BOOKS, you may send me 4 new novels – as soon as they are published – to preview each month FREE for 10 days. If I am not satisfied, I may return them and owe nothing. Otherwise, I will pay the money-saving preferred subscriber's price of just $4.20 each... a total of $16.80 plus $1.50 for shipping and handling. That's a savings of over $8.00 each month. I may return any shipment within 10 days and owe nothing, and I may cancel any time I wish. In any case the 4 FREE books will be mine to keep.

KN050A

Name		
Address		Apt No
City	State	Zip
Telephone ( )	Signature	

(If under 18, parent or guardian must sign)

hell I agreed to bring you, Stuart. You're about as useful as udders on a bull.''

Macauley shrugged. "I do what I can, Captain Hamilton. And sometimes I can't even do that.'' He rapped lightly on Claire's door. "Claire, it's Macauley. The captain believes I need to examine you. Will you let me in?''

There was a long silence, then: "You? Alone?''

"Yes,'' Stuart said before Rand could respond otherwise. "If that's what you wish.'' Cocking his head, he glanced at Rand. "You'll have to leave. I don't think she'll let me in otherwise.''

Reinforcing his words, Claire's voice came from just on the other side of the door. "Captain Hamilton?''

"Yes, Claire?''

"Go away.''

Rand did not look at the doctor, and he took himself off without looking back.

Claire opened the door as soon as Rand's footsteps had receded into the companionway. "Come in, Macauley.'' She turned away and went back to the commode. She dipped her cloth into the pitcher again, wrung it out, and laid it against her forehead, then her throat.

"Sit down,'' Stuart told her. "Over here, on the bed. I can see for myself that you're flushed. What happened?''

Sighing, Claire put the cloth down and did as she was told. "I don't know. I've never experienced anything like it before.''

Macauley reached under the bed and retrieved his medical bag. He took out his stethoscope. "You'll have to unbutton your nightdress. I want to listen to your chest.''

She nodded and unfastened the first three buttons. She remained very still as Macauley pressed the instrument between her breasts, then at the underside of her left one, against her ribs. His hand on her shoulder steadied her.

"You can breathe,'' he chided her.

Claire's smile betrayed her unease. When Macauley tugged on her shift to move it over her shoulder, she tensed.

"I thought you were over your shyness.''

She shrugged. The movement caused her nightdress to fall

as Macauley wanted it. She felt him slip the stethoscope under the material and press it against her back. The coolness of it made her shiver. It was not modesty that made her reluctant to submit to the examination, but a certain mistrust that it made any difference. Since leaving Raiatea she had permitted dozens of doctors a hundred opportunities to poke and prod her. Little was different in her life as a result. She was still blind, and they all admitted they didn't understand the nature of her tropical illness. Claire held no belief that Macauley Stuart was better or worse than any of his colleagues before him. She didn't welcome his attentions, merely suffered them.

Macauley removed the stethoscope. Before he could help Claire with her nightgown, she was already pulling it in place and fastening the buttons. "There's nothing wrong with your heart or lungs," he told her. "Captain Hamilton said you were nauseated."

She nodded. "For a while. It passed."

"Did you vomit?"

"A little."

"Nothing much in your stomach to get rid of, I suspect." He touched the back of his hand to her forehead. Her skin was cool, but he remembered that she had had a cloth pressed to her face. Macauley replaced the stethoscope, then looked through his bag for laudanum. "Tell me about your other symptoms. Does your head ache?"

"No. And there was never any pain behind my eyes." She hesitated, not knowing how to explain it. "I was afraid," Claire said at last. "Deeply afraid."

"What do you mean?"

"Just that. I was afraid. My stomach turned over and my hands shook. I couldn't calm myself. It was as if my heart were in my throat. The only time I've ever experienced anything like that was when I was afraid." Her voice lowered as she tried to sort it out in her own mind. "This time there was nothing to run from or fight."

Macauley frowned. "You're saying you were frightened of nothing?"

"No. Of something. But I don't know what."

"Captain Hamilton was with you when it happened."

"Yes."

"Were you afraid of him? You wouldn't let him back in here."

"No, it was nothing like that." Agitated, Claire moved away from the doctor. She lifted the blankets and slid under them. "You may as well go," she told him. "There's nothing more I can tell you that will help explain what happened."

"Very well. I have some laudanum for you to take."

Claire didn't want it, but if Stuart insisted she knew there was an entire crew who would make certain she took it. She sat up just enough for him to spoon the opiate in her mouth. If it served no purpose but to help her sleep, Claire thought it would be enough.

The doctor waited in Claire's cabin until he saw the medication starting to take effect; then he went to make his report to Rand. He found the captain topside, talking to Cutch while the second oversaw the work going on in the rigging.

Rand stopped talking as soon as he saw Stuart approaching. "Well?" he asked without preamble.

"She's fine now. Resting comfortably. I gave her some laudanum." Macauley glanced overhead at the men working in the yardarms. He grimaced, thinking it was only a matter of time before he was called on deck to set another broken bone. "There's no indication that she's taken a turn in her recovery. What she described to me has nothing to do with the illness as I understand it."

"What did she say to you?" asked Rand. Out of the corner of his eye he noticed that Cutch's attention had strayed from the men to the doctor.

"That she was afraid," Macauley said simply.

Rand's brows rose. "Of me?"

The doctor shook his head. "I didn't get that impression. She certainly couldn't explain it. Her symptoms, though, were consistent with someone who has been frightened."

"That doesn't make any sense. Nothing happened. We were talking."

Cutch caught Rand's eyes squarely. "About what?"

Rand actually had to struggle to remember. It seemed so unimportant now. "I was asking her about Tiare. It was one of the names she called out when she was sick."

Both Cutch and Macauley nodded.

"As it happens, Tiare is the name of her brother's mother. Since she said Tiare's name in the same breath she mentioned tapu, I thought there might be a connection."

Cutch's eyes narrowed intently, while Macauley was clearly lost. "You told her that?" asked Cutch.

"Asked her," Rand replied. "I asked her if Tiare cursed her with blindness."

Cutch shook his head slowly, his disappointment palpable. "Do you really think, if that's true, Claire could have said so? It's powerful magic. I thought you had more respect for it. Mammy Komati raised you to." He stalked away almost angrily and took to the rigging to help the men in the yards himself.

Macauley stared after him, astonished as much by Cutch's tone in addressing Rand as in the content of his short speech. "What did he mean?" he asked. "And who is Mammy Komati?"

"Cutch meant that I've been a fool," Rand said succinctly. He let those words sink in, then gave the doctor a frank look. "But don't think I'd let just anyone point that out." He raked back his hair and crossed to the rail. He was aware of Macauley following him. "Mammy Komati was a nursemaid, mother, friend . . . tyrant. She called herself a Christian and sang spirituals with feeling enough to support that claim, but she never turned her back on the gods of her ancestors."

"She was a slave in your home," Macauley said, beginning to understand.

"That's right. She was my mother's wet nurse, later her confidant and companion. When my father married my mother, he had to take Mammy Komati, too. She was not leaving her baby. I think my father was a little afraid of her." Rand's grin was a bit self-mocking. "I know I was."

He turned his back on the rail and leaned against it, crossing his arms in front of him. The last person he thought he'd be talking about Mammy to was Macauley Stuart. "She said she knew the magical arts, but always cautioned that she used them in the aid of goodness. If anyone became sick, she'd retire to her quarters to mix potions and burn feathers. Sometimes an animal was sacrificed. The crucifix she wore around her neck was nestled among half-a-dozen pagan charms and amulets.''

''She knew about tapu?'' asked Macauley.

''Not by that name,'' Rand said. ''Mammy's magic was African. Tapu belongs to the South Seas.'' He shrugged. ''But it's not dissimilar.''

''Is Mr. Cutch right about it being powerful?''

''You're a man of science, Dr. Stuart. What do you think?''

Macauley chuckled softly, amused. ''You're talking to a man who was raised in the Highlands, who grew up believing there was magic in the mists. Scratch the surface, I'm afraid, and beneath this doctor you'll find someone willing to burn a few feathers if it will cure a cold.'' He studied Rand a moment. ''But you put the question to Miss Bancroft. You must hold some opinion about the power of tapu.''

Rand did not answer immediately. ''I believe it exists,'' he said at last. ''As for its power, I think it rests in the culture. Mammy believed in its power, so it was powerful. Cutch believes, too. I've seen the work of tapu on islanders. A man can be struck dumb by a spell or lose the will to live and die at the very hour predicted by the priestess. In the same way, a child might walk again or be delivered from some unknown source of pain.''

''Miss Bancroft is English,'' Macauley reminded him. ''It's difficult to imagine a race of people with less interest or respect for the mystical. Witness what they've done in India.''

Rand had no desire to hear the doctor's discourse on British imperialism again. ''Miss Bancroft's spent a good portion of her life in and around the Sun Islands. It may be that she holds to the scientific principles of her father with less conviction than she would have others believe.''

''So my French colleague, Dr. Messier, may be right after all,'' Macauley said thoughtfully.

Rand looked at him in surprise. He hadn't considered it from that perspective. "In a manner of speaking, yes, he would be right. Miss Bancroft's blindness might have no physical cause."

"And no catastrophic event for her to recreate. It's the work of a tapu."

"It *might* be," Rand cautioned. "There's nothing to be gained by pressing her on that point. Cutch is right. If it *is* tapu, then she can't speak of it."

"Then what's to be done? I'm out of my depth again, Captain Hamilton. As you so eloquently stated earlier, as useful as teats on a bull."

Rand didn't remember saying it in quite that fashion, but the doctor had, and it raised his own smile. "I suspect we have to find Tiare," he said quietly. "That would be the place to start."

Claire did not know what would happen when she saw Rand again. She was tense at first, wary of the panic that had seized her the day before, but as he strolled with her on deck, it seemed the only thing she had to fear was the memory itself.

Rand noticed her guarded responses and hesitation, but he wisely chose to ignore them. He directed the conversation to inconsequential matters, sharing stories about David and Shelby until Claire was laughing easily. It was only when he mentioned Bria that she sobered.

Claire turned at the rail and touched Rand's forearm. She lifted her face toward him, a question in her expression. "What happened to Bria?" she asked. "Please don't ask me what I mean or pretend that you don't know what I'm talking about. I know that something happened to Bria during the war, something terrible, I think, and that no one ever talks about it now."

"There's a reason for that," he said tersely, some of the pleasure of the evening sinking with the sun. "It's no one's business."

Claire did not take offense. She was not no one in his life. He might have never said in so many words that he loved her, but she knew she was not no one. "You rarely mention Bria when you tell stories about growing up."

"That's because she was so much younger. A year is about

all that separated David, Shelby, and me. Bree came along much later. She was more like a pet than a sister.''

Claire smiled. ''Does she know you felt that way?''

''Probably. We didn't exactly keep it a secret.'' Rand rested one hip on the rail. He braced an arm behind his back to steady him. ''It didn't stop her from dogging our steps. She would do most anything to spend time outdoors with us instead of in the house. About the only thing she liked to do there was play the piano.''

''Did she?'' asked Claire. ''I had no idea. I never heard her play once at Henley. I even asked her about the music room. She said it was for show.''

Rand winced. He could imagine Bria saying that very thing. ''That's true now. At one time she and Father played almost every evening after dinner. It was his talent she inherited for music, not my mother's. She loved it, though. Considered it Bria's one true feminine accomplishment.''

''Yes, that would seem important to Elizabeth.''

''It was.'' He paused. A strand of hair had tumbled free of Claire's combs. He watched it flutter against the corner of her mouth. When she lifted her hand to move it aside, he stopped her and did the thing himself. ''Bree was eleven when the war started . . . fifteen by the time the fighting ended. She died sometime in between.''

''Oh, Rand . . . surely not.''

''You wanted to know.'' He changed his position and crossed his legs. *Cerberus* rode high in the water, her speed steady. The onset of nightfall was changing the color of the sea as fast as the sky. ''Yankee raiders moved south in small bands separate from the large forces. It wasn't easy to get out of their way. Henley fell directly in their path. Until that time, the plantation had largely been untouched. Some slaves had run off early, others left at the time of Lincoln's Proclamation, but there were still enough laborers for David to keep Henley going. England was the only market left, and moving the rice past the blockade was difficult, though not impossible. Shelby was dead by then, killed at Manassas. I was in prison in the North and our father, though we didn't know it yet, had fallen at Vicksburg.

"The Yankee raiders, when they finally came, were like locusts, stripping Henley of everything they could carry. They took supplies they could never hope to use and destroyed family treasures for the pleasure it gave them. I suppose they thought they were doing something to further the end of the war, but it's hard for me to say what it might have been.

"Two of them found my mother in her room. David shot one and was killed by the other. Perhaps that's what made the soldier lose his taste for rape. He left Mother alone with her dead son and went on foraging. I don't know if he stumbled on Bree in the fruit cellar or if it was another of the band. Or several others. Mother says there were five that rode away. Bree never talks about it at all."

Rand's voice was almost inaudible now. "After she was raped once, I don't know if it mattered about the others."

Tears stung Claire's eyes. "I'm so sorry, Rand. For Bria . . . for you."

He looked at her oddly. "It didn't happen to me."

"Yes, it did." Claire turned toward the rail and raised her face. The wind pressed back her tears. "Does a day go by that you don't blame yourself?"

"A day," he said finally, reluctantly. "Now and again."

"Brie doesn't hold you responsible."

"It doesn't matter."

"No," she said. "You're right, it doesn't. You have to forgive yourself." Rand was quiet for so long that Claire began to think he had left her alone. When he spoke, she realized that he had moved from the rail. He was standing behind her. His hands came to rest on her shoulders and then he leaned forward a fraction so his mouth was near her ear. His voice carried nowhere but to her.

"I want to come to your cabin tonight, Claire."

His request, coming on the heels of being told to forgive himself, did not seem entirely odd to Claire. She wondered what part of lying with her was punishment for him and what part was peace. "Yes," she said simply.

His fingers squeezed her shoulders gently, and when she shivered he knew better than to suppose it was the cold.

They stood that way at the rail for a long time, undisturbed by the crew and unaware of their interest. For a while it was not so difficult to believe they were alone.

Claire was sitting on her trunk, brushing out her hair with the door open. She smiled, her head cocked to one side. "I didn't expect you so early."

Macauley Stuart stepped into her cabin and shut the door behind him. His usually pleasant countenance was drawn with concern. "I didn't know you expected me at all."

Claire gave a small start. Her fingers felt nerveless around the handle of her brush. She lowered it to her lap before she dropped it. Feeling off-center and thick-witted by the doctor's unexpected arrival, Claire was slow to recover. "You mentioned something at dinner about reading to me again," she said after a moment. "I've been looking forward to it."

Macauley's fiery brows remained drawn. He regarded Claire consideringly. It was clear that she was preparing for bed. The blankets were already turned down, and although she was still modestly dressed in her chemise and shift, her gown hung on a hook outside the armoire and her shoes were under the bed. In all the time he had been reading to her, she had never greeted him like this. "I haven't come to read to you," he said.

"Oh?" Claire laid down her brush and reached behind her to find her robe at the foot of the bed. She picked it up and pulled it on, belting it loosely about her waist. Tugging her hair free from beneath the collar, she began to plait it. "Then what is it you want? I don't require further examination. If that's why you're here, you may want to simply preserve me in one of the captain's jars so I can be studied at your leisure."

Stuart did not smile. "May I sit down?" he asked.

Claire nodded. "You sound perfectly serious, Macauley. Has something happened?"

"I think it has. I had hoped not, but I think it has."

"You're speaking in riddles."

Stuart pulled the chair out from under the desk and sat down.

"I came to talk to you about the captain, but I fear I may be too late."

"Would it help if I gave you permission to speak plainly?" asked Claire. "Though why such a thing should be necessary, I don't know."

Macauley gave her full marks for composure. "It helps," he said. "I don't think that I need to tell you that the duke had a number of expectations when he hired me to be your companion. I was to see to your physical well-being, naturally, and continue your education as Mrs. Webster would have. Your godfather confided that he hoped you would come to rely on me after a time, that we would become more than teacher and student, or doctor and patient, but friends after a fashion."

"Then I would say Stickle will be pleased with you," Claire told him lightly.

Macauley went on as if she hadn't spoken. "The duke's greatest concern was that Captain Hamilton would set his sights on you, and that you would be too—"

"Blind?" Claire injected, her tone caustic. "Too blind to see?"

"Too naive," Macauley corrected. "I believe your godfather thought you would forget that the captain had his own reasons for agreeing to bring you along. Hamilton has little or no interest in finding your father and brother. It's the treasure he wants, Claire. The duke said that if the time came when it seemed as if you'd forgotten that, then I was supposed to remind you."

"And you think that time has come," she said flatly.

"I think perhaps it's come and gone." Macauley looked around the cabin, then back at Claire. "You were waiting for him, weren't you? That's who you were expecting when I came in."

Claire did not answer. She finished braiding her hair, then let the tail fall down her back.

"It gives me no pleasure," he told her. "I'd hoped I wouldn't have to confront this. For a while it seemed that you and I . . ." His voice trailed off, and he shrugged almost helplessly.

"You and I?" she asked. "There never was such a thing.

Now you've given me reason to doubt I could ever properly call you my friend.''

"You're mistaken. I will always be that.''

"Please. Get out.'' She heard the chair scrape against the floor as Macauley stood. Claire held herself stiffly when he crossed the room to her side.

"Listen to me,'' he said almost pleadingly. "I'm speaking for your godfather now. He begs you to exercise some caution with the captain. Hamilton thinks you know something about the treasure and that's where his real interest lies. You wouldn't be here if it wasn't for that.''

Claire shook her head. "You have it wrong. It's the duke who thinks I know something. I wouldn't be at all surprised if he believed I would reveal it to you.'' Claire raised her face in the direction of the doctor. "I wish I could see you now. I'd know if it were true. I'm not as naive as my godfather would have you believe. I'm fully aware of how much he'd like to have the Hamilton-Waterstone treasure himself, and I don't think for a moment that he is above playing God to get it.''

Claire stood and carefully moved around Macauley on her way to the door. Her fingers curled around the handle and she twisted it. "I know the duke argues his points persuasively and his expectations are high. You shouldn't take it to heart that you've failed him in one area, when you've been so ... so *adequate* in others.'' In her mind's eye Claire saw the doctor flushing deeply. She opened the door and gestured for him to leave. "Good evening.''

Macauley Stuart stopped just before he would have stepped out. He touched the back of Claire's hand. Her skin was cool, and there was a faint tremor running under it. "I think you are not so confident of the captain's attentions as you would have me believe,'' he said. "And don't confuse the duke's interests with my own. I don't.''

Claire shut the door slowly. Her fingers twisted the lock. Later she lay in bed turned on her side and stared sightlessly at the wall, the blankets pulled to her neck. When Rand came she pretended she didn't hear him.

* * *

"You've been avoiding me," Rand told her as he walked into his workroom. "It's been three days since we talked. I can only imagine it's some miscalculation on your part that enabled me to find you here alone."

Claire was sitting at Rand's worktable. The books that cluttered the top were all closed. She stopped fiddling with the microscope and let her hand drift away. She hated that he had come upon her here, in the one place she felt the loss of her sight most keenly. "Mr. Cutch told me you were below checking the pumps," she said quietly. "I thought you would be there for some time."

Rand wondered at her almost painful honesty. She didn't even attempt to deny his assertion. "The first night I thought perhaps I had arrived too late. The next day, when you wouldn't pause long enough to speak to me alone, I realized I'd been wrong. You weren't asleep at all; you simply didn't want me there. Your door was locked that night also, and again last night." He mocked himself with his short, humorless laugh. "Even when I understood what you were doing, I refused to believe it."

Rand pulled out a stool from under the table and sat opposite Claire. He shoved a few books aside and rested his elbows on the edge of the table. "Have I offended you?"

Claire didn't raise her head. "No."

"I want to be with you again, Claire."

She nodded. "I know that."

"Are you afraid of me?"

"No."

Rand let out a long breath. "Then I don't understand. Why are you doing this?"

"I've been thinking about the treasure," she said, lifting her face in his direction for the first time.

"The treasure? Why in the world . . ." He raked back his hair, genuinely perplexed. "What has it to do with—"

"With anything?" she interrupted. "Everything." Claire started to lean forward and found the microscope in her way.

She loosened the vise that kept it in place and pushed it farther down the table. She set her forearms on the surface and imagined that across from her Rand was similarly postured. They could have been negotiating a peace treaty for all the gravity of the occasion. "I know what the treasure means to you," Claire told him. "I needed to understand what it could mean to me."

"You're going to have to explain yourself better than that."

She nodded, prepared. "For me it's a matter of acceptance. Do I accept that you're using me to further your own ends? Do I accept you unconditionally or with terms?"

Rand's eyes widened fractionally. It was almost perverse, how calmly she was talking about what amounted to a betrayal of her trust. Did she really believe he had done that? "Claire, I haven't deceived you. You're on this voyage because your godfather paid me a great deal of money. He wants your sight returned. You want to find your brother and know what's happened to your father. I want a treasure. It seems to me we're all working to the same end."

"No, not the same end. The same destination, perhaps, but definitely not the same end. What we all want may overlap on some points, but our priorities are ordered differently. That's what I was in danger of forgetting. And now I have to ask myself whether or not I can accept it."

Rand did not tell her she was wrong. He wasn't at all certain anymore that she was. "Unconditionally or with terms, I believe you said."

She nodded.

"What terms are you considering?" he asked.

"Only one, really." She paused a beat, then said matter-of-factly, "Marriage."

"I see."

She smiled a little at that. "No, you probably don't." Claire pushed away from the table and stood. "If you come to my cabin tonight, the door won't be locked. I'll let you know then what I've decided."

Watching her go, Rand realized his opinion of her remained unchanged. Claire Bancroft was a piece of work.

* * *

It was after midnight before Rand rapped lightly on Claire's door. He had just left Cutch in command for the next watch. The winds were easy from the east and the seas were smooth. *Cerberus* was running at a good clip, and a full moon lighted her way.

That same moon cast everything in Claire's cabin in a pale blue-and-gray light. Rand eased himself inside and leaned against the door, locking it behind him. Claire was sitting at the foot of her bed, her face and figure limned by the light. She pulled the brush through her hair one more time before she set it aside and came to her feet. Her thin lawn nightgown drifted from her knees to her ankles.

"Rand?"

That she said his name as a question surprised him. He had become accustomed to her knowing him. "Could it be anyone else?" he asked.

"You were so quiet. First in the companionway, then at the door. I had to be certain."

Though he realized she hadn't answered him precisely, Rand let the matter rest. "Come here, Claire."

She hesitated, but only for a moment. She crossed the room to where he was standing.

Rand raised one hand. His fingers brushed the scooped neckline of her shift from her shoulder to just above her breast. The movement raised her nipple against the heel of his hand. "I believe you have something to tell me," he said lowly.

Claire's own voice was not raised above a whisper. "It doesn't matter what use you might make of me," she said. "I find I want you too much to mind terribly. You don't have to worry that there will be terms. Even one."

His fingers curled around the edging of her nightgown and tugged. He drew her closer. "And if *I* want marriage?"

Claire was careful to keep her face expressionless. She shook her head. "I wouldn't do that to you."

"Do what?"

"Allow you to take on one more responsibility."

"One more burden, you mean. That's what you're thinking."

She didn't deny it. Rand's fingers loosened on her gown. His hand drifted lower until he was cupping her breast. Claire felt her breathing become unsteady and shallow. It didn't seem that he held only her breast, but her heart as well. Without any discernible movement on his part, Rand was able to lift her on tiptoe. Using his other hand, he palmed the nape of her neck. It only took the smallest pressure to make her lift her face.

His mouth slanted across hers. Open. Hungry. Deep. His tongue plunged into her mouth. His lips pressed hers hard. He felt her hands rise between their bodies. She gripped his jacket and held on tightly. She could have been drowning, he thought, and she reached for him when she couldn't draw a breath.

He picked her up, carrying her the short distance to the bed. The covers were folded down, but he laid her on top of them. He had thought about this—her body, slim and pale in moonlight, her beautiful breasts tipped with silver. She lifted her arms languidly as he raised the nightgown over her head, and when he was silent, just staring at her, she seemed to know and gave him the practiced smile of a temptress.

"My God, Claire." Then he covered her mouth again.

She felt that he would crawl inside her skin if he could. It did not seem to be enough that he could touch her everywhere, that she opened and responded with sybaritic sensuality. He wanted what he couldn't touch as well: her sigh, her secrets, her soul.

Claire helped him out of his jacket and shirt. He removed his boots and stood to get out of his trousers and drawers. She was still kneeling when he sat back down. He reached for her, circling her back, and brought her close enough to take her breast in his mouth. Her fingers curled in his hair, holding him there. He heard her breath catch, and then he drew her down to the bed.

His palms ran across her skin from her shoulders to her wrists. He kissed the inside of her elbow and, later, the inside of her thigh. She contracted around the two fingers he slipped inside her. Her throat arched and a voice that she did not recognize as her own said his name.

There was pressure at the juncture of her thighs. The heel of his hand rubbed her. She pushed into him, hips grinding. He whispered something against her hair that she could not make out over her own harsh breathing. She held his shoulders as the heat and tension inside her mounted. He kissed her again, this time with the same slow rhythm as his fingers moving inside her. She whimpered at first.

Then she cried out. There were starbursts behind her closed eyes, pulsing white lights that beat in time with her heart. For a moment it was just as if all the stars in the sky were rushing toward her. For a moment it was as if she could see.

Rand kissed the corner of her mouth, her chin. His lips touched her eyelids and he tasted the salty dampness of her tears. His entire body went still.

"Claire? What—"

But she was shaking her head and there was nothing sad in her faint smile. She found the side of his face and brushed his mouth with her thumb. "Later," she said softly. "Come inside me now."

Rand levered himself up. He raised Claire's knees and pressed them back. He looked down at himself, at her, and realized he wanted her to see this, to know how powerfully erotic the sight of their joining was. "Look at us, Claire," he said. Then he took her hand and made her see for herself.

Afterward they lay quietly, curled together, her bottom against the cradle he made for her. There was a heaviness in her arms and legs. And between her thighs there was a pleasant throbbing. "I can still feel you inside me," she whispered.

Rand stroked her naked shoulder. "I wish I was." His first thrust had been deep. The fingers she had curled intimately around him had not insisted on gentleness, and she asked for nothing except his passion. He had wanted to stay with her, joined just as they were, balanced on the curl of a wave, but her body contracted around him, her arms, her legs, and then the damp, velvet walls that held him to her. He rocked against her, again and again, unable to help himself or wanting to. Claire spoke only once and then the sound of her voice had seemed unreal. "Did you really tell me you wanted me to—"

His mouth nestled close to her ear and he whispered the last words.

"I think I must have," she said. Claire didn't have to touch her cheeks to know they were flaming. "There wasn't anyone else here."

He chuckled and kissed the spot on her shoulder his thumb had been idly rubbing. Silence lay over them like another blanket. Rand did not especially want to disrupt it, not when it felt so comfortable and right, yet he didn't see that he had a choice. "You said you'd tell me about your tears."

A peculiar stillness settled over Claire. It was not rooted in wariness or fear, but in absolute calm. It took her a moment to recognize it for what it was: serenity. "I suppose this means it's later," she said.

"Yes." Rand's palm lay over the curve of her hip.

Claire reached for his hand and laced her fingers with his. "For a few seconds it was as if I could see," she whispered.

He couldn't believe he had heard her correctly. He started to speak, but she silenced him by squeezing his hand.

"It wasn't sadness that made me cry, Rand. It was joy. That's what you gave me." Almost involuntarily, Claire moved a little, pressing back against his chest and thighs. She lifted his hand and brought it around her waist. She used his body like a sling to support her while she rested and healed. "Have you ever pressed the heels of your hands against your eyes?" she went on. "Pressed hard enough to get a burst of color or light behind your lids?"

"I've done that," he said.

"That's what it was like," she told him. "Red and orange and yellow. And lots of white light hurtling toward me." Claire lifted his hand to her mouth and kissed it. "It was as if I had remembered how to see. You gave me that when you gave me pleasure. It was a gift as beautiful as it was unexpected."

He simply held her then. She didn't seem to expect any reply, and Rand was glad for that. The hard ache at the back of his throat would have prevented one.

Sleep claimed Claire first. For a time Rand remained propped on one elbow, looking down on her while she slept, just to remind himself that he could.

It was the absence of Rand's warmth that woke Claire. She stretched, sleepily at first, then with more purpose. Her finger-tips curled around the edge of the bed. Her toes found the frame. "Rand?"

At the sound of her voice, Rand turned away from the stove. "I'm over here," he said. "I was adding some coals." He dropped the small shovelful in and shut the door. "In a few more days we'll be in warmer waters. You won't need this at night."

"I don't need it now," she said. Claire ran her hand over the depression his body had made in her bed. "I was fine until you left."

He put the shovel down and went back to the bed. He sat on the edge. "But when you get up you're going to thank me."

"I'm not getting up."

"Yes, you are. Now that you're awake, I want to show you something."

Claire snorted softly at his tactics. She would have been sleeping soundly if he hadn't left the bed. To her way of thinking, adding coals to the stove had been his not-so-subtle way of waking her. "Is it late?" she asked, pushing herself up to her elbows.

"Define late." He watched moonlight cover her breasts as the blanket slipped to her waist.

"Late as in the sun has been up for an hour or more."

"Oh." He leaned forward and kissed her on the mouth. "Then it's very, very early." Rand felt a smile nudge her lips. Her hands circled his neck and held him close. She deepened the kiss and would have brought him down on her if he hadn't taken her by the wrists and gently released himself. "Come on," he urged her. "I promise you, you won't be sorry."

"I'm sorry already," she said. "May I have my robe? It's in the armoire."

Rand handed Claire her nightshift, then found her robe. He helped her into it and belted it for her. He used the ties to draw her close just long enough to kiss her hard; then he nudged her toward the door while she was still too dazed to protest.

Claire tried to dig her heels in when she realized they were going into the companionway. "Where are you taking me?" she whispered.

"To my workroom."

"In the middle of the night?"

"Seems so." He tugged her hand and pulled her a few steps forward. "Pretend it's the middle of the day."

"But I'm in my nightgown. What if someone sees us?"

"Don't worry about that. How will you know if I don't tell you?"

Claire's brows rose. Speechless astonishment gave way to laughter. When he finally dragged her into the workroom, she was nearly breathless with it. Claire threw her arms around him and hugged him tightly. She kissed him on the neck, on the underside of his jaw. "Thank you for that," she said softly against his mouth. "Thank you for expecting so much from me. Until you, no one believed I could laugh at myself. I'm not certain I believed it either." She kissed him one more time, hard. "Now, what is it you're so driven to show me?"

Rand led her to the worktable and pulled out a stool for her. "Sit here." Claire responded dutifully. She sat up straight and placed her folded hands on the table. Her mouth was primly set as she put forth her best imitation of a compliant schoolroom miss.

Amused, Rand told her, "There's moonlight enough in here for me to see if you smirk."

"Then I shall be very careful not to."

"Hmmm."

Claire's head cocked to one side as she followed his movements. He left her alone at the table and walked behind her to the shelves of specimens, then beyond that to the books. She heard him murmur a few titles under his breath before he found what he was looking for. He returned to her and placed what was in his hands on the table in front of her.

"Go on," Rand said. "You can look at it."

Claire's hands unfolded and she reached for the book. She

ran her fingers around the edge of it, judging its size and thickness. It was a cloth-bound book, not covered in leather. The cut of the pages was uneven and the spine was not professionally bound. "This is one of your journals," she said. There were a few others like it on the shelf, she knew, mixed among his books on botany and wildlife. "Mr. Cutch let me explore your library a time or two. I thought I might like him to read from your science books, but I came to realize I wasn't ready for that."

"He told me."

She nodded, glad Rand didn't press. "What's special about this journal?"

Rand reached over her and opened it about a third of the way back. "This journal isn't actually mine, in that I didn't write it. It's a collection of some of the writings of more than a score of scholars. All of them naturalists, some of it going back a few hundred years. Go ahead, you can touch the pages."

Claire laid her fingertips lightly on the pages that were open to her. "The duke has some illuminated manuscripts among his collection," she said.

"They're more valuable than what I have here." Rand placed his hands on her shoulders. "The page you're open to right now, for instance, is something that was written only a hundred years ago. It's a recipe for distilling cherry bark into a cough syrup. The writer drew a beautifully detailed picture of the tree, the leaves and fruit, and the bark. I bought it from a family in Boston a few years ago. They found it lining the bottom of a trunk they were prepared to burn."

"It seems a miracle that you came by it."

"No miracle. Word of mouth. This journal is filled with other fortunate finds. I started it in London when I was studying at Oxford." He turned several more pages and let her lay her fingers on them again. "This is information on quinine. As best as I can tell, the author penned his notes on its medicinal values sometime between 1625 and 1640." He made another search. "Here, this tells about the benefits of arsenic."

"A recipe for murder."

"Yes, but no one knew it at the time."

"Is everything in English?"

"No. There's Latin, French, German. Some of the scholars made their notes backward."

"Mirror writing, you mean? Like Da Vinci?"

"Exactly like that. I don't have anything by him, but there are a few other . . ." His voice trailed off as he carefully turned more pages. "Here's one. These are notes by Henry Baker."

"The English naturalist?"

"The same." Rand watched Claire's fingertips move slowly over the paper as if she could absorb the writing into her bloodstream and the knowledge into her brain. There was a kind of reverence in her touch. When her exploration slowed, he turned her hand aside and went deeper into the collection. "These are notes by Kölreuter about his fertilization experiments on plants."

Claire's voice was awed. "I studied his work. My father tried to replicate the experiments in Solonesia." She lifted her head. "You've given me such an honor. I can only imagine how much Sir Griffin would like to see your collection. I had no idea what you had here. Thank you for sharing it with me."

Her gratitude was heartfelt and Rand realized that for her this was enough. There was no need for him to go any farther, share anything else. She already believed that what he had shown her was a part of himself. It was true, in a way, but it was also true that he used it to hide something as well. Rand turned the pages again. When he found what he wanted he placed Claire's hands on top.

"This is why we came here," he said quietly. "This is what I want you to see."

Claire smiled a little at his words. It was almost as if she could. "What is it?" she asked. "James Cook's ship log? Darwin's notes on the Galapagos?"

"It's the Hamilton riddle."

Chapter Ten

With a small surprised cry, as if she had been burned, Claire jerked her hands away from the pages. She might have moved from the table altogether if not for Rand's hands on her shoulders pinning her down.

"Steady," he said. "I didn't expect it would frighten you."

Claire laughed a little uneasily. "It did, didn't it?" She placed her fingertips on the edge of the table first, then slid them slowly toward the journal. "Who knows it's here?" she asked.

"You."

The enormity of what he was telling her was not lost on Claire. It had the power to rob her of her next breath.

Rand bent and kissed the crown of her head. "Captain James Hamilton kept it in his ship's log for a number of years. At various other times the familys kept it in a locked box, in a shoe, pressed between the pages of a Bible, beneath a portrait of the captain himself and—during the Revolution—sewn in the lining of my great-grandfather's cocked hat. Shelby was the one who thought it was time to hide it in plain sight. He suggested creating a collection of writings where we could insert the riddle. Had he lived, this would have been a selection of poems from the last 400 years. I decided to hide it among what interested me. This page isn't so different from any of the oldest entries in the collection. The handwriting is no more neat than others. At first glance it could be a foreign language.''

"The riddle's in English?"

"Yes. It's difficult to know that until you hold it up to a mirror. It's written entirely backwards.''

"Just like some of the other notes."

"That's right."

"Hiding in plain sight."

"Hmmm. Would you like to hear it?"

Claire hesitated. "All of it this time? Are you certain?"

"Quite certain."

Claire still did not give her agreement. She reached backward and touched one of his hands with hers. "All right," she said finally, resolved to be worthy of this enormous trust. "I'd like that."

Rand's eyes remained fixed on the dark crown of Claire's hair. There was no reason to look at the journal open in front of her. He hadn't lied to the duke or Claire when he told them it was committed to his memory.

Seven sisters, cursed every one
Seven sisters, all alone
One more lovely than the other
Each, at heart, as cold as stone

Blood will run
Flames will come
Blazing sun, blinding some
Blades lifted high across the plain
Flood waters rising, months of rain
A plague will ink clouded skies
Grieving, shadows beneath thy eyes

Seven sisters, cursed every one
Seven sisters, all alone

Await the day, when reunited
They will be placed upon their throne

Rand waited patiently as Claire took it in. When she spoke, he was not disappointed. She connected very quickly to a brief conversation they had shared in London.

"Seven sisters," Claire whispered. "The tikis on Pulotu. I told you about them, do you remember?"

"I couldn't forget."

Claire nodded. "That was when you made your decision to bring me, wasn't it?"

"Yes."

"I'm not sorry I told you, then." She leaned into Rand's embrace. "I'm glad I'm here with you."

Rand stroked her hair. "So am I."

"I want to learn the riddle," she said. "Will you repeat it?"

There was no hesitation. Rand went through it again, then a third time until Claire could say it herself without missing a word.

"But what does it mean?" she asked, mulling it over. "You told the duke it had something to do with gems."

"It's a description of the most valuable part of the treasure," Rand said. "The seven sisters aren't the tikis you've seen on Pulotu. They're seven precious stones."

"I'm afraid you've lost me."

Rand nudged Claire off her stool. He lifted her easily onto the work table and took up her vacated seat.

She laughed. "Why did you do that?"

"Because I like to look at you," he said simply. Rand saw disbelief and pleasure war in her expression. "You can believe me, Claire. I really do like to look at you." He laid his hands on her thighs, just above her knees. "You may be indifferent to the fact that you're a woman, but I'm not."

Claire's lush mouth parted fractionally as she expelled a soft breath. "I find I'm not so indifferent as I used to be."

Rand's hands dipped under her robe and slid farther up her thighs. Her small shiver was communicated to him. "Now what was it you wanted to know?" he asked.

There was a catch in Claire's throat. "About the gems," she said. "I don't understand." Rand was methodically raising her nightgown. The hem tickled her calves, then her knees. She felt it on her thighs. "Everything . . . everything about the riddle sounds like a curse."

"Blood will run," he said. "What color comes to mind?"

"Color?" Rand had leaned forward and placed his mouth on her knee. "Red," she said a trifle shakily. "Blood is red."

"Hmmm. A ruby."

"Flames will come?" she asked.

"Orange." Rand's mouth moved higher. "Did you know there are orange sapphires?"

"Blazing sun." Claire felt Rand's fingers against her hips. He was pulling her inexorably to the very edge of the table. "Yellow."

"There are sapphires that color also. It only takes trace amounts of certain elements to change the color." He spread her thighs slowly. The scent of their earlier lovemaking lingered. "Blades lifted high across the plain?"

In her mind's eye Claire saw a legion of swords raised, all of them glittering like mirrors in the sunlight. "Silver. A diamond?"

Rand shook his head. His cheeks brushed her thighs. "Blades of grass," he told her. "Green. An emerald."

Claire's fingers threaded in his coppery hair. "Flood waters . . . rising." Her shift was bunched around her hips now.

"Months of rain," Rand said.

"Rain . . . pale . . . like an aquamarine."

"Yes." The word was soft against her warm skin. "A plague will ink clouded skies."

Claire closed her eyes at the first intimate caress of his lips. "I don't know," she said.

"Stormy indigo skies," he whispered. "Deep, deep blue."

"A perfect sapphire."

He raised his head and unbelted her robe. "Lean back, Claire."

She obeyed slowly, feeling him lift her thin shift and place a kiss on her flat belly. It was so very difficult to think. Claire struggled to remember the next line of the riddle. "Grieving, shadows beneath . . . beneath thy eyes."

Rand smiled at the thread of triumph in her voice. "Violet," he told her softly. "Violet shadows. Like an amethyst." The next sound was Claire's soft cry and the triumph was Rand's.

He touched her with his lips and tongue and teeth. Stroking. Caressing. He listened to the sound of pleasure rising, the little breaths that she took and held for a moment at the back of her throat. He felt her fingers drift from his hair to the tabletop and heard her nails scrape lightly across the surface as she searched for purchase.

She never found it. Her fingers curled around nothing and she pressed them into tight fists, marking her own palms with savage little crescents. Claire bit her lip, turning every sensation inward as quickly as Rand brought them to the surface. There was a ripple across the plane of her abdomen and a swelling in her breasts. Claire's throat was charged with the vibration of all the words she held back. Heat skimmed along her skin, then slipped beneath it. There was warmth in the taut muscles of her calves and thighs and along the length of her inner arms. Her blood simmered. And just at the place where Rand's mouth created an almost unbearable pressure, there was fire.

Claire cried out his name hoarsely. Her body lifted, arched, every slender cord held momentarily in the taut line of passion. Distantly she heard the distinctive thud of the stool as it hit the floor, and the table was jarred roughly as Rand came to his feet. Standing between her parted thighs he unfastened his trousers. Then he was thrusting himself deeply inside her, driving her last breath out.

The movement of his body was as hard as he was. He held her hips still except for the rhythm he forced on her and she accepted. Every stroke was deep, and the sensation of losing himself in her was one they shared. He surged against her, rocking Claire back when the table itself would not lift. Her tiny cry urged him on until he was a single nerve ending. His body quickened and he moved in her shallowly, draining himself and her of every last pulse of pleasure.

Claire lay quietly under him. His head rested between her

breasts and he was still inside her. Unmoving, she could feel the hammering of his heart and her own. Each ragged breath was warm and somehow reassuring.

Rand pushed himself up to his elbows and looked at Claire's face. Moonshine bathed her features in iridescent light. Her skin glowed in the aftermath of spent passion. Only her dark eyes were opaque and without depth. The faintly almond shape lent them mystery, but nothing could soften their remote character. Without quite knowing why, he suddenly ached for her.

Straightening, Rand eased himself out of her. He helped her sit up, stepping from between her parted thighs. He watched her push somewhat self-consciously at her nightgown while he repaired his trousers.

"What is it?" she asked quietly. Claire belted her robe carefully as if it was the most important task she had ever undertaken.

"What do you mean?"

"Something's changed. I can feel it."

Frowning, Rand raked his hair. How was it possible for her to be so sensitive to the shift in his mood? "You're mistaken." He placed his hands on either side of Claire's waist with the intention of helping her down. She stopped him by gripping the edge of the table and refusing to be moved.

"And you're lying," she said flatly. Claire was once again keenly aware of her surroundings. She had just allowed him to have her on his work table and had never thought to gainsay him. "Have I given you a disgust of me? Is that it?"

"No!" Rand said vehemently. "My God, no. Leave it, Claire. It was nothing like that."

"Then what was it like?" she asked stubbornly.

Rand picked up the fallen stool and set it down hard. Out of the corner of his eye he saw Claire start at the sound. His voice was terse, stiff. "Sorry."

She shrugged. "So now you're angry."

He swore softly. "You're like a dog with a bone."

Claire nodded, not at all offended.

"A large, unpleasant dog," he added.

She smiled, baring her teeth and clicking them together lightly.

Rand stared at her, shaking his head. His own smile flickered. "There was a moment," he began quietly, in the manner of a confession. "A moment afterwards when I was reminded that you're blind."

Claire felt a tightening in her chest. It was difficult to breathe. She made herself listen because she had asked to hear. "Go on."

"That's it," he said.

"It can't be." Claire's chin lifted at a defiant angle. "Did you feel sorry for me, Rand? Is that what happened?"

"No."

"Sorry for yourself, then. Sorry your fortunes are all tangled up with a blind woman who is—"

"Stop it, Claire."

"Who is so lacking in every respect—"

"Claire."

"Including self-respect, that she'll let you take her in any manner you choose."

As if she had struck him, Rand took a step back.

Claire's dark eyes glittered with unshed tears and her lower lip trembled. "Do you feel pity for me now, Rand?"

"No," he said quietly. "Leave it at that."

Her head drooped suddenly, as if it had become too heavy for the slender stem of her neck, and she could no longer keep her shoulders squared off. Her grip on the edge of the table loosened and she slid off slowly. Rand was so silent that she no longer had any idea where he stood in the room. She did not expect that her first step would put her into his arms.

Rand held her closely, her face pressed against his shoulder. She was crying softly, and tears stung his own eyes. "It was an ache," he whispered. "That's what I felt. Not pity. Not anything like it. It was selfishness that made me wish I could take away your blindness. I wasn't satisfied that I could see proof of pleasure in your flushed complexion or your damp mouth. Or that I had felt it all just moments earlier. I wanted to see it reflected in your eyes. You were right at the outset.

What I thought I was feeling for you was really about me . . . about what I can't do for you.''

Claire shuddered a little as she tried to rein in her sobs. ''I don't . . . don't know what I'll do if . . . if I can never see again.''

Gripping her by the shoulders, Rand held her back far enough to study her face. ''What does that mean?'' he asked roughly.

Her own voice was just a thread of sound. ''You must never feel sorry for me, Rand. I count on that. I need it. I do so much of it myself . . . you can't imagine.'' She laughed a little unsteadily. ''Or maybe you can.''

No, he thought; he couldn't. Claire gave so few clues. ''Do you love me?'' he demanded.

Except for the blink she could not help, Claire went perfectly still. She had the sense that she wasn't standing on her own any longer, but was being held up by him. She felt as weightless as the breath she exhaled. ''Yes,'' she said.

Rand hauled her back into his arms. He laid his cheek against the crown of her dark hair and held her steady. ''Then don't tell me you don't know what you'll do.'' Every word was delivered with clipped ferocity. ''No matter what happens, you'll be with me. You'll live with me, grow old with me, and when my sight fails, you'll teach me everything you've learned in these dark years.''

Claire was too shaken to speak.

''I thought you understood what it meant that I brought you here.'' His voice softened. ''Teaching you the riddle, showing you its location, was meant to prove that you matter to me beyond that damn treasure.''

She drew back slightly. Reaching up, Claire touched the side of Rand's face with her fingertips. ''When you say it like that,'' she told him, ''it's almost as if you think I might betray that trust.''

''I was trying to say I don't care if you do.''

''But I wouldn't.''

''It doesn't matter.''

''But say that you know I wouldn't,'' she insisted.

''I *want* to say that I love you.''

"You can say that in a moment. Just now I want to hear that you trust me."

Rand stared at her. She seemed perfectly earnest. "You are a perverse creature."

"Yes."

"Whom I trust without reservation."

Relief washed Claire's features. She nodded faintly. "And?" she prompted softly.

"And whom I love very nearly to distraction."

"Only very nearly?"

"It's your perverseness," he said, "that keeps me anchored."

Claire's thumb brushed the corner of his mouth. She traced the shape of his slight smile. "That's all right, then," she said. Standing on tiptoe, Claire laid her own mouth across that smile. She held him to her just like that, stretched flush against his solid frame, her fingers wrapped around the base of his neck, her eyes closed, and her mouth moving dreamily, unhurriedly over his.

"Can we go back to my cabin?" she asked when she finally broke the kiss.

A little dazed by what had transpired, Rand murmured something that he hoped she would accept as agreement.

Claire lowered herself back to a flat-footed stance. The ship rolled familiarly beneath her. "Check the companionway," she told him. "I'll return your journal to the shelf." She found the heavy journal with no difficulty. It was still lying open on the table just where she and Rand had pushed it when they were otherwise occupied. Claire ran her hand over the page, blushing a little. How would she call the riddle to mind again without thinking of him? Every line bore the imprint of his mouth and hands. *Blood will run . . . Flames will come . . .* She shivered. The tips of her fingers grazed the lower corner of the page, slipping off the journal onto the table.

Behind her, Claire heard Rand open the door to the cabin. She shook her head. The erotic image faded, and with its passing came a certain clarity. Memory was not something that was confined to her head, she realized. She carried it in her fingertips as well. "Rand?"

"It's clear," he said. "Not a soul around."

She barely heard him. Dragging the book closer, Claire fingered the corner of the open page again. There was an edge of urgency in her tone. "Come here."

Rand glanced over his shoulder. Claire hadn't moved from the table. He shut the door and returned to her side. "What is it?"

She pointed to the area of the page she had been examining. "What's this?"

Rand looked. His polished chestnut eyes narrowed as he tried to make out what Claire was pointing to. The pale cast of the moon's light was insufficient. "I need a lantern," he said. "I don't know what you think you've found."

Claire stopped him. "That's because you're not trying to see it through my eyes," she said. "Close yours."

"All right."

"Give me your hand."

It required some peeking on Rand's part to place it in Claire's. If she knew, she didn't admonish him for it. "Now what?" he asked.

Claire lifted the corner of the page carefully. "Feel this," she said. "Both sides."

Now Rand understood and he was astonished. "Do you mean you noticed the holes?"

"Well, yes. You knew they were there?"

"Of course."

"Then why didn't you say so when I asked?"

"I didn't realize that's what you were looking at. There's nothing to see."

Claire squeezed his fingers in frustration, hoping that would open his eyes.

"Ouch," he said softly.

She smiled sweetly and let him go. "Why are there holes in the paper?" she asked. "What do they mean?"

"I don't know, and I don't know."

Claire sighed. "Is there any writing around them, something to distinguish them?"

"No."

She touched the small, raised bumps on the obverse side very carefully. "What made them?"

"I have no idea. I've never speculated."

"Speculate now."

"Well, they're each larger than a pinprick. I told you the riddle was once sewn in the lining of a cocked hat. It could be the needle was pulled through the paper. It also was kept in the heel of a shoe. A cobbler's nail might have pierced it."

"In this fashion?" she asked. "Seven holes arranged in just this way?"

Rand had never observed any particular arrangement. "What are you saying, Claire? That the holes serve some purpose?"

"Might they?"

He shrugged. "What?"

"I don't know."

"Then concede they might be no more than they appear. That paper is three hundred years old. It would be understandable if it were in shreds by now."

"No." Claire shook her head. "No, it wouldn't. Your family has taken great care to make certain that hasn't happened. Generations of Hamiltons have found a way to preserve it. The edges aren't tattered. I don't think it spent very much time in that hat or shoe. The paper hasn't been permanently creased. The folds have been flattened out again. You've done the most damage to it by binding it into this journal. If these holes had been on the other side of the paper, they could be overlooked completely."

"They've been overlooked for three centuries," Rand pointed out wryly. "What I don't understand is why you think they have any significance."

"Can you hold the page up to the light?"

"I suppose."

"Do it."

Rand picked up the journal and carried it over to the porthole. He held it up so that only the page with the riddle hung free.

He turned it a little to the left, then the right. Moonlight coming through the leaded glass defined the exact position of each hole. There were seven of them, he noticed. Seven. Why had that never imprinted on his brain before? It made him wonder how long ago the knowledge of them had been lost. At what point had one Hamilton father neglected to relate the importance of the tiny holes to his son? And when had someone neglected to relate their existence?

"Can you see them?" Claire asked. She sat on a stool.

"Yes," he said, lowering the book.

"Does it remind you of anything?"

"The Big Dipper." Rand closed the journal and returned it to the shelves. "Is that what you meant?"

She nodded. "I thought the same thing."

"And you believe that's significant to the treasure?"

"Couldn't it be?"

"I don't know. We're far below the equator. The Dipper isn't visible in the southern skies." He came to stand in front of her and considered her thoughtfully. "I've always given you full marks for intelligence," he said. "And quickness."

A small crease appeared between Claire's brows. There was something in his voice that made her doubt he would go on in this complimentary manner.

"But this is astonishing," he continued. "Even for you." She nodded. "I've seen something like it before."

Rand's eyes narrowed fractionally. "Where?"

"Abberly Hall. In my godfather's personal museum."

"When?"

"Not long before I left London. It was the first time I'd been in his treasure room in years." She reached for him and found his forearm. "Could we go back to my cabin now? I don't mind explaining it to you. I would just rather do it there."

He took her by the wrist and led her to the door. The companionway was still clear. Rand ushered Claire into it. There was no reason to hurry other than his own need to know what she did. It seemed to take an interminably long time to reach her cabin.

Claire shrugged out of her robe and hung it on the inside

door of the armoire. She crawled back into bed and scooted back to leave a space for Rand. "We can talk as well here as there," she said practically. "It's warmer here."

Rand shucked his trousers and joined her. Claire's knees bumped his as she made herself comfortable. He drew the blankets up to their shoulders and propped himself on one elbow.

Claire had no trouble sensing that he was waiting. "You're going to be disappointed," she said. "I really know so little. I found a paper similarly marked in one of Stickle's illuminated manuscripts. I suppose your brother Shelby was not the only one with the idea of hiding something in plain sight."

"So it seems."

"This was not attached as yours was. Which is how I found it. It came away in my hand as I was looking through the book." Claire's mouth curled to one side as she realized how odd that would sound to him. "I know," she said flatly. "Why does a blind woman look through a book?"

"I hesitated to ask."

Claire pressed her fist lightly into Rand's hard belly. She had to be satisfied with the small grunt he gave in response. "I was reacquainting myself with the duke's treasures, if you must know. You can't imagine what he has there. Broadswords from the Norman invasion. Suits of armor. Tapestries. Bracelets from Egypt. Coins. Precious stones. Books. I was touching almost everything, trying to remember what it was like when I could see all of it. It sounds silly now, but then . . . then it seemed so very important."

"I understand," said Rand.

Claire lay back. Her smile was gentle. "I believe you do." She paused, picking up the threads of her thoughts. "I came across my discovery by accident. The paper was of a different quality than those that properly belonged to the manuscript. I suspect it wasn't as old actually. A sighted person would have known immediately it didn't belong. Stickle wasn't quite so clever as you."

"Clever enough."

"The holes were arranged in the same manner as they are

on your paper. I thought it might be some sort of celestial map."

"Not likely."

"I realize that now. Do you think I was really holding the Waterstone riddle?"

"That's what you think, isn't it?"

She nodded almost imperceptibly. "I suspect the duke is your biggest rival for the treasure."

"Is he? Then why have I never known that? I've been searching for it for years. This is the first time he's ever approached me. Why do you think that is?"

"I don't know."

"Neither do I." It bothered Rand because he suspected Claire was right. The Duke of Strickland probably *was* his foremost rival. It begged the question of why he would have been content to remain so long in the background. "I don't suppose you know how your godfather might have come by the Waterstone riddle?"

"No." She sighed. "Do you know, I meant to ask him about the paper in the manuscript. I was rather pleased with my discovery, but then there was so much to be done before I sailed that it left my mind. I might never have thought about it again if it hadn't been for your riddle."

Rand was not unhappy that she had failed to mention her find to Strickland. He said nothing to let her know that. "Do you think the duke's interest is because of the gems?"

"I suspect so. Especially the sapphires. I don't think there is a collection anywhere to match his."

"You remember it well?"

"I don't know how well, but yes, it's not the sort of thing one forgets. I was a child the first time I saw it. My mother accompanied me to Abberly Hall." Her laughter was a trifle self-mocking. "Do you hear how self-important I thought I was? It would be more correct to say I accompanied my mother. I was the duke's goddaughter, of course, but she was his friend. He let me wander through his museum and touch anything I liked. It made Mama nervous, but Stickle didn't seem to mind. I wore an ornamental headdress that belonged to an Egyptian queen and ropes of silver and gold around my neck. My mother pronounced me spectacularly garish. Stickle said I was bedazzling.'' Her smile deepened. ''I'm certain Mama was in the right of it. I remember sitting on the floor, playing with the duke's sapphires and rubies while he and my mother walked and talked. Some of the stones were nearly as big as my fist. Remember, though, in those days it was a small fist.''

Rand was still impressed. ''Even so, those are large stones. If that's his pleasure, then I can understand why he wants the seven sisters. Even if three hundred years has exaggerated their size, I expect they will still dazzle.''

''Just like in the old rhyme,'' she said, a shade sleepily.

''Hmmm. *One more lovely than the other . . . Each, at heart, as cold as stone.*''

''Not your riddle,'' she told him. Claire stretched and turned on her side again, this time with her back to Rand. She closed her eyes. ''I meant like the nursery rhyme. You know, the one that ends with something like: *With the sisters, this verse brings . . . Wealth beyond the dreams of kings.*''

''*And all the king's horses and all the king's men, couldn't put Humpty Dumpty—*''

Claire's husky laughter cut him off. ''I think you're mixing your Mother Goose verses.''

Rand laid his head on his arm and curled against her. ''If you say so.''

''I do.'' She made an abrupt little yawn. ''Will you wake me before you leave?''

''If you'd like.''

She nodded. His fingers had slipped under her hair, and she felt them run lightly across her nape. She felt herself relax. Her arms and legs grew heavy. When she finally spoke, even her voice was thick. ''I would like to help you find your treasure.''

Rand didn't answer. He wondered what she would think if he told her she already had.

The days and nights grew warmer as *Cerberus* sailed into tropical waters. Following the path of the glowing star Sirius, the ship stayed on a true course for Raiatea in the Society Islands. While the clipper maintained a steady speed of ten to twelve knots, Claire noticed that the crew moved more slowly. Island time, Rand called it. The men were already anticipating the less demanding pace of life in the Sun Islands.

Rand sat on the edge of the bed, Claire on the floor between his splayed legs, and lazily pulled a brush through her thick hair. "I met Cutch in the companionway this morning as I was leaving your cabin."

"It was only a matter of time," she said. With Rand joining her in her cabin almost every night for the past week, it would have been odder if the change in their relationship had gone undiscovered. "I think Mr. Cutch—and probably most of the crew—has known for days."

"Truly?"

Claire laughed at his naivete. "It's not as if we've taken any special pains to hide our affair."

Rand didn't especially like the term *affair,* but he didn't bring it to her attention. She would ask him for a better description, and he didn't have one. "You're not upset?"

"No." Claire reached up and caught his wrist as he would have made another pass with the brush. "I'm not ashamed, Rand. I have no reason to mind that anyone knows about us." She felt him stiffen slightly, as if he were prepared to take issue with her. Claire shook her head, cutting Rand off, and released him. "Tell me what Mr. Cutch said."

"How do you know he said anything?"

"Because he's your mentor, your friend. He wouldn't let the moment pass."

Rand's deep chuckle signaled that he had finally found some humor in it. "He asked me if I knew what I was doing."

"And you said . . .?"

"I said 'yes.' "

"That's all?"

"It satisfied Cutch. He went on about his business and I attended to mine."

Claire smiled. "It must have been the *way* you said it. I

imagine Mr. Cutch would have liked to press for more information.''

Rand agreed, but said nothing. He did not explain that this time with Claire was so precious to him that he did not want to share any part of it with others, even Cutch. He did not want to explain himself or be forced to think of the consequences. ''Has he said anything to you?''

''No. I wouldn't expect him to. Mr. Cutch likes me, but he loves you.''

The brush strokes slowed, then finally stopped. ''Are you telling me I *should* talk to him?''

''I'm telling you that I don't mind if you do. I have much more experience with affairs than you do, Rand. I think I know what to expect. I'm not certain about you.''

Rand put the brush aside. He tipped her head back and studied her features for a moment. She was perfectly serious, he realized. Rand let her go. ''What in God's name are you talking about?''

Claire moved outside the vee of Rand's splayed legs and stood. The back of her gown was partially undone, and she pulled the neckline back where it had fallen over her shoulder. She smoothed the sateen material across her midriff. It was cool under her fingers. Her features were composed, solemn, when she turned to face him, but there was a shakiness to the breath she drew. ''I heard what you said about forever,'' she told him. ''I know you believe you will always want me, that you will always feel about me as you do now. I treasure that, Rand. I *do*. I just think about it differently. Experience says that I should.''

It was difficult for Rand to remain seated. He did because he couldn't think of one thing that would be gained by towering over her. ''What experience?'' he asked with credible calm. ''Claire, I know there's never been anyone else. Whose affair are you talking about? Your father's?''

''My mother's.''

Rand stared at her. He wondered why he had never suspected. There had been hints, now that he thought about it, but he hadn't heard Claire with the same keen ear she turned on him.

He really hadn't known. "The Duke of Strickland," he said at last.

Claire nodded. Her smile was rueful. "My godfather." She found the edge of the desk and skirted it. The chair scraped against the floor as she pulled it out. Claire sat down, her hands folded in her lap. "Perhaps I should have told you."

"I can't think of any reason that you should have—until now. If your mother's affair is making you have some doubts about us, then now is precisely the time you should tell me."

Claire drew in a long breath and let it out slowly. "There is not so very much to tell. It's not even a particularly unusual story. If I hadn't observed the pain of it firsthand, I might think it simply melodramatic and trite."

"May I decide for myself?"

Claire closed her eyes briefly, her acquiescence a barely perceptible nod. "My mother's family had large aspirations but very little consequence. My grandfather was a baron whose penchant for horses and horse racing nearly bankrupted the small fortune of his forebears. What my mother had was a singular beauty that her parents thought could be parlayed into a marriage that would support them all.

"Mother made an impact her first Season. There were any number of suitable matches she could have made to please her family, but she wanted Evan Markham. It must have seemed to her that the Duke of Strickland wanted her as well. If Mother understood that her lack of position made an offer impossible, then she never acknowledged it. Perhaps she believed he would change his mind. I don't know the extent to which their affair progressed at that time. At the end of the Season they were on separate courses. Stickle had proposed marriage to the daughter of an earl. My mother had accepted the most unlikely candidate among all her suitors."

"Sir Griffin."

"He was just Mr. Bancroft then. A mere professor. His interest in the natural sciences was not the frivolous pastime of a peer. He actually *worked* at it." Claire's tiny smile was wry. "My mother's family was convinced he was beneath them in every conceivable way. There was some belief that Mother had accepted him just to spite everyone else.''

''Strickland included?'' Rand asked.

Claire shrugged. ''Perhaps. I don't know. Actually, I've always thought that my godfather may have encouraged the match.''

Rand's eyes narrowed, his expression thoughtful. ''What makes you say that?''

''Just little things I heard over the years.''

Rand understood then that Claire's talent for listening was not simply the result of her blindness. She had merely learned to hone a skill that she had always practiced. ''Then what you know is not because of what either of your parents told you.''

She laughed at that. ''God, no. Even Stickle, who can be painfully forthright on occasion, has never discussed this with me.''

''But you know there was an affair.''

''Oh, yes. My mother took me to Abberly Hall quite frequently. I suppose she thought that my presence would somehow conceal the real nature of the visits. I was the duke's godchild, after all. And he doted on me in his own way. What could have been more natural than to see him at his country home?''

''Did your father know?''

''That we visited? Yes, of course. That there was an affair? Yes, eventually. He never asked me. I shall always respect him for that. He seemed to know that I was charged with a terrible secret and he never made me choose between my mother and him. He never once asked me to take sides.'' She sighed. ''The truth is, Rand, I don't know that he cared very deeply about my mother . . . or even about me. Until Tiare and Tipu, I would have said that Sir Griffin's work was all he was capable of loving.''

Rand said nothing. Contradicting her, insisting that her father must have loved her because she deserved to be loved, would have been false reassurance. He didn't know that Sir Griffin had loved her at all.

''Stickle's duchess died in childbirth,'' Claire went on. ''The baby was stillborn. Had she lived, things may have proceeded differently, but in his grief the duke sought out my mother. I was still an infant. I think Stickle asked if he could take some responsibility for my upbringing and my mother agreed to name him my godfather.''

"You must have wondered . . ." Rand's voice trailed off.

"If I was his child?" she asked. "Yes, I've wondered. How could I not? I've never asked, though. I'm not certain that I want to know or even if it matters. I can't think of a thing that would change if it were revealed to me as the truth."

"Tipu wouldn't be your brother."

"It would be a fact of biology," she said. "It would have nothing to do with the way I feel about him. Or anyone else."

"Very well," Rand said. "But I don't understand what your mother's affair has to do with us."

Claire's brows rose fractionally. "You don't? I thought it was clear. There was no future in it. In time it made everyone involved miserable."

"And that's what you expect to happen to us?"

"Expect? I don't know if I would put it that strongly."

"But you wouldn't be surprised."

"No. Not at all."

Rand stood. His fists clenched and unclenched at his sides. He shook off his agitation before he went to Claire's side. He sat on the edge of the desk and propped one foot against her chair. "I never thought of being with you as an affair," he said.

"Give me a better word," she said.

"I thought you might say that. I don't have one. I'm only saying I never thought about being with you in that manner . . . as if it were something illicit or faintly sordid. I love you, Claire. I thought you understood that."

"Stickle loved my mother, I think. She loved him. It didn't change anything."

"We're not them. I'm not arranging your marriage to someone else so I can keep you as my mistress. Claire, do you think that either your mother or the duke had anything but marriages of convenience? It wasn't loving each other that was the tragedy. It was the way they felt obligated to meet the rigid expectations of the social order. I never noticed that you particularly cared about that.''

"I don't," she said softly. "But you do."

"Me?"

"Rand, you fought a war to protect your precious Southern social order. You risk your life to restore your family honor. I don't fool myself into believing I'm the woman you ever imagined at your side.''

"Then take issue with my imagination," he snapped.

Claire's head lifted at the harshness of his tone. She frowned, uncertain. "You're angry."

"God, yes."

Claire felt her chair rock back as Rand's foot pressed harder against it. She steadied herself by holding the arms tightly. "I don't understand."

"Is it simply that you don't believe I can love you, or that I can love anyone?"

"You're twisting what I've said."

"I don't think so, Claire. Why is it so hard for you to accept that I love you?"

Tears made Claire's dark eyes luminous. Her effort to blink them back was not successful. "Because no one ever has."

Rand took her by the upper arms and lifted Claire to her feet. He drew her close, embracing her loosely. She laid her head on his shoulder and closed her eyes. A few tears were squeezed out, dampening her cheeks, then his shirt. He felt them and said nothing.

"My father. Mother. The duke. They were all caught up in their own interests. Most days I was an afterthought. I supposed it was my fault. No one ever told me it wasn't."

"Oh, Claire."

She shrugged, impatient with herself. "Until now I've been practical about it. They were all kind to me when I came to their attention, but I always knew that somehow I was being used. Mother and the duke hid their affair behind me. Father used me to further his research. I can't help it if I'm a bit unsteady with the thought that you love me. I'm afraid it will come to matter too much. As much as I want it, I'm also frightened.''

"Frightened?''

"My mother loved the duke. It destroyed her.''

Gently Rand drew Claire back. He searched her gravely set features. It was clear she believed what she was saying. "How?'' he asked. "Tell me how.''

"She couldn't refuse him. Even when what he asked was unreasonable, potentially dangerous, she couldn't say no.''

"What are you talking about?''

"At first she argued with him about my father going to the South Pacific. I know because I overheard them. When she realized the duke expected her to accompany Sir Griffin, she was furious. What I remember the most was that she couldn't stay angry. In the end she acquiesced. Her small point of rebellion was to insist that I accompany them. My father and the duke were both against it. They wanted me to stay in boarding school. I wanted to be with my mother. I suppose that's what tipped the scales in her favor. In the end she and I sailed with my father. We were gone five years. It could have been longer, but Mother became ill. She died a few months after we returned to London. Stickle was with her. In spite of what happened, she forgave him for sending her away.''

"He couldn't have been responsible for her illness.''

"Her illness couldn't have happened anywhere but the South Pacific. The poisonous fish that cut her in the shallows lives in those waters only. My father did everything he could to cleanse her blood. It wasn't enough. It was a miracle that she survived as long as she did. I think it was because she wanted to see the duke again.''

Rand shook his head. He wished it was in his power to make it right for her. "Do you blame your godfather?''

"No.''

"Your mother, then.''

"She should have been stronger,'' she said quietly. "She let what he wanted be more important to her than what she wanted.''

"She wanted to be with him,'' said Rand.

"Yes."

"And could she have done that if she had stayed behind?"

"Of course."

Rand touched Claire's cheek. His thumb brushed away the last traces of tears. "Really? They probably had more opportunity to see one another with your father in the country than they would with him outside of it. The duke would not have wanted to cast your mother in an ill light. You know as well as I do that it was her reputation that would have suffered the most. I think she did not want to leave him, but I think she understood that it was the wisest course. I don't think you would be who you are if your mother had been a foolish woman. You were a child, Claire, and you've held a child's way of thinking for too many years. Can you not abandon it now and come to know your mother and father and the duke as mere mortals?"

Claire's smile was a shade watery. Her tone was wry. "You mean they may have made mistakes?"

Rand lifted Claire's hand to his face and let her explore the cast of his features. He wanted her to know the depth of his feeling. "Many of them," he said. "But the most serious was not helping you discover how deserving of love you are."

Chapter Eleven

One hundred miles northeast of Tahiti, and part of the same island chain, Raiatea was known as the "mother of lands" because it was the first to be settled in the Society group. It required five more days, with *Cerberus* following the true course of the star Sirius, for the clipper to reach the island's natural harbor.

Claire had wondered how she would feel when the ship finally came upon Raiatea. It was here that her own canoe had landed after the long, harrowing journey over Pacific waters. The islanders had received her with a mixture of great joy and awe bordering on fear. If not for the presence of the British frigate, Claire knew she might have been elevated to the position of a spirit god by her rescuers. She was placed in the care of her countrymen instead and taken away from the island before she could properly thank anyone who had helped her.

"I'm looking forward to expressing my gratitude," Claire told the doctor. "There were times I despaired of being given this opportunity."

"Hmmm." Macauley Stuart was listening to her with only half an ear.

Claire smiled at his distraction. She wondered how much he

had heard of her account. "Are the outriggers coming to meet us?" she asked.

"Yes. There are four of them. Swift as spiders on the water."

Claire remembered. She felt Macauley brush her arm as he leaned forward at the rail. Above her in the yardarms men were calling out, shouting greetings to women on shore who could not possibly hear them. The activity on the ship was still orderly and purposeful, but it was only the presence of the captain and Cutch that kept it that way. Left to their own urges, most of the crew would have thrown themselves overboard and swum for shore.

Claire touched Macauley's forearm to get his attention. "Has the captain said why we're putting down anchor here?"

"Supplies, I suppose," he said. He tore his eyes away from the throng of honey-skinned women on the shore and regarded Claire with some surprise. "You don't know? I thought you had Captain Hamilton's ear."

Claire's mouth flattened briefly. It was not his words she found distasteful, but the meaning he injected into them. Dr. Stuart had never directly said he knew she was involved in an affair with Rand, but he found ways to indicate it nonetheless. "He's said nothing to me," she said levelly. "It was only this morning that Mr. Cutch mentioned we were close to the island."

"There's something secretive about the whole business of being here," Stuart said.

In spite of her wish to be gone from Stuart's company, Claire was intrigued. "Secretive? How?"

Macauley's genial smile was not in evidence. He rubbed his chin, musing. "Whispering when I'm around. Talk that stops when I come into a room. It's only been this last week, I'd say. Do you think it has something to do with the treasure?"

"That may be so, though I suppose it could be any number of things. I didn't realize you were interested in the treasure."

He shrugged. "I wasn't in London. I was clear to the duke on that account. Folderol and folly, I told him. But as we've approached the South Seas, the whole idea of buried treasure seems more reasonable. There's something magical and mysterious about water as clear and blue as the sky and islands that

are ringed with rainbows and mist every morning. I can imagine
now that men would hide their treasure here just for the privilege
of coming back to find it.''

Macauley glanced sideways at Claire. "I've surprised you,
haven't I?"

"A little." She recalled how the doctor had first described
Bria to her. "I'd forgotten you could be a romantic."

His brogue became more noticeable. "Romantic and practical. That's the curse of the Scots."

Claire laughed. It was good to find some enjoyment in his
companionship again. "The outriggers are here, aren't they?"
She could hear them bumping into the hull of *Cerberus*. "Will
you go ashore?"

"If my legs will hold me. I fear they'll crumple on solid
ground."

She patted his arm. "You'll be fine."

Rand chose that moment to join them. "Claire, we're going
to put you in a sling and lower you into one of the canoes."

Her eyes widened. "A sling? I've never done that before. I
don't expect I'll want to do it again soon. Will we be here
long?"

"I don't know," he said, reaching for her hand. "How long
does a wedding take?"

Claire turned on her side sleepily. Her eyes opened as she
rolled into Rand's solid frame. When he didn't stir, she smiled
and pressed a light kiss to the back of his shoulder. He did not
seem to be bothered by the stillness as she was. It was the
unfamiliar silence that woke her. *Cerberus* was virtually
deserted tonight. Except for a man on watch, she and Rand
were the only people on board. It was comforting and somehow
disquieting at the same time.

Just above the steady rhythm of the lapping waves, Claire
could hear the celebration continuing on shore. At this distance
it did not sound so different from the chuckle of the water. It
was a pleasant roar in her ears, one she might not have noticed
if not for the calm surrounding her now.

Fifteen minutes, she thought. That was how long the wedding took. Rand had spent much more time trying to find the missionary. The Reverend Alvin Simmons was finally tracked to a secluded lagoon where he was summarily captured and carried back to his small thatch church. The poor man insisted on having his clothes returned to him before he would carry out the ceremony. Claire thought it was a reasonable request when Cutch told her about it. Rand apparently considered it a monumental waste of time.

Claire pressed the knuckles of one hand against her mouth. It did nothing to stifle her rather giddy smile, but it helped with the urge to laugh. Until the moment Claire made her vows, Rand's manner had been rather commanding and impatient, almost as if he expected her to refuse him. Not that there had ever been a proper proposal of marriage. It had amused Claire that he was not willing to put the question to her. His logic— that she couldn't say no if he didn't ask her outright—was as absurd as it was endearing.

The only other person surprised by Rand's announcement was Macauley Stuart. His observation that there was something secretive about the stop in Raiatea was proven true. The crew had been informed of Rand's plans well in advance of his prospective bride. Claire supposed that was done in the event she tried to launch herself over the side of the ship. In fact she had only launched herself into Rand's arms. The roar of approval on board *Cerberus* had been deafening. Claire had no idea if the doctor added his voice to the congratulatory cacophony or maintained a stoic silence. Until now she hadn't considered what his opinion of the day's events might be.

Claire stretched, then snuggled comfortably against Rand's naked back. She did not want to think about Macauley Stuart or his opinions. If he was worried about what her godfather would say, she would defend him then. It was not as if he could have stopped her, and it was wrong for the duke to expect that he could.

She wondered how strongly opposed her godfather would have been to the match. If the marriage had taken place at Abberly, would he have been able to give her away? What cautions would he have had for her that she had not already heard from Macauley Stuart or thought of herself?

Claire did not linger long on that course of thinking. She certainly had no regrets about her decision. For all that Rand's manner had been rather high-handed, nothing that was done was done against her will.

Recalling the ceremony, Claire's smile was wistful. After the Reverend Simmons's initial bewilderment and accompanying protests, everything about the exchange of vows went as she would have planned herself. It had been the depth of Rand's feeling for her, not nervousness or fear, that had edged his voice with a faint tremor and brought tears to her own eyes. She was radiant, he told her later. She had been from the moment she appeared in the church on Cutch's arm.

Claire had known the rough-hewn pews were filled with the crew from *Cerberus* because Cutch told her, not because any one of them made the slightest noise. They held their collective breath throughout the ceremony, just as if some doubt about the outcome remained. When she asked Rand about it, he had laughed. It wasn't uncertainty that kept them quiet, he said, but awe. They could have extinguished every candle in the church and still seen the ceremony through her luminescent eyes.

It did not seem outside the realm of possibility.

Claire's toes nudged the back of Rand's calves. She drew her foot along their length and rubbed his ankles lightly. Her murmur had the sound of sleepy pleasure.

"That's a very erotic hum," Rand said. His eyes were closed and his voice was heavy with sleep.

"Hmmm." This time Claire's lips touched his back. His skin was deliciously warm. "I didn't realize you were awake."

Rand was skeptical. "It seems as if you've been trying hard enough to make it so."

Claire laid one hand on his hip. "Have I?"

She sounded terribly innocent, Rand thought, but the fingers that were grazing his thigh were experienced. He groaned softly when they reached his groin. Rand laid his hand over hers. She

circled his penis. "The Reverend Simmons would be shocked,"
he said deeply.

"*I'm* shocked," Claire said.

Rand chuckled. He didn't doubt that she was. It seemed that
Claire was often surprised by her capacity for pleasure. She
made love with a certain degree of curiosity and wonder, and
she seemed overwhelmed at times by her ability to arouse him.
She had once described the point at which she lost control and
his fierce passion took over as not being able to put the genie
back in the lamp. It was wildly exciting and just a little alarming.
She hadn't offered her insight as a complaint, merely as a
statement of fact.

Rand turned. He was swelling under her steady stroking. He
kissed her mouth, circling her tongue with his. His knee nudged
her legs apart, and then he was entering her, one warm fist
replaced by the damp velvet walls of another. She sighed. Their
breaths mingled. She contracted around him. For a while they
lay very still, joined together but with no urgency to move. He
nudged her lips, kissed the underside of her jaw. Her tongue
darted out, first to wet her own mouth, then to lick at his. He
took it into his mouth again and sucked. Beneath him her breasts
swelled, and her body held him more tightly. His hips made
an involuntary thrust forward. Hers lifted. They made small
murmurs of pleasure at the same time.

Rand's smile was wry. "I suppose one of us has to move."

Claire's response was a barely audible sigh. She was content
when he accepted it as agreement. In time her breathing became
as measured as his strokes. She concentrated on nothing but
that. She was unaware of how she helped him with the supple
arch of her body. The bending of her knees, the fingers in his
hair, the cradle she made with her thighs, all of this was done
without conscious thought. Her search for pleasure was all
instinct now, just as his was. The rhythm was as primal as the
ebb and flow of the tides, the tug on their senses as unrelenting
as the moon's pull on the seas. There was something profoundly
satisfying in reveling in their bodies' responses.

Claire caught and held her breath as Rand climaxed. He was
deep inside her when he came, and his shudder tripped her

senses. The single nerve that seemed to control every aspect of her pleasure vibrated with perfect pitch. She pushed on Rand's shoulders, then gripped them hard. She surrendered the small cry that was lodged at the back of her throat, and then she was silent. Her body fell still long before her breathing quieted.

"Are you sleeping?" he asked after a moment.

"No. Dead."

Rand grinned and kissed her lightly on the mouth. "You flatter me." He sat up and went to the basin.

Claire didn't think any of her limbs worked. "How can you move?"

"Sheer force of will." He washed himself and then carried a damp cloth back to their bed. She gave a little start when he raised the covers and placed it on her thigh, but then she let him continue. His ministrations were tender, and from Claire's point of view, blessedly quick. She didn't completely relax until Rand tossed the cloth back in the basin and she heard the accompanying splash.

"Do you think I would be more embarrassed if I could see?" she asked.

"I don't see how."

Claire laughed. She felt him crawl into bed beside her. When his thigh rubbed hers she realized he was wearing his drawers again. It came to her that she did not mind being naked when he was not. She liked the idea that he could touch her so freely.

"Your cheeks are flaming," Rand said, looking down on her.

"You would not credit what I was thinking."

"Tell me."

"Not for all the bloody tea in China."

Rand's eyes widened; then he burst out laughing. Claire's prim, butter-wouldn't-melt voice was so completely at odds with her language that he couldn't help himself. Tears actually gathered at the corners of his eyes.

"You're a wretch to laugh," she told him.

"I know." His attempt at a solemn apology failed. It didn't

help that the corners of Claire's mouth were edging upward. "That's a smug smile you have."

Claire blinked. "Do you have a lantern burning in here?" she demanded.

"No," he said, straight-faced. "Candles. Two of them." His tone became more serious when he saw she was about to protest. Rand's fingers slipped into her dark hair and cupped the back of her head. "I wanted to look at my wife while I made love to her. There's no moon tonight, and only one of us in here can see in the dark."

She smiled a little at that. "You might have told me," she said softly.

"I will from now on. Do you want me to put them out?" The candles didn't have much longer to burn, but Rand would have snuffed them immediately if that was Claire's wish.

"No, it's all right . . . now that I know."

"Why does it bother you?"

Claire was silent a moment, collecting her thoughts. "I don't know if I can explain. I suppose I feel less vulnerable when I think you can't see. During the day my disadvantage is clear. I'm more on guard then, more aware of everything I do. At night, especially here in the cabin with you, I don't experience my blindness so keenly. I imagined if there was an advantage, it was mine."

"You don't have to be on guard with me."

"I know. It just doesn't make it any easier. I never know when I'm being watched. Sometimes I think it's all the time." She mocked herself with a short laugh. "I know perfectly well I'm not deserving of so much attention, but I—"

"I watch you all the time," Rand said.

Claire remembered overhearing Bria tell him that. *You notice her. You notice everything about her.* "Do you?" she asked.

"Hmmm." He bent and kissed her forehead. "Do you mind?"

"It's a little unsettling."

"Bree said your knees would buckle if you knew."

Claire hadn't forgotten. "She was right. From now on I'll use my cane for support as well as guidance."

Rand brushed her mouth with his thumb. "I love you," he said.

Claire's heart swelled as she accepted the words. A moment later she echoed them softly.

Other than the fact that she was now addressed as Mrs. Hamilton, Claire did not find her life significantly changed. Mr. Cutch still read to her. The crew still watched out for her. And Macauley Stuart still hovered over her. She saw Rand with no more frequency than she had before they were married. None of this bothered her in the least. In a way it confirmed how firmly held her position had been. She appreciated that no one treated her any differently now that she was the captain's wife.

Claire was aware of a certain edginess that was overtaking her as *Cerberus* neared Pulotu. No one save Macauley Stuart remarked on it, and then only to ascertain the state of her health. It was not that she believed the doctor was more astute than anyone else, only that he was the least comfortable with her shifting moods. Rand, Cutch, and the rest of the crew seemed to expect that she would become unsettled, and they took it in stride.

The spirit island was at the southern tip of the Solonesia group. Rand had its location marked on his charts, but he had never visited it before. His experience with the volcanic islands and atolls that made up all of Polynesia told Rand he could live out his life in the South Pacific and never set foot on every one of them. The smallest hardly rose above the water and could pass unnoticed until a ship was run aground. The larger ones erupted from the blue velvet of the Pacific like brilliant emeralds. Their mountains were lush with dark greenery, and the sun bleached their shores white.

On Rand's chart Pulotu was a triangle of land roughly centered by four atolls. Seen from the crow's nest on *Cerberus*, it was a jagged black rock thrust upward from the sea like the hand of Satan. At least, that was what Paul Dodd reported from his position at the top of the ship.

Claire shook her head when the words reached her. "It's nothing like that," she told Rand. "He can't see it clearly through the mist."

Rand put one arm around Claire's shoulders. "And you can."

She nodded. "I remember how deeply green the sides of the mountain are. The vegetation is thick and lush. If it weren't for the tapu of the island, it would be a settlement. It can support some crops and has fresh water. My father made his base camp at the southwestern foot of Mauna Puka. It was the best place for a landing. Your charts show the reef, don't they?"

"All along the northern shore," he said. "Treacherous from the looks of it. Is that where I'll find the tikis?"

"No. You should be able to see them as we approach from the south. They're not as large as the ones on Easter Island, but they're forbidding nonetheless."

"The island itself looks forbidding," Rand said. Wreathed by the morning mist, it seemed shrouded by volcanic steam. He could imagine hell had opened up and released its fiery heat around this rock. "Dodd's description is more believable than yours. You said the mountain is called Mauna Puka? That's not on my maps."

"It means Danger Mountain."

Rand rolled his eyes. "Don't share that with my men. Dodd has them spooked now."

"Does it bother you?"

"Let's say that if it weren't for your mission and our treasure, I wouldn't trespass on such a powerful tapu."

"My father didn't give it a thought," Claire said. Her tone indicated that she wished it had been otherwise. "How far away are we now?"

"A league perhaps. One of the smaller atolls is not half so far off our port side." Rand raised his scope and peered through it. He could make out the verdant slopes of Mauna Puka now. When the sun beat back the mist, the island would be an emerald of flawless character.

"Is everyone topside?" she asked.

"Almost." He collapsed the scope and looked around. "Dr.

Stuart's just joined us on deck. I would say that makes everybody.'' Rand glanced down at Claire's profile. She was trying to put on a calm face, but the entire length of her slender frame leaned into the rail. Warm breezes pushed her hair back and pressed the bodice of her gown flush to her breasts. Rand let his arm fall from her shoulders and hoped he didn't regret it. ''I'm not going in after you,'' he told her dryly.

Claire accepted his gentle warning and straightened. Her grip on the rail remained unchanged.

''Are you worried, Claire?''

''Excited and frightened, too.''

Rand said nothing. For now she only needed him to remain at her side, but he stood poised to offer his shoulder if it came to that.

Except for waves breaking against the hull and the southeast trade winds straining the canvas, *Cerberus* was silent. Every man had his eyes trained on the island, looking for some sign that life still existed there, each with the idea of being the first to bring the news to Claire. As Pulotu loomed larger in their sights, their search was fraught first with heady anticipation and then with concern. It was Claire who interpreted the shift in the silence and understood when concern became dread.

Cerberus had not slowed, but it was as if nothing else moved. The quiet aboard the ship was so unnatural that Claire could imagine for a moment that she was alone. Her grip on the rail was no comfort to her now, and panic was instantaneous. It closed her throat and made her stomach lurch. Her heart pounded so loudly that she was deaf to the sound of the sea below her and Rand's voice at her ear. She groped for him as her knees started to fold.

Rand caught Claire before she dropped to the deck. He turned her around, hauling her against his chest to support her. Cutch was at his side quickly, the doctor a step behind.

''Has she fainted?'' Macauley asked.

Rand shook his head. ''She's frightened. Cutch, take over. Bring *Cerberus* around and drop anchor. We'll take two boats in, six men each, to explore.'' He lifted Claire into his arms and started to carry her toward the companionway hatch.

''No.''

Rand didn't hear her. It was the sudden rigidity of her posture that communicated a problem to him. He stopped in his tracks.

''Put me down,'' she whispered hoarsely. Claire found the lapels of Rand's jacket and tugged on them. ''Down.''

He lowered her slowly. When he was certain she was steady on her own feet, he let his hands fall to his sides. Rand watched her struggle for composure. She had to be aware that he was not the only one studying her now. Though Cutch had the crew firmly in his command and was setting them to work, there wasn't a man who didn't need to assure himself that Claire was all right. One after another, they stole glances in her direction.

''I want to be here,'' Claire said. Her features were set in a stoic mask, but her voice trembled slightly. ''I can do this. Don't make me go below.''

''Are you sure?'' asked Rand.

Macauley Stuart cleared his throat. ''I don't think she should be allowed to make that decision, Captain.''

Rand looked sideways at Macauley. The doctor was in earnest. ''You're going to make it for her?''

''She's ill. You can see for yourself that she has no color. Her faculties are impaired. Don't let her dictate—''

Claire realized that if she was shaking now, it was with anger. ''I'm not so impaired that I can't find your shin with my foot,'' she told him tightly.

Rand grinned as Dr. Stuart took a step backward. ''I'd be inclined to believe her, too.'' He took Claire's arm. ''You can stay here—on deck—while the boats go ashore. I'm not taking you on the island until I have a look myself.''

She nodded. ''Is the camp deserted?'' she asked. ''Is that why everyone became so quiet?''

''There is no camp,'' Rand told her. ''No evidence of one that any of us can see. If it weren't for the tikis and my own charts, I could believe we haven't found Pulotu.''

Claire took a deep breath but her lungs did not seem to fill with air. If she fainted now, Macauley Stuart would always have his way. The thought of that was motivation enough to remain standing. "Please take me back to the rail," she said quietly. "Don't leave me with Dr. Stuart when you go ashore."

Rand was aware the doctor heard Claire. The protest was already forming on his lips when Rand simply raised his hand and cut him off. "I'm going to leave you with Dodd," he said. "Cutch will take out one boat. Stuart is going to accompany me in the other. There's no way of knowing what we'll find once we start inland. His services will be better put to use on Pulotu than here."

Claire squeezed Rand's arm, thanking him for trusting her. Under her, she felt the change in speed as the sails were taken up. *Cerberus*'s motion shifted as she slowed. There was no more spray at the rail and the breeze seemed to gentle. When Claire leaned forward now, Rand didn't caution her. "What do you see?" she asked.

"About forty yards of white sand before a barricade of trees. From here it looks impenetrable. The land slopes steeply. The tikis are visible on the outcroppings of rock. The lowest one is placed about fifteen feet above sea level. I make the highest one to be about one hundred fifty feet."

"She's supposed to be Faia. The most powerful of the goddesses."

"Is she related to the others? You said you thought of them as the seven sisters."

"Yes, but that had more to do with the nursery rhyme than any specific knowledge." Claire gave a little start as the anchor was dropped. She had not heard Cutch give the order. "Do you think the camp might have been moved to another face of the mountain?"

Rand's voice was gentle. "Claire, it's been more than a year and a half since you left Solonesia. Your father and brother could be on any one of a score of islands. Pulotu was only a place to start. I would not give too much weight to the fact that there's no camp here now."

Her shoulders sagged a little. "I've always known that," she said. "But knowing and hoping . . ." She didn't have to finish. Rand would understand. They stood silently at the rail until it was time to lower the boats. Standing on tiptoe, Claire offered her husband a chaste kiss on the cheek. He was the one who turned it into something passionate enough to elicit some whistles from the audience in the yardarms.

"Just when I think I'm alone with you," Rand said softly, "twenty-six men remind me that I'm not."

Claire smiled. She managed to maintain that face until Paul Dodd assured her Rand was far enough away that it didn't matter anymore. When she was certain she could speak without a tremor in her voice, Claire said, "Open the scope, Mr. Dodd, and tell me what you see."

Cutch's boat reached shore a little before Rand's. The men jumped out in the surf, hoisted the boat to their shoulders, and carried it ashore. They were squeezing water out of their trousers by the time Rand's boat was deposited beside them.

Rand and Cutch stood apart from the others surveying the face of the island. The stone tikis stared out across the sea, their fiercely carved features unwelcoming. Rand's gaze went from one to the other, studying each as if it could provide a clue. "Do you think they were carved here on the island?" asked Rand.

Cutch shook his head. "I doubt it, but I'd have to look at the rock here first to be certain. Amazing, aren't they? How big do you think the largest one is?"

It was difficult to know from their angle of observation. "Bigger than you."

"I was thinking that. Eight feet?"

"Probably. A quarter to half a ton of rock. How do you suppose they were placed on those outcroppings?"

Cutch scratched his bald head, pretending to give the question real thought. Finally he said, "I have as much notion about that as I do about how those little clipper ships get inside a bottle."

Rand laughed. "Don't strain yourself."

Cutch stopped scratching. "What I was thinking was a bit more interesting."

"Oh?"

"Don't you find it fair to middlin' strange that we can see all of them?"

It took Rand a moment to catch Cutch's meaning. Sitting on their rocky ledges like statues on a pedestal, the tikis were all clearly visible. Surrounding them, however, was the lush island foliage. Casuarina trees with their feather-like fronds and tall coconut palms hugged the lower incline of Mauna Puka. The undergrowth was thick with flowering vines. Left undisturbed, the tikis should have been covered with greenery. "You think they're kept clear by islanders?" asked Rand.

"Possibly."

"There's another explanation?"

"Tapu."

Rand did not ask Cutch if he were serious. "I'll understand if you don't want to look around."

Cutch shrugged his heavy shoulders. "I'm already here," he said. "I figure the time to worry about tapu's long past."

"Then we'll split up. You and your men take the shore route. Go into the trees no more than a hundred yards. If you don't see any signs that Sir Griffin moved his camp, come out again. Go as far as the lagoon, then come back here. I'll take my group along the incline. We'll investigate the tikis."

The going was slow. Whether the direction was along the shore or up the slope, the undergrowth frustrated them all. Cutch's men had to hack their way into the interior at four different points to cover the ground effectively. Rand's crew had to cut and climb. He knew that on *Cerberus* even with the scope, the path of their journey would be largely unknown until they appeared beside one of the tikis. Each time he arrived at one of the clearings where a tiki stood, Rand flagged the ship to signal they were safe. He hoped Dodd did not mistake his communication as some sign of real progress. There was none of that to be had.

It was late afternoon before the two groups met up again. Hungry and thirsty, exhausted by their efforts, the men lay sprawled on the beach summoning the energy to return to the ship. None of them could report any signs of Sir Griffin's encampment.

"Could Claire be wrong?" Rand asked. "It's as if they were never here."

"I expected some signs, too. Except for where we've trampled and cut, it doesn't look as if anything's been disturbed."

"We should tour the entire island." It was the only thing that made sense, but Rand wasn't hopeful. "If they moved the camp, why erase any signs of this one?"

"We need Claire here," Cutch said. "She knows answers to questions we haven't asked yet."

Rand sat up and looked out at the ship. Claire was still at the rail. Her red and white striped poplin gown made her stand out like a barber pole. He smiled to himself. It was not a comparison he would mention. "You saw how anxious she was as we approached the island," he said to Cutch. "And she didn't argue when I told her to stay behind. I don't know if she can bring herself to come out here, even if I agree that it's a good idea. Right now, I'm not so sure it is."

Cutch remained silent. This was his captain's decision. He wondered how being Claire's husband would affect the outcome.

"I don't want to hurt her," said Rand.

"I know."

Rand continued to stare at Claire. Had she moved at all since this morning? What was she thinking now? Dodd would have described his observations. She had to know that they were all on the beach again. Their inactivity would tell its own story. "All right," he said finally. "Take your boat back to the ship. Bring enough supplies for six of us, including Claire, to camp here. We'll stay twenty-four hours. That will give you time to circle the island with *Cerberus*. With the onset of night there may be fires or lanterns that will help us locate another camp."

"Who do you want with you?"

"The doctor stays here. I'll keep Adams, Whittier, and Brown from my crew. Everyone else can go back with you."

Cutch stood. He shook off sand from his shirt and trousers. Without a word he motioned to the men. Most of them had overheard the discussion and were ready to go without explanation.

Rand's decision to stay behind was intentional. He reasoned that Claire was more likely to come to him than she would have been willing to go *with* him. If she had asked him to remain on the ship with her, he wouldn't have been able to refuse. He put more stock in her courage than his own. He had from the beginning.

When the boats returned, Rand waded into the water to meet them. He carried Claire ashore, then led her to a shady alcove of coconut trees. "We'll have the camp set up in an hour."

Claire nodded. She didn't speak, afraid that she would reveal how close to tears she was. The last time she was here, she had not only helped establish the camp, but directed much of its setup. Her father had immediately gone off into the trees to look for unusual flora, Tipu on his heels. Tiare had remained on the ship, refusing to set foot on the island until days later.

"Don't wander off," said Rand.

She forced a smile, wondering if it was as watery as it felt.

Someone handed a blanket to Rand. He snapped it open and laid it out. "Over here, Claire." When she scooted onto the blanket, he knelt beside her and took her chin in his hand. "You're very brave to have come out here at all."

She didn't feel very brave. "Liar."

"I don't lie to you. A little while ago I was sitting on shore thinking your dress took its inspiration from a barber pole." He watched her eyebrows arch predictably. "Do you see? I won't lie to you."

"You take a very odd tack to make your point. I liked this dress." Barber pole, indeed.

Rand kissed her briefly, hard. She had something of no consequence to occupy her now. He moved away to help the others while he could.

Claire sat patiently waiting for the tents to be pitched. The doctor was in charge of building a cooking fire. She wasn't surprised when he walked into the undergrowth to look for wood. "It's a rain forest," she told him. "You won't easily find fallen limbs or branches dry enough to burn here. You'll have more luck if you go along the shore and gather driftwood."

It wasn't long before she was directing the activity in other ways. She told Adams where he could find fresh water and explained to Whittier which fronds made the softest bedding. She pointed Brown toward the lagoon for netting them fish for dinner and described how to build a trap that would give them fish for breakfast as well.

Rand joined her again when the fire was being laid. "You were born to command, m'lady."

"I've always thought so."

He laughed. "Earlier I began to wonder again if we had the correct island, but you seem to know where everything is. You have your bearings about the location of the lagoon. This must be where the camp was."

"It is."

"Then why is there no evidence?"

"My father had no respect for the tapu of the island, but that doesn't mean he didn't respect its nature. When he made a camp, he did as little to disrupt the environment as possible. However, he wouldn't have swept the site clean. He had no reason to. The priests might have done that."

"The priests? Explain that."

"The tapu is supposed to be powerful. If it's to be believed, the priests can't have foreigners trespassing on Pulotu, especially if nothing unfortunate appears to have happened to them."

"So they would eliminate the evidence in order to make it seem no one violates the sanctity of their sacred island."

"Yes."

"Are they the ones who make certain the tikis stay visible? I saw there's no vegetation around any of the statues."

"No. That's tapu."

Rand's head swiveled in Claire's direction. He gave her an arch look that she could not appreciate. He had to say her name with a certain wry twist to prompt her faint smile.

"All right," she conceded reluctantly. "But who's to say what is tapu? The secret of Pulotu's statues is that they're carved from rock with a high base content."

"Like limestone."

"Yes, but not limestone. It's peculiar to Solonesia—a metamorphic rock that was formed when the volcanoes in this part of the world were active. It's not the typical igneous rock found almost everywhere. This rock was quarried on Fala. The humidity of Pulotu keeps the statues moist. Their base chemicals leech into the soil and prevent the vines and grasses that cover everything from encroaching. The tikis always remain visible.''

"Tapu," Rand said softly.

Claire nodded. ''The scientific explanation doesn't matter here. What Solonesians acknowledge is the power of the spirit rock to hold back the forest." Claire raised her knees and smoothed her gown over them. She faced the ocean, staring out as if she could see the seamless melding of clear blue water and sky. "Mr. Dodd told me of your progress to each one of the tikis. Did you find anything to hint at the location of your treasure?"

"No. It wasn't the only reason I went, but no, there weren't any hints. The tikis themselves aren't marked in any unusual way. You probably realize that, though. You studied them while you were here.''

"A little. Not as much as I would have liked. It made Tiare furious, especially when Tipu would come with me. I tried to respect her wishes, but I was curious, too. It was difficult for her because she was the daughter of a priest. If not for meeting my father, she would have become a priestess. Tiare kept the ancient traditions of the islands close to her heart. It was important to her that the Europeans didn't eliminate the culture.''

"Yet she became your father's mistress. By your own admission, Sir Griffin did not honor the tapu or much else about Solonesian society.''

Claire shrugged. "I asked her that myself, and she pretended not to understand the question. What I know is that my father loved her. Perhaps it was enough for her . . . or perhaps she was only keeping the enemy close.''

"It could have been both," Rand said. He watched Claire's features take on a thoughtful, distant look as she considered this. "What's the last thing you remember happening on Pulotu?"

Claire ignored the commotion that was happening around the fire as Brown returned with his net full of fish. "Studying in my tent. It was late. I had my lantern burning. I don't know if you realize there were eight people in our group. You know about my father, Tiare, Tipu, and me."

"And Trenton," said Rand. "Your father's assistant. He was with you then, wasn't he?"

"That's right. He would have liked to have been elsewhere, but Sir Griffin was treating his illness then and he needed to stay with us. The other three men had all been with my father for years. Mr. Davis was usually responsible for overseeing the laborers. Since the Solonesians were reluctant to step foot on Pulotu, the work fell on Mr. Davis and the others."

"Tiare came ashore."

"Yes, but not for days. Usually our group traveled from island to island in outrigger canoes. When the islanders who worked for my father realized he meant to explore Pulotu, they refused to help. Sir Griffin had to wait two months before he found a Yankee whaler willing to transport his entourage and equipment. Tiare boarded the ship, but when we arrived she wouldn't get off. The captain threatened to take her whaling with them if she didn't leave. My father had to go back out to the ship to convince her to come with him. It was the only time I remember him being impatient with her. He simply refused to accept that she was terrified of the island's curse."

Claire felt Rand's fingers lightly touch the nape of her neck. He moved her hair to one side and ran his hand along the length of her spine. His gentleness evoked a shiver of pleasure. "I remember there was some shouting," she said, picking up the thread of her story. "I couldn't tell you who was involved or what the shouting was about. I've thought a lot about it, but I don't know if the voices were alarmed or angry. I know I left my tent, but again, I don't know if I was curious or if someone called me outside."

Rand waited, expecting more. "That's all?" he asked when Claire remained silent. "That's all you remember?"

"I'm afraid so."

"What made you get into the canoe? Leave the island?"

"Fear, I suppose."

"Of what?"

"Isn't that one of the reasons we're here?" she asked a little impatiently. "Did you think it would all come flooding back to me once I came ashore?"

"No . . . I don't know. I didn't . . ." Rand's voice trailed off.

Claire sighed, regretting her shortness with him a moment ago. "It's all right. I didn't know what to expect myself. There was part of me that hoped that coming back to Pulotu would be enough. Then I thought coming ashore was what I needed to do. Now it merely seems that Dr. Messier was wrong and every other physician was right. It's not your fault. You came down on the side of everyone who tried to talk me out of it."

"I'd have rather been wrong," he said quietly.

"I know." She felt his arm come around her shoulder and she leaned into him. She pointed in the direction of the fire pit. Flames were crackling, but she still couldn't smell their dinner roasting. "Have they decided who's gutting and who's cooking?"

Rand looked over at the quartet hunkered down beside the fire. "It looks as if they're casting lots. How hungry are you? I can tell them to—"

"No. Let them work it out. I can wait."

"I saw some wine in the supplies that Cutch delivered. Would you like that?"

"Yes. Very much."

Rand left Claire's side long enough to root through the crates for glasses and wine. He poured them both some, then set the bottle securely in a sand mound beside him. He touched her glass with his and was rewarded with Claire's serene smile. It left Rand wishing he was alone with her. "I should have ordered Cutch to take everyone with him."

Claire understood the direction of his thoughts. "Tonight I'll let you take me to the lagoon," she said. "While they're all sleeping, we'll go swimming."

Rand wondered how he could hurry nightfall. "Have you done that before?" he asked.

"Alone," she said. "Many times. I used to go off by myself often, mostly at night when no one would miss me. I've explored most of the shoreline of the island on foot or by boat."

"But not the interior?"

"No. Not without the others. It's too dense to go far without help. I explored the tikis on my own or with Tipu, but that's all." Claire sipped her wine. "Do you think the treasure's here?"

Rand was quiet for a moment. The truth discouraged him. "I don't know," he said.

Claire found his forearm and ran her hand along its length. "Tell me the legend."

"You know it."

"I know some version of it. Everyone does. But I've never heard it from a Hamilton or a Waterstone. What is it your family passed on to you?"

Rand topped off his glass before he answered. "You have to know that James Hamilton and Henry Waterstone were friendly rivals first, friends second. They each enjoyed favored status as privateers. Queen Elizabeth issued them letters of marque which allowed them to prey on the Spaniards at will. They were successful independently, in part because of their rivalry, but the large prizes, the kind that would bring them great fortune and notoriety, eluded them.

"I don't know who first suggested collaborating—that's been lost in the retelling—but James and Henry agreed to take the Spaniards together. They made a modest fortune for the crown until they seized the prize meant for Pope Gregory. In addition to gold, there were gems that were chosen because of their graduated colors. Placed side by side they would be a rainbow of precious stones. The captains knew too well what they had. It both awed and frightened them. The wealth of the prize was beyond anything they could have imagined."

Rand glanced at Claire. Her expression was rapt. She nudged him with her elbow to make him continue. "They decided not to return to England immediately. Although they captured their prize in the Atlantic, the voyage they had set out to make was supposed to take them to Peru. They saw no reason to alter their course. They continued to capture Spanish ships and gold around South America, but they gradually grew more cautious, afraid of losing what they'd already taken. Finally they stopped pirating altogether and set out across the Pacific.

"James and Henry couldn't agree on how to divide the prize or what portion should be returned to the queen. When it looked like the two crews were going to turn on each other, the captains reconciled long enough to form another alliance. They split one fifth of the booty among the men on both ships. Another fifth they agreed to carry back to Elizabeth. Three fifths, including the seven sisters, they determined to hide. They knew that if they returned to England with the entire treasure, they would see very little of it for their efforts."

"But they didn't hide it together," Claire said. "Why not?"

"They didn't trust each other. There was a cartographer on Henry's ship who was in the queen's employ. They chose him to find a place to hide the treasure. The man must have suspected it was a death sentence, or perhaps he believed he'd be left behind. He was either clever or desperate when he devised his own plan. He hid the treasure but left the captains separate riddles to recover it. They could find the treasure again if they let him live or if they worked together to solve the riddles. Evidently James and Henry thought they could work together because the mapmaker was killed."

"Who did it?" asked Claire.

"Henry Waterstone," said Rand. "And if his descendants had survived, I'm sure they'd say with equal certainty that it was James Hamilton. It's another of those things lost in the retelling."

"Like the significance of the holes in the paper," she mused.

"Or even if there's any significance. Henry and James were further divided after the murder. It's an irony that their names are both attached to the treasure."

"Who was the cartographer? Does anyone remember his name?"

Rand chuckled. "I've never been able to discover it, but I have a name for the clever bastard." He saw Claire's quizzical expression. "I call him Mercutio."

Understanding Rand's dark humor did not take Claire long. *"A plague on both your houses,"* Claire quoted softly. "From *Romeo and Juliet.*" Her features became troubled. "I don't like it, Rand."

He shrugged. "You have to admit it's fitting. It's not the treasure that's been cursed all these years, but the houses of Hamilton and Waterstone."

Chapter Twelve

The lagoon was quiet, almost unnaturally so. It was as if the stillness had substance. Claire found herself reluctant to move once she discovered it. She stood on a slip of smooth rock, her body poised for flight, and breathed deeply of air redolent with hibiscus and humus.

From the water Rand watched her slender figure rise on tiptoe. If there was fear, it was not evident to him. If there was hesitation, he couldn't find it. Claire's body made a graceful arc before it broke the lagoon's placid surface and disappeared entirely.

Claire broke the water again a few feet away. "Rand?"

Until that moment Rand was unaware that he was holding his breath. Now he let it out slowly and closed the distance between them. "Right here."

Treading water, Claire turned. "Will you take my hand?"

Rand found her wrist and pulled her toward him. He drew Claire toward shallower water, where he could comfortably stand. He didn't mind that she didn't test the depth, but chose to attach herself to him instead. Her legs circled his hips and she placed her hands on his shoulders. She dipped backward, wetting her hair again so that every strand was pulled away from her face. When she came back up, Rand's mouth was waiting for her.

He kissed her deeply. At the small of her back his hands tightened. Her thighs cradled him more intimately. She lifted her hips, searching instinctively. It was the thrust of Claire's body that joined them. She was the one who stole his breath.

Claire broke the kiss. Her fingers covered the wet trail from his shoulders to the nape of his neck. Her thumbs brushed his jaw. "Are you watching me?" she whispered.

"Hmmm."

She tugged on his hair. "Are you?"

"Yes." Even with no moon it was still possible to make out the shadowed features of her face. The canopy of palms did not cover the entire lagoon. There was a natural skylight at the center and starshine was mirrored in the water. "Yes," he repeated, his voice husky. "I'm watching you."

"Don't."

"How's that?"

"Close your eyes. See me the way I see you."

Rand shut his eyes. A moment later Claire's fingers brushed his lids. He smiled. "Didn't you think I would do it?"

"Sssh," she said, touching his mouth. She raised her head and replaced her fingers with her lips. She kissed him gently with her damp mouth. Her breasts rubbed against his chest. Her nails lightly scored the length of his spine.

Rand felt every muscle in his body grow taut. Beneath his skin there was a shudder of sensation, not of release but of anticipation. He waited for her to move, to rise and fall on the part of him she held as if it were a part of herself. She didn't. His penis remained rigid inside her and she remained motionless.

He became aware of her breathing. He heard the same cadence in the gentle surge of water against the rocks. It was a softly primal rhythm, untouched by time. It resonated through him until he was deaf to everything save that sound and it became a dull roar in his ears.

Claire's mouth was on his neck. She sipped his skin. Her tongue flicked at the base of his ear. Her teeth caught his lobe and tugged. She was weightless in his arms, yet he had never been so aware of her. The planes and angles of his own body were defined by the curves of hers. His chest tightened when Claire's breasts swelled. She rubbed her nipples against him, arched, and began to move in his arms.

Rand thought it was possible he would come out of his skin. Her lips slanted hungrily across his and her tongue was thrust into his mouth. Her body moved insistently, sinuously. His response came without thought. He did not know where she was going to touch him or how. He only knew that he did not want her to stop.

Claire buried her face in the curve of Rand's neck as he came. She held him tightly, as if it were her body supporting them both and not his. The water seemed cooler than it had moments earlier. She shivered a little as she felt herself being lowered. When her feet finally touched bottom she was shoulder deep in the water. She still leaned against Rand and covered his heartbeat with her palm. Neither of them spoke.

Rand bent his head and kissed the damp crown of Claire's hair. The scent of English lavender had been replaced by the island fragrances of hibiscus and torch ginger. He led her to a blanket of ferns at the edge of the lagoon, and with his eyes wide open this time, he made love to her.

"It's like drowning," she whispered. Her words were faintly slurred as she turned sleepily in his arms. Claire had let Rand help her into her shift, but she wouldn't let him take her back to camp. At daybreak they could return, she'd told him. "Even with the ground at my back, it's like that."

Rand's smile was wry as he listened to Claire's dreamy tone. "We almost *did* drown," he pointed out.

Claire lifted herself on one elbow. She found Rand's mouth with her fingers, then with her own lips. The kiss was sweetly tender. She touched the side of his face. "That was for not minding."

Rand's chuckle rumbled in his chest. "Go to sleep."

She did, but only for a short while. In spite of the pleasant weariness that made her resist moving from Rand's side, Claire found herself wide awake. *A plague on both your houses.* She turned Mercutio's dying curse over in her mind again.

Montagues and Capulets. Hamiltons and Waterstones. Rand was not far off the mark in comparing the animosity that existed between the two families. James Hamilton and Henry Waterstone would have been contemporaries of Shakespeare, and the legend was born during that time. Was it possible the bard found inspiration for his feuding family there?

Claire sat up. Drawing her legs toward her chest, she smoothed her shift over her knees and tucked the hem under her toes. Her mouth twisted to one side as she remained deep in thought. She worried her bottom lip between her teeth. *A plague on both your houses.* It had taken three centuries to eliminate the Waterstones, but it was done. Claire did not want to believe that the Hamiltons were on a course toward the same fate, yet it was difficult to ignore that the line of men whose responsibility it was to secure the riddle was approaching extinction. Shelby, David, and Rand's father were all gone. Bria might never have children.

Claire felt a stirring in her womb and a longing so intense that it was almost painful. The fear that followed robbed her of breath.

"Claire?"

She had not realized she made any sound until he said her name. A second sob rose in her throat and threatened to choke her when she tried to hold it back. Tears rushed to Claire's eyes and she shuddered.

Rand sat up. Without a word his arms went around her. He could feel her entire body trembling. "I'm taking you back to camp. Dr. Stuart—"

Claire gulped for air. "No," she said, shaking her head. "No. I'm not sick. Not—"

Then Rand understood. Claire was frightened. She was experiencing the same intense fear she had on *Cerberus* after her illness. "Nothing's going to happen," he whispered. "I won't let anything hurt you."

But that wasn't the problem, Claire thought. "It's you," she said raggedly, turning in his arms. "Nothing can hurt *you.*"

He tried to soothe her, his tone vaguely patronizing. "All right, nothing can hurt me."

Claire pushed at his chest and released herself from his embrace. "You don't know about curses," she told him, her body rigid now. Her hands were folded into fists and her knuckles dug into her thighs. She spoke the words of the riddle like a mantra. *"Blood will run. Flames will come. Blazing sun, blinding some. Blades lifted high across the plain. Flood water rising, months of rain. A plague will ink clouded skies. Grieving, shadows beneath thy eyes."* It was difficult for Claire to breathe again. She started to get to her feet.

Rand grabbed her wrist and pulled her back down. "There's no curse, Claire."

She shook her head. "Mercutio," she whispered. "You said so yourself."

Rand's eyes widened. He swore softly as he held her to him again. "I didn't mean it, Claire. Not a word."

"You meant it."

He just held her then. Rand recognized the futility of trying to argue his point. He changed his strategy and applied his energy toward helping Claire become calm again. He absorbed her restlessness and dried her tears. His fingers combed through her damp hair. He rubbed her back, warming her. Rand had no measure for the passage of time. It might have been only minutes that he held her, or the better part of an hour. What he knew with certainty was that Claire's slender frame grew heavy against him as her breathing steadied. He held her long past the point that she was sleeping deeply.

Sunrise brought pale yellow light into the lagoon. The dark green canopy was speared by shafts of light wherever there was an opening. One of them fell across Claire's shoulder as she slept on.

Rand knelt at the edge of the lagoon and cupped his hands in the water. He sluiced his face and neck and raked back his hair with damp fingers. In the distance, where the shallow channel opened up to the sea, Rand could make out the tall masts of *Cerberus*. Cutch had returned with the ship sometime during the night. Rand did not allow himself to hope that Cutch's mission had been more successful than his own.

Claire was sitting up when Rand turned around. She was

stretching her arms and trying to hold back a yawn. In every way the effort was a comic contortion. She froze when she heard Rand's deep chuckle.

"May I have a private moment?" she asked with some asperity.

Rand cleared his throat. "Of course. I'll turn around."

Claire didn't believe him, but she finished stretching anyway. Rising to her feet, she asked for direction, then padded softly and unerringly to Rand's side. She knelt and performed her morning ablutions in the same manner as Rand had. She imagined his eyes on her as water trickled down her throat and dampened the neckline of her shift. "I can feel sunshine on my face," she said.

Her skin glowed. The light lifted red highlights in her hair to the surface. In profile her features were serene, and when she turned to Rand he saw that it was no trick of the sunlight. Claire's expression was untroubled, her smile genuinely unaffected.

He couldn't imagine not kissing her, so he did.

"Why did you do that?" she asked as he drew back. She had an urge to touch her mouth, to reaffirm the fading imprint of Rand's tender kiss.

"Because I wanted to."

Her smile deepened. "Hedonist." She thrust her hands forward, intending a playful shove. She miscalculated her own strength and Rand's position and nearly toppled them both in the water. Laughing, Claire scrambled to her feet and neatly eluded his grasp.

Rand shook his head as his arms came up empty. His eyes were admiring as they followed her progress back to the bed of ferns. Her sense of direction was unerring. She had found her neatly folded pile of clothes and was beginning to dress by the time he joined her.

Rand sat down and picked up his socks and boots. "We need to discuss what happened last night," he said.

Claire was smoothing her stocking from ankle to knee. Her fingers paused briefly. Her faint smile was self-mocking. "So it wasn't an unpleasant dream."

"No," he said. "Not a dream."

She nodded slowly. It was not what she wanted to hear, but it was what she expected. "Can you forgive me?"

Rand's puzzlement was real. "Forgive you? For what?"

"For being so . . . so . . ." Words failed her.

"So female?" he suggested.

"You only said that because I haven't anything to throw at your head."

Rand grinned. There was some truth to that. "I said it because it's as ridiculous as you supposing you need forgiveness." His effortless smile faded as his tone grew more serious. "I want to explore Pulotu more thoroughly this morning, especially around the tikis. I can send you back to the ship if you'd like. There's no reason for you to stay if being here frightens you so badly."

"I want to be here," Claire said. "With you. Last night . . . last night my thoughts tumbled out of control. I'll do better today."

Rand could tell it was still difficult for her to talk about. The strain showed at the corners of her mouth and in the small crease between her dark brows. "Tell me about your thoughts."

Claire slipped on her other stocking and smoothed it over her calf. There was a sensation of tightness in her chest, but it was no more than she could bear. "I never realized so clearly how the curse has affected your family. With your father and brothers gone, and your sister unlikely to ever marry, I recognized for the first time how much the curse rides on your shoulders. Those words in the riddle—the ones you think describe a rainbow of precious stones—they could just as easily be describing the war you fought."

"They could describe any war," Rand said. "I imagine those who came before me considered that. There have been wars and plagues and floods enough these past three hundred years to make every part of the riddle seem prophetic. That was the cartographer's talent."

"There are no more Waterstones," she said quietly.

"Families come and go. It's the nature of nature. You've studied Darwin. It's only arrogance or superstition that sets forth an argument that excludes humans from natural law—just as if we weren't part of the animal kingdom.''

"The last of the Waterstones was killed for the riddle.''

"Then it's greed that killed him. One more facet of human nature, not a curse. I wish I hadn't mentioned Mercutio. Clearly you took it to heart.''

Claire bent her head and said in a rush, "I want to find the treasure.''

Rand yanked on his boot. "So do I.''

"And end the curse,'' she finished.

His head swiveled and he stared at her. "Didn't you hear anything I said?''

"All of it. And I want to believe you're right.'' Claire spread the skirt of her gown across her legs and pressed out the wrinkles with her palms. "But we're on Pulotu now, and there's no evidence that anyone's been here before us. There will be a reasonable explanation, just as there is for why nothing grows around the tikis, but I also know that hearing it will give me small comfort. I know you have respect for the religion of these islands. What you don't respect is that it can affect you.'' Claire turned her back so that Rand could fasten the buttons on her gown. "I don't mind if you humor me in this,'' she told him. "Does it matter that we want to find the treasure for different reasons? In the end we'll both have what we want, just like in the nursery rhyme: *Reunited, freed of curse; Thy reward the richest purse.''*

Rand was silent, weighing her words carefully. Claire was right that he respected the beliefs of the Sun Islanders. She hadn't said that she considered his thinking superior to theirs but it was what lay between her words. He was searching for a fortune. She wanted peace of mind. What did their differences matter indeed? Finally he said, "I don't know that rhyme.''

Recognizing that Rand was not going to expend more effort in convincing her she was wrong, Claire released a breath slowly. The corners of her mouth lifted in a tentative smile. When he finished buttoning her gown, she turned and gave him a glimpse of its rare beauty. "Didn't Elizabeth read to you from Mother Goose?'' she asked.

"I thought she did," he said. "I just don't know that one."

"My mother had a particular fondness for it. I've mentioned it before, when we first spoke of the tikis. There are seven sisters in it also."

"Then I know I've never heard it. I would recall that."

"But I *did* recite part of it to you. Remember? On the ship. After you taught me your riddle. *With the sisters, this verse brings; Wealth beyond the dreams of kings.*"

"I thought it had something to do with Humpty Dumpty."

Claire laughed. "You *are* confused. Listen:

At the end of one God's promise
Stand seven pagan sentinels
Seven rings but just one key
Silver, tin, and mercury
Iron bracelet, leaden chain
Treasure lost, treasure gained
Copper circlet, crown of gold
Seven sisters flee the fold
Reunited, freed of curse
Thy reward, the richest purse
Seven rings but just one key
Metals all of alchemy
With the sisters, this verse brings

Rand finished the verse, his voice trailing off at the end. *"Wealth beyond the dreams of kings."*

Claire heard the change in his tone and she felt his silence keenly. "Rand? What is it? Have you heard it before after all?"

"Never," he said, stunned. "Never once."

"Then what—" She stopped as Rand's fingers closed tightly around her upper arms. He gave her a little shake. His rough urgency surprised Claire. Her mouth snapped shut.

"Claire. Tell it to me again. All of it."

She blinked. He was rising and hauling her to her feet in front of him. He let her go long enough to pull on his other boot; then he was taking her arm and yanking her through the undergrowth toward the open beach.

"Again," he said.

Claire's recitation was somewhat breathless this time. She finished just as they made the clearing. Her heels dug into the sand to stop Rand's forward progress. He picked her up. Claire rebelled at the thought of being thrown over his shoulder. She started to struggle, but then his lips were on hers, first at the corner of her mouth, then across it. He kissed her brow, her temple, the tip of her nose. He pressed his lips to her closed eyes and then touched the crown of her hair. Rand set her down slowly. She was flush to his lean frame, and in the end she simply leaned against him.

"Goodness," she said, catching her breath.

Rand hugged her. "The very essence of it."

Claire couldn't quite tell if he was serious. She raised her face and let him see her skepticism. "You may as well tell me what this has all been in aid of. I'm certain I don't understand."

Rand held her from him briefly. "You really don't, do you?"

Claire's mouth flattened. "There's no particular pleasure in the admission," she said. "You needn't emphasize it."

He laughed. "God, I love you."

"I should hope so." The line of her mouth softened a little.

Rand kissed her again, then looped his arm in hers. He didn't have to urge her to begin walking back to the encampment. "It's the verse," he told her. "It's not one from your cherished Mother Goose."

"Of course it is. You may not recognize it, but my mother read it to me with all the others."

"I'm beginning to think your mother was infinitely more clever than anyone has credited. She gave you the Waterstone riddle in a way you could hear it. She put it in your safekeeping years ago and counted on time and circumstance to unravel it."

Claire pulled Rand up short again. "That can't be right," she said. "Why would she do that? More to the point: *how* could she? My mother was not a Waterstone. I know my family tree. There's not a Waterstone twig anywhere on it."

''I didn't think there was. But I wonder how well you know your godfather's family.''

''Stickle?''

''Unless you have another godfather.''

Claire did not take him to task for his gentle mocking. Her mind was spinning in another direction. ''The paper I found in the duke's manuscript . . . the one with the holes . . . then it really was the Waterstone riddle.''

''So it seems,'' Rand said. ''The Duke of Strickland is either descended from Waterstones or he had the last one killed to take the riddle for himself.''

''Stickle is not a murderer.''

Rand was not going to argue that point. Claire knew the truth no better than he, but her view was more palatable. He could let her keep it until they learned otherwise. ''Then he's a Waterstone,'' said Rand. ''And he's kept his head by keeping the secret.''

''He must have told my mother.'' Claire's voice shook slightly. ''To have shared this secret with her . . . to have trusted her . . . I only imagined I understood how much he loved her.''

Rand supposed that was one interpretation of events. He did not explain to Claire that there could be others. He took her arm again. ''Come. I want to get back. You shouldn't repeat the riddle to anyone, Claire, now that you know it for what it is. You can teach it to me later. I'll take you with me when I go back to look at the tikis.''

She nodded. ''Why didn't I understand sooner?''

''Why should you? Your mother had her own version of hiding the riddle in plain sight. A very clever woman, your mother.'' He shook his head, his smile admiring, then laughed outright. ''Mother Goose. It was inspired.''

''That rhyme made as much sense as any of the others,'' Claire said. ''Ring around the rosie is about the plague. Did you know that?''

''I'd heard.''

''And London Bridge *was* falling down before it was rebuilt.''

''What about Humpty Dumpty?''

Claire laughed. "You like that one, don't you?"

He shrugged. "I just remember all the words."

"I think it's a reference to King Richard III."

Rand thought about that. "I like them all better as nonsense."

Claire squeezed his arm. "So do I."

The men were just rising as Claire and Rand approached. They stumbled, sleepy-eyed and shaggy-headed, to their feet and wandered off to see to their personal needs. Rand was aware of Macauley's pointed stare in their direction but couldn't say if his expression was disapproving or envious. Wisely the doctor kept his own counsel.

Cutch came ashore with a small crew as they were sitting down to eat. He didn't deny he had watched through the scope until the fresh fish was smoking in the pit before he headed out. No one denied him the opportunity to enjoy their labors.

Rand finished his breakfast and leaned back in the sand on his elbows. "Claire is going with me to look at the tikis." No one save Macauley Stuart seemed to find anything odd about this statement. "I'll need two men to assist us. Volunteers."

A number of heads lifted, including the doctor's. Rand chose Whittier and Brown. "It will take the better part of the morning. The rest of you should explore along the shore again and into the forest. Cutch will direct you." He turned to his second in command. "I haven't heard a report. I take it to mean you found nothing during your tour around the island."

Cutch nodded slowly. "There's no other camp on Pulotu. We looked for more tikis, but these seven are the only ones we could find."

"Ideas?"

"We should explore the islands closest to this one first. Even the atolls. Inhabitants of the other islands may be able to tell us something and shorten our search."

"Very well." Rand jumped fluidly to his feet. "We'll plot our course this evening on *Cerberus*. Brown, you and Whittier organize our supplies. We'll need a sling and harness for Claire. She can't climb without assistance."

Claire also knew she couldn't climb in a dress. She disappeared into her tent and when she stepped out again she was wearing clothing that Cutch had packed for Rand. Nothing fit properly. Claire made do by rolling up the sleeves and trouser legs and cinching a belt tightly around her waist. "Well?" she asked a shade defiantly. She spoke to the men at large. "Your silence is hardly flattering."

Rand's gaze took her in head to foot. "We're all rendered speechless," he said dryly. "You might have warned us."

Claire counted off six paces from the tent and dropped herself in the sand at Rand's side. She crossed her legs tailor-fashion and began plaiting her hair. "You have to agree this is more practical for scaling rocks."

Rand's tone was doubtful. "Well, if I *have* to agree . . ."

Macauley Stuart spoke up. "She's really not going to wear trousers, is she?"

Rand's expression was wryly amused. "Who's going to tell her no? You?"

Stuart's mouth snapped shut.

Claire bent her head so her smug smile was not so clearly in evidence. She continued to work on her braid while Rand finished planning their trek. No one questioned why Rand wanted to study the tikis a second time. Every man, including Macauley Stuart, shared a sense of anticipation in regard to the treasure. The seven tikis seemed significant in the search as nothing else had. Even if it was proved later that they were only misdirection, no one believed they should dismiss this opportunity out of hand.

Rand used a stick to draw seven furrows in the sand. Each furrow represented a different elevation and corresponded to the height of the tikis on Mauna Puka. Cutch placed one shell on each line to represent a tiki.

Claire had been following the discussion, trying to visualize the map Rand was laying out in the sand. She tilted her head toward him when he fell silent. "What is it?" she asked.

"See for yourself." He laid the stick he'd been using across her lap. "Connect the shells."

Claire tied off her braid and swung it over her shoulder. She picked up the stick and held out her hand for Rand to direct her. He chose the starting point and guided her carefully from shell to shell until all seven were connected.

Cutch rubbed his chin thoughtfully. "Ain't that something." He looked over his shoulder at the tikis on the foothill. The pattern of the stone carvings was not obvious on the three-dimensional face of the mountain, but on the map Rand and Claire had drawn, it could not have been clearer. "Sure enough, that's the Big Dipper."

Rand was helping Claire retrace the connections so her sense of the map was the same as everyone else's. He gave her full marks for containing her excitement in front of the others. It was only beneath his own hand that he felt the small tremor in hers.

"What do you think it means?" Claire asked.

Rand looked at the men. Cutch was still staring at the map, pondering its importance. Brown, Whittier, and several others were already spending their share of the treasure. Only Macauley Stuart was giving Rand his full attention, and Rand felt it like a tangible force. He shrugged, unwilling to say what he thought of this chance discovery. He took the stick from Claire. "I suppose that's what we should find out."

Macauley glanced at the map; then his gaze swiveled to Claire. "Why should it mean anything?" he asked.

It was Cutch who answered. "It's a Northern constellation," he said. "Sirius and the Southern Cross are more important in these waters. If the Solonesian priests placed the tikis in this arrangement—'' He broke off when he looked up and intercepted the warning in Rand's eyes.

Macauley finished Cutch's sentence for him. "It was an accident. Is that what you're saying?"

Cutch nodded, regretting he had spoken up at all. Belatedly he understood that Stuart had put his question to Claire. Would the doctor never learn he had to say Claire's name when he wanted a response from her? "Somethin' like that," he muttered.

"What do you suppose the likelihood is of it being an accident?" Stuart asked.

Cutch threw up his hands. "Can't say."

Stuart looked at Rand. "Captain?"

"I wouldn't know."

There was a thread of enthusiasm in the doctor's voice now. He leaned forward eagerly, intent on making his point to the others. "But if it's not an accident, then the islanders were directed to place their tikis in just this fashion . . . Or they were put there by someone other than the Solonesian priests."

"If it's not merely happenstance," Claire reminded him.

The doctor's fiery brows came together as he shook his head vigorously. "It's not."

"Well," Rand said dryly, "perhaps you can use this discovery to explain Stonehenge."

In spite of the chuckles Rand's comment prompted, Macauley Stuart pretended to give the suggestion full consideration. He responded in equally dry tones, "Perhaps I will. It would secure my place in history."

Claire's dark brows rose a notch. "I didn't know you aspired to such a place."

Macauley's genial smile took on a wry twist. "A footnote, to be sure. Nothing so preeminent as Hamilton-Waterstone."

Rand said nothing. He drew his stick across the sand map, erasing the furrows and moving the shells. What remained had no bearing to the path he and his small crew would take across Mauna Puka. Tossing the stick toward the water, Rand stood. Beside him Claire came to her feet. He took her hand and placed it in the crook of his arm. "Brown. Whittier. Get the gear. Cutch, take the others with you."

The rest of the group stood. The men divided off. Macauley looked to Rand as if he hoped to be reconsidered for joining the captain. When Rand said nothing, the doctor reluctantly placed himself with Cutch's crew.

Rand turned with Claire and began walking toward the foot of the mountain. "We're going to take the route that connects tikis as if they were on a single plane. Just like you connected them in the sand. That's not the route I took the men on yesterday."

"I've never done it that way before," she said. "Tip and I worked our way side to side until we reached the top."

"There may be nothing to it," Rand cautioned her. "I examined the tikis carefully and saw nothing. You've studied them too."

"Shouldn't Cutch be with us?" Claire heard footsteps behind them and realized Brown and Whittier were almost on their heels.

"It's not that I don't want him here," he said. "But that I want him with the doctor more."

Claire's smile was gentle. "Dr. Stuart was hired to look after me, Rand. I don't think he sees our marriage as making any difference to his assignment."

"That would be one perspective," said Rand.

Claire raised her head, her expression questioning. "What do you mean—" She broke off when Rand squeezed her arm. Brown and Whittier were now within earshot. Claire's thoughts went immediately in a different direction. She imagined the mountain looming darkly in front of her and the ferns and vines as almost impenetrable. "Do you really think I can do this?" she asked.

"You're dressed for it."

She laughed. On impulse she stepped around Rand so that he was forced to stop or knock her down. Claire threw her arms around his neck and kissed him soundly on the mouth. She heard Brown and Whittier chuckling as they marched past.

Rand grasped Claire's waist, holding her to him as she broke off the kiss. "What did I do to deserve that?" he asked.

"Complaining?"

Her coquettish smile was so at odds with her manner of masculine dress that Rand was moved to laughter. "No complaint. I was merely wondering how I might prompt a similar consequence in the future."

Claire took his arm again and nudged him to follow the path that Brown was widening in front of them. "It's your confidence in me," she said simply. "I find I like it very much."

Rand sighed. "You might have told me it was an aphrodisiac before now."

Claire pinched his arm lightly as heat flushed her cheeks. Out of the corner of her mouth she said, "Think about the treasure."

"Oh," he said. "I am." He left it to Claire to imagine his wicked smile. The footing was more difficult now as they began to climb. He concentrated on keeping Claire sheltered at his side and on solid ground. To reach the first tiki did not require the use of the sling, but Rand harnessed Claire with the rope when they arrived at the outcropping of rock. That she understood the danger was evident by the fact that she didn't protest.

Brown and Whittier stayed at the edge of the clearing while Rand led Claire closer to the statue. The carving sat in isolation on a plateau of land that jutted forward from the mountain. Rand looked back once to be sure that Whittier had secured the harness and that his attention wasn't straying. The young man's eyes were fixed on Claire. He was prepared to haul her back if there was the slightest misstep.

The tiki stood a foot taller than Rand. The lines of the face were deeply carved, but the impression it left was one of wisdom, not alarm. Like all the tikis, this goddess's hands were resting across her rounded belly. To the rear her naked buttocks protruded at a sharper angle.

Rand placed Claire's hands on the tiki's shoulders. They looked pale and delicate against the dark stone. "Tell me the riddle again," he said.

Claire spoke as she began exploring, looking for something

this time that her eyes had never seen. *"At the end of one god's promise stand seven pagan sentinels. Seven rings but just one key. Silver, tin, and mercury. Iron bracelet, leaden chain, treasure lost, treasure gained. Copper circlet, crown of gold. Seven sisters flee the fold. Reunited, freed of curse; thy reward, the richest purse. Seven rings but just one key. Metals all of alchemy. With the sisters, this verse brings wealth beyond the dreams of kings."*

Rand listened, surveying the statue with a critical eye. "She's not wearing any jewelry. No circlets, crowns, bracelets, or chains. The only circles she has are the ones around her eyes."

Claire raised herself on tiptoe and fingered the stone furrows carved out around the goddess's eyes. "There aren't seven rings here. Only two around each eye. Solonesian priests have similar circles tattooed around their eyes."

"If this tiki is one of the pagan sentinels," Rand said, "then where are her rings?"

"Lift me," Claire said. "Let me look at the top of her head."

Rand knelt and gave Claire a leg up. He gave her time to explore before he lowered her to the ground. "Anything?"

"As smooth as Mr. Cutch's head."

"That's not encouraging." He went over what he could remember of the riddle in his own mind, then asked Claire to repeat it. "One god's promise," he mused aloud. "Who's the most powerful god among the Solonesians?"

"Orono. He is the Solonesian equivalent to Oro in the Society Islands. Like Zeus and Jupiter in Greek and Roman mythology."

"Orono," Rand repeated. "And what promise did he make?"

"I've never heard of one. Most of the stories I've listened to end with the spirit gods driving out the *papalagi*. The white man."

"I'm familiar with those. It seems to me this sort of promise should be older than the European threat. These islands were inhabited thousands of years before the Spanish and Portuguese found them."

"I agree, but I don't know of one."

Rand looked at the tiki again. The goddess's deeply carved smile no longer looked benign to him. "I think she's mocking us," he said.

"That's because we're foolish *papalagi*. Let's go on. The riddle says there is just one key. What we're looking for could be on one of the others."

It was that thinking that kept them going right up through the fifth tiki. As Rand judged the angle of incline to the sixth statue, his interest in pursuing the last two began to wane. Claire sensed his hesitation.

"I'm not quitting now," she said.

"Claire, it's fifty feet almost straight up to the next tiki."

"We knew that when we started this morning."

"I thought there would be something by now. Your riddle . . ." It was impossible to keep disappointment from straining his voice.

Claire touched his arm. "Rand," she said softly. "If you're afraid for me, I'll wait here. But don't stop short because of me. I swear I'll go on alone."

Rand studied the tilt of Claire's chin. Tendrils of hair had escaped her braid. Damp wisps lay against her temples and forehead. There were tiny beads of perspiration across her upper lip. His shirt clung to the curve of her breasts. He watched her pluck at it, then fan her exposed throat. The harness looked as if it was chafing her shoulders. He gestured to Brown to bring a canteen of water forward. Claire drank greedily when it was thrust into her hands. She held it out for Rand when she was through.

"Mr. Brown and Mr. Whittier will take me if you don't," she said while he drank.

Rand darted both men a glance and they looked quickly at the ground. He didn't know quite how to interpret their refusal to meet his eyes. He wondered if they would really go against his express wishes. Rand decided not to test them. He took a few swallows from the canteen and gave it back to Brown. "We'll rest a little longer," he said, watching Claire. "Then we'll start climbing." Her beatific smile rewarded his decision.

Rand leaned back against the tiki. There was no danger of

the statue tipping. It easily weighed half a ton. Brown and Whittier stretched out beneath some palms. Whittier gave Claire a bit more lead on the harness so she could sit down. Her legs dangled over the outcropping.

"How high are we?" she asked.

"Ninety, ninety-five feet."

Claire let a breath out slowly and eased herself back a little. She heard Rand's short laugh. "It was always my idea to come up here," she told him, "but Tipu had to coax me out to the tikis. He was a little monkey. Completely fearless. It wasn't like that for me. I wouldn't be sitting here if I could see."

Rand didn't respond. His eyes were trained off shore, first on *Cerberus,* then on the dark shadows riding the waves toward her. The shadows took shape slowly, rising and falling at first, then steady on the surface as they cut through one crest after another. Rand estimated the speed of the small outriggers at close to twelve knots. They glided across the water as a single mass, separated by only a few feet at starboard and port and again at stern and bow. There was a powerful beauty in their approach. Their masts bent like reeds, and their triangular sails bowed with captured wind. They sped forward as if guided by one hand. Like an army of ants their approach was relentless. They could have been the tentacles of a single organism.

What they were was an armada.

Over Claire's head Rand motioned to Brown and Whittier to direct their attention to the horizon. He placed a finger to his lips to warn them not to comment. Once the two men saw the advancing fleet of outriggers, an entire pantomime of orders and questions began.

Claire lifted her head, her brow furrowed. "Why is everyone flapping their arms?" she demanded. "Mr. Brown? Are you going to take flight?"

Brown, who had indeed been waving his arms to gesture his intention to leave the group and warn Cutch, let his hands fall to his side abruptly. He cleared his throat, his Adam's apple bobbing, and looked to Rand to provide an explanation.

"Mr. Brown is going to heed nature's call," Rand said. He

saw Brown's thin face turn a ruddy hue. "He was trying to be delicate about it."

"Oh." Claire ducked her head.

Rand waved Brown on. The man tore through the ferns with little regard for the path that had already been cut. Rand bent and touched Claire's shoulder. "Let me help you up."

"Are we ready to go?" She gave him her hand and allowed Rand to pull her to her feet. "I confess I thought we would take a longer rest."

Rand didn't comment. He had no way of knowing if they had been seen on the ledge. The Solonesians had embraced some of the *papalagi's* ways. Telescopes were now a valued possession of the seafaring islanders. Rand took Claire's arm and hurried her away from the clearing where the tiki stood. The canopy of ferns and trees offered immediate shelter, but his haste raised Claire's suspicions.

"Something *is* wrong," she announced. "You may as well tell me, Rand. My cooperation is so much easier to come by that way."

Rand grabbed Claire's harness at the back and thwarted any thoughts she had about taking it off. "I need you to do precisely as I say, Claire. Do you understand?"

"Yes," she said, hearing his urgency clearly now. Nothing about his tone suggested this was negotiable. "Of course. Whatever you want."

He kissed the crown of her head, thanking her for not delaying him with questions. "I want you to stay here with Whittier. That's all you have to do."

Claire's hands folded into fists at her sides. It was the only way she could keep from reaching for him. She listened to him charge off with the same reckless speed that had driven Brown. "It is *not* a call of nature," she said with quiet sarcasm.

"No, ma'am," said Whittier.

"It wasn't fair for my husband to leave the explanations to you, Mr. Whittier, but there you have it." Claire shrugged out of the harness. Now that she was forbidden to go anywhere, it was an unnecessary precaution. "I'm waiting."

Whittier craned his neck to see past Claire and the tiki beyond her. The canoes were almost upon *Cerberus* now. It was as if the clipper was going to be swallowed by a bloom of algae. "It's the Solonesians," he said. "Their navy's here."

Claire frowned. "The Solonesians don't have a navy."

Whittier tugged on one of his brows nervously. "Begging your pardon, Mrs. Hamilton, but when one group of people put together this many boats, it's a navy."

"It's a fishing fleet."

"I make about fifty outriggers carrying six men each."

"Fifty?" Claire felt her heart trip. She had never heard of so many canoes being amassed. "That can't be."

"It surely is."

Claire realized belatedly that she had offended her guard. It did not surprise her that she thought of him in that light now. She understood it was what Rand intended when he left her with him. "I'm sorry, Mr. Whittier. I don't doubt you. The men must come from all the islands in the Solonesian group. No one island has such a fleet."

"That's what I'm saying, ma'am. It's a navy."

Claire shook her head. "What makes you think they're not here to welcome us?"

"It would be the spears," he said flatly. "I've seen the like before, and their kind ain't for fishin'."

The ground suddenly felt soft and uneven beneath Claire's feet. Her stomach lurched. "Where has the captain gone?"

"After Brown," he said. "They both mean to find Cutch and the others. Like as not Cutch won't be able to see what's happening until it's too late."

"It's already too late, isn't it?" Claire said.

Even as she asked the question the fleet divided. Fully half the canoes surrounded *Cerberus* while the others sped toward shore.

"What's that sound, Mr. Whittier?" Claire strained to make it out. At first she thought it was the beating of the wind in the sails. "Is it drums?"

"Not drums," he said. "The men are chanting. Reckon it's a battle-ready song." He watched as the islanders around *Cerberus* tossed ropes over her rails and shinnied up the sides as swiftly as spiders. The crew on board the clipper could not possibly repel the force. Their only hope was to surrender quickly and pray for mercy.

Claire shivered as a great cry was carried to her ears from across the water. "Is it *Cerberus?*" she asked. "Have they taken her?"

"Aye," Whittier said softly. "She's theirs now. Not that they'll have any use for her. Great clumsy thing compared to the skiffs they use on these waters."

"What about the crew? Can you see if they're all right?"

Whittier couldn't know with any certainty what had happened on board, but he spoke to ease Claire's fears. "There's been no fighting. That's what the captain would have wanted."

Claire nodded. "Are there canoes just off shore?" she asked.

"That's right. The half that didn't take *Cerberus*. I thought they were coming in, but they stopped short. They're flanking the entire shore from the lagoon to about sixty yards west of here."

"They won't come ashore," she said. "Not all of them. This is sacred ground. The priests are the only ones who will brave the tapu." Claire knew that by setting foot on Pulotu in front of so many witnesses, the priests would have their authority from the spirit gods confirmed. Rand would have to tread carefully if he wanted to come to terms with the priests. She hoped he remembered that. "Take me to my husband."

Whittier swallowed hard. "Now, Mrs. Hamilton, that's just what the captain said I wasn't supposed to do. And you shouldn't ask me."

Claire managed not to stamp her foot in frustration. She found Whittier's sleeve and tugged on it. "What can you see?" she demanded with growing impatience. "Is there one outrigger moving forward?"

Whittier edged them both cautiously to the edge of the clearing. "One canoe," he said, holding out his arm to bar Claire from going forward. "The men are all in fancy headdresses."

"Those are the priests."

"Mostly," Whittier said, his eyes narrowing on the central figure.

''What do you mean?''

''I mean they're mostly men. The one that's leading is sure enough a woman.''

Claire's breath caught. Her fingers tightened on Whittier's arm. Her voice barely reached the level of a whisper. ''Tiare,'' she said. ''It must be Tiare.''

Chapter Thirteen

Rand took a single step toward the open beach and found his way immediately blocked by Cutch. "Step aside," he said.

Cutch did not move. He was aware of the others watching him. "Tell me what you're thinking," he said quietly.

Rand had to tilt his head back to look into Cutch's dark eyes. "I'm going to ask for the return of my ship and the men."

He made it sound so reasonable that Cutch could almost believe this bold tactic had some chance of success. "There are three hundred of them."

"I only need *her* permission."

Cutch looked over his shoulder. Beyond the shade of the palms that protected their small band, he could see the Solonesian priestess and her entourage begin to fan out. She was directing them toward the tikis. "Claire," Cutch said softly. The danger to her was unclear, but he knew Whittier would not let the priests reach her without a fight. He felt Rand simply step around him. This time he did not try to halt his progress.

There was a faint disturbance on the edge of the forest as Rand moved through the undergrowth. When he reached the perimeter of the pale sand, his arrival was greeted without surprise. The priests had closed ranks again, clearly protective of the woman in their midst. Their attention, for the time being, was on Rand, not on the tikis.

His stride was confident, not threatening. Rand kept his hands at his sides, palms out, clearly showing he had no weapons and no reason to think he needed them. He did not know if this gesture made him courageous in the eyes of the Solonesians, or merely foolish. He halted when no more than ten feet separated him from the priests.

"Captain Rand Hamilton," he said, bowing his head slightly in acknowledgment of the woman in his presence. He saw his name cause a stir among the priests. There was an exchange of glances. Only the woman remained unmoved by this information. Rand went on, "Master of *Cerberus*."

"No longer," came the softly spoken reply. "I am Tiare. And the ship is mine." Lifting one arm in a graceful gesture, Tiare parted her protectors. She closed the distance to Rand before anyone could stop her. For a moment her eyes strayed past his shoulder to the edge of the forest. "How many are watching your back?" she asked.

The directness of the question did not startle Rand. He found he had no capacity for surprise left. "Tiare." He said her name under his breath, his lips barely moving. Did Claire know? he wondered.

Tiare's sloe eyes returned to Rand, but the mask of calm she wore was impenetrable. Her small chin lifted slightly, arrogantly. Her bare, honey-skinned shoulders were set back. She wore the mantle of authority as if it were tangible, her proud carriage brooking no refusal. "How many?" she repeated.

"Six," Rand said. "Watching my back."

"You will tell them to come forward."

"To what purpose?"

"To *my* purpose."

Rand shook his head. If she was angered by his refusal, she didn't show it. But then, Rand reminded himself, she had three hundred men to do her bidding. His lack of cooperation was hardly worth noting. Perhaps she was even amused, though Rand could not glimpse any hint of a smile on the wide curve of her mouth. He watched her head tilt slightly to one side as she regarded him with detached curiosity. He recognized the look. It exactly mirrored his own expression when he stumbled upon a particularly peculiar specimen. Her eyes pinned him back.

It was not entirely possible to determine her age. Her honeyed complexion did not hint at her years. There were no creases at the corners of her eyes or mouth, and the slender stem of her neck was smooth and unlined. Her thick hair, dark and glossy, fell all the way to her hips. She wore it without ornamentation, simply parted in the middle and tucked behind her ears so that it rippled softly past her shoulders. Unlike the priests, she had no headdress and displayed no tattoos. Their chests were bare while she was modestly covered by a pale yellow sheath. The lava-lava draped her from breast to ankle, and it was only when she walked, and the material parted along her calf, that a glimpse of the elegant line of her leg could be seen.

"What are your intentions?" Rand asked.

"I have the same question."

"We pose no threat to you."

"No threat?" She used one arm to indicate the expanse of shoreline. "This island is sacred," she said. "Your presence off shore was a threat. Your presence here is a violation."

"In a few hours we would have been gone."

She gave no indication if she believed him. "You will be gone now. Order your men to come out."

"What about my ship?"

"I have not decided. However, as long as your men offer no resistance, they are safe."

Rand wondered if she could be trusted.

As if she could read his mind, Tiare asked, "What choice do you have, Captain?"

Rand looked out to *Cerberus* again. The men lining the rail were all Solonesian. His own men, he imagined, were bound on deck or already in the hold. His gaze wandered to the armada of outriggers along the shore. It hardly mattered that Tiare's followers would not set foot on the island. As long as they held his clipper, Rand knew he had no leverage. His resistance could cost the men on board their lives. As Tiare said, what choice did he have? He lifted one hand and indicated to Cutch that he and the others should reveal themselves. He stepped to one side so Tiare could watch their approach without moving herself.

As though a light breeze moved through the trees, palm fronds swayed one after the other until the group passed into the open. Cutch didn't pause at the edge, but the others did. Taking their cue from him, they hurried to catch up. Macauley Stuart brought up the rear.

"You can see they're unarmed," Rand told Tiare.

"They have no weapons I can *see*," she said. "There is a difference."

"We are not soldiers."

"There was never any doubt about that, Captain Hamilton. If there had been, your name was enough to put it to rest. Hamilton-Waterstone. It was only a matter of time before you reached us."

Rand assumed that she had learned of his search for the treasure from other islanders. *Cerberus* was not an unfamiliar sight in the South Seas. Even separated by hundreds of miles of water, the island chains had astonishingly swift communication. The inhabitants of Polynesia were no longer as isolated as they once were. The European trade joined them in ways that hadn't been possible when the islands were first explored and settled. "You were expecting us," Rand said.

It was the first time Tiare smiled. "For three hundred years, Captain."

Rand merely stared at her, not certain he could have understood her correctly. Clearly her smile indicated that she relished her answer and his stupefied response.

"You have come for the treasure that bears your name." She said it without inflection, merely as a statement of fact. "Your name and the name of one other." Tiare pointed to Cutch as he closed in on them. "Is *he* a Waterstone?"

Rand shook his head. "There are no Waterstones."

Tiare's eyes lifted to take in Cutch's large frame. It wasn't enough. In the end she conceded to his size by tipping her head back. She blinked once when he grinned broadly and introduced himself.

"Cutch, ma'am. I'm called Cutch."

Rand did not think he imagined the faint color that tinged Tiare's cheeks. His eyes shifted to Cutch, regarding his friend and mentor in a new light. If Cutch was aware of Tiare's reaction, he didn't show it.

"I am Tiare."

Cutch's smile faltered, then faded. He glanced at Rand for confirmation. "Tiare?"

"Apparently so."

Macauley Stuart pushed his way through the men behind Cutch. "Claire's Tiare?"

Stuart's intrusion in the conversation registered first with Tiare, then the import of his words. A small furrow appeared between her dark brows. "Claire?" she asked. "Claire Bancroft?" It was not properly a question the way Tiare said it. It was as if she knew the answer but found it suspect.

Rand ignored Tiare and resisted the urge to look back at the face of Mauna Puka. If Whittier was following orders, then Claire was safe. Tiare did not give him the impression that she would have welcomed Claire's presence. It might go badly for all of them if the priestess knew Claire was on Pulotu. "Tell me what you're going to do with my ship," he said.

Tiare gave Rand as much attention as he had given her. Her eyes narrowed on the doctor's face. She pointed to him and motioned him to come forward. She saw him look to Rand, then to Cutch for instructions. "They are not in command here," she reminded him. "Not on Pulotu. Now come here." She indicated the ground in front of her. When Macauley obeyed, the priests moved to surround the group. "What is your name?" she demanded.

"Macauley Stuart."

"Tell me what you meant."

The doctor did not pretend to misunderstand. "I have heard your name before," he said. "I wondered if you might be the one of whom Miss Bancroft spoke."

"How do you know Claire Bancroft?"

"I am her physician."

Rand watched Tiare closely. Stuart had confirmed the answer to the question she would not ask. Now Tiare knew Claire was alive.

"Claire is here?"

Belatedly it seemed Macauley realized he had said too much. He hesitated, weighing his answer, then looked squarely at Tiare and lied to her. "No, not on Pulotu. On Raiatea."

Tiare said nothing. Her upper lip lifted in a sneer as soft as the lilting accents of her native language. She stepped back from the circle of men and peered into the dense forest undergrowth. Her eyes moved slowly along the tree line and then lifted to the foothills of Mauna Puka. She studied every one of the tikis. Finally she pointed to the two priests closest to her and spoke an order in her own tongue.

The men seized Macauley Stuart and began dragging him toward the water. Cutch started forward to rescue the doctor, but Rand grabbed him by the arm and held him back.

Tiare smiled thinly. "Your captain is wise," she said. "You might render some assistance on shore, but you will surely be pulled into the surf. Once there, my men will overpower you."

Rand let his arm fall away from Cutch and watched as the priests pressed Macauley's head under the water. The doctor thrashed and heaved but they held him down. 'What did you tell them to do?"

"I told them to drown the liar." She saw that Rand was skeptical. "Do you think I wouldn't kill him for his lack of respect?" she asked quietly. "You don't know me at all, Captain Hamilton."

The priests yanked Stuart to his knees and let him suck in a breath. He tried to struggle to his feet but they held him fast. A wave washed against his chest and the breath he took was a mixture of air and water. Before he could clear his lungs they pushed him under again.

Tiare watched calmly. "He does not want to give her up," she said. "Even to save himself. How odd."

Rand could not decide if she found the doctor's loyalty

peculiar or the fact that Claire inspired it. "Stop them," he told her.

Tiare merely glanced back at him, her satisfied smile still very much in evidence; then she turned to watch Stuart's labored struggle again.

Rand lunged at Tiare, striking so quickly that even Cutch was caught off guard by the movement. There was a terrible cry from the men in the canoes. Their roar carried across the water and surged with the next wave onto the shore. The sound of it chased a shiver down Rand's spine, but he did not release Tiare. He pulled her away so that she was out of easy reach of the remaining priests. Out of the corner of his eye he saw Macauley lurch to his feet. His captors only had a loose grip on his wrists now. He could have shaken them off if surprise hadn't kept him immobile.

"Teee—arrrr—eee." Her name was carried on the back of the wind. Tiare and Rand heard it together, and they both looked up to find the source. The voice came again, lifting the name of the priestess so strongly into the air that it could be heard by the now hushed armada. "Teee—arrr—eee."

Rand scanned the face of Mauna Puka, his gaze moving quickly from one tiki to another in search of Claire. He saw her step out into the clearing where he had left her. She looked impossibly fragile next to the strength and fierceness of the stone tiki. Whittier hadn't let her leave, but apparently he couldn't stop her making herself known. She wasn't even wearing her harness. Rand released Tiare. His hands were shaking.

Tiare put one hand to her throat. She massaged the place where Rand's forearm had tightened against her skin. "Tell her to come down," she said to Rand. "Unless you want your men murdered in front of Claire, tell her to come down."

"I don't have to tell her," he said, watching Claire turn. Whittier stepped onto the outcropping and took her by the elbow. "She was letting you know she's coming of her own accord."

Tiare pointed to the priests holding Stuart. She spoke to them in her own language again, this time directing them to move the doctor to one of the outrigger canoes. When this was done, they returned to shore and took another of Rand's men. By the time Whittier was escorting Claire across the open sand, only Tiare and two of her priests remained. Whittier was removed next, his protests coming to nothing.

Tiare studied Claire, her features impassive. "You do well not to look at me," she said. "You shame yourself by returning to this sacred place. You shame all of us by bringing them with you."

Claire continued to keep her eyes averted. It was not terribly difficult. She felt as if she were going to be sick; her stomach was in her throat and there was a weight pressing against her chest. Stepping out to the tiki to reveal herself to Tiare was the hardest thing she had ever done, yet she had never once considered *not* doing it. Whittier's description of what was happening on shore convinced her that she had no choice. Somehow she knew that she was at the heart of the standoff. She could not let the doctor drown or Rand think he could hold off the armada by taking Tiare hostage.

"Can you not recognize what we have here?" Tiare demanded. "Or has the treasure blinded you as it did your father?"

Recoiling as if she'd been struck, Claire's head snapped up and her knees buckled. The darkness that consumed her vision remained as it was. She had the sensation of vertigo. Her stomach lurched again, and then she was weightless and falling, falling through the void that was her sight.

"Claire?" Rand touched her shoulder lightly as she stirred. With Tiare's permission he had been allowed to take her to *Cerberus* and place her in their cabin. He had not been able to rouse her to consciousness during the trip to the clipper or when he carried her below. It occurred to him initially that Claire had faked her swoon. It was this thought that kept him calm until they reached the ship. When she failed to respond to him after they were alone, the truth was borne home to him. Cursing himself for not demanding that Stuart attend her, Rand knelt at her bedside and bathed her face with cool water.

The clipper's sails had been taken in. She was being towed like a wrecked scow toward a destination determined by Tiare. His men, bound hand and foot on deck, could do nothing to stop *Cerberus*'s progress over the water. Tiare's armada rowed on into the late afternoon sun.

Claire would have sat up if not for Rand's palm on her shoulder.

"Slowly," he cautioned. "You've been sleeping deeply."

"Did I faint?"

He nodded. "Yes. I thought you planned it."

"I wish I had. I don't have a plan. Do you?"

"No." He watched her take this information in stride. He let his hand fall from her shoulder and helped her up. Rising from his knees, he sat beside her. "I was allowed to return you to *Cerberus*."

Claire had recognized the familiar fragrance of her own pillow as soon as she woke. "We're moving," she said. "Has Tiare given you command of your ship?"

"Not at all. Cutch is at the wheel, but only to guide her. Tiare's men are towing *Cerberus*."

"Towing her? But where?"

"She hasn't made me privy to her plans."

Claire closed her eyes and rubbed the bridge of her nose. "What can she be thinking?" She rested her elbows on her knees. "What did Tiare say to you while I was still in hiding?"

Rand repeated their brief conversation for Claire. "Until your name was mentioned, it seemed that we would only be escorted off the island. Stuart brought Tiare's wrath on him when he lied to her."

"It's a grievous offense," Claire said. "He should not have tried to protect me."

"He shouldn't have used your name in the first place."

"I don't think Tiare would have had him drowned."

"Is that right?" asked Rand dryly. "Then why did you show yourself?"

"Because Whittier told me you had Tiare by the throat. I considered my intervention timely."

"It was."

Claire sat up straight, a slight smile softening her worried expression. Rand's admission was offered rather reluctantly, as if it pained him that she was correct. Other than her smile, Claire let it pass.

"What did Tiare say to you?" Rand asked.

"She was angry with me for bringing you to Pulotu."

"Why? Why isn't she rejoicing? She said she'd been waiting for me for three hundred years."

"She said that?"

Rand realized it was the first time he'd mentioned it. "I'm sorry. Yes, it's what she said in response to learning my name."

Claire frowned. "But what does it mean? In all the time I knew Tiare, I never once heard her mention the treasure until today. Why would she say that to you?"

"I suppose because I'm a Hamilton. She seemed disappointed to discover there were no Waterstones among my men."

"I don't understand this at all. Is she taking you away from the treasure or toward it?"

Rand had wondered the same thing himself. "I don't know." He stood up and went to the small writing desk. Since their marriage he had moved many of his belongings into Claire's cabin. There was no good reason that she should have to learn his own cabin's layout when she was so comfortable in hers. He reached under the desk to pull out the navigation charts he had rolled and secured there.

"What are you doing?" asked Claire.

"Looking for a chart. Perhaps I can get a fix on our position."

Claire nodded. Pushing herself farther back on the bed, she crossed her legs tailor-fashion and folded her hands in her lap.

Rand glanced at her and smiled. "You've struck a thoughtful pose. Is it helping?"

"Not yet." She hesitated. "I was afraid to face her."

Rand stopped rummaging for a moment. "I know."

"There were so many times I thought I would be sick. Mr. Whittier was very kind and patient. He tried to dissuade me. I know he was trying to follow your orders, but I think he was worried about me."

"I'm sure he was."

"And then nothing happened."

Rand's fingers curled around the chart he wanted. He placed it on top of the desk. His attention, though, was for Claire. "I'm not certain what you mean. You fainted, remember? That's hardly nothing."

Claire's voice was not much more than a whisper. "I can't see."

Rand's chair toppled behind him as he pushed away from the desk and jumped to his feet. He went to Claire's side and pulled her into his arms. His fingers threaded in her hair and he stroked her back. Her small shudders tore through him. She pressed her face in the curve of his neck. Her tears slipped between her cheek and his throat. He did not bother to wipe them away. He would have absorbed them if he could.

"She asked me if I was blinded by the treasure as my father had been." Claire's words were offered somewhat shakily, but Rand had no difficulty understanding them.

"And that's when you fainted?"

She nodded. "I don't even know why. What word was I reacting to? Blinded? Treasure? Father?"

"All of it."

"Then why does it mean so little to me?" She lifted her head and impatiently brushed away tears. "Why am I not sick with fear now?"

"Perhaps because you've faced your worst fear."

"Tiare?"

Rand lifted Claire's palm to his cheek. He shook his head and let her feel the motion. His voice was gentle. "Your *worst* fear, Claire."

She sucked in her breath as the truth came to her. She spoke on a thread of sound. "I'm never going to see again."

Rand pressed his mouth to the heart of Claire's palm, then let her circle his neck again. She held him tightly, but she did not cry. He felt her breathing grow soft and even, and in time he became aware that she had fallen into a healing sleep.

Rand laid Claire back on the bed and covered her with a blanket. He bent over her and kissed her temple. He breathed deeply of the fragrance of her hair. "You will always see things I cannot," he whispered.

Rand rose slowly then and returned to his chart.

The island was called Tarahiki and they reached it at dusk. At first Rand thought Tiare meant to run *Cerberus* aground, but at the last moment the outriggers shifted their direction and the men towed the clipper past the dangerous shoals and into the island's secluded natural harbor. Rand saw immediately that *Cerberus* was no longer easily visible to any other ship passing Tarahiki. She was protected, or hidden, on three sides by towering coconut trees and volcanic rock. A waterfall split the horseshoe-shaped lagoon in two. The shoreline was narrow. Less than ten yards of white sand separated the water from the forest, and the rock at the sides of the inlet rose steeply.

Rand described it all to Claire as they stood at the rail of the clipper and awaited Tiare's arrival on board. None of her surroundings were familiar to Claire.

"Perhaps my description is poor," Rand said.

"No. You've said it all beautifully. I've never been here before. The name means nothing to me either." She repeated it to herself softly now. "Tarahiki." Claire shook her head. "No, I don't know it."

"I may have it wrong. It's difficult to be certain."

Cutch joined them at the rail. He was uncomfortable being able to enjoy some freedom on the deck while the crew remained bound. At the capstan their Solonesian guards were lowering the anchor. "It seems Tiare intends us to stay."

"That's what I was thinking," said Rand. He put his back to the rail and his chin lifted in the direction of his men crowded around the mainmast. "Have you considered how we might free them and take back the ship?"

"I find the presence of three hundred Solonesian warriors does not make for clear thinking."

Rand understood. The outriggers surrounded the clipper. The harbor was so crowded with the canoes, it was possible to reach the shore without getting one's feet wet. Even with the oars raised, there was little room for maneuvering. "I can't make out if we're going to be set free or getting our first glimpse of our prison."

Cutch had the same concerns. "How are you feeling, Claire?"

"I'm fine."

"The crew was relieved when Rand brought you topside. To a man they were worried about you."

Faint color touched Claire's cheeks. Everyone had been witness to her collapse. It embarrassed her to think about it. "Where is Tiare?"

"She's never been on *Cerberus,*" said Cutch. "She's on one of the outriggers with the other priests. I suspect she'll come aboard soon. What did she say about your father and brother?"

Claire shook her head. "Nothing. There was never a moment to ask."

There was some commotion at the starboard side. Rand turned and looked over the rail. A moment later Cutch joined him.

"What is it?" asked Claire.

"Tiare," Rand said succinctly. "Right on schedule." Arms folded across his chest, Rand watched the warriors on board throw out the rope ladder for her ascent. She was lifted above the canoe by the other priests until she could grasp the ladder. Rather than climbing it, it was hauled aboard by her men. His tone was dry. "That's a variation on getting aboard that I hadn't seen before."

Cutch watched as Tiare was set gently on the deck. She didn't falter as she walked toward them. She had a long, elegant stride. Cutch's heavy lids lowered to half-mast. He watched the pale yellow material of her lava-lava split along the length of her thigh. Every inch of her was sun-kissed. He stepped back as she approached Claire.

Tiare lifted her hand toward Claire and saw for herself that Claire's eyes did not follow the movement. "I didn't know," she told Claire. "Standing on the beach at Pulotu, I didn't know." She took Claire's hand and raised it to her own heart.

"I was angry, but I did not mean to be cruel. We have never been friends, you and I, but we have not always been enemies. I do not want to be your enemy now."

Claire nodded, her eyes closing momentarily. She felt Tiare's hand loosen around her own. She withdrew it carefully and let it fall to her side. "I didn't want you to know then," Claire said when she could trust her voice. "But I'm not sorry Captain Hamilton told you."

Tiare glanced at Rand. His features remained impassive, but his posture was protective. His hands rested lightly on Claire's shoulders. She addressed Claire again. "He is your husband?"

"Yes."

Pointing to Cutch, Tiare asked, "And this black man?"

"A friend," Claire said.

Tiare nodded, satisfied with the answer. "Why have you come back, Claire? Is it really for the treasure? I've never heard you express interest in it before."

"I could say the same of you."

Tiare's slight smile could be heard in her voice. "Then we've both had our secrets. But you haven't properly answered my question. Is it only the treasure?"

"No," said Claire. "Of course not. I've come for Tipu . . . and my father."

Rand and Cutch gave Tiare full marks for trying to school her expression. However, she could not control the color that drained from her face and left her complexion sallow. Rand's fingers tightened on Claire's shoulders, bracing her and himself for what Tiare could not yet put into words.

Claire sensed the tension. "Tiare?"

"Your father is dead, Claire. How can you not know that?" There was a hesitation, then a worried thoughtfulness to her expression that communicated to both Rand and Cutch that she was considering her words carefully. "You were with Sir Griffin when he died."

Claire blinked. "You're mistaken. I would remember that. I would *know*."

"Claire," Rand said quietly. Beneath his palms, her shoulders were rigid. ''You have always been aware there are events you can't recall.''

''But not *this*. I tell you, I would know.'' Her chin came up. ''Where is Tipu? I want to see my brother.''

''I will take you to him later,'' Tiare said.

Rand recognized Tiare's cool tone now. Her beautifully flowing accents were chilled and there was nothing but authority in her voice. Belatedly he understood that when Claire told Tiare she was mistaken, it was virtually the same as naming her a liar. Rand started to speak, but Tiare held up her hand, cutting him off.

''Your men will be freed after the lagoon is cleared of mine. This is Arahiti. It will be your home until it is decided what's to be done with you. You may leave the ship, of course, but not the island. Your great clipper cannot navigate the shoals without our help. Try to make your escape, and you will founder.''

Claire reached for Tiare, but the woman easily avoided the contact. Claire let her hand fall slowly back to her side. ''Why?'' she asked. ''Why are you doing this?''

Tiare did not answer. She turned and walked away, moving among her men with ease. She directed them in her own language, the clear command evident in her voice and in the haste with which others did her bidding.

A crease appeared between Claire's brows as she listened to Tiare. ''I don't know this woman,'' she said. ''Tiare was quiet. Most often she was biddable. She served others. Never once did she issue an order.''

One of Rand's brows arched. He looked over the top of Claire's head at Cutch. ''It appears she's learned the way of it in your absence.''

Cutch was watching Tiare, but he heard Rand's comment. He shook his head. ''She didn't learn this,'' he said. ''No one does. Look at how they move for her. She was born to it. The Tiare you knew, Claire? I'd wager *she* was the impostor.''

Claire's frown only deepened. ''But why act one way when you're really something else? Could she have really loved Sir Griffin so much?''

"Perhaps," Rand said quietly. "And perhaps she was following orders of her own." As he spoke, Tiare was being lifted over the side of *Cerberus* and lowered carefully to the waiting canoe. "Didn't you tell me once that Tiare's father was a priest? That she would have been a priestess if it weren't for your father?"

"Yes," Claire said slowly.

"Well, what if she's always been a priestess? What if her attachment to your father was by *her* design, not his?"

"But she had a child by him."

"Did she?" he asked. "How can you be certain? How can anyone but Tiare be certain?"

"It can't be. Tipu looks like—"

"Yes?" Beneath his palms Rand felt Claire's shoulders sag. "Claire?"

"He looks like Tiare," she said at last. "He looks nothing at all like Sir Griffin or even like me." Claire eased out from under Rand's light grip. She turned to face him, her expression still clouded with doubt and questions. "Even if it's true, why? What does it mean, Rand?"

"I wish to God I knew." He set Claire away from him. Following Cutch's gaze across the harbor, Rand could see the Solonesians paddling their canoes toward the mouth of the lagoon. The last of Tiare's men had just gone over the side. She was obviously confident of her ability to keep *Cerberus* in the harbor without guards. "Wait here. Cutch and I have to free the men."

It required less than ten minutes before every last man had the use of his limbs again. They stood and stretched. Some went port side to relieve themselves away from Claire's hearing. Macauley Stuart immediately sought out Claire while Rand and Cutch explained their situation to the crew.

"I think you should be lying in your cabin," he told her. "You have little color in your face."

"Rand will take me there when he's done talking to the others. Don't you want to hear what he has to say?"

"To what end? I know less than nothing about where we are or where we're likely to be once we leave here."

"That's my point, Macauley. We're not leaving. At least not until Tiare gives her permission."

"How can that be?"

"Rand can explain it better, but it has to do with the shoals around Arahiti. Without help from the Solonesians, he'd run *Cerberus* aground."

"But he has maps . . . charts. I've seen them."

"Of course he does," she said with more patience than she felt. "But they're only as good as the mapmakers and explorers who came before us. If this island has never been charted, then there's nothing on his map, is there?"

"No, I suppose not." He leaned against the rail. "And the name of this place again?"

"Arahiti. That's what Tiare called it. Rand thought we were on Tarahiki."

"Two different names for the same place?"

"Possibly." Claire didn't think so, but if it helped the doctor remain calm because he thought Rand knew where they were, Claire did not want to say anything to the contrary. "What about you, Doctor Stuart? Tiare's men were not gentle with you. Shouldn't you be resting below?"

If Macauley shut his eyes, he knew he would feel the priests' hands on the back of his neck, pressing his face under the surf. The last thing he wanted to do was to lie down. "In time," he said.

Claire was quiet a moment; then she said, "Thank you."

"Thank you?"

"For what you did on Pulotu. I know you tried to protect me."

"I spoke out of turn in the first place," he said.

She smiled. "That's what Rand said."

"He was right. As Cutch explained to me later, I was being punished for lying. I had not realized I was such a poor one."

Claire said nothing, but the echo of the statement stayed with her long into the evening.

It was late when Rand entered their cabin. At first he thought Claire was sleeping. When he sat on the edge of the bed, he realized she wasn't there at all. The blankets were rumpled into a pile and the pillows were scattered, but she was under none of it. Having been topside, Rand knew she wasn't there. He went down the companionway and found her in his work room. She was sitting at the table, her head in her hands, deep in thought. Moonlight touched her fair complexion. Her eyes were clear and no trace of tears was evident on her cheeks.

"At least you're dressed for bed," he said, shutting the door behind him.

She nodded once, rather vaguely, as if she hadn't really heard him.

Rand approached her. He kicked out the other stool and spun it around to Claire's side. He sat down, leaned back against the table, and stretched his long legs in front of him. His arms were folded across his chest. "Aren't you tired?"

Claire continued to rest her chin on her hands. "Was it only last night that we slept by the lagoon?"

"Hmm-mmm."

"How could I not have known about my father?"

Rand realized Claire's thoughts were tumbling in every direction. It wasn't surprising she couldn't sleep. "I think you did know," he said. "You've always suspected that you wouldn't find him alive."

"But if what Tiare says is true . . . I was with him when he died. How could I not remember *that?*"

"Perhaps you don't want to." Rand saw Claire's mouth twist to one side. Clearly his explanation was not to her liking. He didn't blink when she changed the subject again.

"Is Arahiti the same island as Tarahiki?"

"No. I miscalculated. There is no Arahiti on my charts, and Tarahiki doesn't have this lagoon or the shoals. Why do you want to know?"

"Macauley was uncomfortable with the idea that you might not know where we are."

Rand grinned wryly. "I find it a little disconcerting myself."

Claire lifted her head just enough to lay her cheek on her hands. Her face was turned in Rand's direction now and she was frowning. "You really don't know?"

"There's no island with this shoreline on any of my charts.

Arahiti doesn't exist as far as the mapmakers are concerned. Tiare's men have taken some of my instruments and I can't fix longitude or latitude with any great certainty. The path of Sirius in the night sky, the fact that I know the position of Pulotu and how long it took us to get here, will help me narrow our location, but pinpointing it? No, I can't do that. Arahiti is a Solonesian secret, I'm afraid.''

Claire nodded slowly, taking it in. ''I told Macauley this might be the case, but I didn't really believe it. I was rather patronizing to him. Now I don't think I like this news any better than he did.''

''Tiare never spoke of this place?''

''Never.'' She sighed. ''I'm learning there's quite a bit I don't know about Tiare. I suppose she's only ever told me what she wanted me to know.''

''Then she's not so different from any of us.''

Claire considered that. ''I've told you that my father was never particularly interested in the culture of the Solonesians, but I thought he loved Tiare. I realize now how much he tried to mold her into a proper European woman. He only ever accepted those Solonesian traits that served *him.*''

''It doesn't mean he didn't love her.''

''I suppose not, but it seems peculiar.''

''Now that you're so wise in the ways of love,'' Rand chided her.

''Exactly,'' she said a shade smugly. Without warning, Claire found herself being thoroughly kissed. She was not of a mind to draw back. Instead, she slipped her arms around Rand's neck and let him set her on the table top. ''Not here again,'' she murmured against his mouth.

''You had no complaints the last time.''

''I wasn't married then.'' His deep chuckle vibrated against Claire's lips.

''So you're respectable now.''

''Yes, I am.''

''More's the pity.'' He straightened and allowed his hands to rest lightly on her thighs.

''It doesn't mean you can't take me to bed.''

"Actually, it does. I have the watch. I only came down to check on you."

"May I go topside with you?"

"Of course." He helped her down from the table and waited in their cabin while she pulled on a gown over her shift and found a shawl.

The sky was overcast. A sliver of moon could be seen when there was a break in the clouds. Claire stood at Rand's side at the forecastle. There were few men on deck. Some had retired to their hammocks; others had been sent to shore in the rowboats to make camp. Lantern light dotted the narrow beach. Claire was only aware of the gentleness of the evening. Waves licked at the ship's hull, a light breeze beat the furled canvas against the masts. Farther off there was the steady rush of water over the fall. She wondered what purpose was served by intruding on this peaceful night. "Why do you need a watch?" she asked.

"Habit." Rand put his arm around her. "I volunteered because I didn't think I could sleep."

Claire recognized it was no small admission that he made. "Can you see Sirius?"

"Not tonight. The sky's thick with clouds."

"Do the men understand you don't know our location?"

"Yes. They've accepted we're not going anywhere just yet."

"But you haven't."

"I don't like being kept prisoner, Claire. The surroundings have nothing to do with it. Once was enough for anyone's lifetime. I don't know what Tiare has planned for us, but I'm not letting her plans be our only option. The men who left the ship are moving out tonight to explore the outer beaches. Cutch is leading one group. Dodd, the other. There are lanterns at the campsite, but they're for diversion."

"You think Tiare's followers are watching us?"

"Some of them, yes. Don't you?"

Claire hadn't thought about it. Now that she did, it made sense. "I suppose so."

"In spite of what she said about the shoals, she has to know there is always a possibility that I could navigate *Cerberus* out of here. Tiare does not strike me as leaving anything to chance.

I imagine we would find ourselves under attack if we didn't founder first.'' Rand let his arm drop away from Claire's shoulders. He leaned forward, bracing himself against the rail. ''I keep thinking about her reply when I noted she seemed to be expecting us. *'For three hundred years, Captain.'* What in the hell did she mean?''

''Perhaps she meant no more than that, Rand. What if you accept the words as she said them? It's been three centuries since the treasure was hidden here. What if the Solonesians have always known of its existence? What if they've been guarding it?''

''Guarding it,'' Rand said softly. ''From whom?''

Claire considered that. ''From anyone who wasn't a Hamilton or a Waterstone, I suspect.''

''You mean they were *entrusted* with protecting the treasure? Who would have charged them with that responsibility?''

Claire rubbed Rand's shoulder. ''It's your legend. Who do you think is the most likely candidate? James Hamilton or Henry Waterstone?''

''I'd like to believe it was my great-times-seven grandfather, but the truth is, it doesn't sound like something he or Henry would have done. They didn't trust each other. Can you imagine either one of them giving the Solonesians the keys to their kingdom?''

''When you put it that way . . .''

Rand breathed deeply of the redolent island air, then exhaled slowly. He realized he was no longer capable of thinking clearly. Rather than try, he simply pulled Claire into the shelter of his arms and held her there. ''What about Tipu?'' he asked quietly.

''Tiare said she would take me to see him. I have to trust that she will.''

''Claire, what did you imagine you would do with your brother when you set out?''

''At first I thought I only wanted to find him again, to be certain he was safe.''

''And later?''

''Later I suppose I had some vague idea that I would take

him back to London with me and ... and raise him ..." Her voice trailed off.

"And raise him as if he were your own son?"

Claire's throat had closed and there was an ache behind her eyes. She could only nod.

"And what of his mother?"

"I wasn't considering Tiare's wishes," Claire said, her voice small and tight. "Only those of my father. He wanted Tipu to be educated in England and know English customs." Claire felt Rand's arms tighten fractionally. Her smile was apologetic, watery. "Sir Griffin was not an easy man to understand."

Rand let his silence on the subject serve as his agreement. "Does Tiare know your father's wishes?"

"He never made any secret of them."

"Then she must suspect you've returned to take Tipu away. No wonder she became anxious the moment she realized you were on Pulotu. She's afraid of you, Claire."

"Afraid? Of me? I think you're mistaken."

"I'm not."

A throat clearing behind them interrupted Claire's response. "What is it?" she asked.

"Apparently our watch is over." Still sheltering Claire, Rand turned around. "Mr. Brown."

"Aye, Cap'n. You can rest easy. I have the next watch."

Rand nodded. He took Claire's elbow and waited for her to bid Brown good night; then he escorted her back to their cabin. She was in bed several minutes before she realized he was making no move to join her.

Turning on her side and propping herself on one arm, Claire cocked her head to listen to Rand's slight movements. When she quieted she heard the familiar sound of him smoothing one of his heavy charts across the desk. "You can't rest until you know where we are, can you?" She did not wait for an answer. Sliding her legs over the side of the bed, Claire joined Rand at the desk. "Is it because you want to go back to Pulotu?"

"Pulotu? No, I'm not interested in going back."

"You're not? But what about the treasure?"

"Wherever it is, it's not on Mauna Puka. I don't think it's anywhere on Pulotu."

"But—"

"The tikis are a diversion. You made me realize that."

"I did?"

Rand took Claire by the wrist and drew her onto his lap. The chart was laid out before both of them. It covered the entire surface of the writing desk and was draped several inches over either side. "What you said about the Solonesians being charged with guarding the treasure . . ."

"But I don't know that. I only suggested it to explain away what Tiare said to you."

"And it's a very good suggestion. The placement of the tikis on Mauna Puka never made sense to me. It wasn't the work of the Solonesians. They might have supplied the labor, but not the plan."

"Because it's like the Big Dipper."

"Yes."

"If the tikis keep others out, doesn't it follow that's where the treasure is?"

"Not necessarily. What if the plan was to keep attention on the island so the treasure could be kept more safely somewhere else? It's like a magician encouraging you to watch his hat while the rabbit is up his sleeve."

"But the tikis only serve to keep Solonesians away."

"Not the priests," he reminded her. "Doesn't it make sense that the secret of the treasure would be entrusted to a few, not the population at large? Every culture has small societies founded and maintained in secrecy. The priests of Solonesia may not be so different from the Masons. They have a tradition to uphold, a responsibility that's been passed along for three centuries: protect the treasure."

"And now that you're here, they have to decide what to do."

"Now that I'm here," he repeated softly. "If I only knew where that was."

Chapter Fourteen

"Let me look at the chart," Claire said. "Where is Pulotu?"

Rand guided Claire's index finger to the island. "Here. Almost 14° south of the equator and 160° longitude." To help her visualize their position, he drew her finger across the equator and used her thumb like the point on a compass. "Here are the four smaller islands closest to Pulotu. Haipai. Arotu. Hanna and Amo. Amo, to the south, is really an atoll."

"What about the rest of the Sun Islands?"

Rand looked at the map. There were so many tiny islands that made up the larger group known as Solonesia, he hardly knew where to begin. He started with the most populated one. "Here is Gaiati."

Claire nodded. "Yes. I know that one. Tiare was born there."

Still keeping her thumb on Pulotu, he showed her Rapa Tiri and Mauna Ti. "It's likely most of the men in the outriggers today were from one of those three islands. The call to arms probably began at Gaiati and continued southwest. Men joined in waves until Tiare's armada was built, and then they came on a fairly straight course for Pulotu."

"Show me."

He took her finger to each of the islands. "Here and here and here . . . and here."

"Gaiati to Rapa Tiri to Mauna Ti to Pulotu? Is that right?"

"Well, they would have passed Hanna before they reached Pulotu."

Claire asked him to show her islands around Pulotu again. "Not the atoll," she said. "It confuses me."

"You're confusing *me*," he said. "What are you looking for?"

"The forest," she said simply.

When she offered no further explanation, Rand went through the motions again. He studied the latitude and longitude of each of the islands, their shorelines, and the distance separating them as he took Claire from one to the other. Belatedly he noticed that her hand was trembling in his. He squeezed it. "What is it, Claire? Are you all—"

She found his mouth with hers and kissed him hard. "Don't you see?" she demanded.

"What?" he asked, glancing at the chart again.

"The forest!"

"Claire, it's the Pacific. There's no—"

"The forest," she said again. Almost breathless now, Claire pushed herself off Rand's lap and hurried to her armoire. She didn't mind that she stumbled into things in her haste or that she almost collided with the door of the wardrobe as she flung it open.

"Careful," Rand called to her. He watched her pull open drawers and begin to ransack them. She pitched ribbons and scarves and combs over her shoulder and onto the floor. The colorful litter spread out at her feet was testimony to her excitement. Gone was the Claire who insisted that everything be in its place.

"Here it is!" she announced.

Rand could not properly see what she had in her hand until she returned to the table. She sat down on his lap again and showed him the object of her frantic search. "A brooch?" he asked. "What has that to do with—"

He stopped because she was more intent on opening the

brooch than on listening to him. When the pin was free, Claire found his hand and began to lift it toward her. Rand resisted, uncertain what she was going to do.

Claire felt him pulling against her. "Do you think I mean to stick you?" she asked, amused.

"I have no idea."

"Put your hand over mine and take me to Pulotu."

"Very well." He drew her hand with the brooch in it to the island, then watched in some horror as Claire poked a hole in his valuable navigation chart. His fingers closed tightly over her hand to keep her from doing more damage. "What do you think you're—?"

"Showing you the forest," she said patiently, as though speaking to a child. "By connecting the trees."

It was then that Rand understood. "My God," he said under his breath, studying the map again. This time he did not allow his vision to be distracted by the lines that indicated sea depths, coastlines, and shore elevations. His eyes were no longer focused on meridians, parallels, and rhumb lines. Now he saw what Claire was looking at. "Here," he said, taking the brooch from her hand. "I have something that will work better than this." He reached in the drawer under the desk and found his dividers. He let Claire hold them and feel the shape of the plotting instrument.

"Like two question marks facing one another," she said.

Rand chuckled. "I suppose it is. Careful, the ends of those question marks are pointed."

Her fingers fiddled with the adjustable screw that joined the hooks. She could make the distance between the two pointed ends wider or narrower by turning the screw. "I suppose we know now what Captain Waterstone's cartographer used to make the holes in the riddles." She gave it back to him. "You do it."

"Dividers are usually used to help measure the distance between two charted points. However . . ." He poked through the hole Claire had made at Pulotu, widening it slightly. "It will . . ." He punctured Rapa Tiri and Mauna Ti. "Do nicely . . ."

The dividers were stabbed into Haipai and Arotu and Hanna in quick succession. "For this purpose." Rand made the last hole in Gaiati.

- Gaiati

- Rapa Tiri

Hanna •   • Mauna Ti

Haipai •   • Arotu

• Pulotu

He dropped the dividers on the floor and held up the chart to the lantern. Pinpoints of light came through like stars in the night sky. It was unmistakably the Big Dipper that appeared. Rand threw back his head and laughed. "You are the *most* amazing woman I have—"

Claire turned in his arms so that he was forced to drop the chart. She circled his neck. "I am the most amazing woman *ever*," she whispered.

Rand's laughter deepened. "Yes," he said. "You are." He kissed her full on the mouth. Her lips parted under his and her fingers tightened on his neck. Rand slid one arm under her legs and the other behind her back. He stood, lifting her with him, and kicked things out of his way on his way to the bed.

"What are you doing?" Claire asked as he lowered her.

"Wrong question. You should be interested in what I'm *going* to do."

"But you don't know anything—"

Rand's brows kicked up. "I know this," he said, kissing Claire just below her ear. "And this." The damp edge of his tongue flicked the hollow of her throat. "And how to do this." He unfastened the first three buttons of her nightshift and parted the material to reveal her breasts.

Claire blocked him by putting up her hands and pressing against his shoulders. "I'm talking about the treasure," she said. "You don't know where it is"

"Oh, I think I can find it from here." Because his tone left no doubt about what he was referring to, Rand wasn't surprised to see Claire's skin pinken from her cheeks to her beautifully full breasts. He took her by the wrists and held them lightly at her sides while he lowered his head. His mouth closed over her nipple and sucked gently. He heard her quick intake of air. She held it like that, the breath caught in the back of her throat, until he levered himself up to her mouth. He kissed her and took the breath she was holding.

Claire's tongue swept across Rand's upper lip. She traced the shape of his smile and delighted in the slightly wicked curve of his mouth. Slipping her wrists free of his loose hold, Claire began to undress her husband. She helped him shrug out of his jacket and unfastened the buttons of his shirt. They both sat up while she drew the shirt off his shoulders. It joined the debris from her armoire on the floor. The pile grew to include Rand's boots, stockings, trousers, and drawers, and finally Claire's shift.

Claire stretched her body along the length of Rand's. Her bare toes wriggled against his ankle. His hands were at the small of her back. They moved lower, cupping her bottom. "Coming aboard?" he asked huskily.

Laughing, Claire raised herself with Rand's help until she was lying full across his body. Her breasts were flattened by his chest, the hard points of her nipples exquisitely tender. She slid one hand between their bodies and lifted her hips. She guided him into her. The small, involuntary movements made Rand groan softly. Claire hummed her pleasure.

She pushed herself up while Rand's fingers traced the curve at the small of her back. She rocked slowly, rising and falling with the same gentle rhythm of the ship under her. Rand stroked her thighs. His thumbs went across the plane of her belly, then drifted higher until they found the underside of her breasts. His thumbnail lightly scraped her nipple. Claire's shiver vibrated through him.

He pulled her down and kissed her deeply. Her mouth was warm and sweet. He turned so that she was under him. He thrust into her hard enough to force a whimper. She jerked under him and clutched at his shoulders. "I'm sorry," he whispered. "I don't know what—"

Claire held him tightly, shaking her head. "No, it's all right." She nudged his mouth with lips that were almost bruised by the intensity of his kisses. "I won't break."

Rand's touch gentled anyway. He did not temper his passion so much as tame it. She did not make it easy for him. Claire clutched his hips with her thighs. She arched under him, digging her heels into the mattress. Her breasts lifted, teasing him. Lantern light bathed her, and where his mouth had been her skin glistened. He took one damp nipple between his lips again. His teeth closed carefully over it. Claire's fingers twisted in his hair and she held him there. The hot suck of his mouth made her cry out his name.

She held him when he came. Her arms and legs tightened. Her mouth closed over the skin of his shoulder. Where she held him most intimately contracted as well. Then it was her turn, and his fingers caressed her. She was damp and her skin had a heady, musky fragrance. He stroked her, finding the rhythm that had been his body's moments earlier. She never said once that it was too much. True to her word, she didn't break.

She shattered.

He watched as pleasure changed the shape of her lush mouth, curving it into a perfect O. Her lashes fluttered once, then closed. Her throat arched and the line of her jaw tightened. The wave of tension that was passion's release passed. Light color blossomed in under her skin.

For Claire the sensation of weightlessness slipped away gradually. She was grounded again. She became aware of Rand's arm lying across her abdomen, his breath near her ear. Her arms and legs felt pleasantly tired, and her heart hammered out a slow, heavy beat.

"Go to sleep," he whispered.

Claire nodded. He did not have to tell her twice.

* * *

When Claire woke, she was alone in the cabin. She had no idea if she'd slept one hour or seven. She felt rested enough to get up and find Rand. Claire washed quickly and dressed her hair. She noticed that her abandoned search through the armoire was no longer in evidence. Rand had put everything neatly away. She smiled to herself, humming softly, as she drew her gown over her head. Claire smoothed the cream linen skirt over her hips and fastened the buttons on the bodice. The last thing she did before picking up her cane and leaving the room was to check the desk for Rand's chart. When she didn't find it, she knew where he would be.

"Did you sleep at all?" she asked, walking into his workroom.

Rand didn't look up from the map spread in front of him. He tapped the stool beside him, absently indicating that she could join him.

Claire found the stool with the tip of her cane and sat down. "I passed the night quite comfortably."

Rand's response was a distracted grunt.

"Yes, well, thank you for asking." She let a few minutes pass in silence. Occasionally there was the telltale scratch of his pen on the paper as he made calculations with the parallel rulers and the plotter. Claire placed her elbows on the table and rested her chin on the back of her hands. "Am I covering anything important?" she asked.

"Hmmm?"

Claire realized he had not really heard her. She supposed that was an answer of sorts. Apparently she was not disturbing him in the least. Less offended than annoyed, Claire laid one forearm across the chart. "*Now* am I covering anything important?"

Rand rubbed the bridge of his nose with his thumb and forefinger. It eased a little of the headache that was pressing the back of his eyes.

Sensing his distress, Claire was immediately sorry for the aggravation she had added. She leaned the cane against the table and stood. Placing her hands on Rand's shoulders, she began massaging the tight muscles across his back. "Can I get you anything?" she asked. "Dr. Stuart has headache powders."

"No, I don't want any of *his* medicine."

Claire smiled, teasing him. "Isn't that a bit like cutting off your nose to spite your face?"

"Right now I would gladly cut off my head."

She worked her fingers more vigorously and was rewarded by his grateful sigh. "How long did you sleep?"

"A few hours. It's after seven now."

"Have you been poring over the chart since you woke?"

Rand shook his head. "I checked the watch. Dodd's band returned to the camp sometime after midnight. We know a little more about the shoals than we did before. Not much, though. Cutch and his group slipped back just before daybreak. He's not reported to the ship yet."

"Shall I bring you some coffee?" she asked.

"I'll get it." He realized how good it sounded. There were healing powers in the aroma alone. "Maybe you can calculate a course for us while I'm gone."

"Very amusing." She let her hands fall away as Rand stood. He kissed the crown of her head, then left. Shrugging, Claire returned to her stool. Her stomach rumbled. She pressed her midriff against the table and hoped Rand thought about returning with more than coffee—and that he brought enough to share.

Claire picked up the parallel rulers and tapped one beveled edge lightly against the chart. She wondered when Tiare would return and when she could expect to see Tipu again. She had thought a great deal about the conclusion Rand had drawn. Claire supposed it wasn't outside the realm of possibility that Tiare was frightened of her. Tiare had always been protective of Tipu and resentful of what she perceived as Claire's interference. Claire wondered at her own arrogance in assuming she had some inherent right to take Tipu from his mother, just to raise him in the cold, industrial, but infinitely civilized climes of London.

Claire shook her head, her smile rife with self-mockery.

Vowing to tell Tiare that there was no reason to fear her intentions, Claire recognized that she had lightened her own burden. This time when she tapped the rulers, the beat was a livelier one.

The door opened and Claire spun on the stool. Her welcoming smile grew wider as the aroma of freshly brewed coffee reached her nose. "I hope some of that is for me."

"If you want it." Macauley Stuart crossed the room and set his mug on the table. His placement effectively stopped Claire's hasty attempt to roll the chart up. "There's no coffee stain, I promise you," he told her.

Claire kept her fingers on the part she had already rolled. "I might knock it over," she said. "I'm blind, you know."

That gave the doctor pause. He looked at her gravely set expression and said, "I believe I am finally becoming accustomed to your rather droll sense of humor." He took the ruler from her right hand and gently tapped the wrist of her other hand with it. Her fingers unfolded reflexively and the chart unrolled beneath her palm. "I assure you, no harm will come to it." He slid the mug across the chart toward her. "Enjoy," he said as her hands closed around it.

Claire did not lift the mug. She knew the position of her forearms across the table would frustrate Stuart's efforts to examine Rand's chart. "What are you doing here?"

"I was looking for you. I never had an opportunity to examine you after you fainted yesterday. I thought I would see you before you dressed for the day, but you were already gone from your cabin. I had not realized you were such an early riser."

"Perhaps that's because you spent so much of the voyage in your own cabin," she said.

Stuart let that pass. "Don't you want the coffee after all?" he asked. "I didn't drink from the mug, if that's why you're hesitant."

"No, it's not that. It's very hot, isn't it? I don't want to burn my mouth."

"I didn't notice as I was carrying it. Here, let me take it. I can add a little water from the pitcher on the bench."

"Oh, no. Then it will be diluted. It's better when it's strong, don't you agree?"

"It's better when it's hot," he said. "If you're not going to drink it, I will." His hands closed over hers.

Claire was determined not to lose this battle of wills. She held on to the mug tightly, pulling one way when the doctor pulled the other. Hot coffee sloshed and spattered the back of his hands and the tips of her fingers.

"Ouch! Dammit!"

Macauley surprised Claire by releasing his grip on her and the mug. The pull she had exerted on it was now too much. Her hands flew upward, the mug with them. She jumped out of the way of the hot coffee but there was no saving the chart. Claire could hear it dripping over the edge of the table and realized most of it was spreading out across Rand's valuable map. "Quickly!" she snapped. "Give me something to wipe it up!"

Too late Claire realized he wouldn't give her anything. Instead, he took control of the situation and she could do nothing but step aside. "Has it been ruined?" she asked anxiously.

"It's difficult to tell," he said, mopping up the coffee with his handkerchief. He went twice to the dissecting basin to wring out the scrap of linen. "There are some holes in this map, but I don't think the coffee did that." He said it tentatively, as if he weren't really certain. "It couldn't, could it?"

"I don't know," Claire lied. "Be careful not to tear it."

"I'm afraid the captain's writing has been smeared. That can't be good."

Claire sighed. "No, it can't be."

"This book's a little worse for wear," he said.

Claire's heart lodged firmly in her throat. "What book?" she asked weakly.

"The one holding down the far corner of the chart. I don't suppose you knew it was there."

Certain her heart was never going to resume beating, Claire asked, "May I have it please?"

"In a moment." Macauley wrung out his handkerchief a

third time, then applied it carefully to the open pages of the book. "This must be one of the captain's journals," he said.

"A log book?"

"No, one of his naturalist journals."

"Is the writing still legible?"

"That's difficult to say. I couldn't read it before it had coffee all over it."

So that's where his eyes had wandered while he was talking to her, Claire thought. He had found something else to occupy him while she was trying to protect the chart. "May I have it?" she asked again.

"Why? Do you think you can read it? You're blind, remember?"

Claire's mouth flattened. "It's only amusing when I say it." She held out both hands, palms up.

"In a moment." Macauley's eyes narrowed. His fair features took on a perplexed expression as he lifted one of the pages and noticed coffee had seeped through to the page under it. "How peculiar," he said.

"What?" Claire asked quickly. "What's peculiar?"

He told her what happened. "But the stain's in the shape of the Big Dipper," he went on.

"I agree that's peculiar," Claire said. "Now, may I have my husband's journal?" She hoped that by reminding Macauley of her relationship with Rand, he would be moved to respond more quickly. Her hands, however, remained empty. "What are you doing?"

"I'm blotting the coffee."

He worked more slowly than Claire would have liked. She was sure he was studying the writings. She realized a few moments later that she was only partially correct. Macauley Stuart was studying the map.

"Do you know what Captain Hamilton was plotting?" he asked.

"Plotting?" Claire forced a small laugh. "Does he really seem interested in intrigue to you? Against whom would he be plotting?"

The doctor shook his head. "The map, Claire. I'm talking

about the course he was plotting. He has joined six . . . no, seven . . . islands on this chart with a line running from one to the other." His voice slowed toward the end as he bent his head and looked at the map more closely. "He put these holes here . . . I wonder why . . ." He blinked, seeing the larger picture for the first time. "It's the Big Dipper, isn't it? Just like the tikis on Pulotu." He looked at the journal page again, lifting it carefully and examining it. He saw the tiny holes that had allowed the coffee to seep through in the same familiar pattern. "This is passing strange. His journal is torn in an identical manner."

"I'm sure it's all very interesting," Claire said in bored accents. "You must ask him about it. Have you quite finished cleaning the mess?"

"Yes, just . . . about . . . yes, I've got it . . . finished now."

Claire frowned. Her head was cocked to one side in an attitude of deep listening. "What did you do?" she demanded.

Macauley closed the journal and put it in her hands. "I finished wiping it down."

She shook her head. "No, you did something. I heard you. You removed a page."

"Claire, I assure you—"

"No, I assure *you*—" She stopped, clutching the journal protectively to her chest. She didn't need to examine it to know the Hamilton riddle was no longer among its contents. "It was you," she said accusingly.

"Me?" His response was an absent one. He was leaning over the chart again. He traced the lines Rand had drawn with his fingertip. His lips moved as he read the unusual island names to himself.

Claire hit the table with the flat of her hand. She felt Macauley jerk in response. Satisfied that she had his attention now, she continued. "You were the one looking through our belongings."

Macauley's brows kicked up, though his features remained pleasant. He tucked the journal page into the inside pocket of his jacket. "Really? And when did I do that?"

"On the voyage from London to Charleston," she said. "The cabins were disturbed from time to time . . . this workroom . . .

you told me last night that you had seen the captain's charts . . .'' Her voice trailed off momentarily as her mind worked out the problem. ''While we were at Henley, you were the one responsible for searching Orrin Foster's study. And later, after we returned to *Cerberus,* it was you who came into my cabin.''

''I was in your cabin many times,'' he pointed out calmly.

She waved aside his interruption. ''You were in there looking for something,'' she told him. ''And I surprised you. You hid from me while I searched the cabin. You *knew* I was frightened, yet you never revealed yourself. The irony is that I left and went searching for you, looking for your help. You weren't in your cabin then, no matter what you said to the contrary. You went there later, probably during the short time I was on deck, and that's how Mr. Cutch was able to find you. There was an accident topside, remember? You were needed to set a broken leg.''

''Oh, I remember,'' the doctor said. ''About setting the leg, at least. My recollection of the rest is rather vague, probably because I was involved in none of it.''

''Were you ever seasick even a single day?'' Claire asked. ''That's how you moved about so freely, isn't it? While Rand and the others thought you were confined to your bed, you were able to search the ship almost at will. *I* was certainly no threat.''

''Have I done something to offend you, Claire? Is that why you're making these accusations?''

Claire laid the journal down. She put out her hand again. ''Please give me the page you removed. You have no right to take it.''

Macauley glanced at the chart again. ''Hamilton's figured it out, hasn't he? This is his riddle. The *Hamilton* riddle.''

''I'm sure I don't know. My understanding is that the journal is scientific in nature.''

''Then perhaps your husband has not been as trusting as you might have hoped.'' Macauley regarded Claire's composed features with a critical eye. ''Or perhaps you are a more facile liar than I credited.''

"Rand will be returning soon. If you give me the page, I'll accept blame for the damage. I'll say nothing to him."

"You overplayed your hand, Claire. Now I *know* you're lying."

Claire felt her cheeks warming. "What is your interest in the treasure?"

"I imagine it's the same as yours," he said. "Finding it."

It was the answer she was expecting, yet Claire felt as if her breath had been stolen. Pressing her hands against her midriff, she sat down slowly. "Who are you?" she asked. Even to her own ears her voice sounded odd, adrift.

"Macauley Stuart," he said simply. Then he understood what was at the root of her question. "Oh, you mean am I a Waterstone or is there a Hamilton on my family tree? The answer is no. Neither. I'll tell you something else. I'm not Mercutio either."

"Mercutio?" Confused, Claire's brows creased. Her voice was just above a whisper. "But how . . . when?" Her eyes widened fractionally. "You were spying on us . . . on Pulotu . . . at the lagoon."

Stuart shrugged. "I was doing a bit of exploring on my own that morning. I didn't know you and the captain were gone from the camp."

"You're lying." Then she realized he had said *morning,* not evening. He had overheard more than her discussion with Rand about Mercutio.

Macauley saw the change in Claire's expression. "Yes, I know the Waterstone riddle. But then, I've always known it. It was only a revelation to discover you've known it as well."

Claire tried to understand what he meant. She found her breathing was coming more easily, but now her head hurt. She rubbed her temple. The ache moved behind her eyes. The darkness that was her constant companion seemed to have substance. It was actually painful. Claire tilted her head toward the cabin door. She listened for the sound of Rand's light step in the passageway. Where was he?

"The captain's been delayed, I think," Macauley told her. "An outrigger was coming into the harbor when I left the deck.

I heard someone say it was Tiare. I suppose your husband is welcoming her back.''

Claire started to rise. Immediately she felt the weight of the doctor's hand on her shoulder, halting her. She did not try to resist. "I want to see Tiare. She's going to take me to my brother.''

"In a moment. Hamilton will bring her here. He knows where you are.'' He lifted his hand but didn't remove it completely. It hovered just inches above Claire's shoulder. "Tell me what you know about the treasure," he said. "Is it on one of these islands?''

"I don't know.''

"Why did Rand connect them on the chart?''

"I don't know.''

"What's the significance of the Big Dipper?''

"I don't know.''

He raised his hand to strike her, then held back. He watched Claire sit there unflinchingly, unaware of his intent to send her reeling. He lowered his hand slowly. "We can join forces, Claire. You and I and the captain. Hamilton will accept my help if you suggest it. And I *can* help you. You can depend on it.''

Claire's lips merely tightened.

"What say you, Claire?''

"I don't believe you.''

Macauley shrugged. "I wish you'd reconsider.''

Claire was still for a moment; then she nodded. "All right, but there's nothing I can tell you that you haven't worked out for yourself already. I really *don't* know the answers to the questions you asked.''

He wondered if he could believe her. The opportunity to question her further was lost when Stuart heard footfalls in the companionway. "I believe the captain is coming now," he said. "Think about what I've said.''

Rand opened the door to the workroom, then paused on the threshold. "Doctor," he said, nodding in Stuart's direction. "I didn't expect to find you here.'' He stepped to one side and ushered Tiare into the cabin. "Tiare, you remember Macauley Stuart, don't you?"

"The liar," she said succinctly. Watching the doctor flush, Tiare was satisfied. She ignored him after that, crossing the room to Claire's side. Her hand curved gracefully as she reached to touch Claire's forearm. "I am going to take you to Tipu," she said, her voice lilting. "As I promised."

Claire forced a smile. She experienced no joy at Tiare's announcement. In that moment she hated Macauley Stuart for robbing her of that. "I would like my husband to come. I want him to meet Tipu."

Tiare's voice was somewhat imperious. "It is already arranged."

Macauley cleared his throat. "Then I shall come along," he said. "To attend Mrs. Hamilton."

Rand's brows rose. "Why do you think that's necessary?" He didn't wait for an answer. "Claire?" he asked. "Is something wrong?"

Everything, she wanted to say. *I've lost the Hamilton riddle.* "No, nothing at all." It was so patently a lie that Rand saw through it immediately, just as Claire knew he would. She also anticipated that he would place the wrong construction on it. She was not disappointed.

"Your cheeks are flushed," he said. He waved the doctor aside and went to Claire. He touched her forehead with the back of his hand. She was warm, but not overly so. Rand studied her again. He laid his fingers against her cheek.

Claire placed her hand over his. "It's nothing, I tell you. I was sitting at the table with my cheek propped on my hand."

Rand looked over his shoulder at Macauley. "Is she sickening again?"

"That's my assessment," he said. "Perhaps the visit to her brother should wait."

"No!" Claire removed Rand's hand. "I'm going. You may come if you want, Macauley, but I'm not staying here."

Rand glanced at Tiare. Her beautiful features held no clue as to what she was thinking. "Tiare? May the doctor join us?"

"I do not trust him. He is a liar."

Claire appealed to her. She did not want the doctor left behind with nothing to do but study the stolen riddle. Claire was certain he had his own reasons for wanting to go, or he wouldn't have suggested it. They were working at cross purposes and arriving at the same end. "Dr. Stuart was trying to protect me," she said. "He didn't understand the gravity of lying to you."

Tiare was silent for a long time. "Very well," she said finally. "He may come."

Macauley was the last one to leave the cabin. He picked up Claire's cane and gave it a little toss in the air, smiling broadly to himself as he made a show of catching it again. Claire had maneuvered Rand and Tiare perfectly, he thought. It was not entirely unexpected. The Duke of Strickland had warned him at the outset that Claire Bancroft was in every way her father's daughter.

Macauley Stuart told himself he would do well to remember that.

The outrigger was crowded once they were all aboard. There were six men at the oars. Rand, Claire, and Macauley were each squeezed between a pair of rowers while Tiare sat alone in the bow.

Macauley tapped Rand on the shoulder. "Will it be a long trip, do you think?"

Rand only shrugged. Any other movement would have caused him to collide with the men pulling the oars. He glanced up at the sun and tried to mark the course they were taking. In the distance he could make out the dark shape of an island. He kept it in his line of sight and compared it to what he remembered of its location on his charts. The outrigger canoe was skimming the water at a good clip, helped by an easterly wind. He made their direction as north by northwest. He was also aware when they began their slow, wide arc.

The outrigger slowed when it reached the inlet. The breeze was diminished by trees on either side of the shallows. Claire leaned back so Rand could describe the verdant landscape as they passed it. Every sort of greenery covered the nearly vertical walls of the narrow inlet. Delicate ferns swayed gently overhead, almost as if they were fanning the voyagers. Seven warmly colored varieties of hibiscus lent their fragrance to the humid air. The sun was at its zenith. As the canoe went deeper into the interior of the island, a bright shaft of light guided them.

High above them water cascaded from an opening in the rock. Sunlight glinted off the shower. Where the mist rose from the churning and crashing waters, a rainbow was born. One luminescent arc disappeared into the trees but the other end, a liquid ribbon of shimmering color, quite clearly sank beneath the water's surface.

Rand extended his arm to Claire to help her from the canoe. He lifted her past the shallow water and set her down when they reached shore. "Is it really so beautiful?" she asked him.

"Yes," he said.

"A rainbow," she whispered, sighing. "Water and sunlight. Proof of God's covenant."

For a moment neither of them moved. *At the end of one god's promise.* It was so obvious now that Rand wondered why he had never thought of it. A rainbow. It was perfect. He almost laughed out loud. Instead, he gripped Claire's elbow. The small squeeze he gave her was unnecessary. The revelation had effectively silenced her.

"Has something happened?" asked Macauley.

Rand turned to find the doctor watching both of them, but particularly Claire. "Just a misstep," said Rand.

Macauley immediately went to Claire's side. He slipped his arm through hers. "In the event you feel faint," he said kindly.

Claire knew exactly what his gallantry was in aid of: the doctor did not want her talking to Rand outside of his hearing. She accepted his assistance without demur.

"What is this place?" Rand asked Tiare.

Tiare didn't answer the question. "Come. We are almost there."

Tiare turned and moved with confident grace into a slim opening in the trees. The path was well marked because everything around it was grown. Only a steady parade of Solonesians kept one narrow route beaten down. They walked single file.

Rand led Claire by holding one end of her cane and giving her the other. Macauley followed with all six of the oarsmen in his wake.

The path took them upwards at a gentle slope at first, then at a sharper angle. After a hundred yards they were actually climbing stairs cut from volcanic rock. The dark green overhang of ferns and fronds blocked most of the sunlight until they reached the summit. There, the canopy parted and the vastness of the blue sky was revealed.

Claire raised her face to feel the warmth of the sun on her skin. Rand had dropped his end of the cane and was now standing beside her. She found his arm. "What is this place?" she asked him.

"A temple," Rand said. "There is an open-air altar at the center of a large, raised platform. The altar and platform are made from volcanic stones. It would have taken years to carry them all to this summit. Four wooden pillars are set a few feet from each corner of the altar. A tiki rests on the top of each of them. The forest is cut back ten yards on all sides and the platform is in good repair. I've seen temple ruins before in the islands. This isn't one of them."

Macauley Stuart listened to Rand's description. "Do you mean they still worship here?" he asked in hushed tones.

"That's what I think."

The doctor looked critically at the altar, taking in its height and length. "Do they practice human sacrifice?"

"When they find the right human," Claire said dryly.

Ahead of them Rand saw Tiare's shoulders shake slightly, as though she were trying to contain her laughter. He found himself smiling. Indicating to Claire that it was time to move on, he led her carefully up the steps of the platform. It wasn't until they approached the altar that Rand caught a glimpse of the boy shyly hiding behind it.

Rand knew Tiare had picked this location with a single purpose in mind: to remind Claire of Tipu's Solonesian heritage. It didn't matter that Claire couldn't see the temple. She could feel the smooth volcanic stones beneath her feet and touch the ancient altar that once held sacrifices to the Solonesian gods.

Beyond that, there was a sacred history here that transcended the stone.

Rand glanced over his shoulder and saw that the islanders who accompanied them had not stepped up to the platform. They stood back at a respectful distance, watchful, yet with the intention to give privacy to the reunion.

Rand released Claire's arm as Tiare brought her son forward. The boy came out from behind the altar with some reluctance. Rand could see that it was more than shyness that held the child back. He was afraid. "Here is your brother, Claire," he told her quietly.

"Tipu?" Claire held out her hand.

Tiare nudged the boy forward. "He is frightened of you, Claire. I told him you cannot see. He thinks the spirits who have taken your sight will not let you know him."

Tears welled in Claire's eyes. She dropped to her knees beside the altar. "I will know you," she said. "You are my brother, Tipu. I would know you among a hundred children."

Tipu's dark eyes regarded Claire warily. He did not like being afraid, especially not in front of the *papalagi*. His mother should not have said he was frightened. He inched forward as curiosity slowly overwhelmed his fear.

The skirt of Claire's gown was spread in a circle around her. She felt a shift in the fabric as Tipu's small, bare toes touched the hem. She gathered a few inches in her fingers, making the circle smaller and drawing him in. Claire didn't stop until she felt him nudge her knees. She knew they were almost eye to eye now. She could hear his light breathing, could almost feel it on her face. "I won't hurt you," Claire said quietly. "You can touch me. There is no tapu."

She had, of course, gone to the heart of his fear. It wasn't only that she might not recognize him that kept him away, but that somehow the powerful tapu could steal his sight as well. He looked back at his mother for reassurance. This time Tiare provided none. Her beautiful features remained solemn and unencouraging. It must be his decision, she said, without saying anything at all.

Claire sat as still as the stone around her. She did not sense

Tipu raising his hand, but then the heat of his palm was near her cheek. She fought the urge to press it against her face. "Tipu?" she whispered.

"Hullo, Claire." His decision made, Tipu threw his arms around Claire's neck so forcefully that he knocked her off balance. Her shoulder hit the altar but Claire hardly noticed the pain. She hugged him to her, laughing, pressing kisses on his forehead, and stopped only when she sensed his face contorting in an effort to avoid her spontaneous display of affection.

"I don't suppose it matters where in the world you are," she told Rand. "Boys of a certain age don't like kisses."

"We get over it," Rand said. He looked at Tiare. She was watching Tipu and Claire, a slender, even indulgent smile on her face.

Claire set Tipu from her. She ruffled his dark hair, then pushed it back were it fell over his eyes. It was thick and soft. In her mind's eye she imagined it still had the lustrous blue-black sheen of Tiare's. Smiling, Claire tugged on Tipu's earlobe, eliciting a giggle from him. "You've grown so tall," she said, drawing an imaginary line from the top of his head to the top of hers. He puffed out his small chest and held himself straighter so that he was an inch or so higher.

"Taller than you," he said.

Claire nodded. She didn't point out that she was kneeling. They had always measured his height in this manner. Claire's fingers swept his cheek and rested momentarily on his small chin. Tipu's face was rounder than she remembered, his chin sturdier. She touched his wide brow and ran her finger along the length of his nose. There was nothing about his features that reminded her of her father: no bump along the bridge of his nose; no gently receding chin. She knew his complexion was no fairer than the warm honey tones of his mother's.

Claire realized that one of Tipu's fears had almost come true. Had she waited much longer to return to the islands, she wouldn't have recognized him. He had grown up speaking Tiare's Solonesian dialect and English equally well, but now Claire detected more Solonesian influence. The few words he spoke to her had the soft vowel sounds of the islanders. It was as it should be, she thought. Claire hugged Tipu to her again. He was wearing a lava-lava wrapped around his waist. His sun-kissed shoulders and back were warm. "Tiare?" she said.

"Yes?"

"Thank you," Claire whispered hoarsely. She let Tipu squirm free. "I needed to know he was all right. Thank you for that. I've been . . . I've been afraid for so long."

Tiare nodded. "It is understandable. I have never doubted that you love him. I was less certain about your intentions."

Rand helped Claire to her feet. He felt Tipu watching him closely. He looked at the boy, a question in his own eyes.

Tipu continued staring boldly, less afraid of the *papalagi* stranger than he had been of his own sister. "Is the big ship in the harbor yours?"

Tiare touched her son's shoulder and shook her head.

"I don't mind his questions," Rand told her. "Yes. I call her *Cerberus.*"

Tipu tried out the unfamiliar word. "Is that your mother's name?"

Rand laughed. "No. It's the name of a three-headed dog that guards the entrance to the underworld."

The boy blinked widely. "I like tiki better."

"I do too." He pointed to the tikis mounted on the pillars. "Will you tell me about these?"

Tipu was happy to oblige. He led Rand away to study the first one.

Tiare watched them and nodded approvingly. "Your husband is giving us an opportunity to talk," she said, taking Claire's arm. She looked over her shoulder at Macauley. "The other one . . . the liar . . . is still hovering." She waved him back with an imperious flick of her fingers, then drew Claire to the far side of the temple platform.

The tip of Claire's cane tapped lightly on the black rock. She found the edge of the platform with it, then backed up several inches.

"I am not going to push you over the side," said Tiare.

Claire smiled. "I didn't think you were, but it will make the doctor more comfortable if I'm away from the edge. I was light-headed earlier.''

"Were you?" Tiare asked.

It was the absence of inflection in Tiare's voice that let Claire know she was suspicious. "A trifle," Claire said.

"Really?"

Claire sighed. "No, not at all." She turned so Macauley could not read her lips. "Is he watching us?"

"Yes."

It was as Claire expected. "He wanted to come with us," she said. "Rand would not have permitted it if I hadn't invented some reason."

"I am surprised *you* permitted it."

Claire shrugged. She was not going to tell Tiare about the stolen riddle. There had been no mention of the treasure, and Claire was not going to bring it up. It had never been part of her relationship with Tiare, and she did not want it to intrude now. "I wanted to keep the peace," she said. "Dr. Stuart and Captain Hamilton have not always dealt well together."

Tiare accepted this as fact. "Now that you know Tipu is safe, what are your plans?"

Behind her Claire could hear Tipu discussing the spirits residing in the tikis. His youthful voice was filled with a mixture of reverence and pride. He had not merely grown taller and broader in her absence. There was also the maturing influence of responsibility. "You intend he should become a priest," Claire said.

"It is his blood."

"*In* his blood, you mean," Claire said.

Tiare shook her head. "No. I do not mean that. Your father spoke often of such things. You English make it weak. Like your tea with milk. It *is* his blood."

"As it is yours."

"Yes."

Claire nodded, understanding in a way she had not before. Her voice was just a whisper. "I am not going to take him from you, Tiare. I know what my father wanted, but it would not be right."

''It is difficult not to honor the wishes of one's father, is it not?''

Frowning slightly, Claire nodded again. Tiare spoke as if from her own experience.

''I was not supposed to have his child,'' Tiare said softly. ''I was taught how to prevent it, but I ignored the teachings of my own mother and the wishes of my father. Griffin wanted a child, and I wanted to give him one.'' She paused when she saw Claire's features go from clouded to clear. ''What is it you think you know?''

''It's just that I had begun to question if Tipu was really my brother. I wondered if—''

''But he isn't,'' Tiare said, interrupting her. ''Trenton is Tipu's father.''

Claire's mouth opened, then closed. This confession was like nothing she expected to hear. ''I don't understand,'' she said finally. ''Did Sir Griffin know?''

Tiare hesitated. ''You really don't remember, do you? It was the last evening we spent on Pulotu . . .''

Chapter Fifteen

The evening air was humid. Claire untied the flaps of her tent and opened them. Even the breeze from off shore felt thick. She stood there a moment, listening to distant thunder and watching lightning rend the night sky. Ducking back inside, Claire returned to her worktable. She did not sit down but leaned over the microscope instead, absently massaging the small of her back as she studied the slide. She stopped to adjust the lantern light. The droplet of blood under the microscope came into clearer focus.

Claire's slender shoulders drooped. "No change." She sighed deeply and made a note in her journal. Removing the slide, she marked it and replaced it with another one. What she saw remained the same. She did not like this feeling of discouragement. It was because she had hoped for something more than she was finding. She thought this time the blood would clot.

Now Claire sat down. Sir Griffin would have to be told. He would not be as discouraged as she was. He did not invest so much of himself in each experiment. He would, however, be disappointed. He would wonder aloud if Claire had followed his instructions exactly.

Claire slid the notebook toward her. She thumbed back several pages and reviewed what she had done. Every step was recorded in her precise handwriting. Measurements. Time. Method. Pressed between two pages was a flower like those she had used to make the serum. There were detailed pictures drawn by her own hand. The location of this particular hibiscus variety was noted. She could not find a mistake.

It was the sound of Sir Griffin's voice that pulled Claire's attention from her work. At first she thought the sound was only in her head and she tried to ignore it. It was difficult enough to accept her father's censure when he delivered it in person. She did not want to hear his critical voice when he wasn't around.

Sir Griffin had been more single-minded of late—distracted, but not in the familiar manner when his work absorbed his interest. He was willing recently, even insistent, that Claire do more of the research. He went out to explore the island for new flower varieties and made copious notes himself, but he left the distilling and slide preparation to Claire. She liked the work, the time alone to reflect and discover, and she did not miss Trenton's presence in the palm-frond shelter that was also their laboratory. It would have been a mostly satisfactory arrangement if Sir Griffin had evinced trust in Claire's findings. There were times he seemed to find fault as a matter of course rather than as a matter of science.

Frowning, Claire closed her notes. What she heard was not coming from inside her head at all. It was clearly her father she heard, but his voice, like the thunder, was at some point distant. Claire stepped outside the tent. She turned her head. The heavy air carried his voice to her.

There were no lanterns burning in any of the other tents. Tiare and Sir Griffin shared one. Trenton had his own. Tipu often slept on the open beach and sometimes with Claire. Tonight he was lying in a sand pit he had dug for himself earlier in the day. He had taken care to line it with fresh ferns. His mother had warned him a storm was coming, but she placed a blanket over him anyway and stayed with him until he fell asleep. He didn't stir as Claire passed by.

Neither did the man posted as guard for the small camp. He slept as soundly outside his tent as his two comrades did inside. Claire supposed this often happened. She found her own foolishness remarkable in that she had trusted these men to follow Sir Griffin's orders.

Claire crossed the beach to the lagoon almost soundlessly, her footsteps absorbed by small shifts in the sand as she went. She did not try to be particularly quiet. Her intent was not to eavesdrop on the argument, but to stop it. Both voices were recognizable by the time she reached the tree line. Claire heard Trenton swear forcefully and her father respond in kind. She slowed her steps, surprised by the animosity and wary of it. Sir Griffin was Trenton's mentor. She could not recall that they had ever exchanged words. Trenton deferred to her father in all things scientific.

Thunder rumbled. Supported by the heavy, humid air, it rolled overhead and seemed to shake the tops of the palms. It covered Claire's attempt to make herself known. Neither her father nor Trenton heard her clear her throat.

"You're a damn fool," Trenton was telling Sir Griffin. "There's nothing here. It's time to move on."

"You're guessing," Griffin snapped back. "We've explored less than a third of Pulotu."

"And we haven't seen anything that merits a second look or continuing." He pointed to the outrigger anchored in the lagoon. "I'm prepared to leave even if you're not."

"Don't threaten me. There's Claire's work to consider."

Trenton's laughter was dismissive and bitter at the same time. All thoughts Claire had about revealing her presence fled. Stepping off the path, she leaned behind a palm and waited to hear how her father would respond.

"She's the only one who hasn't lost sight of why we're here," Griffin said.

"That's because she doesn't know why we're here. You've managed to keep her in the dark for years. Your wife kept her in the dark."

"Claire was a child then. She didn't need to know."

"And now? What excuse is there?" Trenton's laughter was

derisive this time. "You're afraid she won't want to continue the work you started. Your scientific legacy will end in your lifetime, not hers."

"Go back to the camp," Sir Griffin ordered. "You don't know what the bloody hell you're talking about. I have no belief that will change when you're sober, but at least I won't have to smell every breath you're wasting. Here, let me have that bottle."

Claire edged forward slowly. The shadows in the lagoon were deep and made it difficult to see. A streak of lightning gave Claire her first clear glimpse of Trenton clutching his whiskey bottle. Behind him the outrigger bobbed. The lagoon waters were no longer still. She was left with those images when the sky went black again.

"No, thank you," Trenton said with mock politeness. "I like being drunk. You would too if you were dying."

"I've told you, you're going to be an old man before the syphilis kills you."

Trenton snorted. "Not if Tiare has her way."

"What do you mean?"

"She didn't tell you? She's cursed me."

"Oh, for God's sake," Sir Griffin said, disgusted. "You're an idiot. Why Strickland ever thought you could carry out his work . . ." His voice trailed off as he turned to go.

"We're not finished here," Trenton called after him. "Where are you going?"

"I'm finished."

Claire's hand flew to her mouth, stifling her gasp, as she watched Trenton tackle her father. The whiskey bottle thumped to the ground a moment before their bodies hit it. Sir Griffin and Trenton followed the path of the bottle, rolling down the embankment toward the water. They stopped just short of the edge.

Sir Griffin's breathing was labored but his voice carried clearly. "Get off me." He pushed at Trenton's shoulders. "These actions hardly alter my opinion."

Excessive drink had added creases to Trenton's features, making him look older than his years, but there was no accom-

panying toll on his fitness. He was still lean, still strong, and he had no difficulty keeping Sir Griffin pinned to the ground. Even when he sat up, he kept Sir Griffin immobile by straddling him and resting most of his weight on the older man's abdomen.

"I say we move on," Trenton repeated, his words only slightly slurred. "Tiare's leading you around by the nose and you're too full of yourself to realize it. You think it was your idea to come here when she's been pointing you in this direction all along. There's only one idiot here—and I'm sitting on him."

It was an effort for Sir Griffin to speak, but he managed to get out, "Tiare had to be threatened to leave the ship. She didn't want to set foot on Pulotu."

Trenton shook his head vigorously. "She wanted you to believe that. The longer you're occupied here with the search, the less chance you have of ever finding the treasure."

"You want a woman," Griffin said. "That's all it is. Claire won't have anything to do with you and Tiare is mine. You think you'll find someone again once we've left Pulotu." His laughter was strained. "Don't you realize that no woman in Solonesia will have you? Tiare will make certain of it."

"I told you, she's cursed me."

"She's protecting her people from the spread of your pox and you damn well know it."

"Tiare hates me," he said. "She wants me dead."

Sir Griffin pushed at Trenton again and tried to wriggle free. Trenton lifted himself momentarily, easing Griffin's breathing, then sat down hard. Whatever Griffin had been trying to tell him was released in an unintelligible rush of air.

"Do you want to know why?" Trenton asked.

Claire leaned forward. Her fingers still pressed the trunk of the palm, but she was more exposed now. No one noticed her. Then like a wraith from the spirit world, Tiare appeared without warning. She wore a shift that was bleached of color when lightning rent the sky. It rippled around her slender figure as she walked toward them.

Trenton's chin lifted aggressively. "Tell him," he challenged her. "Tell him why you hate me."

Tiare said nothing to Trenton. She knelt beside Sir Griffin. "Are you all right?"

Sir Griffin nodded. "Trenton's out of his mind."

"Yes," she said softly. Her eyes strayed to the whiskey bottle. "I can see that."

Swearing under his breath, Trenton finally stood. He brushed himself off, then picked up the bottle. Holding it by the neck, he took a long swallow. Out of the corner of his eye he watched Tiare help Sir Griffin to his feet. He lowered the bottle. "I've been telling him what a fraud you are, Tiare."

Tiare ignored him. "Let us return to the camp, Griffin." She slipped her arm in his.

It was when they both turned that Trenton struck. He brought the butt of the bottle down hard on Griffin's shoulder, just at the curve of his neck. Pain shot down Griffin's spine. He staggered forward as his knees buckled. It was Tiare's surprising strength that kept him on his feet.

"I said, don't walk away from me."

Uncaring of the consequences, Claire ran out of the trees and launched herself squarely at Trenton. He fell backward into the water while she teetered on the edge of the bank until Tiare grabbed a fistful of her gown and yanked her back. Water splashed all of them as Trenton surfaced. He stood waist high in the lagoon and raised his fist. He had managed to hold on to the bottle, but its contents were now more water than whiskey. His features were a mixture of anger and triumph as he waved the bottle at them.

"Do you think you're protecting him?" he yelled at Claire. "You need to hear the truth as much as he does. Tipu's my son, Griffin! Tell him, Tiare! Tell both of them!" He waded toward the bank. "She seduced me when you couldn't give her the son you wanted, Griffin. When she was certain she was carrying a child, she sent me on my way, pointed me in the direction of a dark-eyed beauty she knew was infected with the pox. She thought it would kill me as quickly as it does her own people." Lightning flashed as Trenton's mouth twisted in a parody of a smile. For a moment his teeth actually gleamed. "You've wanted me gone because of Tipu!"

"I want you gone because of the treasure," Tiare said. Releasing Sir Griffin, Tiare stepped in front of Claire and effectively blocked Trenton's exit from the water. *"Your search is destroying him. He came here to discover the secrets of our plants, secrets our gods put there for healing our people. This is the work for which he is meant. Not your work, or the work of the one who sends you to watch over him."*

"Get out of my way," Trenton fairly growled. He started to heave himself up to the bank, but Tiare pushed him back.

"Leave," she told him, pointing to the outrigger. *"I heard you say it is what you want to do."*

"No!" Griffin put his hand on Tiare's shoulder. *"He can't leave. There's a storm coming. He may be lost."*

Trenton laughed. *"Stay. Go."* He looked at Claire. *"You must have an opinion."*

"I have one," she said. *"I don't think you want to hear it."*

"So self-righteous, Claire. You still don't see, do you? Your father doesn't want me to leave because he knows I control the money that supports his work. Your work now."

"But you're his student."

Griffin looked at his daughter. Heavily, reluctantly, he said, *"He's more than that, Claire."*

Trenton was satisfied Claire understood when he saw her take a step backward. *"The scales are being lifted from your eyes, eh? Seeing more clearly now?"*

"Leave her alone," Sir Griffin said tiredly. He nudged Tiare to one side and extended his hand to Trenton. The younger man ignored it. Still holding the bottle, he hauled himself out of the lagoon. Water dripped from his clothes.

"It's all true," Trenton said to no one in particular. He shook himself off, spraying water in every direction. He stamped his feet several times. *"Every word."*

Claire looked at Tiare, then her father. *"Is it?"* she asked, her voice hushed.

Sir Griffin's broad shoulders sagged. *"It shouldn't matter to you, Claire. You're not part of it. I've made sure of that. The work you're doing here is all that should be important."*

"But—"

He shook his head. "It is your work. It's been that way for longer than you've known."

"I've never known."

Trenton laughed outright then. "I told you she was blind."

Griffin threw a right hook that lifted Trenton off his feet and put him flat on his back in the water. Before either Tiare or Claire could stop him, Sir Griffin jumped into the lagoon after his assistant. They thrashed around awkwardly, each of them trying to push the other under or land a blow that would end the match. Trenton had youth on his side. Sir Griffin had anger.

Lightning creased the sky, illuminating their struggle at odd moments. Claire stepped closer to the edge, wanting to join the fight. Tiare stayed where she was, watching intently, her lips moving around the sacred words of a powerful spell.

"No tapu, Tiare," Claire said when she realized what Tiare was saying to herself. She placed her hand on Tiare's forearm. "No tapu."

Tiare shook off Claire's hand. Her words had the strength of a whisper now. In the water Trenton was fending off Griffin's attack by waving the bottle.

Claire shook her head. "I don't . . ." She closed her eyes as Trenton's weapon grazed the top of Sir Griffin's head. "I don't believe this." Claire put one hand over her eyes. It was too painful to watch now. Neither of them seemed to realize they were behaving foolishly. Behind her, Claire could still hear Tiare speaking softly. The cadence was lilting, the intent deadly. "There is no tapu," she said almost angrily.

It was then that Claire heard the dull thud of Trenton's bottle make contact with her father's skull. Her hand flew away from her face and she saw Sir Griffin start to sink below the water. "Tiare!"

Claire's sigh was almost inaudible. Lying beside her in bed, propped on one elbow, Rand watched the gentle rise and fall of Claire's chest as her breathing calmed. His eyes lifted to hers and he was witness to the tears that formed there. She blinked once, and a few of them slipped from the corners of her eyes, fell past her temple, and disappeared into her dark hair. She knew the lantern was burning in their cabin. She knew he could see her pain clearly and she didn't try to hide from it or him.

"Is this Tiare's version of events?" he asked her. "Or your own?"

"My own," Claire said. "At the temple . . . as she was telling me things . . . I realized my mind was running ahead of her words. I knew what she was going to say before I heard her. I suppose that's when I understood I was actually remembering what happened."

"I knew something was different when you joined us again."

"You didn't say anything."

"I thought you would tell me in your own time." He hesitated, wondering what he wanted to tell *her*. "And I didn't want—"

Claire interrupted him, her smile slight but genuine. "You didn't want Dr. Stuart to know anything had changed."

One of Rand's brows kicked up. He shouldn't be surprised, he reminded himself. Claire always heard more than was said. She knew the extent of his distrust for Stuart. "That's right," he said. "I didn't." He thumbed away the traces of tears at the corners of her eyes. "There's more to your story," he said gently. "Do you know what it is?"

Claire nodded. "The blow to my father's head was a fatal one, but Trenton didn't wait to find that out. He started swimming for the outrigger as soon as Sir Griffin slipped under the water. Tiare jumped in to help my father, and I went after Trenton."

"Then you didn't know Sir Griffin was dead either."

"No," she said quietly. "I didn't know. Not for certain. Tiare screamed for me to come back, but I didn't understand. Or perhaps I didn't want to. I remember thinking I *had* to stop Trenton. There was nothing else on my mind. I hung onto the canoe until we were in open water. I thought I could tip it."

Rand shook his head. "Not an outrigger."

"No one was there to explain that to me. I discovered it on my own." Listening to herself, Claire was astonished at her own folly. She could only imagine how foolish she sounded to Rand. "Trenton wasn't able to stop me from pulling myself into the canoe. He needed both his hands for maneuvering. It wasn't raining yet, but the lightning and thunder were closer and the wind was picking up. Trenton was operating the sail, so the oars were free. I picked one up and hit him with it across the back. He fell, but then so did I. The sail whipped around and knocked the oar out of my hand. It went right in the water. We both tried to get it back. I warned him we needed to head for shore. We could have returned to Pulotu easily at that point, but Trenton had his own ideas about where he wanted to go.''

"Here?" asked Rand. "Did he know about this place?"

"I don't know. He never said. We headed straight into the storm. I think he had some navigational equipment but he wasn't adept at using it. He was not a skilled sailor either, merely a competent one. By the time we passed through the storm we were hopelessly lost. He blamed me but he was afraid to get rid of me. I was able to help him with the outrigger and he knew it. There were some supplies on the canoe. He rationed them in his favor but he never tried to starve me or keep the water away, at least not in the beginning. I think if we had seen land at any point, Trenton would have pitched me overboard and made for it alone. He kept me alive because I was useful. That changed when it became clear to him that the supplies were going to run out. He hoarded everything then. He slept with the waterskin under his arm to keep me from getting it.''

"But you survived him," said Rand. "How did—"

Claire shook her head. "I don't know," she said. "I really don't. I was too weak to move or even talk. I went in and out of consciousness. Trenton was there . . . and then he wasn't. The canoe just kept drifting. I don't know if he was missing days or hours before I reached Raiatea. By the time I arrived I had forgotten he was ever with me.''

"When did you know you were blind?"

"I was unconscious when my rescuers pulled me from the outrigger. It was when I came around later that I realized I couldn't see.''

"And couldn't remember," said Rand.

She nodded. "The doctor on board the British frigate had many more questions than I could answer. There were things

I recalled gradually that helped explain what happened, but it wasn't until I stood with Tiare at the temple that the picture became complete.'' Claire's sigh was a little uneven, not quite a sob, but not entirely composed. ''I understand why you thought Tiare had placed a tapu on me. I confused a lot of things during my illness.''

''I put the wrong construction on the only things you said aloud. The tapu was for Trenton.''

''Yes. As far as Tiare is concerned, the tapu worked.''

''I wouldn't argue otherwise.''

''Neither would I,'' she said quietly. ''Tiare and Tipu were taken from Pulotu by the priests the morning after my father died. She told me we were always being watched. My father's assistants were exiled to other islands. They'll never be able to tell what happened that night. Evidence of the camp was eliminated. Tiare wanted to show me where she scattered my father's ashes. It's here on Arahiti. She said you can see it from the temple.'' The words caught in her throat. Claire felt an ache building behind her eyes. She blinked, drew in a shaky breath, then continued. ''A new variety of hibiscus is blooming there now. Sir Griffin would like that. It's a fitting tribute.''

She paused. Rand's fingers slipped between hers and squeezed. Claire returned the gentle pressure, assuring him she was all right. ''I know now that Tiare was right: toward the end my father was losing sight of his work . . . and himself. Finding the treasure took more and more of his time. It was how he decided which islands we would visit and how long we would stay. Trenton was always there, pushing him. I don't suppose Sir Griffin thought he could say no, but I don't think it takes away from what he *was* able to accomplish. He earned his knighthood. He contributed something to science as a naturalist.''

''No one is going to take that away from him,'' Rand assured her. ''But it's only part of his legacy, Claire. You're the other part. He trained you, guided you, probably bullied you, but he made it possible for you to carry on his work. He never completely abandoned what he loved; he passed it on to you.''

''Then I've failed him.'' It was impossible to keep all the

bitterness she felt out of her voice. "I can't exactly carry on now, can I?"

Rand did not try to hold Claire. Placing his arms around her just then would have provided neither comfort nor consolation. It would have added to her despair, made her seem less strong than she was. She could not see the tears that blurred his own vision. He would not let her know that at the moment when he was offering to be her eyes, he could see nothing at all.

It was still dark when Claire woke. She eased herself out of bed, careful not to disturb Rand, and washed her face at the basin. Her eyelids were faintly swollen and tender from weeping. She wondered if she would ever be reconciled to the losses in her life. Her mother. Sir Griffin. Her sight. Even Tipu would be gone to her. Claire shook her head, hating the self-pitying slant of her thoughts. It was time to take something back.

She left the cabin quietly. Although she carried her cane, she didn't use it to tap her way down the passage. She needed no special assistance to find Macauley Stuart's cabin. His door opened soundlessly and Claire entered without announcing herself. She was prepared for a confrontation, but it didn't come to that. Macauley was snoring deeply, unaware of her presence.

Claire found the jacket he had been wearing easily enough. It was stretched across the back of the only chair in his room. The Hamilton riddle, however, was no longer inside it. Claire wondered how much opportunity Macauley had had to study it. She had given him little during the day or evening. It was only after they retired to their respective cabins that he was alone with his stolen prize.

Claire patted down Macauley's writing desk. The open bottle of rum helped explain his deep slumber. She wondered if he had gotten drunk in celebration or frustration. Claire set down her cane so she could hold the bottle in one hand and raise the desktop with the other. None of the papers inside had the distinctive markings of the riddle. She rearranged them neatly and closed the lid.

Macauley stirred. Claire didn't move at all. She held her

breath until she heard him snoring again. The resonance had changed, and now Claire realized he was facing the wall. She grew a little braver in her exploration, methodically searching the cabin as she circled outward from the desk.

Claire found his medical bag at the foot of his bed. She was so certain it was where he had put the riddle that she contemplated just leaving with the bag. She reconsidered when it opened easily under her questing fingers. Macauley had slipped the riddle under the lining of the bag. She would have missed the opening if she had been searching with her eyes. It wasn't visible that way. It was the subtle change in the plane surface that her fingertips acknowledged. The riddle was easy to find and remove after that.

Claire slipped it under her own sleeve, closed the bag, and left Macauley's cabin.

She ran full tilt into Rand in the companionway. He didn't say anything, and she didn't explain. When he gripped her by the elbow, Claire sensed she was about to be dragged back to their cabin if she didn't accompany him willingly.

Once inside, Claire made a small show of rubbing her arm where he had held her.

Rand was having none of it. "I didn't hurt you," he said. "Don't make me wish I had. What were you doing in Stuart's cabin?"

Claire stopped massaging her arm. He had never spoken in quite that tone to her before. She was sure she didn't like it. "Are you accusing me of something?"

Was he? "If I am," he said finally, "I'm not prepared to admit it."

She smiled a little at that. It seemed he was as surprised by his reaction as she was. Claire took pity on him. "I didn't want to tell you about this until I could make it all right again."

"If you think you're relieving my mind, let me explain: you're not."

Claire crossed the room to him. He was sitting on the desk, one hip anchored on the edge. His other leg was stretched out in front of him. He made room for her but his mouth didn't soften much the first time she kissed him. It was better the second time. "Does that help?" she asked.

"I'm reserving judgment."

She sighed. "That's probably wise," she allowed. Placing some distance between them, Claire removed the riddle from under the sleeve of her robe and handed it to Rand. "Yesterday, before Tiare arrived and while you were gone to find breakfast, Dr. Stuart surprised me in the workroom. At first I thought he was you. I didn't have time to hide the map we were looking at when I realized I was wrong. I didn't know your journal was lying on the table." She told him about the coffee spill and Macauley's discovery.

Rand carefully unfolded the riddle. The left edge was ragged where it had been torn from the book. The coffee stains were evident, but so was the writing. What the spill *had* done was to swell the paper and make the holes disappear. If Claire had never found them, no one would ever know they had existed. He told her that.

"Dr. Stuart knows they existed," she said. "The spill must have seeped through to the page under it. He commented on the pattern. He saw the same one on your chart." She drew in a deep breath and said in a rush, "I think he's working for my godfather. Stickle wants to be certain you don't cheat him of his share of the treasure. Stuart must have an arrangement similar to the one Trenton had. Do you remember what I told you I overheard at the lagoon? Sir Griffin said Trenton was an idiot; he didn't know why Strickland thought he could carry out his work. They had been talking about the treasure earlier. It must be all related, Rand. It *must* be."

Claire's earnestness made Rand smile. He wasn't able to keep it entirely out of his voice. "It sounds plausible enough, I suppose."

Claire's eyes narrowed. Her hand lifted and struck like a cobra, but there was no sting in her touch. She felt the shape of Rand's mouth with her fingertips. He had no time to school his features. In any event, he didn't try. "You know!" she said. "You've always known."

His smile deepened. He held her hand to his lips and kissed

the pads of her fingers. "Are you accusing me of something?"
Rand didn't wait for her answer. "I haven't always known,"
he said. "In fact, until you returned the riddle, I've only ever
had suspicions."

"But you've never said anything."

"What could I have said that you would have accepted? You
weren't even prepared to believe he wasn't a doctor. You found
reasons to defend him when he cared for my mother at Henley,
remember?"

Claire did remember. She blushed a little. "Perhaps he's just
not a very good one."

Rand chuckled. "I think that's probably true. It doesn't really
matter, does it? He hasn't caused anyone harm. As you pointed
out, his care of my mother was at least adequate. On board
here he's set some bones and managed to help you through your
illness. He never understood very much about your blindness,
though. Your godfather expected too much from him in that
regard. I suppose in his own way Macauley's tried to protect
you—from me."

Claire found the chair behind the desk and sat down heavily.
Her shoulders drooped. "My godfather," she said, more to
herself than Rand. "What can he be thinking?"

"He wants the Hamilton-Waterstone treasure, I imagine."
Rand's voice was matter-of-fact. "Just as I do."

"But you have some claim to it."

Rand shrugged. "After all these years? I don't know that
my claim is any more valid than any other. The treasure was
stolen in the first place. I think it properly belongs to the person
who can find it. The Duke of Strickland wants to be that person.
He can't do it himself, so he's made his bargain with others."

"My father."

"Yes."

"He arranged for my mother to marry my father."

"Yes." He wasn't certain if Claire would understand how
long ago Strickland's manipulation had begun. Finding the
treasure had consumed most of the duke's life. Rand could
almost pity him. He understood too well what that was like.
"Strickland would have chosen your father after a great deal

of thought. Not just anyone could be persuaded to go on a treasure hunt, then be expected to deliver that treasure intact. The duke didn't want to lose it all after it was found.''

''My father must have seemed heaven-sent to Stickle.''

''Probably. Griffin Bancroft had a deep interest in the flora of the very part of the world Strickland wanted explored. Your father cared more about his own work than the treasure, so the duke wasn't afraid that Griffin would steal it from him. He probably only had to promise funding all future expeditions. Your father would have been satisfied with that.''

Claire smiled wistfully. ''Yes,'' she said quietly. ''Yes, he would have.''

''It took some time to arrange. We both know that the duke was in possession of the Waterstone riddle. Your mother couldn't have passed it on to you in any other way.''

''But why? Why did she do it at all?''

''A bit of sly revenge, perhaps.'' Rand saw Claire's brow pull together as she considered this. ''For many things. The duke wouldn't marry her. He arranged her marriage. And he wanted her to go with Sir Griffin to the South Pacific. You told me she didn't want to accompany your father on the trip at all.''

''No, she didn't. They argued about it. Stickle was insistent.'' Her face cleared. ''Revenge,'' she said softly. ''Yes, that makes sense. My mother realized the duke was using her to watch my father.''

Rand nodded. ''His eyes and ears. I don't think he expected her to resist going. I certainly don't believe he expected her to take you. Your mother saw to it that he had no choice.''

''The final proof that he wanted the treasure more than he wanted her . . . or me.''

''You don't know that you're his daughter, Claire. He may not even know. Your mother is the only one who could have known the truth and—''

''And he killed her.''

''He couldn't have known what would happen.''

''He knew there were dangers.'' Her head came up. ''Why are you defending him? You have as much right to be angry with him as I do. Even hate him. If it weren't for the duke, Stuart wouldn't be here. For that matter, *I* wouldn't be here.''

''Exactly.''

''Oh.''

Rand reached for Claire's wrist and drew her to her feet. He brought her between his legs and rested his palms lightly on her hips. ''It doesn't really change anything, knowing that, but it gives me some allowance not to despise him. You have to make your own decision.''

''He sent Sir Griffin back here after my mother died.''

''Don't you think your father wanted to return?'' asked Rand. ''You did.''

''But he sent Trenton, too.''

There was nothing Rand could say to that. The duke was not blameless. Even his motives in allowing Claire to board *Cerberus* were suspect. Strickland had been insistent that she accompany Rand, but they might never know the why of it. Was it that he didn't want to deny her the opportunity to regain her sight, or was it the only way he could put his own spy aboard Rand's ship? He had to have known Rand would never permit Stuart on *Cerberus* otherwise.

Rand watched Claire's expression change as she struggled with some of the same questions. Whatever conclusions she drew, she kept to herself. All save one.

''I think he must be responsible for the murder of the last Waterstone,'' she said.

Rand drew his knuckles lightly across Claire's cheek. He tucked a tendril of dark chocolate hair behind her ear. ''There's no proof.''

''He has the riddle.''

''Possession of it does not equal murder. He could have bought it from the murderer.''

''You don't believe that.''

''No,'' he admitted. ''I don't. But we'll never know, Claire. You'll have to accustom yourself to that.''

Claire didn't know if she could. It seemed of late that she was being asked to accustom herself to too many of these revelations. She wanted something in return for it. ''I want to find the treasure,'' she said. She stepped out of Rand's reach. ''Yours is not the only house it's cursed.''

''Claire.''

She shook her head. ''You don't want to talk me out of it,'' she said. ''You know you don't.''

''I might,'' he said. ''If you think it's more important to me than you are.''

That gave her pause. The surge of anger that had been rising in her was suppressed again. Claire bent her head, ashamed. ''No, I don't think that.''

Rand leaned forward and cupped Claire's chin. He lifted it and drew her back. He kissed her lightly. ''All right,'' he said. ''We'll find the treasure.''

She was a little suspicious of his confidence. ''You know something, don't you? Something other than what we realized yesterday.''

He knew she was talking about the rainbow. *At the end of one god's promise.* ''I know where to find the rainbow,'' he said.

''You do?''

''We were there yesterday.''

''That's the one?'' she asked excitedly. ''At the waterfall? But how can you know that?''

''Because I know where we are.''

''You mean where we *were.*''

''No,'' he corrected her. ''I mean where we are. It's one and the same.'' He tapped her lips lightly with his finger when she would have interrupted. ''I spent a considerable amount of time yesterday thinking about the Big Dipper. Why would the cartographer use it? I connected the islands on my chart and I still didn't see what he did, not until I thought like a navigator. Our mapmaker saw a shape in the islands that was familiar to him and he exploited it. He used it to identify the island where the treasure would be hidden.''

Claire could not remain silent any longer. ''But there are seven stars—I mean islands. It could be any one of them.''

''It's none of them,'' Rand told her. ''He was cleverer than that.''

"Cleverer than me, certainly. I don't understand."

"The Big Dipper is only important for what it points to, not for what it is."

Claire's jaw actually sagged a little as the truth came to her. "Polaris. He was showing us the North Star."

"Well, actually a small island called Arahiti, just as Tiare said. It's not on the chart. I fixed its location the same way I would have fixed Polaris—by using the pointer stars in the Dipper and following a straight line approximately four times the distance between them. In this case, four times the distance that separates Haipai from Pulotu. Remember I thought we had arrived on Tarahiki? That island is close enough that I could see it when Tiare took us to the temple. In fact, I kept it in sight for most of the journey. That's how I know we never really left Arahiti."

"Never left? But we were on the water for hours in both directions."

"That direction was a circle. More precisely, a half circle. If that isn't enough for you, think back to what Tipu asked me. He wanted to know if the big ship in the harbor was mine. How would he know it was there if he hadn't seen it? I'm sure the temple we visited is somewhere on this island, Claire. That means the waterfall is also. Tiare may want us to think the treasure is on Pulotu, but she brought us to it."

"Do you think she intends to show us where it is?"

"You know her better than I do."

Claire drew in her lower lip and worried it as she thought. "She could have shown my father to it at any time and never did. But then, he was neither Hamilton nor Waterstone."

"I'm only one half of the equation," Rand pointed out. "Our mapmaker meant for Hamilton and Waterstone to work together. I don't suppose—"

Claire shook her head. "I've told you before, not a drop of Waterstone blood in these veins."

"What if you're the duke's daughter?"

"No. I've seen the portraits in his homes. Markhams and Abberlys for generations. No Waterstones."

"Then I think Tiare will have reason not to share what she knows," said Rand. "We'll have to look for ourselves."

"When?"

"Now. We have a few hours before daybreak. Cutch will come with us. He's scouted some of the island. It could help us." Rand surveyed Claire's nightshift and wrapper. "Go on. Get dressed."

Claire made short work of it. She tore through his things and found trousers and a shirt that were no better fitting than the ones she had worn on Pulotu. Rand said nothing, though. He waited for her at the door, then escorted her topside. The man on watch helped them lower one of the boats over the side, and Rand rowed them to shore. He woke up Cutch and told him what they were going to do.

"I only just went to sleep," Cutch said. "Been up most of the night looking for a way off this island." He rubbed the back of his smooth head. "Don't seem right, you wakin' me up again and tellin' me you don't want to leave."

Rand made allowances for Cutch's sleep-deprived state. "So you found something?"

"Mebbe." He yawned hugely and allowed Rand to help him to his feet. The men around him slept on. "Tell you about it as soon as I wake up."

Chuckling, Rand thrust an unlighted torch and a pick in Cutch's hands. He was carrying a shovel. Claire had a coil of rope resting on her shoulders. She had complained once of feeling like a plow horse but she accepted the weight gamely.

"Who knows we're out here?" Cutch asked as Rand led them into the forest.

"Dodd's on watch. I told him to raise the alarm if we haven't returned by noon. Not that he would know exactly where to find us." He intercepted Cutch's dark look of concern over Claire's head. "Tiare will know. Dodd only has to tell her that we're looking for the treasure and she'll find us."

"Probably kill us, too," Cutch said rather mournfully.

Claire smiled. "I don't think so, Mr. Cutch. She likes you."

Cutch followed closer on Claire's heels. "Did she say something to you?"

''Not exactly. But I could see the interest in her eyes when I mentioned your name.''

For a moment Cutch almost believed her. His deep chuckle rumbled pleasantly when he realized what she'd said. ''You *saw* that, did you?''

Rand interrupted before Claire could answer. ''I wouldn't challenge her, Cutch.''

Claire turned her head and gave Cutch a wide, teasing smile. She felt him place his large hand over the crown of her hair and make her face front. She stumbled a bit on the path while Rand easily stepped over a fallen branch.

''One of you should watch where you're both going,'' Cutch said.

Claire concentrated more on Rand's lead after that. They moved in relative silence. The forest was home to enough nocturnal predators that their own movements often blended in. There was always the steady sound of moving water in the background. They did not light the coconut-sheath torch that Cutch carried. Its light would have made their progress visible to anyone watching from the ship or from across the island's harbor. Moonshine was adequate for their travels as long as they went slowly. Occasionally they would stop so Rand could orient them with the compass he kept in his pocket.

''So you *do* know where we're going,'' Cutch said, watching Rand squint as he studied the compass. ''I was wondering.''

''You should keep on wondering,'' said Rand. He made a quarter turn and rechecked the compass. Even after he pocketed it, he stood where he was, his head cocked to one side as he listened intently. He suddenly turned back. ''This way . . . I think.''

While they continued to walk, usually climbing, Claire explained everything as she understood it to Cutch. He didn't voice his skepticism but he wasn't exactly enthusiastic. He reminded them that he had already made an exploration of some of the island. He hadn't seen the temple or come across a waterfall other than the one that was in the harbor.

''Did you come this way?'' Claire asked simply.

"Well, no. Rand's leading us to the interior. We were looking for a way out."

"If you go in far enough, it's eventually the same as going out."

Rand chuckled. "Argue with that," he told Cutch.

Cutch shook his head. "No, thank you. Not on a bet."

Their passage became easier when Rand brought them closer to the stream. The noise that had always been in the background seemed to shift in importance. Cutch didn't say a word, but his steps were a little more lively.

It was almost daylight when they came upon the source of the narrow stream. It wasn't a waterfall, but a small spring that fed it. It trickled from the rock and gathered in a small pool that eventually became the stream. Rand was undeterred. He pointed upward so Cutch could see what they had to climb. "We'll have to harness Claire."

Some of the rope was taken off Claire's shoulders and tied around her waist. Rand joined the other end to his chest. "It's not much different than when you scaled Mauna Puka to study the tikis," Rand told her. Over the top of her head he almost dared Cutch to say anything different. Cutch looked at the rough face of the lava rock. He had to tip his head back to see the top. It was a hundred feet if it was a step, and most of it was on a steep incline.

"Not much different," Cutch repeated under his breath. "I'll bring up the rear."

They began climbing. There were natural footholds in the rock, but they were uneven and sometimes at an uncomfortable distance from one another. Rand and Cutch both studied the path ahead of them to make certain they could navigate it with Claire in tow. The easiest route was also the longest one. They crossed the face of the lava formation in a wide zigzag pattern. It took them more than an hour to reach the top.

The temple platform and altar were immediately in front of them.

"What is it?" Claire asked when she felt Cutch's stillness beside her.

"I'm looking at the temple. It's just like Rand described it to me."

"Of course," said Claire. She brushed off her trousers and removed the rope from her waist. "Did you doubt it?"

Rand grinned while Cutch swore he had only ever been confident. He unhitched the rope at his waist and helped Claire coil it. "It's not much farther, Cutch. You'll find the going a lot more straightforward."

The rush of water came to them clearly as they began their descent. The manmade steps leading from the temple were easily negotiated compared to the ground they had just covered. Even the last part of the path, which Claire remembered as being steep, seemed unremarkable to her now. They broke out of the trees and into the channel at exactly the place Tiare had started their trek yesterday.

Claire listened to the water cascading in a steep arc from the rock. "Is there a rainbow?" she asked Rand.

"No. The sun's too low in the sky." He placed her arm at his elbow. "This way," he said. "We need to find seven pagan sentinels."

Cutch had been leaning on his pick, waiting to hear something that made sense. "Seven pagan sentinels," he said under his breath. "They're back on Pulotu." No one paid him any attention. Shaking his head, he straightened and slung the pick over his shoulder; then he fell into step behind Claire and Rand.

Claire felt the spray of fresh water on her face and throat as they came closer to the falls. The steady roar of the water was almost painful to her ears. She would have covered them if she hadn't had to hold Rand. She was aware that they were all raising their voices to exchange words.

"It's a narrow ledge," Rand told her. "You'll have to walk directly behind me. Take a fistful of my shirt."

"Maybe we should put the rope around her again," Cutch said.

Claire shook her head. "I'll be fine! How far is it?"

"About twelve feet!" Rand said loudly. "We're going right behind the falls."

For good measure, Cutch took a fistful of Claire's shirt. He could haul her back if her feet slipped on the damp rock. They inched their way behind the shower of water. Besides making certain he didn't fall, Cutch had to keep the torch dry. As soon as they were hidden by the curtain of water, and safe on a wider platform of rock, Rand told him to light it.

At first Cutch saw nothing but the face of more sheer, polished rock. Nature's alcove behind the falls seemed to have no way out but the way they came in.

Rand motioned to him to step forward. "Shine your light here," he said. "On these markings."

"What is it?" Claire asked. "What do you see?"

"I have no bloody idea," Rand said.

Chapter Sixteen

"What do *you* see?" Claire asked Cutch.

"Writing on the wall," Cutch said. "Only I can't read it."

Rand put down his shovel. Confronted with the stone, he realized the shovel was useless. Out of the corner of his eye he saw Cutch lean the pick against the rock. Neither of the tools they had brought seemed like much help now. Rand's short laugh held more mockery than humor. "I always thought of it as *buried* treasure," he said ruefully.

Frustrated, Claire yanked on Rand's sleeve. "Tell me," she demanded. "Show me."

Cutch held the torch steady while Rand described what was in front of them. "It's just more rock, Claire. There are some runes carved into the surface." His eyes narrowed as he studied them. The torch created shadows at the underside of the writing. The runes were not carved on the flat surface of the rock at all. He ran his hand over them and found the characters were inscribed on smaller circles of stone that were embedded in the rock like cylinders, each about the size of a gold piece.

Claire listened carefully to Rand's description. Beside her Cutch was equally rapt. "How many runes?" she asked.

Rand counted them, making certain he didn't miss any or

count any twice. They were scattered over the face of the rock. "Seven," he said slowly. He looked at them again as if he couldn't quite believe it. "Seven." He anticipated Claire's next questions. "No, the pattern isn't the Big Dipper this time. There is no pattern."

"There must be."

Rand stepped back and looked over it again, joining the raised characters in different arrangements in his mind's eye. "Nothing, Claire."

Claire felt the heat of the torch as she approached the rock. "You can put it to one side," she told Cutch. "It won't help me see anything." She laid her palms flat on the rock. It was smoother than she expected. She wondered what part the smooth surface owed to the constant spray of water and the passage of centuries, and what part was owed to the work of man. She ran her fingers over the slightly raised runes but couldn't visualize the ones she touched. The grooves on either side of the circles were curious to her though. "Did you see these?" she asked Rand.

Rand and Cutch both leaned over Claire's shoulders and followed the path of her index finger. She was tracing a larger circle in the face of the rock. It brought her back to the carving where she started. "It's very faint," she said. "I think the rock has eroded so the groove is more shallow than it used to be. Even these runes probably don't extend as far out as they used to." Her hand passed to another carved symbol, and she found another groove that followed another circular path. "Each character is like a single pearl on a necklace. There are seven necklaces, one inside the other, each with its own pearl."

"Seven concentric circles," Rand said.

"*Seven rings,*" Claire pointed out. "*And just one key.*"

Cutch interrupted, trying to follow their thinking. "What about the pagan sentinels? I thought you needed to find them."

In response, Rand pulled Claire away from the rock so he could view it in its entirety again. His hands rested on her shoulders to keep her still and his own excitement in check. "It's the solar system," he said. "Those runes are symbols for the planets. Saturn. Jupiter. Mars. *Those* are the pagan sentinels. The Roman gods.''

Cutch looked at the rock with new appreciation. ''That so?'' He bent toward one of the characters and examined it more closely. ''That crescent sure enough could be a moon. Not exactly a planet, though, is it?''

''No,'' Rand said. ''It's not. But it's always represented in ancient star maps. There were seven heavenly bodies charted, not including the earth. At that time it was considered to be the center of everything.''

''So we pretend it's in the middle of all these other necklaces,'' Cutch said.

''Orbits,'' Rand corrected. ''That's what the grooves really represent. The moon has the inner orbit around the earth. The rune that's a circle with a point in the center is the sun. Then Venus. Mars. Mercury. Jupiter and Saturn.'' Rand could feel Claire fairly trembling with the need to touch the runes again. He let her go. ''It's too bad it doesn't help us,'' he told her. ''The riddles don't mention the planets. I don't know what to make of it.''

Claire's excitement was palpable as she explored the symbols again. ''I know these characters,'' she said. They were familiar to her in a way they hadn't been before. When Rand had described the sun and moon, she realized where she had seen them as well as all the others. It wasn't on a map of the ancient universe. ''These are alchemy symbols. Just as the riddle says: *Seven rings but just one key.*''

''*Metals all of alchemy,*'' Rand finished for her.

Claire nodded. ''Each planetary character corresponds to a different earth metal. The old alchemists made a connection between the influences of the planets and the metals they were using. The moon is silver. The sun is gold.''

''My God,'' Rand said softly. He had learned these things at Oxford, but it had always struck him, and most of his fellow students, as something more akin to mysticism than the first rudiments of real science. Claire's education, at Sir Griffin's knee, was fuller and richer than his own experience. ''Venus?'' he asked.

"Copper."

He nodded, knowing she was right as soon as he heard her answer. His brows came together as he concentrated. "Mars is iron."

"I never studied this," Cutch said. "But even I know Mercury's mercury."

Claire laughed. "Very clever. But do you know Jupiter?"

It was Rand who answered. "Tin. And Saturn is lead."

"That's all of them," said Claire. Thinking it through, she added slowly, *"Seven rings but just one key."*

"I don't see a key," Cutch told them. The torch flickered as he moved it around and looked high and low.

Rand stopped him. "It's not that kind of key. Look at this." Rand stood beside Claire and pulled at the cylinder that was marked by the sun's character. It required a little jiggling to loosen it, but the rod finally gave. There was enough play in it to pull it out or push it in. "I suspect what we're looking at is some kind of sequencing mechanism. If we remove these cylinders in just the right order, we'll be able to move the stone. I suspect we'll get one opportunity to do it right."

Cutch's brows lifted. He held the torch closer to his face to make certain Rand could see his disbelief. "Now how are you going to do that?"

"I'm not. I'm going to let Claire do the honors." He turned to Claire. "I'll help you if they stick. Go on," he urged softly. "You know what to do. You've earned this right. *Seven rings but just one key . . ."*

Claire's hand closed over the end of the cylinder with the crescent moon carved on its surface. *"Silver,"* she said and pulled it out. She found Jupiter next. It closely resembled the number four. *"Tin."* The eight-inch cylinder slid out more easily than the first one. She gave them both to Rand to hold. *"And mercury."* She had to stand on tiptoe to pull it free. *"Iron bracelet."* She yanked at the cylinder represented by the god Mars, then found Saturn. *"Leaden chain. Treasure lost, treasure gained."* Claire worked it loose and held it out to Rand. There were only two cylinders left. *"Copper circlet,"* she said. Venus was removed easily. "Help me with the last one. We'll do it together."

Rand laid the cylinders of polished rock on the ledge where they stood. He took Claire's hand and placed it over the only remaining cylinder. "The sun," he said.

She nodded. *"Crown of gold."* The cylinder moved under her questing fingers, slowly at first; then, with Rand's help it came away in one smooth motion.

Rand placed this last cylinder in the pile with the others. *"Seven sisters flee the fold."* He waited.

They all waited. Claire was actually holding her breath.

Nothing happened.

Rand recited softly, *"At the end of one god's promise stand seven pagan sentinels. Seven rings but just one key. Silver, tin, and mercury. Iron bracelet, leaden chain. Treasure lost, treasure gained. Copper circlet, crown of gold. Seven sisters flee the fold. Reunited, freed of curse; thy reward the richest purse. Seven rings but just one key. Metals all of alchemy. With the sisters, this verse brings wealth beyond the dreams of kings."*

Nothing happened.

Cutch handed Rand the torch. "Hold this." He picked up the shovel and slammed it hard against the stone. The force of his strike made his powerful forearms vibrate. He shrugged innocently when Rand just stared at him. "Chanting's nice," he said. "But sometimes a mule needs a good kick." He raised the shovel again.

It was a low rumble at first. It was difficult to distinguish from the sound of the water at their backs. Claire was the first to be able to make it out. She pointed at the rock face. Cutch lowered the shovel and took a step back. Rand did the opposite. He cupped a hand around his ear and counted the thuds as the crude tumblers dropped into place. At seven, the vibrating stopped.

Rand glanced at Cutch. "Watch this." He pushed on the rock with both hands, exerting very little effort, and felt it give as easily as a sail in the face of the wind. He opened it wide enough to allow them to enter, then tested the door to make certain it didn't swing easily in the other direction.

"Why don't I stay here," Cutch offered. "Just in case."

"All right. Claire?"

"I'm going with you." She indicated the ropes around her shoulders. "I'd like to replace these with something in gold."

Rand glanced at Cutch. "You were right, Cutch. She married me for my money."

"You don't have any yet," she pointed out. "Go on." Claire slipped her arm through his.

"I need the torch," he said. "But you can carry it." He waited while Cutch placed it in her free hand. "In the event this treasure really *is* buried, I'll take the shovel and pick."

The antechamber was small and it was empty. "There's only one corridor," Rand said.

"Then I suppose we should follow it."

Rand smiled at her eagerness. "You really do want wealth beyond the dreams of kings."

Claire snorted indelicately and nudged him forward.

The corridor was narrow and long. They didn't go very far before the light from outside the cave could no longer reach them. The torch Claire carried threw light a few feet in front of Rand and cast their shadows on the wall.

"What is it?" Claire asked when Rand stopped suddenly. She could feel a subtle difference in the air. Water trickled somewhere ahead of them. The space around her had opened up. "Is it the treasure?"

"It's another chamber," he said.

"Oh."

"The treasure's sitting in the middle of it."

Claire almost dropped the torch. "Truly?"

"Steady with that thing," said Rand. The shovel and pick thudded noisily as he dropped them. He saw Claire jump at their eerily hollow echo. "Sorry. I didn't mean to startle you. I wasn't thinking."

She waved aside his concern. "Would you like the torch now?"

He took it from her hands. "It's a very ordinary sea chest," he said, approaching it slowly. "About three hands high and eight long."

"It's not encrusted with jewels?"

"No. Not one." He secretly admitted to a little disappointment himself. When he and his brother played at finding it, it was always encrusted with jewels. Rand sank down on one knee. He felt Claire drop beside him. Neither of them touched the chest, though it was only a finger's distance from them.

"What *is* this place?" asked Claire, her voice hushed.

"Why are you whispering?"

"It seems that kind of place."

"It's not a burial vault or a church."

"Are you sure?"

In truth Rand hadn't looked around since his eyes had alighted on the chest. He held up the torch and drew it in a small circle over his head. There were three passages leading deeper into the mountain. No light came from any of them. "Water ran through here a long time ago," he told her. "It made all these passages."

"I can still hear it," she said.

"It must be an underground river that feeds the waterfall. This place wasn't dug out by the islanders. They probably showed it to Waterstone's mapmaker, but he was the one who came up with the stone to put at the entrance."

"Mercutio," Claire said. "I don't mind if you want to call him that. It's as good a name as any."

Rand held the torch directly over the trunk lid. He ran his hand along the rough wooden surface. Rusty iron strips held the mottled wood in place. He picked at a bit of mossy growth on one corner. It came away easily. Rand stared hard at what he was seeing. He scraped off a bit more with his thumbnail. He had no difficulty recognizing the symbols he uncovered. They were simply letters of the English alphabet and their particular order told him what he needed to know.

"Actually," he said softly, "I have a better name for our cartographer. How do you like William Abberly?"

"Abberly?" Claire actually sat back on her bottom. "The duke's Abberly? Abberly Hall?"

"I imagine." He took her hand and placed it on the carved letters. "You won't be able to make it out, but that's what it says right here."

"He carved his name in the chest?"

"He did."

Claire sat up on her knees again. "So Strickland has some real connection to the treasure after all. I never thought of this. Do you think he knows?"

"Don't you?"

She nodded. "All these years . . . centuries . . . the part of the legend no one talked about."

"William Abberly was probably a younger son. Educated but with few prospects. Going to sea with Henry Waterstone would have been a grand and dangerous venture. Making maps of the New World for the queen would have been a great privilege."

"He was still the son of a duke. When he didn't come back with Waterstone, there would have been some kind of inquiry."

"Not if the family was out of favor with Elizabeth," Rand said. "Strickland told me that his ancestors almost lost Abberly Hall. They might not have been able to get any satisfaction . . . at least not immediately. Who can say when they understood the role William Abberly played in hiding the treasure? He was the key figure and they had nothing to show for it."

"Neither did the Hamiltons or the Waterstones."

"We had Abberly's riddles. They didn't. When Henley Hamilton moved himself and his family to the colonies he thought he was protecting them from the Waterstones. I think they all had much more to fear from William Abberly's family."

Claire was silent as she took it all in. "If Stickle is truly my father, then . . ."

"Then you're an Abberly." Rand could see by her expression that she was not comfortable with the idea. "Would you like to open the chest?"

She shook her head. "What if . . . you know . . . he's . . ."

"Inside?" Rand chuckled. "He's not. I think William Abberly lived out a long and fairly productive life here. In spite of the fact that Henry Waterstone left him for dead, the mapmaker survived. He has descendants to prove it.''

Claire expelled the name with the softness of releasing a breath. "Tiare."

"And Tipu. And all the priests who have guarded this treasure before him. That's what Tiare meant when she said they had been waiting for me for three hundred years. That's the real reason the Hamilton name meant something to her. The other priests understood it, too. William Abberly passed down a story of his own.''

This last revelation made Claire twist her head and listen for footsteps behind them. "I think we should hurry, then. We can't know what he intended his children and their children and all the children after him to do to you.''

Rand had also considered that. He passed the torch back to Claire. Placing both hands on the edge of the chest, he applied some pressure upward. The lid was raised with little effort.

Claire heard the hinges creak. "Well?" she asked.

"It's filled with smaller wooden cases," he said, removing one. "The ones I can see on top are all the same size. The carvings on them are different." He opened one. In a bed of emerald velvet, none the worse for being secreted away for three hundred years, was a strand of the most perfect pearls Rand had ever seen. He lifted them carefully, half expecting them to spill all over the stone floor, then asked Claire to hold out her palm. He dangled the string above her hand for a moment, then lowered it slowly.

It was like rainfall in her hand. The beads were as cool as water drops. "Pearls," she said. The strand was too long to be held properly in one hand. "I'll wear it with the rest of the ropes." Claire slipped it over her head and around her neck. "What else is there?" She pretended to be affronted by his low laughter. "I'm curious," she defended herself.

Rand was still smiling to himself as he removed another case. "Diamond eardrops," he told her. He turned the case this way and that. The exquisitely cut diamonds flashed. "Do you want to wear them?''

"No. Not with what I have on.''

Rand's burst of laughter echoed in the chamber. He snapped the lid shut. ''Something else perhaps.'' He set the case down and picked up another. ''Rubies? This is a bracelet.''

''The pearls are enough, thank you.'' Claire leaned forward. ''I don't understand. I thought all of this was for Pope Gregory. He wasn't going to wear these things, was he?''

''It's merely tribute,'' Rand explained. ''He could do anything with it he liked. Hoard it. Display it. Or give it to a mistress.'' He caught her surprised expression. ''Are you really so naive?''

''Not any longer.''

Grinning, Rand leaned over and kissed her. Before Claire could take him to task, he began opening more cases. Pope Gregory's gifts from the Spanish government included a silver belt, snuff boxes, music boxes, rings, a chalice, ivory combs, a crucifix, and two small cases filled with nothing but uncut stones. All of the items, including the cases, were encrusted with precious gems. Every one of them was the work of an artisan.

Rand stared at the bottom of the chest. There were only eight wooden boxes remaining. Unlike the boxes he had opened previously, these were marked with carvings he recognized. He reached for the one engraved with a crown and lifted it out. He raised the lid carefully.

The crown was a headband of hammered gold. Slender. Plain. Except for its circumference it could have been mistaken for a collar. Rand held it up and described it to Claire. ''There are places for each of the stones to be set, but none of them have been.'' He placed the crown on top of its case and retrieved another box from the chest. ''If I'm right, this should be the ruby.''

''*Blood will run,*'' Claire said. In spite of her solemn tone, her expression and posture were eager.

''I wonder if the curse is true,'' Macauley Stuart said.

Rand and Claire turned simultaneously toward the chamber's entrance. The doctor stood on the threshold, a pistol in his hand, Tiare and Tipu just off to one side. Tipu held a torch. He was trying very hard to keep it steady.

"Dr. Stuart?" asked Claire.

"He has a gun, Claire," Rand said quietly. Out of the corner of his eye he saw her stiffen. Without realizing it, she started to lower the torch. Rand put down the box in his hand and gently touched her elbow to remind her to keep it up. "Tiare and Tipu are with him."

Tiare made a small, almost imperceptible, negative shake of her head when Rand looked at her.

Rand corrected himself. "Tiare and Tipu are here," he said. "They're not *with* him." His glance swiveled back to the doctor. "Why don't you let Tiare hold the torch? It's too heavy for Tipu. He'll drop it."

Macauley placed his free hand on Tipu's thin shoulder. "The boy's doing fine."

"Where is Mr. Cutch?" asked Claire.

"Just where you left him."

"Did you hurt him?"

"He's alive," Stuart said.

It was not precisely an answer to her question. Claire opened her mouth to press for more information, but Rand's light touch at her side silenced her.

"Where are your men, Tiare?" asked Rand.

It was Macauley who answered. "They're not coming," he said. "I suppose things will proceed more smoothly if you're not anticipating a rescue from anyone. You can concentrate on what I'm saying."

Rand continued to look at Tiare. She was clearly frightened. Torchlight flickered on her face and revealed features that were almost colorless and a bottom lip that trembled. He was surprised when she responded to his question, even when it was clearly Stuart's intent to keep her quiet.

"I came to your ship with Tipu. Just the two of us. None of my men know we're here. I wanted to speak to you privately."

"Enough," Macauley said. He waved his gun a little. When he was done, it was pointed at Tipu. "She didn't think you could find the treasure," he told Claire and Rand. "I wasn't convinced. You're both very clever . . . most of the time." He looked at Claire. "You left your cane in my cabin this morning.

That's how I knew you were there. I discovered the riddle was missing from my bag right away. You could have given yourself more time if you hadn't been so careless.'' He watched self-recrimination bring heat to Claire's cheeks. ''I still wouldn't have been able to follow without Tiare's help. She brought me by canoe. I was surprised to find out I've been to this place before. Obviously it was something you discovered on your own, Captain.''

''I would rather have arrived in an outrigger. The land route was difficult.''

Macauley nodded. ''That's what Tiare told me. She said even if you knew where you were going, it would take some time to arrive. She was right. You haven't been here so very long.'' His eyes wandered over the treasure boxes that surrounded Claire and Rand. Some of them were open. He could see for himself the jeweled bounty that had already been uncovered. He returned his attention to Rand. ''Tiare was wrong about this underground vault, too. She said you wouldn't be able to get inside. Apparently no one here knows the secret to opening the stone. Not even the priests.''

''That was as my ancestor wished,'' Tiare said.

''William Abberly,'' Claire said.

Tiare and Tipu nodded in unison. ''Only Hamilton and Waterstone working together can open the vault,'' Tipu said in important tones. ''You must be Waterstone, Claire.''

''My mother entrusted me with the riddle,'' she said. There was no point in explaining she had no Waterstone blood. Revealing that to Tiare might prove dangerous.

''You never helped your father find the treasure,'' Tiare said.

''I never knew he was looking for it. And I didn't understand I had the riddle in my possession. It wouldn't have mattered. It's as Tipu has learned from you. Hamilton and Waterstone had to work together. That was Abberly's real intent.''

Macauley Stuart's ironic laughter punctuated Claire's words. ''You think so? He only wanted members of both families in the same place so he could bury them with the treasure. In this case, both of you.'' His chin jutted toward them. ''Tell them,

Tiare. It's why you came to see them this morning in secret. Tell them what your priests decided.''

Tipu turned his head around to look at his mother. She would not meet his eyes. The torch wavered in his hand again.

''She doesn't want to say it in front of the boy,'' Macauley said. ''But I'll tell you what she told me alone. The priests decided that you would be brought here, and if you could prove yourselves by opening the stone, you would remain here. Forever. The only way you and the ship were going to be released was if you couldn't get into the vault. Tiare came on her own to warn you. She thought she could persuade you to leave the stone untouched, even if you knew its secret.'' He shrugged. ''You know now that she was too late.'' His gaze rested for a moment on the pick and shovel. ''I don't think you're going to be able to dig your way out.''

Macauley nudged Tipu forward, pressing the barrel of his gun against the back of the boy's head. ''Go on,'' Stuart said. ''Hold the torch up.''

Tipu tried to glance back at his mother and couldn't. He took a few small steps forward. His light joined Claire's, and the treasure at her feet took on a glowing quality. In spite of his fear, the colors mesmerized him. ''Where are the seven sisters?'' he asked.

The doctor nodded. ''I had the very same question.'' He used his weapon to point to the golden headband. ''Is that the crown?''

Rand nodded. He held it up. ''Do you want to see it?''

Macauley was not going to be distracted so easily. For good measure he took a step back. ''There are no stones on it. I was told to expect a rainbow of stones.''

''We were just getting to those when you came in. Do you want us to finish? I can place them in the crown temporarily.'' Without waiting for Macauley's direction, Rand picked up the box that he hoped held the ruby and opened it. The ruby's brilliance was enhanced by the torchlight. Rand plucked it from its velvet bed and placed it gingerly in its oval setting in the crown. ''*Blood will run,*'' he said. He chose another. This time it was an orange sapphire of exceptional color. The round cut matched perfectly with its setting. *"Flames will come.* Claire, would you get another?" He guided her hand to the box that he knew held the yellow stone. It was another sapphire with a strong saturation of color and a square cut. He squeezed Claire's hand gently as he helped her set it in its proper place.

"Blazing sun, blinding some," she said.

One of Macauley's brows lifted. "Your own curse, Claire. How fitting."

She ignored him and accepted Rand's help in choosing another. "It should be an emerald. *Blades lifted high across the plain.*"

It was a pear-shaped emerald, almost fifteen carats in weight. The clarity of the gem was astonishing. Claire was the only one not distracted by it. She set it in its place by touch alone.

"Flood waters rising, months of rain." Rand held up an aquamarine. By itself, it was the least valuable of all the stones in the collection, but without it the setting was incomplete. There was no other gem whose color was so perfectly suited to fill this band of the rainbow's spectrum. Rand set it as carefully as the others.

A deep indigo-blue sapphire was revealed next. It was cut in the kohinor manner, a style that reflected its Persian meaning: mountain of light. Rand held it up briefly before he set it in the crown. *"A plague will ink clouded skies."*

"The last one," Macauley said impatiently. "Open the last one."

Rand took out the only remaining box and lifted the lid. It was an amethyst. The violet color was clear, the stone almost flawless. *"Grieving, shadows beneath thy eyes."*

Macauley nodded. "I read your riddle," he said. "Memorized it, too." He didn't mention that he hadn't understood it. Mostly he had concentrated on deciphering the mirror writing. *"Seven sisters, cursed every one. Seven sisters, all alone. Await the day, when reunited they will be placed upon their throne."* He held out his hand. "They're reunited now, aren't they? Give me the crown."

"Of course." Rand flung the crown at Macauley's head. It hit the doctor squarely on his brow. The precious stones, none of them tightly set, flew in seven different directions. Stuart raised his gun just as Rand tackled him at the knees. He went down heavily, Rand on top of him. The gun fired as it skittered across the floor. Tiare screamed and ran to protect her son. Claire groped for Tipu, found the torch, and took it from his shaking hands.

"Rand?"

His reply was cut off as Macauley struck him hard in the ribs with his elbow.

Claire recalled the fight at Henley between the two men. Bria had at least told her what was happening. Tiare was strangely silent. Claire could hear Tipu whispering to his mother, unintelligible words that had the cadence of comfort. That frightened Claire as much as anything else that was happening. Had Tiare been injured? Had Tipu?

There was more scuffling. Neither man could rise to his feet. They rolled on the cold stone floor, first one on top, then the other. They were every bit as evenly matched as they had been at Henley. Claire knew Rand might not be the victor here.

She tilted her head, listening hard to the give and take of the fight. The blows they landed sounded equally damaging and their grunts were indistinguishable. Someone kicked her and she fell against the chest. The boxes slid around. She heard the sound of metal scraping against the floor and realized one of them was grappling for the gun. The next recognizable sound she heard was Macauley's triumphant cry and Rand's alarmed one.

She knew who had the gun.

Claire dropped both torches in the trunk and slammed the lid. She heard the flames sizzle and pop. The lid was warm but not for long. The fires died quickly in the airless chest, and the chamber was immediately quiet. No one moved because they couldn't see.

Except Claire. She picked up the shovel. Long before Macauley Stuart understood what had hit him, she had.

Bending, Claire found the gun in his limp hand and removed it. "Rand? Take this, please." She heard him push away from Stuart and sit up himself. She imagined he was rubbing his own head, thinking what a narrow escape he had had. She could have told him it wasn't that close.

"Did you use the shovel?" Rand asked, getting to his feet. The impenetrable darkness was disorienting. He found himself turning around as if that would help him locate Claire. "Or the pick?"

"The shovel." She tapped it on the floor to help him find her. "Here I am." She had to go to him when he was still a few feet from her. She found his hand and placed the gun in his palm. "You keep this."

Rand tucked the weapon at the small of his back. "Was Tiare hurt?"

"I don't know." She started in Tiare's direction and stepped on one of the small treasure boxes. "Be careful, Rand. The treasure's been scattered all over the floor." She slipped one length of rope off her shoulders. "Use this to tie Macauley."

Rand took the rope and knelt again, groping his way across the floor until he found the doctor. He remembered his men teaching Claire to make knots on board *Cerberus*. He discovered how difficult it was for her when he tried to secure Macauley in the dark. "How is Tiare?" he asked to cover his frustration.

"She's not injured. Neither is Tipu." Claire finished running her hands over him. She kissed her brother lightly on the cheek. "They're both frightened. This place has a powerful tapu for them. We have to get them out before they can't walk any longer."

Rand sat back on his haunches. He felt something press against the sole of his boot. He lifted his foot and found one of the gems. He dropped it in his pocket. "Out? How do you propose we do that? I don't have anything to light the torches, and there are three passages leading from this room besides the one that brought us in. We can't expect Cutch to come for us, Claire. We don't know what ..." He didn't finish that thought, but began a new one instead. "No night has ever been as black as this. I'm completely turned around. I don't know which way is out."

Claire merely smiled. "I do." She crossed the chamber to

his side and handed him more rope. "Tie this around your waist and connect it to Tiare and Tipu. Leave enough length between you so you're not stepping on each other's heels. Is Macauley trussed?"

"Like a Christmas goose."

"You'll have to carry him."

Rand sighed. "I was afraid you'd say that. He would have left us here, you know."

"I know."

"But we're not going to do that to him."

"No," Claire said. "We're not. We're not like him, Rand. We're not going to kill someone over this treasure. It's not worth it."

She started to turn away but Rand found her. He gripped her elbows and brought her flush to his chest. "Sometimes you make me a better man than I am," he said softly.

Rand had no trouble finding her mouth with his own. He only pulled away when he felt Macauley stir at his feet. "Give me the shovel," he told her, setting Claire away from him.

She found it. "Not too hard, please."

It took Rand a few moments to find the proper position. He brought the shovel down on Macauley's shoulders with a satisfying thwack. There was a groan, then silence. Rand let the shovel fall and began uncoiling the rope Claire had given him. "This won't take long," he said.

Claire was waiting for him at the passage entrance when he finished. "Tie the last length around my waist," she said. She turned, her arms folded across her chest and out of the way.

"Done." Rand looked a shade longingly over his shoulder at the treasure he couldn't see. He thought of the gem in his pocket. It would be worth a fortune by itself. He could be satisfied with one of the sisters, even the aquamarine. He very much doubted Claire would let him return for the rest of the sibling rainbow. "Lead on," he told her.

Claire waited for Tipu and Tiare to fall in line behind her. When she heard Rand lift the doctor to his shoulders, Claire started forward. The rope tightened slightly when Tipu faltered. Tiare's hands pressed her son's shoulders lightly. "It's all right," she encouraged him. "Claire is not blind here. There is no tapu."

"No tapu," Claire said softly. "There never was."

She led them through the passage without hesitating once. It was only when Claire reached the threshold of the antechamber that her steps grew less certain. The roar of the waterfall was in her ears. Behind her there was another roar, a deafening rumble this time. The ground shook. The tremor went right through her.

"It's going to collapse!" Rand yelled. No one could hear him. They had come far enough through the corridor that he could see the entrance on the other side of the antechamber. The stone was still open and diffuse light from beyond the waterfall streamed through.

Rand pushed Tiare and Tipu ahead when he saw Claire falter, then stop. The ropes that connected them were going to tangle her in their rush to get out. She was holding them back. He tore at his own leash and let it fly. He dropped Macauley and released Claire. He yelled at Tiare and Tipu to run.

"Claire!" He shook her. She didn't respond. Her arms were crossed rigidly in front of her. She was stiff and unyielding. It was as if she was deaf to him as well as blind. Rand picked her up and carried her out of the chamber. Tiare and Tipu had Cutch on his feet and were helping him get past the waterfall. There was blood on his shoulder and more at the side of his head. He lumbered along, holding onto Tiare for support.

Fine black dust was beginning to pour from the entrance of the vault like smoke from a burning building. Rand followed Tipu. The first chance he had to put Claire down safely, he did.

Then he went back inside for Macauley Stuart.

The dust was thick and it blinded Rand. He knelt, groping on the floor for the doctor's body. He found an arm and began to drag Stuart toward the entrance. He felt himself being plucked off his feet. Rand knew there was only one man with the strength to do that, and in spite of his wounds, Cutch was that man. Cutch had come back for both of them.

Rand stumbled past the falls, this time with Cutch and

Macauley behind him. The explosion that collapsed the entrance almost knocked them to the ground. Rand turned, half expecting to see that the hillside had collapsed as well. It hadn't. Nothing on the outside seemed to be altered in any way. He and Cutch watched the waterfall pound the small avalanche of rock and dust into the inlet. The water churned, covering the evidence that the vault had ever existed.

Shaking his head, Cutch tossed the doctor's bound body unceremoniously on the beach and followed Rand to where the others were sitting.

"Couldn't have lived with myself if I'd let you go in there alone," Cutch said, dropping to his knees beside Tiare. "She wouldn't have let me."

"Claire?"

"No, Tiare."

Rand couldn't make his slight smile reach his eyes. He looked Tiare and Tipu over, then left them to Cutch's care. Or perhaps it was the other way around. They were all going to be fine.

He hunkered down beside Claire. "Are you all right?" he asked, searching her fine features. He could see for himself that her shocked state had passed. Her arms were no longer tightly crossed in front of her. All the booty she had been clutching to her chest was now lying on either side of her. What she hadn't carried out, she was wearing.

Rand simply shook his head, marveling. His heart swelled. He had no words for what he felt in that moment. He just stared at her and hoped she would understand his silence.

Claire removed one of the diamond pendants from her ears and placed it on the sand. "I decided they were right for this occasion after all." She then removed the other. She shook out her hair after taking out the ivory combs. The emerald chips along their edges glittered as she set them aside. From behind her back she removed the jewel-encrusted crucifix, then took off the rope of pearls. The rings came next. Two of the largest were stacked on her thumb. She pulled them off without a second thought.

She raised her left leg and tugged at the hammered gold band that circled her thigh like a garter. Claire held it out until

Rand took it; then she reached in her pocket and brought out a fistful of stones. "They're all here, save one," she said. "I couldn't find it."

Rand couldn't think what she meant for a moment. He blinked and looked down at her open palm. Red. Orange. Green. Blue. Indigo. Violet. Only the yellow sapphire was missing. *"Blazing sun, blinding some."* There was a bittersweet quality to his smile as Rand reached into his own pocket and held up the one stone he had been able to rescue. "I can see that."

Claire looked into his eyes for the first time. "So can I."

His face was a revelation to her. She watched one of his dark brows come up slowly as confusion warred with hope. His beautiful mouth parted, but he had no words. He held her riveted so that she could not look away even if it had been her desire, and this time she offered something in return: she stared back.

Sunshine glanced off his coppery hair. Strands of it touched his collar and fluttered in the warming breeze. His perfectly cast features were covered by a film of dust. The thin scar that disappeared into his temple stood out in dark relief. Claire remembered Mrs. Webster once telling her it was the scar that kept him from being beautiful. Now Claire saw for herself that her teacher was wrong. Mrs. Webster had never looked into Rand's eyes the way she was doing now, had never seen the beauty of a soul captured in the warm color of polished chestnuts or in the perfect clarity of the tears that rimmed those eyes. As diamonds could etch glass, Rand's tears etched his face, their tracks clearing the dust. He did not raise his hands to wipe them away.

Claire knew a moment of panic as her own vision blurred. She was not prepared for the return of darkness after so brief a journey into light. She looked around quickly, her eyes darting to absorb the complete palette of the landscape. It seemed that her memory of colors had failed her. The feathery palm fronds that waved overhead had never been quite this shade of deep, rich emerald. Her fingers sifted through grains of sand that surely glittered with the intensity of stars. The inlet mirrored sunlight and the perfect azure sky above them. Magenta and crimson hibiscus exploded with pyrotechnic ferocity from the greenery and black lava rock. The raucous cry of a gull turned Claire's head and she was left with the fleeting impression of bright white wings and a scarlet tail that fluttered behind like a pennant.

She blinked. Form blurred but none of the vibrancy was lost. Her vision held the broad, sweeping strokes of watercolors. There, where Tiare knelt beside Cutch, the distinction between the two figures, one like honey, one as dark as coffee, was lost at the edges. The tenderness of the scene, of Tiare's delicate ministering to her wounded warrior, had its own golden aura. Tipu, with the eagerness and impatience of youth, danced around the couple trying to be helpful and with no notion of how that might be accomplished. His cheeky grin flashed whitely as he turned and twisted in the sand.

The crashing water drew Claire's attention next. The colors of one god's promise were so close it seemed she could touch them. They shimmered and floated, translucent, yet somehow with substance. The color of light. A waterfall of light.

"Claire." Rand said her name gently. He took her face in his hands and held her still. Without a word he willed her to look at him. He saw her uncertainty, her fear, the return of panic as her vision blurred again, and then he spoke with the quiet assurance that would change all that.

"You're crying, Claire. Do you understand? From where I'm looking, the rainbow is in your eyes."

Epilogue

Cerberus rode high in the water. Her canvas was taut. Speed, direction, and the fullness of sail all defined the presence of the powerful wind at her back. The rush of the sea against her hull had a percussive musical cadence that was almost hypnotic. Salt spray lifted high over the rail in a fine mist. In this moment the curve of the horizon was a seamless joining of water and sky, unmarked by islands, atolls, or other ships. *Cerberus* glided on alone. Solonesia was behind her.

Claire leaned forward at the head rail, her arms braced as stiffly as masts to confront the wind's resistance. Where her dark hair had escaped its anchoring pins, it fluttered away from her face. She could taste the sea on her lips.

"I knew I would find you here." Rand came up behind her. He lightly placed his hands on Claire's shoulders. She didn't resist the gentle pressure of his palms as he grounded her to the deck again. If he knew where to find her, he thought, then perhaps she had been expecting him. With no conscious intent, they had established a ritual for themselves.

It was the onset of darkness that beckoned them both to this place. Each evening for a week now, Claire had watched the passage of twilight into night and saw the ocean absorb the deep indigo presence of the sky. Rand could always feel the slender thread of tension that held her still until she glimpsed the first evening star. She stood here on the edge of night and confronted her fear of the darkness coming upon her forever.

Claire relaxed in the shelter of Rand's embrace. Sirius was a distinct point of light overhead. "I don't want to take it for granted," she said softly.

"I know. Neither do I."

"Do you think I'm foolish coming here?"

"You're incredibly brave." He said it as a matter of fact, not opinion.

Claire smiled. "Why do you come?"

"Because you're here. I don't want to take *you* for granted."

Claire turned in his arms and tipped her head back. *I won't let you,* she had been going to say. The flippant response simply lodged in her throat. She was not quite used to seeing him yet, not used to the riveting expression of his polished chestnut eyes. She had thought she understood how he looked at her, but this was something else again. She had known the shape of his features, the defined chin and cheekbones, the Roman nose, the thin scar that creased his skin from temple to chin, but this deeply studying stare of his had been outside her imagination.

Claire anchored herself to Rand as she stood on tiptoe. She touched her mouth to his and didn't close her eyes until long after he did. The kiss left them both a little unsteady and breathless. She felt Rand's fingers lace at the small of her back and keep her right where she was for a few minutes more. When he set her away from him, she felt his reluctance.

"I have to speak to Dodd," he said. "There are some—"

Claire shook her head. "You don't have to explain. I understand. Go on." She watched him walk away, his long, confident stride never faltering under the roll and pitch of the deck. Halfway to his destination he glanced back, seeking her out. She lifted her hand to indicate that she was fine and he went on, reassured. She wondered at this gesture, wondered if it was the casual habit that it seemed. How often in the past had his eyes sought her out and never received any response?

Her smile softened, became a shade bittersweet. He had been looking after her in the most literal fashion, and she had been unable to appreciate or encourage it. No, she thought, she would not take this miracle of sight for granted.

Or the miracle that they were together now, bound for Charleston on *Cerberus*. It was Tiare's fine hand that had guided them toward this end. With the collapse of the mountain vault, she saw the opportunity to help them escape. The priests had expected that the treasure would bring death for both Hamilton and Waterstone. Tiare showed them that this was indeed the case. Once Claire and Rand were safely aboard *Cerberus,* Tiare and Tipu brought the priests together. Tiare solemnly led them to the crushed entrance and recounted the story of how Macauley Stuart had taken her and Tipu to the site. In Tiare's recitation she made the doctor a hero for permitting her the opportunity to witness Rand and Claire's burial in the mountain. There was no disputing testimony from Stuart. According to Tiare, he died while trying to rescue Rand and Claire. It was an impressive performance in that the words did not stick in her throat. She took some satisfaction from the fact that while the doctor was aboard *Cerberus* by then, he was also considerably more confined in his hiding place than Rand and Claire were in theirs.

At her side Tiare had Tipu for support and Cutch's dark, grief-stricken face as further evidence of the deaths. There was never a moment in which she was not believed.

With the treasure buried at last and William Abberly's wishes carried out, there was no reason for *Cerberus* to remain on Arahiti. The tikis had stretched their powerful tapu across time and brought an end to Hamilton and Waterstone. The work of the priests was done. The treasure had been protected for those it was meant to destroy.

Tiare and her men led *Cerberus* out of the harbor, past the dangerous shoals and into open water. Claire and Rand came topside only when they were certain they could not be seen by the outriggers. It was an unsatisfactory way to say good-bye to the woman who had ultimately saved them. Standing at the taffrail that evening, Claire and Rand had to tell themselves that Tiare understood what was in their hearts.

She had let them leave with their lives and the treasure, and they were both richer and poorer for her generosity. Never returning to Arahiti meant that Tipu was forever out of their reach. Tiare and Cutch as well. In the week they had been aboard *Cerberus,* neither Rand nor Claire had looked at the treasure. It was locked in the hold very near Macauley Stuart's new quarters. They hadn't looked in on him either.

Claire was sitting in the middle of the bed, brushing out her hair, when Rand came upon her again. Her head was tilted to one side as she pulled the brush through in long, lazy strokes. One of his journals was open in the cradle of her crossed legs. She was studying his notes on the coral reefs around Tahiti, her free hand guiding her eyes as she read the page. She was so absorbed that she didn't look up when he entered.

Rand cleared his throat.

"I know you're there," Claire said. "I'm ignoring you."

Rand shrugged out of his jacket and laid it over the back of the desk chair. He sat down and began removing his boots, tossing them toward the bed so they thumped loudly on the floor beside Claire. She continued reading, not even annoyed by his attention-seeking. Shaking his head, Rand let her be. He removed the ship's log from the desk and recorded the day's journey. When he was finished he sat back, stretched hard, and looked up. Claire was watching him, a sweet smile curving her lips. She was holding the closed journal in front of her. The brush lay on the trunk. It was obvious to him now that she had been studying him as intently as she had his notes.

"Did you try clearing your throat?" he asked.

"Several times. You were oblivious."

At least she knew he wasn't ignoring her. He shut the ship's log, put it away, and leaned back in the chair. He propped his feet on a padded stool under the desk. "I had a lot to write today."

Claire knew this seventh day at sea had been relatively uneventful. Rand was catching up his record of all that had happened since they'd found Pulotu. "Will you read it to me when you're finished?"

Rand's brows lifted slightly. "You can read it yourself."

"I'd rather you read it. I like the sound of your voice."

He grinned at that.

"Almost as much as Mr. Cutch's," she said.

His grin merely deepened, forcing a small dimple to appear at the corner of his mouth. "Setting me in my place, Mrs. Hamilton?"

She laughed. "Something like that, Captain." Claire scooted back on the bed so that her back was flush to the wall. Her fingers lightly tapped the journal's leather binding. "What do you suppose Mr. Cutch is doing now?" she asked a trifle wistfully.

Rand pretended to give it some thought. "Let's see . . . it's a warm, lovely evening on Arahiti . . . starshine . . . gentle breeze . . . Tipu's asleep and Cutch is alone with Tiare. I'd hazard a guess about his activities, but then you'd blush." Rand watched as Claire was put to a blush anyway. His smile faded slowly. "I miss him," he said. "I'm happy for him, but I miss him."

Claire nodded. It was the same for her. Cutch had elected to stay behind on Arahiti with Tiare and Tipu. He said at the time that it didn't seem like a choice. It was something he had to do. Claire and Rand understood exactly what he meant. "Did you ever imagine Mr. Cutch would fall in love?"

"Fall? He was tripped."

Claire didn't disagree. "Blind-sided."

Rand laughed. "Exactly." He unbuttoned the neck of his shirt and massaged his nape. His expression sobered. "He'll be a good father to Tipu."

"I've thought the same thing." She wished she had told him how she felt before now. "In fact, I've thought that if he does just half as good a job with Tipu as he did with you, my brother will grow up to be a fine man."

Beneath Rand's coppery hair, he felt the tips of his ears redden. Ducking his head a bit, both pleased and embarrassed, Rand changed the subject. "Not having Cutch here will mean more time for me topside, at least until Dodd is sure of his new position and duties.''

"I know," she said. "I told you earlier this evening I understand. I meant it.'' Claire held up the journal a fraction. "I have more than enough interests to keep me busy. Your work is fascinating, Rand. You have a broader perspective than my father. Sir Griffin's studies were focused almost solely on deriving tonics from the island plants. His contribution is certainly important, but what you've done has much wider application.''

"Do you think so?"

Claire realized she was being asked because he valued her opinion. He trusted her to answer honestly and not pat him on the back with false encouragement. "Yes," she said. "I do. Your work is remarkable, really. I knew so very little about it before. Studying with Sir Griffin isolated me, and when I returned to England . . . well, you know I couldn't resume my work. The duke told me precious little about your explorations . . .''

Claire shook her head and looked past Rand's shoulder for a moment, retrieving a more accurate memory. "No, that isn't entirely true. He told me some things about you, about your studies, but I displayed little interest. I was jealous, I think. Horribly jealous that you were doing what I wanted to do, and seeming to do it in a half-hearted fashion while you hunted the treasure.''

Claire laid Rand's book on the trunk at the foot of the bed. "Stickle understood from the beginning how important your work was to you. I wish I had understood so well. I might not have thrown his ashtray at your head.'' She sighed. "Or at least I would have let you kiss me a little longer.''

The memory of that kiss in Strickland's dining room lifted one corner of Rand's mouth. "I would have liked that.''

"You were trying to shock me.''

"Perhaps," he said. "But I still would have liked it.''

Claire could not quite contain her smugly satisfied smile. She began to fold back the covers while Rand stripped to his drawers. Although she pretended to be very involved with smoothing the sheets and pillows, she watched her husband's every move out of the corner of her eye.

Rand blew out one lantern and prepared to do the same to the other.

"No," she called to him. "Let it burn."

He shrugged and backed away. Rand took one corner of the covers she raised for him and slipped into bed. Almost immediately Claire's arm slid around his waist as she turned on her side.

"I like looking at you," she said in a rush. Under the blanket Claire's fingers danced across his chest and down his abdomen. She felt Rand suck in his breath. She was surprised when he laid his hand over hers and held her questing fingers still. "Rand?"

"Do you, Claire?" His voice was husky, serious. Only an edge of earnestness gave his tone inflection. He saw that his question had startled her and he felt foolish for asking it. "I . . . the scar . . . I wondered what . . ." He couldn't seem to find a coherent thought, so he fell silent. His hand slid away from Claire's.

Claire lifted her fingers to the thin scar that crossed his features. The line was whiter now because Rand was holding his jaw so tightly that a small muscle ticked in his cheek. She laid the backs of her fingers across the spot until she felt him relax; then she replaced her fingers with her lips. She kissed him there once, and again at his temple where the scar disappeared into his hairline. "You should take issue with my imagination," she whispered. "In my mind's eye you were not nearly so handsome. In spite of Mrs. Webster's fine description, you are so much more than the sum of your parts." She kissed his mouth. "Although some of your parts . . ."

It was a long and leisurely kiss that held them bound. Claire's fingers threaded through his copper hair. She cradled his head. He turned so that she was under him. Her hips lifted as he drew up the hem of her nightgown. His thumbs brushed the soft skin of her inner thighs. She made a tiny sound at the back of her throat as he parted her legs.

Rand raised her gown higher. The smooth expanse of her

flat belly was under his hand. Her skin was warm. He felt the curve of her ribs as she drew in a shuddering breath. She held up her hands and let him remove the gown. She watched him as he lowered his head and took her nipple in his mouth.

Claire blinked. Even knowing she was about to feel the damp edge of his tongue didn't prepare her for the sensation. She clutched his shoulders and rose a fraction off the bed as pleasure shot through her. It was the same when he placed his lips on her other breast. She closed her eyes ever so briefly. She did not want to look away.

Rand teased her later. "Are you ever going to kiss me with your eyes closed again?"

"Probably not," she said. She stretched sleepily and made the abrupt little yawn of a child. "Will you mind?"

"No."

She smiled, content. Her cheek rubbed his bare shoulder. She felt his small shiver. "Too much?" she asked.

"No." It almost was. He could still feel her hands on him. His skin remembered where she had touched. There was a light trail of sensation going from his wrist to his elbow. He could feel the tug of her teeth on his ear. She had bent low over him to remove his drawers and the curling ends of her dark hair had swept over his thighs. Then her mouth . . . "No," he said again, his voice husky. "Not too much."

Claire lifted her head anyway. She propped herself on one elbow and looked down at Rand. "I want to come back here some day, Rand. I know we can't return to Solonesia, but there are so many other islands. You want to study here, don't you?"

He didn't answer immediately. "What about Henley?" he said finally.

"Bria will care for it. The treasure will ensure that she has the money to do it. Your sister's largest problem in the future will be keeping fortune hunters away. She won't have to contend with Orrin once you buy him out."

"There's my mother."

"She won't have to contend with Orrin either. And she can always travel with us."

Rand tried to imagine his mother aboard *Cerberus* and Bree alone at Henley. Neither came easily to his mind. "We'll see," he said, not committing himself. "We have weeks to go before we reach Charleston and there's still—"

Claire shook her head, cutting him off. "I don't want to talk about it."

He couldn't help smiling. "I see," he said gently. "It's all right if you arrange my life, but there's no talking about arranging yours."

"It's *our* future," she said.

"Then we should talk about what's to be done with Strickland. If you don't want to see him when I deliver his share of the treasure, that's all right, but I intend to see that he gets it."

"That's just my point," she said. "He deserves none of it. Macauley Stuart would have killed us."

"I don't believe for a moment that was your godfather's desire. Whatever else he's done, Claire, Strickland loves you and he would have had no harm come to you. Stuart was acting on his own. The duke can deal with him."

"And Macauley stays in the hold until then."

"God, yes. You can't talk me out of that."

"I don't want to talk you out of it," she said feelingly. "I was simply making certain." Because the last sounded a little cruel to her own ears, she added, "But you're treating him well enough, aren't you?"

"Well enough," Rand said dryly.

Claire laid her head on Rand's shoulder again. "Do you think it's possible the duke means for me to inherit his collection someday?"

"I think it's very likely."

"Then whatever portion of the treasure you turn over to him will come to me eventually."

"Yes. In fact, I'm going to insist upon it. It's one of the

ways the duke can prove that you've made him a better man than he is.''

Claire smiled. ''I suppose you think you're very clever.''

''I only hope you think so.''

Her agreement was muffled as she trapped another yawn behind her hand. She knew she was fighting sleep and couldn't seem to help herself. ''I don't think I want to visit the London doctors,'' she told him. ''Or even Dr. Messier. There will be such a fuss, and they'll all want to examine my eyes. I don't want that. You won't insist on it, will you?''

''Of course not.''

She frowned a little. ''But there might be something someone can learn from my experience.'' Claire bit her lower lip as she wondered again what exactly her experience had been. For all that she and Rand had gone over the events, they still were uncertain what had brought about the return of her sight. ''I suppose there will be as many explanations for what's happened to my vision as there are physicians.''

''Probably.''

''I don't know that Dr. Messier was entirely right. If he was, why didn't my sight return with my memory? After Tiare spoke of the past, I should have been able to walk down from the temple unaided.'' She didn't wait for Rand to answer. ''Yet it didn't happen then. I think my vision actually returned while we were still in the vault, but I didn't know it until I was leading the way out. When we reached the antechamber, the sunshine from beyond the waterfall disoriented me. I didn't understand what I was seeing, or *that* I was seeing.''

Rand recalled Claire's uncertain, faltering steps as she came upon the entrance to the vault. She hadn't been able to move. ''Ironic, isn't it? You were blinded by the light.''

Her mouth curled to one side. ''You're not helping.''

''Sorry.'' His grin negated his apology. ''You know what I think.''

She did, but it was hard for her to agree. ''The seven sisters,'' she sighed. *''Reunited, freed of curse.* Do you really believe that by returning the stones to that crown I lifted some sort of curse?''

"No. But you believe it."

"I don't. I've never said that."

"Just because you can't bring yourself to say it doesn't mean that somewhere inside you didn't hold it as truth. As much as you wanted to save all of us, Claire, you had to free *yourself*. The seven sisters gave you a way to do both."

She was silent, thinking hard about his reasoning. He'd never explained it in quite that way before. It wasn't that the stones held the key, but that somehow the key had been within her. *Seven rings but just one key.* Her brow curved together. "It would make Dr. Messier correct," she said slowly. "In a way."

"Or not entirely wrong," Rand said. "In a way."

Claire was quiet again. Finally she said, "It can't be right to withhold the information, can it?"

"I don't know about right, but it's certainly understandable."

"Dr. Messier would want to publish his theories. I would be Patient C. I don't think I like that. Although I shouldn't like it if my name were used."

Rand chuckled. "Can you continue this argument with yourself, or must I offer an opinion from time to time?"

Claire's mouth flattened, but only in order to tamp down her sleepy grin. "I'll carry on alone," she said softly. "Go to sleep."

Rand knew that she would be surprised to learn she drifted off first. He looked down at the serene curve of her mouth and felt a surge of tenderness that became a pressure in his chest. He touched her cheek and brushed aside a lock of hair the color of dark chocolate. She didn't stir.

They would return to the South Pacific, Rand thought, as soon as their business was concluded half a world away. Claire couldn't seriously doubt it was what he had planned all along. He needed to know it was what she wanted as well. She probably had some idea about being his assistant, doing much the same thing for him as she did for her father. He would, of course, have to make her rethink that bit of foolishness.

He would never accept Claire as his assistant. She was his partner. Rand thought of the treasure in the ship's hold and the one in his arms. His lips moved softly over the words as he closed his eyes:

> *With the sisters, this verse brings*
> *Wealth beyond the dreams of kings.*